Rod Gallowglass has just landed on a strange new world . . .

A world where elves, witches, goblins and all the other creatures of legend from Earth's Middle Ages are reality. Where good and evil are as sharply defined as black and white. Where a people of witches and warlocks lingers treacherously on the brink of destruction. Only Rod Gallowglass, a hardheaded man of science, can save the land of Gramercy from doom. But Rod does not believe in magic . . .

Ace Books by Christopher Stasheff

The Warlock series

ESCAPE VELOCITY
THE WARLOCK IN SPITE OF HIMSELF
KING KOBOLD REVIVED
THE WARLOCK UNLOCKED
THE WARLOCK ENRAGED
THE WARLOCK WANDERING
THE WARLOCK IS MISSING
THE WARLOCK HERETICAL
THE WARLOCK'S COMPANION
THE WARLOCK INSANE
THE WARLOCK ROCK
WARLOCK AND SON

Heirs to the Warlock Series

A WIZARD IN ABSTENTIA
M'LADY WITCH
QUICKSILVER'S KNIGHT

THE WARLOCK IN SPITE OF HIMSELF

CHRISTOPHER STASHEFF

ACE BOOKS, NEW YORK

This Ace Book contains the complete text of the original
edition. It has been completely reset in a typeface
designed for easy reading, and was printed from new film.

THE WARLOCK IN SPITE OF HIMSELF

An Ace Book / published by arrangement with
the author

PRINTING HISTORY
Ace original mass-market edition / 1969
Ace trade paperback edition / September 1998

The Penguin Putnam Inc. World Wide Web site address is
http://www.penguinputnam.com

Check out the Ace Science Fiction/Fantasy
newsletter, and much more, at Club PPI!

ISBN: 0-441-00560-8

Introduction to the Ace Classic Edition
of
The Warlock in Spite of Himself
by Christopher Stasheff

As I write this, I look back thirty years to January 1968, when I had finished dictating the rough draft of *A Warlock in Spite of Himself* into a tape recorder, and was starting on the extra chapters I needed to intersperse through the whole book. I'm amazed and delighted to discover that it's still in print.

WARLOCK wasn't the first novel I had written, but the other two still haven't been published. The first was "mainstream," for lack of a better word, and the second was historical. I didn't have the audacity to try to write science fiction, even though I'd been reading it since I was ten—after all, to write SF, you actually had to know something about science. But in June, 1967, I was a new arrival in Lincoln, Nebraska, with a few friends but a lot of lonely Saturdays, and one of the SF magazines announced a novel contest. The winner would get $2000 and have the novel published in their pages.

Hey, what did I have to lose? Only time that needed filling. Besides, I had some pronounced ideas abut the nature of democracy and its struggle against totalitarianism, and I knew that political commentary was a legitimate basis for an SF story and had been ever since Thomas More's *Utopia* and Cyrano de Bergerac's *Journey to the Sun* and *Journey to the Moon*, and they hadn't known anymore about science than I did. So I sat down to write the kind of book I enjoyed reading.

I made a list of my favorite fantasy monsters, figured out how they could exist in our rational universe, and found a background they could fit into—Ireland as it should have been, a colony started by IRA malcontents who despaired of ever winning back the Six Counties. I centered the story around a hero who had been developing in my mind since childhood, gave him a squire and a steed rolled into one—a robot horse with a computer for a brain. To make the steed interesting, I made him the antithesis of what a machine should be—infallible. I did that by making him epileptic; the thought came naturally, since I am epileptic. I named him "Fess" after a childhood hero and his model number—being a broadcaster, I made its acronym "F.C.C." I have since been accused of writing the story about Fess and giving him Rod Gallowglass for a sidekick.

A Warlock In Spite of Himself turned out to be one of those magical books that almost seemed to write itself. It didn't really, of course, but I became so engrossed in it that it was constantly there at the back of my mind, growing and developing, no matter what the front of my mind was doing—so I could be walking down the street when Brom O'Berin, the court jester, would leap into my conscious thoughts, standing there with arms akimbo and beard bristling, to announce that he was really the King of the Elves! Themes began to work themselves in—identity and ideals and devotion to causes, things I had wondered about as, in my late adolescence, I tried to hammer out an understanding of the world and some rules to live by. In December of 1967, I went to see a production of Moliere's *The Doctor in Spite of Himself* and sat there, electrified, as I realized what the title should be—and that Rod Gallowglass spent an amazing portion of the book trying to deny what he was experiencing.

By the time I had written a hundred pages, I had to admit to myself that the culture I had described had very little of Ireland in it, and a great deal of England—so I changed the name of the group who founded the colony. Instead of the IRA, they became the Romantic Emigres. When the book was published and I read the back cover, I was amazed and a little angry to find the group had been re-named the Society for Creative Anachronism. I later found out that the SCA really existed—so I am among the many who can claim to have invented it, even if I didn't know about them when they started. It proved to be the first of my many accurate predictions of events that had already happened.

As I wrote, I realized that I needed an earlier chapter to explain what I had just written, so I started a list of additional chapters to go back and write. When I finished the main story line, that list had as many chapters on it as I had already written! Somehow that only gave me greater enthusiasm for the job—after all, this time I knew how the chapters were supposed to end.

I finished writing the extra chapters in June—they doubled the length of the book—then typed it over the summer, five pages a day. Of course, by that time, the contest had been over for almost a year. Nothing daunted, I sent the manuscript off to the first publisher on my list—Ace, alphabetically, but also with the reputation for starting new writers; I was hoping to be half of an Ace Double. Then I settled down to chew my fingernails and ambush the mailman.

It sold! I was jubilant. It was the second most wonderful moment in my life, to that date. I've had moments that surpassed it since, but very few.

When I calmed down three months later, I began to think about doing a sequel—I had grown fond of Fess, and of Rod and his wife Gwen. But I didn't like the usual way of doing sequels to a book that ends with the hero and heroine marrying, usually managed by having her die and him start looking for love all over again or, less drastically, by having her kidnapped and him spending the book trying to rescue her. I also didn't like the fact the sequels almost never featured children or family life. This struck me as being very unrealistic on the one hand and a very bad message for young readers—who constituted most of the SF readership at that time—that once you get married, the adventure is over, the fun stops, and the story ends. The impact was even worse in the television shows of the time. On the adventure shows, strong, capable, intelligent, resourceful unmarried heroes met and overcame all enemies weekly, but they were juxtaposed against family shows in which the father was usually portrayed as a kind of unassuming teddy bear or even, as in THE LIFE OF RILEY, somewhat less intelligent than his wife and certainly less intelligent than his children. The message was even more clear: Get married and turn into a cream puff. For women, the scenario was just as bad, perhaps worse, since the women on the action shows were glamorous, intelligent, active, and dynamic, whereas the mothers and wives on the family shows were, like their husbands, retiring, good-looking in a subdued sort of way, and rarely seen outside the home. The swan married and turned into a hen.

I didn't think that was true, so I decided to write sequels that would show that conflicts, and the resulting adventures, don't end with marriage and children. Ideally, I was going to write a whole series showing the life-long development of Gwen and Rod as they raised a whole family. I tried to make their married life just a adventurous as their courting days, and saw to it that they both remained just as attractive to one another as they had been when they were single.

One of the banes of marriage in my generation was the ending line of the average fairy tale: "They got married and lived happily ever after." It sounded like cause and effect, like a magic spell; all you had to do was find your true love, manage to marry them, and you would automatically have a happy and secure marriage forever.

I was raised being warned against that mindset, having been told that a successful marriage takes work on both sides, and that even the best marriages have rough spots and conflicts that can be worked through and worked out, but only with courage, perseverance, honesty, willingness to try to see the issue from the spouse's side, and hard work. As the series developed and Rod and Gwen grew older, I tried to show that their marriage succeeded not by magic, but by love, dedication, and work. I had made it quite clear, in WARLOCK IN SPITE OF HIMSELF, that Gwen was an important and powerful person in her own right; I tried to reinforce that, making her save Rod and the children as often as he saved her, and ensuring that she learned his form of magic more quickly than he learned hers.

So when I wrote the first sequel, I intended to write not just the story of Rod and Gwen, but the story of a family. I think I've succeeded reasonably well with that. In KING KOBOLD, you'll meet baby Magnus, their eldest, and confront the problems of trying to raise a child with psychic powers—how DO you make him stay in the playpen?—but also the advantages; in the pinch, he saves Rod from a psychic monster. In THE WARLOCK UNLOCKED, Rod and Gwen have all four children, but Gregory is an infant—who nonetheless pulls his family back from the parallel fantasy universe to which they'd been kidnapped. In THE WAR-

LOCK ENRAGED, Rod has to try to cure himself of the hair-trigger temper he acquired in that universe and its effects on his family. In THE WARLOCK WANDERING, Rod and Gwen manage a night out that turns into several months, as they're kidnapped into the past, a few months before the events of ESCAPE VELOCITY (which tells why the Romantic Emigres was colonized) and have to try to find their way home—and Gwen learns quantum physics. In THE WARLOCK IS MISSING, we find out what the kids have been doing while their parents were away and Puck was their babysitter. In THE WARLOCK'S COMPANION, we find out about Fess's past, join the family as they exorcize an old castle, and watch Magnus fall in love with a ghost and suffer his first heartbreak. In THE WARLOCK INSANE, Rod eats a psychedelic chestnut and goes off by himself to wander through fantasies until it wears off—and Gwen follows with the children to make sure he's safe, then to make sure the people he *meets* stay safe. In THE WARLOCK HERETICAL, Rod and his family side with the crown and help the Father General of the Order of St. Vidicon to curb an abbot who is trying to set up an independent Church of Gramarye for his own purposes. In THE WARLOCK ROCK, Rod and Gwen try to cope with teenage independence and peer pressure while trying to cope with a media system that has spiralled out of control. In WARLOCK AND SON, the family confronts a witch who is bent on emotionally warping the grown Magnus to the point at which he'll become unable to fall in love, her first salvo in a battle to keep the Gallowglass family from going into a third generation. She succeeds with Magnus, then keeps trying in THE WARLOCK'S HEIRS series—tries and fails with Cordelia, then Geoffrey, and finally Gregory, whose gentleness and remorseless logic finally defeat her—sort of.

By and large, I think I accomplished what I set out to do. If there's a defect, it's that it's Rod's hangups and weaknesses that cause trouble, not Gwen's. Some fans have taken me to task for that, claiming that I make Gwen impossibly good, that surely there should be times when she gives in to the stress and pressure of family life and turns to snap at Rod and chew him out, that she might become depressed or try to break out of the confines of domesticity and thus create a problem that Rod and the kids have to pull together to try to solve. I plead guilty to that, but I'm afraid I could never bring myself to show Gwen as being to blame for anything. After twenty-five years as a husband and father, and of watching other people's marriages, I'd have to admit that's not realistic—both partners are apt to cause trouble, and the simple fact of two different people trying to live together generates friction that comes as much from the one as from the other.

But then, so many things have changed in marriage and family life since I wrote *The Warlock in Spite of Himself* that I can't be sure that the picture I set out to present in 1969 is still accurate in 1998—or even in focus.

So if you want to read about the Middle Ages not as they were, but as they should have been, read this book. Also if you want to read about family life not as it really is, but as it should have been, read the rest of the series, and you can watch Magnus grow from an adventurous toddler into an adventurous teenager who is ripe for love and heartbreak; see Cordelia blossom from a cute little minx to a beautiful big minx ready to win hearts and lose them with equal ease; follow Geoffrey from a boosty boy in love with war into a handsome muscle-man as ready for action on the battlefield as in the boudoir; and observe Gregory transform from a tender-hearted, keen-minded child into a . . . but hold on, I haven't written his grown-up adventure yet.

I've written the others, though, in the sequel series, THE WARLOCK'S HEIRS. Since it's the series for the second generation, I concentrate on the younger folk as each finds his or her destiny, so their parents become figures in the background, old stars making cameo appearances. Gwen has filled out a bit and has a few wrinkles and a few gray hairs among the red, but is still beautiful, especially in Rod's eyes. Rod is still the capable klutz he always was and still believes in himself only because Gwen does, but he seems to have finally regained his mental health (due to an adventure I haven't finished writing). He is older, grayer, mellower, and more bulky. But Rod and Gwen have made it through to the verge of grandparenthood still healthy, still active, and still in love.

So I guess it does turn out happily, after all.

PART ONE

VISIT TO A SMALL PLANTAGENET

The asteroid hurtled in from Capricorn, nosed around a G-type sun, swerved off toward the fifth planet. Such a trajectory is somewhat atypical for asteroids.

It slapped into the planet's gravity net, swooped around the globe three times in three separate orbits, then stabbed into atmosphere, a glorious shooting star.

At a hundred feet altitude it paused, then snapped to the surface—but only *to* the surface. No fireworks, no crater—nothing more drastic than crushed grass. Its surface was scarred and pitted, blackened by the friction-heat of its fall; but it was intact.

Deep within its bowels echoed the words that would change the planet's destiny.

"Damn your bolt-brained bearings!"

The voice broke off; its owner frowned, listening.

The cabin was totally silent, without its usual threshold hum.

The young man swore, tearing the shock-webbing from his body. He lurched out of the acceleration chair, balanced dizzily on the balls of his feet, groping till his hand touched the plastic wall.

Steadying himself with one hand, he stumbled to a panel on the other side of the circular cabin. He fumbled the catches loose, cursing in the fine old style of galactic deckhands, opened the panel, pressed a button. Turning, he all but fell back to the chair.

The soft hum awoke in the cabin again. A slurred voice asked, with varying speed and pitch, "Izzz awwl (Hic!) sadizfagtoreee . . . M'lorrrr' Rodney?"

"All the smooth, glossy robots in the galaxy," muttered Milord, "and I get stuck with an epilepic!"

1

"Ivv ut bleeezz m'lorr', thuh c'passsider c'n be—"

"Replaced," finished Rodney, "and your circuits torn out and redesigned. No, thank you, I like your personality the way it is—except when you pull off a landing that jars my clavicles loose!"

"Ivv m'lorrd will vorgive, ad thuh cruzhial momend ovvv blanetfall, I rezeived zome very zingular radio waves thad—"

"You got distracted, is that what you're trying to say?"

"M'lorrrd, id was imerative to analyze—"

"So part of you was studying the radio waves, and part of you was landing the ship, which was just a wee bit too much of a strain, and the weak capacitor gave. . . . Fess! How many times do I have to tell you to keep your mind on the job!"

"M'lorrd egzbressed a wizh to be like thuh—"

"Like the heros of the Exploration Sagas, yes. But that doesn't mean I want their discomforts."

Fess's electronic system had almost recovered from the post-seizure exhaustion. "But, m'lorrd, the choncebt of heeroizm imblies—"

"Oh, forget it," Rodney groaned. Fess dutifully blanked a portion of his memory banks.

Fess was very dutiful. He was also an antique, one of the few remaining FCC (Faithful Cybernetic Companion) robots, early models now two thousand years out of date. The FCC robots had been programmed for extreme loyalty and, as a consequence, had perished in droves while defending their masters during the bloody Interregnum between the collapse of the ancient Galactic Union and the rise of the Proletarian Eclectic State of Terra.

Fess (a name derived from trying to pronounce "FCC" as a single word) had survived, thanks to his epilepsy. He had a weak capacitor that, when overstrained, released all its stored energy in a massive surge lasting several milli-seconds. When the preliminary symptoms of this electronic seizure—mainly a fuzziness in Fess's calculations—appeared, a master circuit breaker popped, and the faulty capacitor discharged in isolation from the rest of Fess's circuits; but the robot was out of commission until the circuit breaker was reset.

Since the seizures occurred during moments of great stress—such as trying to land a spaceship-*cum*-asteroid while analyzing an aberrant radio wave, or trying to protect a master from three simultaneous murderers—Fess had survived the Interregnum; for, when the Proletarians had attacked his masters, he had fought manfully for about twenty-five seconds, then collapsed. He had thus become a rarity—the courageous servant who had survived. He was one of five FCC robots still functioning.

He was, consequently, a prized treasure of the d'Armand family—prized as an antique, but even more for his loyalty; true loyalty to aristocratic families has always been in short supply.

So, when Rodney d'Armand had left home for a life of adventure and glory—being the second son of a second son, there hadn't been much else he could do—his father had insisted on his taking Fess along.

Rod had often been very glad of Fess's company; but there were times when the robot was just a little short on tact. For instance, after a very rough planetfall, a human stomach tends to be a mite queasy; but Fess had the bad sense to ask, "Would you care to dine, m'lord? Say, scallops with asparagus?"

Rod turned chartreuse and clamped his jaws, fighting back nausea. "No," he grated, "and can the 'm'lord' bit. We're on a mission, remember?"

"I never forget, Rod. Except on command."

"I know," growled his master's voice. "It was a figure of speech."

Rod swung his legs to the floor and painfully stood up. "I could use a breath of fresh air to settle my stomach, Fess. Is there any available?"

The robot clicked for a moment, then reported, "Atmosphere breathable. Better wear a sweater, though."

Rod shrugged into his pilot's jacket with a growl. "Why do old family retainers always develop a mother-hen complex?"

"Rod, if you had lived as long as I have—"

"—I'd want to be deactivated. I know, 'Robot is always right.' Open the lock, Fess."

The double doors of the small air lock swung open, showing a circle of black set with stars. A chill breeze poured into the cabin.

Rod tilted his face back, breathing in. His eyes closed in luxury. "Ah, the blessed breath of land! What lives here, Fess?"

Machinery whirred as the robot played back the electron-telescope tapes they had taken in orbit, integrating the pictorial data into a comprehensive description of the planet.

"Land masses consist of five continents, one island of noteworthy dimensions, and a host of lesser islands. The continent and the minor islands exhibit similar flora—equatorial rain forest."

"Even at the poles?"

"Within a hundred miles of each pole; the ice caps are remarkably small. Visible animal life confined to amphibians and a host of insects; we may assume that the seas abound with fish."

Rod rubbed his chin. "Sounds like we came in pretty early in the geologic spectrum."

"Carboniferous Era," replied the robot.

"How about that one large island? That's where we've landed, I suppose?"

"Correct. Native flora and fauna nonexistent. All lifeforms typical of Late Terran Pleistocene."

"How late, Fess?"

"Human historical."

Rod nodded. "In other words, a bunch of colonists came in, picked themselves an island, wiped out the native life, and seeded the land with Terran stock. Any idea why they chose this island?"

"Large enough to support a good-sized population, small enough to minimize problems of ecological revision. Then too, the island is situated in a polar ocean current, which lowers the local temperature to slightly below Terran normal."

"Very handy; saves them the bother of climate control. Any remains of what might have been Galactic Union cities?"

"None, Rod."

"None!" Rod's eyes widened in surprise. "That doesn't fit the pattern. You sure, Fess?"

The developmental pattern of a lost, or retrograde, colony—one that had been out of touch with Galactic civilization for a millennium or more—fell into three well-defined stages: first, the establishment of the colony, centered around a modern city with an advanced technology; second, the failure of communications with Galactic culture, followed by an overpopulation of the city, which led to mass migrations to the countryside and a consequent shift to an agrarian, self-sufficient economy; and, third, the loss of technological knowledge, accompanied by a rising level of superstition, symbolized by the abandonment and eventual tabooing of a coal-and-steam technology; social relationships calcified, and a caste system appeared. Styles of dress and architecture were usually burlesques of Galactic Union forms: for example, a small hemispherical wooden hut, built in imitation of the vaulting Galactic geodesic domes.

But always there were the ruins of the city, acting as a constant symbol and a basis for mythology. Always.

"You're sure, Fess? You're really, really sure there isn't a city?"

"I am always certain, Rod."

"That's true." Rod pulled at his lower lip. "Sometimes mistaken, but never in doubt. Well, shelve the matter of the city for the time being; maybe it sank in a tidal wave. Let's just make a final check on the life-forms' being Terran."

Rod dove head-first through the three foot circle of the lock, landed in a forward roll, rose to his knees. He unclipped the guerilla knife from his belt— a knife carefully designed so that it could not be attributed to any one known culture—and drew the dagger from its sheath.

The sheath was a slender cone of white metal, with a small knob at the apex. Rod plucked several blades of grass, dropped them into the sheath, and turned the knob. The miniature transceiver built into the sides of the sheath probed the grass with sonics to analyze its molecular structure, then broadcast the data to Fess, who determined if any of the molecules were incompatible with human metabolism. If the grass had been poisonous to Rod, Fess would have beamed a signal back to the sheath, whereupon the white metal would have turned purple.

But in this particular case, the sheath stayed silver.

"That ties it," said Rod. "This is Terran grass, presumably planted by Terrans, and this is a Terran colony. But where's the city?"

"There is a large town—perhaps thirty thousand

souls— in the foothills of a mountain range to the north, Rod.''

"Well . . ." Rod rubbed his chin. "That's not exactly what I had in mind, but it's better than nothing. What's it look like?''

"Situated on the lower slopes of a large hill, at the summit of which is a large stone structure, strongly reminiscent of a Medieval Terran castle."

"Medieval!'' Rod scowled.

"The town itself consists of half-timbered and stuccoed buildings, with second stories overhanging the narrow streets—alleys would be a better term— along which they are situated.''

"Half-timbered!'' Rod rose to his feet. "Wait a minute, *wait a minute!* Fess, does that architecture remind you of anything?''

The robot was silent a moment, then replied, "Northern European Renaissance.''

"That,'' said Rod, "is *not* the typical style of a retrograde colony. How closely do those buildings re-semble Terran Renaissance, Fess?''

"The resemblance is complete to the last detail, Rod.''

"It's deliberate then. How about that castle? Is that Renaissance too?''

The robot paused, then said, "No, Rod. It would appear to be a direct copy from the German style of the 13th Century A.D.''

Rod nodded eagerly. "How about styles of dress?''

"We are currently on the night side of the planet, and were upon landing. There is a good deal of illumination from the planet's three satellites, but relatively few people abroad. . . . There is, however, a small party of soldiers, riding Terran horses. Their uniforms are—uh—copies of English Beefeaters'.''

"Very good! Anyone else in the streets?"

"Um . . . a couple of cloaked men—uh—doublet and hose, I belive and . . . yes, a small party of peasants, wearing smocks and cross-gartered buskins. . . ."

"That's enough." Rod cut him off. "It's a hodgepodge, a conglomeration of styles. Somebody has tried to set up his idea of the ideal world, Fess. Ever hear of the Emigrés?"

The robot was silent a moment, mulling through his memory banks. Then he began to recite:

"Malcontents abounded toward the end of the 22nd Century A.D. Bored with their 'lives of quiet desperation,' people turned primarily to mysticism, secondarily to escapist literature and entertainment. Gradually the pseudo-Medieval became the dominant entertainment form.

"Finally, a group of wealthy men pooled their funds to buy an outmoded FTL liner and announced to the world that they were the Romantic Emigrés, that they intended to reestablish the glory of the Medieval way of life on a previously-uncolonized planet, and that they would accept a limited number of emigrants in the capacities of serfs and tradesmen.

"There were, of course, many more applicants than could be accommodated. Emigrants were selected 'for the poeticness of their souls'—whatever that may mean."

"It means they loved to listen to ghost stories," said Rod. "What happened?"

"The passenger list was swiftly completed. The thirteen tycoons who had organized the expedition announced that they thereby rejected their surnames and adopted instead the family names of great Medieval aristocrats—Bourbon, di Medici, and so forth.

"Then the ship departed, with its destination carefully unspecified, so that there would be 'no contamination from the materialist world.' Nothing more was ever heard of them.''

Rod smiled grimly. ''Well, I think we've just found them. How's *that* set with your diodes?''

''Quite well, Rod. In fact, a statistical analysis of the probability of this being the Emigrés' colony reveals the following—''

''Skip it,'' Rod said quickly. Statistics was Fess's hobby; given half a chance, he could bore you for hours.

Rod pursed his lips and eyed the section of the hull that housed Fess's brain. ''Come to think of it, you might send the statistics back to SCENT with our educated guess that we've found the Emigrés' colony. Might as well get at that right now; I'd like them to know where we are in case anything happens.''

SCENT, the Society for the Conversion of Extraterrestrial Nascent Totalitarianisms, was the organization responsible for seeking out the lost colonies. The Proletarian Eclectic State of Terra had shown remarkably little interest in any colony that was lacking in modern technology; so that the lost colonies had stayed lost until the totalitarian rule of PEST had been overthrown by DDT, the Decentralized Democratic Tribunal. DDT had quickly consolidated its rule of Terra, governing in accordance with the almost-unattainable goals of Athenian democracy.

It had long been known that the inefficiency of democratic governments was basically a problem of communication and prejudice. But, over a period of two centuries, DDT cells had functioned as speakeasy schoolrooms, resulting in total literacy and masters' degrees for seventy-two percent of the population; prejudice had thus joined polio and cancer on the list of curable diseases. The problems of communication had been solved by the development, in DDT laboratories, of sub-molecular electronics, which had lowered the bulk and price of electronic communication gear to the point where its truly extensive use became practical for the first time. Every individual was thus able to squawk at his Tribune at a moment's notice; and, being educated, they tended to do a lot of squawking just on general principles— all very healthy for a democracy.

Squawking by radio had proved singularly effective, due largely to an automatic record of the squawk. The problems of records and other bureaucratic red tape had been solved by red oxide audio recording tape, with tracks a single molecule in width, and the development of data-retrieval systems so efficient that the memorization of facts became obsolete. Education thus became exclusively a training in concepts, and the success of democracy was assured.

After two centuries of preparing such groundwork, the DDT revolution had been a mere formality.

But revolutionaries are always out of place when the revolution is over, and are likely to prove an embarrassing factor to the police forces of the new government.

Therefore, DDT had decided not to be selfish; rather, they would share the blessings of democracy with the other remnants of the old Galactic Union.

But democrats are seldom welcome on planets run by totalitarian governments, and scarcely more welcome on planets where anarchy prevails—this due to the very nature of democracy, the only practical compromise between totalitarianism and anarchy.

What was needed was a permanent organization of revolutionaries, subversive republican democrats. Since there was a large supply of out-of-work revolutionaries on hand, the organization was quickly formed, and christened the Society for the Conversion of Extraterrestrial Totalitarianisms. The "Nascent" was added a century later, when all the known inhabited planets had been subverted and had joined DDT. The old revolutionaries were still a problem, the more so since there were more of them; so they were sent out singly to find the Lost Colonies.

Thus was formed SCENT, the organization whose mission it was to sniff out the backward planets and put them on the road to democracy.

Since Rod had found a medieval planet, he would probably have to foster the development of a constitutional monarchy.

Rod, born Rodney d'Armand (he had five middle names, but they make dull reading) on a planet inhabited exclusively by aristocrats and robots, had joined SCENT at the tender age of eighteen. In his ten years of service, he had grown from a gangling, ugly youth to a lean, well-muscled, ugly man.

His face was aristocratic; you could say that for it—that, and no more. His receding hairline gave onto a flat, sloping forehead that ran up against a brace of bony brow-ridges, somewhat camouflaged by bushy eyebrows. The eyebrows overhung deep sockets, at the back of which were two, somewhat hardened gray eyes—at least Rod hoped they looked hardened.

The eye sockets were thresholded by high, flat cheekbones, divided by a blade of nose that would have done credit to an eagle. Under the cheekbones and nose was a wide, thin-lipped mouth which, even in sleep, was twisted in a sardonic smile. Under the mouth was a square jawbone and a jutting chin.

Rod would have liked to say that it was a strong face, but it tended to soften remarkably when/if a girl smiled at it. Dogs and children had the same effect, with a great deal more frequency.

He was a man with a Dream (There had been a Dream Girl once, but she was now one with his callow youth.)—Dream of one unified Galactic government (democratic, of course). Interstellar communications were still too slow for a true democratic federation; the DDT was actually a loose confederation of worlds, more of a debating society and service organization than anything else.

But adequate communication methods would come along some day, Rod was sure of that, and when they did, the stars would be ready. He would see to that.

"Well, let's be about our business, Fess. No telling when someone might wander by and spot us." Rod swung up and into the air lock, through and into the cabin again. He went to the plate in the wall, released the catches. Inside was a control panel; above this was a white metal sphere with a dull finish, about the size of a basketball. A massive cable grew out of the top of the sphere and connected to the wall of the shop.

Rod unscrewed the connection, released the friction clamp that held the sphere in place, and carefully lifted it out.

"Easy," Fess's voice said from the earphone implanted in the bone behind Rod's right ear. "I'm fragile, you know."

"A little confidence, please," Rod muttered. The microphone in his jawbone carried his words to Fess. "I haven't dropped you yet, have I?"

"Yet," echoed the robot.

Rod cradled the robot "brain" in the crook of one arm, leaving one arm free to negotiate the air lock. Outside again. he pressed a stud in the side of the ship. A large door lifted from the side of the pseudo-asteroid. Inside, a great black horse hung from shock webbing, head between its forelegs, eyes closed.

Rod pressed a button; a crane extended from the cargo space. The horse swung out on the crane, was lowered till its hooves touched the ground. Rod twisted the saddlehorn, and a panel in the horse's side slid open.

Rod placed the brain inside the panel, tightened the clamp and the connections, then twisted the saddlehorn back; the panel slid shut. Slowly the horse raised its head, wiggled its ears, blinked twice, gave a tentative whinny.

"All as it should be," said the voice behind Rod's ear. The horse champed at the bit. "If you'll let me out of this cat's cradle, I'll check the motor circuits."

Rod grinned and freed the webbing. The horse reared up, pawing the air, then sprang into a gallop. Rod watched the robot run, taking a good look at his surroundings in the process.

The asteroid-ship had landed in the center of a meadow, shaggy with summer grass, ringed by oak, hickory, maple, and ash. It was night, but the meadow was flooded with the light of three moons.

The robot cantered back toward Rod, reared to a halt before him. Forehooves thudded on the ground; the great indigo eyes turned to look at Rod, the ears pricked forward.

"I'm fit," Fess reported.

Rod grinned again. "No sight like a running horse."

"What, none?"

"Well, almost none. C'mon, let's get the ship buried."

Rod pressed studs on the side of the ship; the cargo hatch closed, the air lock sealed itself. The ship began to revolve, slowly at first, then faster and faster as it sank into the ground. Soon there was only a crater surrounded by a ring-wall of loam, and the roof of the asteroid curving three feet below.

Rod pulled a camp shovel from Fess's saddlebags, unfolded it, and bent to his task. The horse joined in, flashing out with its heels at the ring-wall. In ten minutes the wall had been reduced to six inch height; there was a large mound of earth in the center, twenty feet across and two feet high.

"Stand back." Rod drew his dagger, twisted the hilt 180 degrees, pointed the haft at the earth-mound. A red light lanced out; the loam glowed cherry red, melted, and flowed.

Rod fanned the beam in a slow arc over the whole of the filled-in crater till the soil had melted down a foot below ground level. He shoveled the rest of the ring-wall into the hole, making a slight mound, but the next rain would take care of that.

"Well, that's it." Rod wiped his brow.

"Not quite."

Rod hunched his shoulders; there was a sinking feeling in his belly.

"You have still to assume clothing appropriate to this society and period, Rod."

Rod squeezed his eyes shut.

"I took the precaution of packing a doublet in my lefthand saddlebag while you were testing the grass, Rod."

"Look," Rod argued, "my uniform will do well enough, won't it?"

"Skintight trousers and military boots will pass, yes. But a pilot's jacket could not possibly be mistaken for a doublet. Need I say more?"

·"No, I suppose not." Rod sighed. He went to the saddlebag. "The success of the mission comes first, above and before any considerations of personal comfort, dignity, or—hey!" He stared at something long and slender, hanging from the saddle.

"Hey what, Rod?"

Rod took the strange object from the saddle—it had a handle on one end, he noticed, and it rattled—and held it up where Fess could see it.

"What is *this?*"

"An Elizabethan rapier, Rod. An antique sidearm, a sort of long knife, designed for both cutting and thrusting."

"Sidearm." Rod eyed the robot as if doubting his sanity. "I'm supposed to wear it?"

"Certainly, Rod. At least, if you're planning to adopt one of your usual covers."

Rod gave a sign appropriate to a Christian martyr and pulled the doublet from the saddlebag. He wriggled into it and belted the rapier to his right side.

"No, no, Rod! Belt it to your *left* side. You have to cross-draw it."

"The things I go through for the sake of democracy. . . ." Rod belted the rapier to his left hip. "Fess, has it ever occurred to you that I might be a fanatic?"

"Certainly, Rod. A classic case of sublimation."

"I asked for an opinion, not an analysis," the man growled. He looked down at his costume. "Hey! Not bad, not bad at all!" He threw his shoulders back, lifted his chin, and strutted. The gold and scarlet doublet fairly glowed in the moonlight. "How do you like it, Fess?"

"You cut quite a figure, Rod." There was, somehow, a tone of quiet amusement in the robot's voice.

Rod frowned. "Needs a cape to top it off, though."

"In the saddlebag, Rod."

"Think of everything, don't you?" Rod rummaged in the saddlebag, shook out a voluminous cloak of the same electric blue as his uniform tights.

"The chain passes under the left armpit and around the right-hand side of the neck, Rod."

Rod fastened the cloak in place and faced into the wind, the cloak streaming back from his broad shoulders.

"There, now! Ain't I a picture, though?"

"Like a plate from a Shakespeare text, Rod."

"Flattery will get you a double ration of oil." Rod swung into the saddle. "Head for the nearest town, Fess. I want to show off my new finery."

"You forgot to seed the crater, Rod."

"What? Oh! Yeah." Rod pulled a small bag from the right-hand saddlebag and sprinkled its content over the circle of raw earth. "There! Give it a light rainstorm and two days to grow, and you won't be able to tell it from the rest of the meadow. Let's hope nobody comes this way for two days, though. . . ."

The horse's head jerked up, ears pricked forward.

"What's the matter, Fess?"

"Listen," the robot replied.

Rod scowled and closed his eyes.

Distant, blown on the wind, came youthful shouts and gay laughter.

"Sounds like a bunch of kids having a party."

"It's coming closer," Fess said softly.

Rod shut his eyes and listened again. The sound *was* growing louder . . .

He turned to the northeast, the direction the sound seemed to be coming from, and scanned the horizon. There were only the three moons in the sky.

A shadow drifted across one of the moons. Three more followed it.

The laughter was much louder now.

"About seventy-five miles per hour," Fess murmured.

"What?"

"Seventy-five miles per hour. That's the speed at which they seem to be approaching."

"Hmmm." Rod chewed at his lower lip. "Fess, how long since we landed?"

"Almost two hours, Rod."

Something streaked by overhead.

Rod looked up. "Ah, Fess?"

"Yes, Rod."

"They're flying, Fess."

There was a pause.

"Rod, I must ask you to be logical. A culture like this couldn't possibly have evolved air travel yet."

"They haven't. *They're* flying."

Another pause.

"The people themselves, Rod?"

"That's right." Rod's voice held a note of resignation. "Though I'll admit that one who just flew over us seemed to be riding a broomstick. Not too bad-looking, either. Matter of fact, she was stacked like a Las Vegas poker deck . . . Fess?"

The horse's legs were locked rigid, its head swinging gently between its legs.

"Oh, hell!" Rod growled. "Not again!"

He reached down under the saddlehorn and reset the circuit breaker. Slowly, the horse raised its head and shook it several times. Rod caught the reins and led the horse away.

"Whaddappend, RRRawwwd?"

"You had a seizure, Fess. Now, whatever you do, *don't* whinny. That airborne bacchanalia is coming our way, and there's an off chance they might be out to investigate the shooting star. Therefore, we are heading for the tall timber—and *quietly*, if you please."

Once under the trees at the edge of the meadow, Rod looked back to check on the flying flotilla.

The youngsters were milling about in the sky half a mile away, emitting joyful shrieks and shouts of welcome. The wind tossed Rod an intelligible phrase or two.

"Rejoice, my children! 'Tis Lady Gwen!"

"Hast thou, then, come at last to be mother to our coven, Gwendylon?"

"Thy beauty hath but waxed, sweet Gwendylon! How dost thou?"

"Not yet robbing cradles, Randal. . . ."

"Sounds like the housemother dropping in on a party at the Witches' College," Rod grunted. "Sober, Fess?"

"Clearheaded, at least," the robot acknowledged, "and a new concept accepted in my basic programming."

"Oh." Rod pursed his lips. "My observation is confirmed?"

"Thoroughly. They *are* flying."

The aerial sock-hop seemed to have rediscovered its original purpose. They swooped toward the meadows with shouts and gales of laughter, hovered over the ring of newly-turned earth, and dropped one by one to form a circle about it.

"Well, not too many doubts about what they're here for, is there?" Rod sat on the ground, tailor-fashion, and leaned back against Fess's forelegs. "Nothing to do but wait, I guess." He twisted the signet on his ring ninety degrees, pointed it at the gathering. "Relay, Fess."

The signet ring now functioned as a very powerful, very directional microphone; its signal was relayed through Fess to the earphone behind Rod's ear.

"Ought we to tell the Queen of this?"

"Nay, 'twould fash her unduly."

Rod frowned. "Can you make anything out of it, Fess?"

"Only that it's Elizabethan English, Rod."

"That," said Rod, "is why SCENT always sends a man with a robot. All right, let's start with the obvious: the language confirms that this is the Emigré's colony."

"Well, of course," Fess muttered, somewhat piqued.

"Now, now, old symbiote, no griping. I know you don't consider the obvious worth reporting; but overlooking obvious facts does sometimes lead to overlooking secrets hidden right out in plain sight, doesn't it?"

"Well . . ."

"Right. So. They mentioned a Queen. Therefore, the government is a monarchy, as we suspected. This teenage in-group referred to themselves as a coven; therefore they consider themselves witches. . . . Considering their form of locomotion, I'm inclined to agree. But . . ."

He left the *but* hanging for a few minutes. Fess picked up his ears.

"They also spoke of telling the Queen. Therefore, they must have access to the royal ear. What's this, Fess? Royal approval of witchcraft?"

"Not necessarily," said Fess judiciously. "An applicable precedent would be the case of King Saul and the Witch of Endor. . . ."

"But chances are they've got an in at court."

"Rod, you are jumping to conclusions."

"No, just coming up with a brilliant flash of insight."

"That," said Fess, "is why SCENT always sends a robot with a human."

"Touché. But they also said that telling the Queen would 'fash her unduly.' What's *fash* mean, Fess?"

"To cause anxiety, Rod."

"Um. This Queen just might be the excitable type, then."

"*Might* be, yes."

Music struck up in the field—Scottish bagpipes playing the accompaniment to an old Gypsy tune. The young folk were dançing on the cleared earth, and several feet above it.

"Bavarian peasant dance," Fess murmured.

" 'Where the ends of the earth all meet,' " Rod quoted, stretching his legs out straight. "An agglomerate culture, carefully combining all the worst Old Earth had to offer."

"An unfair judgment, Rod."

Rod raised an eyebrow. "You *like* bagpipes?"

He folded his arms and let his chin rest on his sternum, leaving Fess the sleepless to watch for anything significant.

The robot watched for a couple of hours, patiently chewing his data. When the music faded and died, Fess planted a hoof on Rod's hip.

"Gnorf!" said Rod, and was instantly wide awake, as is the wont of secret agents.

"The party's over, Rod."

The young folk were leaping into the air, banking away to the northeast.

One broomstick shot off at right angles to the main body; a boyish figure shot out after it.

"Do thou not be so long estranged from us again, Gwendylon."

"Randal, if thou wert a mouse, thou wouldst woo oliphants! Farewell, and see to it from now thou payest court to wenches only six years thy elder!"

The broomstick streaked straight toward Rod, climbed over the trees and was gone.

"Mmm, yes!" Rod licked his lips. "Definitely a great build on that girl. And the way she talks, she's a wee bit older than these birdbrains. . . ."

"I had thought you were above petty conquest by now, Rod."

"Which is a nice way of saying she wouldn't have

anything to do with me. Well, even if I haven't got the buying power, I can still window-shop."

The junior coven sailed over the horizon; their laughter faded away.

"Well, that's that." Rod gathered his feet under him. "The party's over, and we're none the wiser." He rose to his feet. "Well, at least we're still a secret; nobody knows there's a spaceship under that circle of earth."

"Nay, not so," chuckled a pixie voice.

Rod froze, turned his head, stared.

There, among the roots of an old oak, stood a man, broad-shouldered, grinning, and all of twelve inches tall. He was clad in doublet and hose in varying shades of brown, and had very white teeth and a general air of mischief.

"The King of the Elves shall be apprised of your presence, Lord Warlock," said the apparition, chuckling.

Rod lunged.

But the little man was gone, leaving only a chortle behind him.

Rod stood staring, listening to the wind commenting to the oak leaves and the last faint snicker dying away among the oak roots.

"Fess," he said. "Fess, did you see that?"

There was no answer.

Rod frowned, turning. "Fess? Fess!"

The robot's head swung gently between its fetlocks.

"Oh, hell!"

A deep-toned bell was proclaiming the advent of nine o'clock somewhere in the large, ramshackle town that was, as near as Rod and Fess could figure from speed and bearing, the juvenile witches' home base. In view of their remark about the Queen, Rod had hopes the town would turn out to be the capital of the island.

"Only a guess, of course," he added hurriedly.

"Of course," Fess murmured. The robot voice gave the distinct impression of a patient sigh.

"On a more immediate level, what name should I go by in this culture?"

"Why not Rodney d'Armand VII? This is one of the few cases where your natural name is appropriate."

Rod shook his head. "Too pretentious. My forebears never did get over their aristocratic aspirations."

"They *were* aristocrats, Rod."

"Yeah, but so was everybody else in the planet, Fess, except the robots. And they'd been in the family so long they had a right to claim some of the honors."

"It was honor enough to—"

"Later," Rod cut him off. Fess had a standardized sermon on the *noblesse oblige* tradition of the Maxima robots, which he would gladly deliver at the drop of anything resembling a cue. "There's a small problem of a name, remember?"

"If you insist." Fess was disgruntled. "Mercenary soldier, again?"

"Yes. It gives me an excuse to travel."

Fess winced. "You could pose as a wandering minstrel . . ."

Rod shook his head. "Minstrels are supposed to be up on the current news. Might not be a bad idea to pick up a harp, though—especially if the ruler's a woman. Songs can get you places where swords can't. . . ."

"We go through this every time. . . . Would 'Gallowglass' suit you, Rod? It was the Irish term for a mercenary soldier."

"Gallowglass . . ." Rod rolled the word over his tongue. "Not bad. That's got some dash to it."

"Like yourself."

"Do I detect a touch of irony there? But it *is* a good, solid word . . . and it's not exactly what you'd call pretty. . . ."

"Definitely like yourself," the robot murmured.

"I daresay it'll do. Rod Gallowglass it is. *Whoa!*"

Rod sawed back on the reins, frowning. From some-place ahead of them came the low mutter of a mob.

Rod frowned. "What's all the commotion?"

"Rod, may I recommend caution . . ."

"Not a bad idea. Gee-up again, but lightly with the hooves, please."

Fess went at a walk through the narrow moonlit street, sidling up against the weathered wall of a build-ing. He stopped at the corner, thrust his horse's head around the angle.

"What do you see, Sister Ann?"

"A mob," said Fess.

"Astute observation, Watson. Anything else?"

"Torchlight, and a young man climbing up on a platform. If you'll pardon the analogy, Rod, it closely resembles a pep rally at your alma mater."

"Just might be what it is." Rod swung out of the saddle. "Well, you stay here, big fella. I'll scout the terrain."

He rounded the corner and let himself fall into a soldierly swagger, one hand on the pommel of his sword.

Not a bad idea, from the look of the crowd. Must be a meeting of the local Vagabond's Union. Not an un-patched doublet among them. He wrinkled his nose; a washed body seemed to be even more rare. Definitely a seedy lot.

The meeting-place was a large, open square, bor-dered by a wide river on one side; there were wharves with wooden ships riding at their moorings. On the other three sides of the square were cheap, decaying lodging-houses; sea-tackle stores and other cheap shops, and warehouses. The warehouses, at least, were in good repair. All the buildings were half-timbered, with the characteristic overhanging second story.

The shouting, jostling mob filled the whole square. Flaming pine knots lent a demonic light.

A closer look at the crowd revealed patched eyes, shriveled limbs, heads minus ears—an odd contrast to the figure that stood on the jury-rigged platform.

He was young, broad-shouldered and blond-headed. His face was clean and unscarred, snub-nosed and blue-eyed. It was a round, almost innocent face, open and honest, filled with the eerie light of a Man with a Mission. His doublet and hose were clean, for a wonder, and well-tailored from good cloth. A sword hung at his hip.

"A kid from the right side of the tracks," Rod mused. "What in the Seventh Hell is he doing in this rathole?"

The youth threw up his hands; the crowd roared, pine-knot torches surged forward to light him.

"Whose shoulders have borne up the weightiest burdens?" the boy shouted.

"Ours!" roared the crowd.

"Whose hands are worn hard and scarred with rough toil?"

"Ours!"

"Who is it have built all the wealth that the noblemen squander?"

"We!"

"Who is it have reared up their lofty castles of granite?"

"We!"

"Shall you not have a share in these riches and luxuries?"

"We shall!"

"Why," roared the young spokesman, "there is wealth enough in even one of these castles to make each one of you a king!"

The crowd went wild.

"You catching this, Fess?"

"I am, Rod. It sounds like a mixture of Karl Marx and Huey Long."

"Strange synthesis," Rod muttered. "And yet, maybe not so strange, when you come to think of it."

"This is your wealth!" shouted the youth. "You have a *right* to it!"

The crowd went wild again.

"Will they give you your due?"

The crowd went suddenly quiet. An ugly murmur began.

"No!" the young man bellowed. "You must therefore demand it, as is your right!"

He threw up his arms. "The Queen has given you bread and wine when the famine was upon you! The Queen has given meat and good wine to the witches whom she harbors!"

The crowd fell deathly still. A whisper ran through the ranks: "The witches! The witches!"

"Aye," roared the spokesman, "even the witches, the outcast and spurned. How much more, then, will she give to you, who have borne the heat of the day?

"She will give you your due!"

The crowd echoed his roar.

"Where do you go?" yelled the young Demosthenes.

"To the castle!" someone shouted, and other voices took up the cry. "To the castle! To the castle!" It became a rhythmic chant. "To the castle! To the castle! To the castle!"

A high, keening wail cut across the chant. The crowd fell silent. A narrow, twisted figure hobbled to the edge of a warehouse roof and called out over the square:

"Soldiers, a company or more!"

"Out through the alleys and wharves!" bellowed the young man. "At the House of Clovis we shall meet, within the hour!"

To Rod's amazement, the crowd remained silent. Streams of people began to pour down the twisted alleys. There was no panic, no crush.

Rod shrank into a doorway and watched as the torches were grounded. Score upon score of beggars ran past him, light-footed and silent, to be swallowed up by the dark mouths of the byways.

The square emptied; the light sounds of scampering faded away. In the sudden quiet, Rod heard the drum of approaching hooves—the soldiers, coming to check up on the Queen's loyal subjects.

Rod stepped out onto the cobbles, running on the balls of his feet, around the corner where Fess stood waiting.

He was into the saddle without breaking stride. "The good part of town," he whispered, "fast and quiet."

Fess could extrude inch-thick rubber pads from his hooves when silence was called for; he had also memorized a photo-map of the city from their aerial survey. There are advantages to a robot horse.

They fled through the town; the ground rose beneath them, building into the hill crowned by the royal castle. The quality of the buildings improved gradually; they were coming to the more affluent districts.

"What do you make of all that, Fess?"

"A totalitarian movement, beyond question," the robot replied. "A rabble-rouser, no doubt power-hungry, who will lead the people to make demands on the government, demands which cannot be met. The crown's refusals will be used to incite the mob to violence, and you have your revolution made.''

"Couldn't be just an ambitious nobleman trying to usurp the crown?"

"Usurpation derives its support from the upper classes, Rod. No, this is a proletarian revolution— a prelude to a totalitarian government.''

Rod pursed his lips. ''Would you say there was evidence of outside intervention from a more advanced society? I mean, proletarian revolutions aren't usually found in this kind of culture, are they?''

"Rarely, Rod, and the propaganda is rudimentary when they do occur. Persuasion in a medieval society never refers to the basic rights; the concept is alien to the culture. The probability of intervention is quite strong. . . .''

Rod's lips pulled back in a savage grin. ''Well, old mechanism, it looks like we've come to the right place to set up shop.''

At the uphill edge of the town, they came on a rambling, two-storied structure built around three sides of a torchlit courtyard. A timber palisade with a gate closed the fourth side. A party of laughing, well-dressed young men sauntered out of the gate; Rod caught a snatch of drunken song. Tableware rattled, and voices called for meat and ale.

"I take it we've found one of the better inns.''

"I would say that was a warranted assumption, Rod.''

Rod leaned back in the saddle. "Looks like a good place to spend the night. Is garlic sausage possible in this culture, Fess?''

The robot shuddered. "Rod, you have the most unearthly tastes!''

"Make way, make way!'' a voice trumpeted behind him.

Turning, Rod saw a party of soldiers, cavalry, trotting toward him. Behind them rolled a gilded, richly-carved carriage.

A herald rode in front of the soldiers. "Stand aside from the road, fellow!" he called. "The Queen's coach passes!"

"Queen!" Rod's eyebrows shot up. "Yes, yes! By all means, let's stand aside!"

He nudged Fess with his knee. The horse whirled off the road and jockeyed for a position on the shoulder that would give Rod a good look at the royal party.

The curtains on the coach were half drawn, but there was looking space. A lantern cast a warm yellow glow inside the coach, affording Rod a brief glimpse as the coach spun by.

A slender, frail form wrapped in a dark, hooded traveling cloak; a pale, small-bone face framed with blond, almost platinum hair; large, dark eyes; and small, very red lips drawn up in a pout.

And young, very young—scarcely past childhood, Rod thought.

She sat ramrod straight, looking very fragile but also very determined—and, somehow, forlorn, with the hostile, chip-on-the-shoulder attitude that so often goes with fear and loneliness.

Rod stared after the retreating party.

"Rod."

Rod started, shook his head, and realized that the coach had been out of sight for a while.

He glowered at the back of the horse's head. "What is it, Fess?"

"I wondered if you'd fallen asleep." The black head turned to Rod, the great eyes laughing gently.

"No." Rod twisted, looking back at the turn where the coach had disappeared.

Fess schooled his voice to patience. "The Dream again, Rod?"

Rod scowled. "I thought robots didn't have emotions."

"No. But we *do* have an innate dislike of a lack of that quality which has often been termed common sense."

Rod threw him a sour smile. "And, of course, an appreciation for that quality called irony, since it's basically logical. And irony implies—"

"—a sense of humor, yes. And you must admit, Rod, that there is something innately humorous in a man's chasing an object of his own invention over half a galaxy."

"Oh yeah, it's a million yuks, sure. But isn't that the difference between a man and a robot, Fess?"

"What? The ability to form imaginary constructions?"

"No, the ability to get hung up on them. Well, let's see if we can't find you a quiet stall where you can chew your data in peace."

Fess turned and trotted through the inn-yard gate.

A hostler came running from the stables as Rod dismounted. Rod tossed him the reins, said, "Don't give him too much water," and strolled into the big common room.

Rod hadn't known that rooms could be smoky without tobacco. Obviously, chimney-building was numbered among the underdeveloped sciences on this planet.

The customers didn't seem to mind, though. The room was filled with laughter, coarse jokes, and coarser voices in loud conversation. The great room was taken up by twenty or so large, round tables; there were several smaller tables, occupied by people whose dress marked them above the common (but not high enough to be staying at the castle). Lighting consisted of pine torches, which added to the atmosphere; tallow candles, dripping nicely on the guests; and a huge fireplace, fit to roast an ox, which was exactly what it was doing at the moment.

A small horde of boys and stocky peasant girls kept a steady stream of food and drink passing between the tables and the kitchen; many of them displayed considerable skill at broken-field running.

A large balding man with an apron tied around his ample middle burst out of the kitchen with a great smoking platter—the landlord, at a guess. Business was good tonight.

The man looked up, saw Rod, took in the gold and scarlet doublet, sword and dagger, the general air of authority, the well-filled purse—most especially the purse—and shoved the platter at the nearest serving girl. He bustled up to Rod, rubbing his hands on his apron.

"And how may I serve you, good master?"

"With a tankard of ale, a steak as thick as both your thumbs, and a table alone." Rod smiled as he said it.

The innkeeper stared, his lips forming a round O— Rod had apparently done something out of the ordinary.

Then the old man's eyes took on a calculating look, one that Rod had seen before; it was usually accompanied by a remark to the waiter, *sotto voce*, "Soft touch. Soak him for all he's worth."

Rod had smiled.

He should have known better.

Some things can be undone, though. Rod let his smile droop into a scowl.

"Well, what are you waiting for?" he barked. "Be quick about it, or I'll dine on a slice off your backside!"

The landlord jumped, then cringed, bowing rapidly.

"But of course, m'lord, of course! Quickly it will be, good master; yes, quickly indeed!" He turned away.

Rod's hand clamped onto his shoulder. "The table," he reminded.

The landlord gulped and bobbed his head, led Rod to a table beside an upright log that served as a pillar, and scurried away—cursing under his breath, no doubt.

Rod returned the courtesy, but enlarged the object to include all that the landlord stood for, namely the mercenary ways of mankind.

And, of course, wound up cursing himself for having catered to Mammon by getting tough.

But what could he do? SCENT agents were supposed to remain inconspicuous, and a softhearted medieval bourgeois was a contradiction in terms.

But when the landlord said quickly, he meant it. The steak and ale appeared almost before Rod had sat down. The landlord stood by rubbing his hands on his apron and looking very worried. Waiting for Rod to accept the cooking, probably.

Rod opened his mouth to reassure the man, and stopped with a word not quite past his larynx. His nosed twitched; a slow grin spread over his face. He looked up at the landlord.

"Do I smell garlic sausage?"

"Oh yes, your worship!" The landlord started bobbing again. "Garlic sausage it is, your worship, and very fine garlic sausage too, if I may say so. If your worship would care for some . . . ?"

"My worship would," said Rod, "and *presto allegro*, sir-rah."

The landlord shied, reminding Rod of Fess regarding a syllogism, and ran.

Now, what was that all about? Rod wondered. Must

have been something he said. And he'd been rather proud of that sirrah. . . .

He sampled the steak, and had just washed it down when a plate of sausage *thunked!* onto the table.

"Very good," said Rod, "and the steak is acceptable."

The landlord's face broke into a grin of relief; he turned to go, then turned back.

"Well, what is it?" Rod asked around a mouthful of sausage.

The landlord was twisting his hands in his apron again. "Beg pardon, my master, but . . ." His lips twisted too, then the words burst out. "Art a warlock, m'master?"

"Who, me? A warlock? Ridiculous!" For emphasis, Rod jabbed his table knife in the landlord's general direction. The huge belly shrank in amazingly; then it bolted, taking its owner along.

Now where did he get the idea I was a warlock? Rod mused as he chewed a mouthful of steak.

Never had a better steak, he decided. *Must be the smoke. Wonder what wood they're using?*

Must have been the presto allegro *bit. Thought they were magic words, probably.* . . .

Well, they *had* worked wonders.

Rod took a bite of sausage and a swig of ale.

Him, a warlock? Never! He might be a second son of a second son, but he wasn't *that* desperate.

Besides, being a warlock involved signing a contract in blood, and Rod had no blood to spare. He kept losing it in the oddest places. . . .

He drained his tankard, set it down with a thump. The landlord materialized with a jug and poured him a refill. Rod started a smile of thanks, remembered his station, and changed the smile to a sneer. He fumbled in his purse, felt the irregular shape of a gold nugget—

acceptable currency in a medieval society—
remembered the quickness of the house to gyp the
generous, and passed over the nugget in favor of a
sliver of silver.

The landlord stared at the small white bar in the palm
of his hand, his eyes making a valiant attempt to turn
into hemispheres. He made a gargling sound, stuttered
elaborate thanks, and scurried away.

Rod bit his lip in annoyance. Apparently even so
small a chunk of silver was enough to excite comment
here.

The touch of anger dissipated quickly, though; a
pound or two of beef in the belly *did* tend to make the
world look better. Rod threw his legs out in the aisle,
stretched, and slumped backward in the chair, picking
his teeth with the table knife.

Something was strangely wrong in this common
room. The happy were a little too professional about
it—voices a shade too loud, laughter a trifle strained,
with a dark echo. The glum, on the other hand, were
really glum; their brown studies were paneled in walnut.

Fear.

Take that pair at three o'clock on the third table from
the right, now—they were awfully earnest about whatever it was they were hashing over. Rod gave his ring a
surreptitious nudge and pointed it at the twosome.

"But such meetings do no good if the Queen is
continually sending her soldiers against us!"

" 'Tis true, Adam, 'tis true; she won't hear us, for,
when all's said and done, she won't let us close enough
to speak."

"Why, then, she must be forced to listen!"

"Aye, but what good would that do? Her nobles
would not let her give what we demand."

Adam slammed his open hand on the table. "But

we've a right to be free without being thieves and beggars! The debtors' prisons must end, and the taxes with them!''

"Aye, and so must the cutting off of an ear for the theft of a loaf of bread.'' He rubbed the side of his head, with a hangdog look on his face. "Yet she hath contrived to do summat for us . . .''

"Aye, this setting-up of her own judges now! The great lords will no longer give each their justice, by style and taste.''

"The nobles will not bear it, and that thou knowest. The judges will not stand long.'' One-Ear's face was grim; he traced circles on the wet tabletop.

"Nay, the noblemen will stand for naught that the Queen designs!'' Adam plunged his knife into the tabletop. "Will not the Loguire see that?''

"Nay, speak not against the Loguire!'' One-Ear's face darkened. "If 'twere not for him, we would still be a ragtag horde, with no common purpose! Speak not against Loguire, Adam, for without him, we would not have the brass to sit in this inn, where the Queen's soldiers are but guests!''

"Oh, aye, aye, he pulled us together and made men of us thieves. Yet now he holds our new manhood in check; he seeks to keep us from fighting for that which is ours!''

One-Ear's mouth turned down tight at the corners. "Thou hast hearkened too much to the idle and envious chatter of the Mocker, Adam!''

"Yet fight we must, mark my words!'' Adam cried, clenching his fist. "Blood must be shed ere we come to our own. Blood must answer for blood, and 'tis blood the nobles have ta'en from—''

Something huge slammed into Rod, knocking him back against the table, filling his head with the smell of sweat and onions and cheap wine.

Rod braced an arm against the table and shoved with his shoulder. The heavy form swayed away with a *whuff!* of breath. Rod drew his dagger and thumbed the signet ring to off.

The man loomed over him, looking eight feet tall and wide as a wagon.

"Here now!" he growled. "Why doncha look where I'm going at?"

Rod's knife twisted, gleaming light into the man's eyes. "Stand away, friend," he said softly. "Leave an honest man to his ale."

"An honest man, is it!" The big peasant guffawed. "A sojer, callin' hisself an honest man!" His roaring laughter was echoed from the tables.

On an off bet, Rod decided, strangers weren't popular here.

The laughter stopped quite suddenly. "Nay, put down your plaything," said the big man, suddenly sober, "and I'll show you an honest villager can outfight a sojer."

A prickle ran down Rod's spine as he realized it was a put-up job. The landlord had advised the big ox of the whereabouts of a heavy purse. . . .

"I've no quarrel with you," Rod muttered. He realized it was the worst thing he could have said almost before the words were off his tongue.

The big man leered, gloating. "No quarrel, he says now. He throws hisself in the path of a poor staggering man so's he can't help but ran into him. But, 'No quarrel,' sez he, when he's had a look at Big Tom!"

A huge, meaty hand buried itself in the cloth at Rod's throat, pulling him to his feet. "Nay, I'll show you a quarrel," Big Tom snarled.

Rod's right hand lashed out, chopping into the man's elbow, then bouncing away. The big man's hand loosened and fell, temporarily numbed. Big Tom stared at his hand, a look of betrayal.

Rod pressed his lips together, tucked his knife into the sheath. He stepped back, knees flexed, rubbed his right fist in his left palm. The peasant was big, but he probably knew nothing of boxing.

Life came back into Tom's hand, and with it, pain. The huge man bellowed in anger, his hand balling into a fist, swinging at Rod in a vast roundhouse swipe that would have annihilated anything it struck.

But Rod ducked under and to the side and, as the fist went by him, reached up behind Tom's shoulder and gave a solid push to add to the momentum of the swing.

Big Tom spun around; Rod caught the man's right wrist and twisted it up behind Tom's back. Rod jerked the wrist up a little higher; Big Tom howled. While he was howling, Rod's arm snaked under Tom's armpit to catch the back of his neck in a half nelson.

Not bad, Rod thought. So far he hadn't needed boxing.

Rod planted a knee in Tom's backside as he released his holds; Tom blundered into the open space before the hearth, tried to catch his balance, and didn't make it. Overturned tables clattered and thudded as the patrons scuttled back, all too glad to leave the fireside seat to Big Tom.

He came to his knees, shaking his head, and looked up to see Rod standing before him in a wrestler's crouch, smiling grimly and beckoning with both arms.

Tom growled low in his throat and braced a foot against the fieldstones of the hearth.

He shot at Rod head-first, like a bull.

Rod sidestepped and stuck out a foot. Big Tom went flailing straight for the first row of tables. Rod squeezed his eyes shut and set his teeth.

There was a crash like four simultaneous strikes in a

bowling alley. Rod winced. He opened his eyes and forced himself to look.

Big Tom's head emerged out of a welter of wood-work, wide-eyed and slack-jawed.

Rod shook his head sadly, clucking his tongue. "You've had a rough night, Big Tom. Why don't you go home and sleep it off?"

Tom picked himself up, shin, wristbone, and clavi-cle, and put himself back together, taking inventory the while.

Satisfied that he was a gestalt again, he stamped a foot, planted his fists on his hips, and looked up at Rod.

"Here now, man!" he complained. "You don't half fight like an honest gentleman!"

"Not hardly a gentleman at all," Rod agreed. "What do you say we try one more throw, Tom? Double or nothing!"

The big man looked down at his body as if doubting its durability. He kicked at the remains of an oak table tentatively, slammed a fist into his own tree-trunk biceps, and nodded.

"I'll allow as I'm fit," he said. "Come on, little man."

He stepped out onto the cleared floor in front of the hearth, walking warily around the perimeter, keeping one baleful eye on Rod.

"Our good landlord told you I had silver in my purse, didn't he?" said Rod, his eyes snapping.

Big Tom didn't answer.

"Told you I was an easy mark, too," Rod mused. "Well, he was wrong on both counts.

Big Tom's eyes bulged. He gave a bellow of distress. "No silver?"

Rod nodded. "I thought he told you." His eyes flicked over to the landlord, ashen and trembling by a pillar.

And looked back to see Big Tom's foot heading right toward his midriff.

Rod fell back, swinging both hands up to catch Big Tom's heel and inspire it to greater heights.

Tom's foot described a neat arc. For a moment, he hung in the air, arms flailing; then he crashed howling to the floor.

Rod's eyes filled with pain as Big Tom floundered about, struggling for the breath that the floor had knocked out of him.

Rod stepped in, grabbed the front of Tom's tunic, braced his foot against Tom's and threw his weight back, hauling the big man to his feet. Tom immediately sagged forward; Rod shoved a shoulder under Tom's armpit and pushed the big man back to the vertical.

"Ho, landlord!" he shouted. "Brandy—and fast!"

Rod liked to think of himself as the kind of man people could lean on, but this was ridiculous.

When Big Tom had been somewhat revived and commended to the gentle jeers of his booze buddies, and the guests had somewhat restored the room and resumed their places, and Rod had still not wreaked anything resembling vengeance on the landlord, that worthy's eyes sparked with a sudden hope. He appeared again before Rod, his chin thrust out and the corners of his mouth drawn down.

Rod hauled himself out of the depths of a rather cynical contemplation of man's innate goodness and focused on the landlord. "Well, what do you want?"

The landlord swallowed thickly. "If it please your worship there's a little matter of some broken chairs and tables. . . ."

"Chairs," said Rod, not moving. "Tables."

He slammed to his feet and coiled a hand around the innkeeper's neck. "Why, you slimy little curmudgeon! You set that ox on me, you try to rob me, and you have

the gall to stand there and tell me I owe you money?''
He emphasized each point with a shake of the landlord's neck, slowly pushing him back against the pillar.
The landlord made a masterful attempt to blend into the
bark, but only succeeded in spreading himself thin.

"And to top it all off, my ale's gotten warm!" Rod
shouted. "You call yourself a landlord, and you treat a
gentleman of arms like *this?''*

"Forgive, master, forgive!" the landlord rattled,
clawing at Rod's hand with commendable effort and
negative effect. "I meant no harm, your worship; I
meant only—"

"Only to rob me, yes!" Rod snorted, letting him go
with a toss that fetched him up backward over a table.
"Beware the kind, for they tend to grow cruel when
you cross them. Now! A goblet of hot mulled wine by
the time I count three, and I may refrain from stretching
your ears out and tying them under your chin. Git!"

He counted to three, with a two second pause between numbers, and the goblet was in his hand. The
landlord scuttled away with his hands clapped over his
ears, and Rod sat down to sip at the wine and wonder
what a curmudgeon was.

Looking up, he saw a half a garlic sausage sitting on
the table. He picked it up with a heavy hand and tucked
it into his purse. Might as well take it along; it was
about the only good thing that had happened today.

He surged to his feet and called, "Ho, landlord!"

Mine host came bobbling up.

"A chamber alone, with heavy blankets!"

"A chamber alone, sir! At once, sir!" The landlord
scuttled away, still bobbing his head. "Heavy blankets, sir! Quite surely, sir!"

Rod ground his teeth and turned away to the door. He
stepped out and leaned back against the jamb, letting
his head slump forward onto his chest, eyes closed.

"The law of the jungle," he muttered. "If it looks weak, prey upon it. If it turns out to be strong, bow to it; let it prey upon you and hope it won't devour you."

"Yet all men have pride," murmured a voice behind his ear.

Rod looked up, smiled. " 'Art there, old mole?' "

" 'Swear! Swear!' " Fess answered.

Rod let loose a stream of invective that would have done credit to a sailor with a hangover.

"Feel better?" Fess asked, amused.

"Not much. Where does a man like mine host hide his pride, Fess? He sure as hell never let it show. Obsequiousness, yes; avarice, yes; but self-respect? No. I haven't seen that in him."

"Pride and self-respect are not necessarily synonymous, Rod."

Someone tugged at Rod's elbow. He snapped his head around, muscles tensed.

It was Big Tom, his six-foot-five bent strangely in a valiant attempt to put his head below the level of Rod's.

"God e'en, master."

Rod stared at him for a moment without answering.

"God e'en," he replied, his voice carefully neutral. "What can I do for *you?*"

Big Tom hunched his shoulders and scratched at the base of his skull. "Eh, master," he complained, "you made a bit of a fool of me back a while."

"Oh?" Rod lifted an eyebrow. "Do tell!"

"I do," the big man admitted, "and . . . well . . . ." He pulled off his cap and twisted it in his great hands. "It *do* seem like . . . well, master, you've finished me here, and that's gospel."

Rod felt his back lifting. "And I'm supposed to make it up to you, is that it? Pay you damages, I suppose!"

"Eh, no, master!" Big Tom shied away. " 'Tisn't that, master, not that at all! It's just . . . well . . . I was a wonderin', I was, if you might . . . that is . . . I . . ."

He twisted the hat through some gyrations that would have astounded a topolgist; then the words came out in a rush.

"I was wonderin' if you might be needin' a servin'-man, you know—a sort of groom and lackey, and . . ." His voice trailed off. He eyed Rod sidewise, fearful and hopeful.

Rod stood frozen for a moment or two. He searched the big man's open, almost worshipful face.

He crossed his arms and leaned back against the jamb again. "Why, how's this, Big Tom? Not half an hour agone, you sought to rob me! And now *I* am supposed to trust *you* for a squire?"

Big Tom caught his nether lip between his teeth, frowning. " 'Tain't right-seeming, master, that I know, but—" His hands gestured vaguely. "Well, the fact of it is, you're the only man what I ever raised hand against, could beat me, and . . ."

His voice ran out again. Rod nodded slowly, his eyes on Big Tom's.

"And therefore you must serve me."

Tom's lower lip thrust out, pouting. "Not must, my master—only that I *wants* to."

"A robber," said Rod. "A cutpurse. And I'm to trust you."

Big Tom's hat twisted again.

"You've got an open face," Rod mused, "not the kind of face that hides its feelings."

Big Tom smiled widely, nodding.

"Of course, that doesn't mean anything," Rod went on. "I've known quite a few gentle-seeming girls that turned out to be first-class bitches."

Tom's face fell.

"So you might be honest—or you might be a thorough rogue. It's a *Fess*-cinating puzzle."

The voice behind his ear murmured, "Preliminary interpretation of available data indicates basically simplistic personality structure. Probability of individual serving as reliable source of information on local social variables exceeds probability of individual practicing serious duplicity."

Rod nodded slowly. He would have settled for an even chance.

He fished a scrap of silver from his purse—it smelt slightly of garlic—and slapped it into the big man's hand.

Tom stared at the silver in his palm, then at Rod, then back at the metal.

Abruptly, hs hand closed into a fist, trembling slightly. His staring eyes came up to Rod again.

"You've accepted my coin," said Rod. "You're my man."

Big Tom's face split from ear to ear in a grin. He ducked his head. "Yes, master! I thanks you, master! Forever I thanks you, master! I—"

"I get the message." Rod hated to see a grown man grovel. "You go on duty right now. Tell me, what are the chances of getting a job with the Queen's army?"

"Oh, most excellent, master!" Big Tom grinned. "They're always needing new sojers."

A bad omen, Rod decided.

"Okay," he said. "Duck back inside, find out which room we've been assigned, and check it to make sure there isn't a cutthroat in the closet."

"Yes, master! Right away!" Big Tom bustled back into the inn.

Rod smiled, closed his eyes, and let his head fall back against the jamb. He rolled his head from side to side, laughing silently. He would never cease to be amazed at the bully psychology; how a man could go from arrogance to servility in less than ten minutes, he would never understand.

A low, quavering wail cut the night air, soaring into a shriek.

Rod's eyes snapped open. Sirens? In *this* culture?

The sound was coming from the left; he looked up, and saw the castle, there on its hilltop.

And there, at the base of the tower, something glowed, and keened like a paddy wagon lamenting the death of some squad cars.

The guests tumbled out of the inn to stand in the courtyard, staring and pointing.

" 'Tis the banshee!"

"Again!"

"Nay, all will be well. Hath it not appeared thrice before? And yet the Queen lives!"

"Fess," Rod said carefully.

"Yes, Rod."

"Fess, there's a banshee. On the castle battlements. A banshee, Fess."

There was no answer.

Then a raucous buzz snarled behind Rod's ear, swelled till it threatened to shake his head apart, and cut off.

Rod shook his head and pounded his temple with the heel of his hand.

"I'm going to have to have that boy overhauled," he muttered. "He used to have *quiet* seizures."

It would have been unwise for Rod to go to the stables to reset Fess while the inn-yard was full of gawkers; he would have been thoroughly conspicuous.

So he went up to his room, to lie down till things had quieted down a bit; and, of course, by the time the courtyard was clear, Rod was too comfortable to take the trouble of going down to the stables. No real reason to reset the robot, anyway; it would be a quiet night.

The room was dark, except for a long swathe of light streaming in the window from the largest moon. There was a subdued murmur and clatter from the common room—nightowl guests drinking late. Rod's chamber was very peaceful.

Not quiet, though. Big Tom, curled up on a pallet at the foot of the bed, snored like a bulldozer on idle, making more noise asleep than he did awake.

Now there was a riddle—Big Tom. Rod had never before been in a fight where he hadn't been hit at least once. Big Tom had left himself wide open, every time; and sure, he was big, but he didn't have to be *that* clumsy. Big men *can* be quick. . . .

But why would Big Tom have thrown the fight?

So Rod would take him on as a serving-man?

And what about Adam and One-Ear? Their talk would seem to indicate they'd been at the pep rally down by the wharf, which would mean they were members of the proletarian party. What had the young rabble-rouser called it? The House of Clovis, yes.

But if Adam and One-Ear were a representative sample, the House of Clovis was a house divided against itself. There seemed to be two factions, one backing the Loguire—the juvenile orator?—and one led by the Mocker, whoever that might be. The usual two factions, nonviolent and violent, tongue and sword.

Now, why would Big Tom have wanted a butler job? Social climber, maybe? No, he wasn't the fawning type. Better wages? But he'd seemed to be moderately prosperous as the neighborhood heavy.

To keep an eye on Rod?

Rod rolled over on his side. Tom just might be a member in good standing of the House of Clovis. But why would the House want to keep tabs on Rod? They couldn't suspect anything, could they?

If Fess's guess was right, and the House was backed by an off-planet power, they definitely might suspect something—never mind how.

But wasn't Rod letting his paranoia show again?

He was wide awake, every muscle tense. He sighed and rolled out of bed; he couldn't sleep now. Better reset Fess and have a talk. Rod needed the robot's electronic objectivity; he had very little of his own.

Big Tom stirred and wakened as Rod lifted the rusty door latch.

"Master? Where dost thou go?"

"Just got a little worried about my horse, Big Tom. Think I'll run down to the stables and make sure the hostler's treating him right. Go back to sleep."

Big Tom stared a moment.

"Certes," he said, "thou'rt a most caring one, master."

He rolled over and burrowed his head into the folded cloak he used for a pillow. "To be so much concerned for a horse," he muttered, and snored again.

Rod grinned and let himself out of the room.

He found a stairway a few paces away—dark and musty, but closer to the stables than the main door.

There was a door at the bottom of the stair, one that was not very often used; it groaned like a bullfrog in heat when he opened it.

The inn-yard was flooded with the soft, golden light of the three moons. The largest was only a little smaller than Terra's, but much closer; it filled a full thirty degrees of sky, a perpetual harvest moon.

"Great planet for lovers," Rod mused; and, because

his eyes were on the moon, he didn't notice the gray strand of cord stretched a little above the doorstep. He tripped.

His arms swung up, slapping the ground to break his fall. Something hard struck the back of his head, and the world dissolved in a shoal of sparks.

There was a ruddy glow about him, and a throbbing ache in his head. Something cold and wet moved over his face. He shuddered, and came wide awake.

He lay on his back; a limestone roof vaulted over him, glimmering with bits of captured light. Pinch-waisted limestone columns stretched from the roof to a green carpet—stalactites and stalagmites joined. The green carpet stretched away in all directions for at least a mile. He was in a vast underground cavern. The light seemed to come from everywhere, a dancing, wavering light, setting the sparks in the ceiling into an intricate ballet.

The green carpet spread under him; he could feel it, cold and springy, damp, under his back: moss, three inches thick. He tried to put out a hand to touch the moss, and discovered that he couldn't move his arms or legs. Lifting his head, he looked for ropes binding him, but there was not so much as a thread.

He shook his head, trying to get the ache out of it so he could think clearly.

"Fess," he muttered, "where am I?"

There was no answer.

Rod bit his lip. "Come on, iron horse! Are you asleep at the switch?"

Switch . . .

Fess had had a seizure. Rod had been en route to reset him.

Rod was on his own.

He sighed and lay back on the green moss carpet.

A deep voice began singing, off to his right. Rod looked.

A fire fluttered in a bare stone circle. A tripod stood over it, supporting a cauldron—a covered cauldron, bubbling merrily, with a tube leading from a hole in the cover. Drops of water fell from the roof, striking the tube; and a beaker sat under the far end of the tube, collecting drops.

A primitive still.

And a moonshiner, a moonshiner perhaps eighteen inches high, very broad-shouldered and generally stocky, clad in doublet and hose. He had a round, cheerful face, twinkling green eyes, a snub nose, and a very wide mouth curved in an impish smile. To top it off, he wore a Robin Hood hat with a bright red feather.

The green eyes looked up and caught Rod's. "Ha!" said the little man in a buzzing baritone. "Tha'rt come to thy senses, warlock!"

Rod scowled. "Warlock? I'm not a warlock!"

"To be sure," said the little man, "tha'rt not. Thou comest in a falling star, and thou hast a horse made of cold iron. . . ."

"Just a minute, there," Rod interrupted. "How'd you know the horse was made of cold iron?"

"We are the Wee Folk," said the little man, unperturbed. "We live by Oak, Ash, and Thorn, by Wood, Air, and Sod; and those who live by cold iron seek the end of our woodlands. Cold iron is the sign of all that cannot abide us; and therefore we know cold iron, no matter what form or disguise it may be in."

He turned back to the kettle, lifting the lid to check the mash. "Then, too, thou canst hear what is said a good half mile off; and thy horse can run as silent as the wind and faster than a falcon, when it has cause to. But tha'rt not a warlock, eh?"

Rod shook his head. "I'm not. I use science, not magic!"

"Assuredly," said the little man, "and a rose by any other name . . . Nay, tha'rt a warlock, and as such tha'rt known already throughout the length and the breadth of Gramarye!"

"Gramarye? What's that?"

The little man stared in surprise. "Why, the world, warlock! The world we live in, the land between the Four Seas, the realm of Queen Catharine!"

"Oh. She rules the whole world?"

"Certes," said the elf, giving Rod a sidelong glance.

"And the name of her castle? And the town around it?"

"Runnymede. In truth, tha'rt a most untutored warlock!"

"That's just what I've been trying to tell you," and Rod sighed.

The little man turned away, shaking his head and muttering. He opened a pippet on the collection beaker and drained some of the distillate into a shot-glass-sized mug.

Rod suddenly realized he was very thirsty. "Uh, say—what're you brewing up there? Wouldn't be brandy, would it?"

The elf shook his head.

"Gin? Rum? *Aqua Vitae?*"

"Nay; 'tis spirits of another sort." He bounced over to Rod and held the miniscule mug to the man's lips.

"Thanks." Rod took a sip. He looked up at the roof, smacking his lips. "Tastes like honey."

"Where the wild bee sucks, there suck I." The little man hopped back to the fire.

"Not bad at all. Could you spare the recipe?"

"Aye, assuredly." The elf grinned. "We would do aught within our power for a guest."

"Guest!" Rod snorted. "I hate to impugn your hospitality, but immobilizing me isn't exactly what I'd call a welcome."

"Oh, we shall make amends ere long." The little man lifted the cauldron lid and stirred the mash.

Something clicked in Rod's mind. The hairs at the base of his skull began to prickle.

"Uh, say, uh . . . I don't belive we've been introduced, but . . . your name wouldn't be Robin Goodfellow, would it? Alias Puck?"

"Thous speakest aright." The elf replaced the lid with a clang. "I am that merry wanderer of the night."

Rod fell back onto the moss carpet. It'd make a great story to tell his grandchildren; nobody else would believe it.

"Say, Puck—you don't mind if I call you Puck?"

"Oh, nay."

"Thanks, uh . . . I'm Rod Gallowglass."

"We ha' known it."

"Well, just thought I'd make it official. Now, you don't seem to spare me any particular ill-will, so, uh, may I ask . . . uh . . . why am I paralyzed?"

"Ah, that," said Puck. "We must find if you are a white warlock, or black."

"Oh." Rod chewed the inside of his cheek for a moment. "If I'm a white warlock, you'll, um . . . let me go?"

Puck nodded.

"What happens if you decide I'm a black warlock?"

"Then, Rod Gallowglass, you shall sleep till the Trump of Doom."

Rod felt as though a weak electric current had been applied to his jaw. "Great. The Trump of Doom. And I never was much good at bridge."

Puck frowned. "How . . .?"

"Skip it. 'Sleep till the Trump of Doom.' A very

neat euphemism. Why don't you just come right out and say you'll kill me?''

"Nay." Puck thrust his lower lip out, shaking his head. "We would not kill you, Rod Gallowglass. Thou shouldst but sleep forever, and with pleasant dreams.''

"I see. Suspended animation?''

Puck's brow wrinkled. "I know not that word. Yet rest assured, thou shalt not be suspended. The Wee Folk have no fondness for a hanging.''

"Well, I suppose that's something of a comfort. So how do I prove I'm a white warlock?''

"Why," said Puck, "by our enlarging you.''

Rod stared. "How's that again?

"Aren't I big enough already?''

The elf's face split into a broad grin. "Nay, nay! Enlarging you! Removing the spell that binds you!''

"Oh." Rod lay back with a sigh of relief. Then he jerked back up. *"Freeing* me? That's going to prove I'm a white warlock?''

"By itself, no," said Puck. " 'Tis a question where we free you.''

He clapped his hands. Rod heard the scurrying of scores of small feet coming from behind him; a fold of dark cloth was drawn over his eyes, knotted behind his head.

"Hey!" he protested.

"Peace," said Puck. "We do but bear you forth to your freedom.''

A host of tiny hands lifted Rod. He resigned himself and lay back to enjoy the trip.

It was a rather pleasant way to travel, actually—like an innerspring mattress with four-wheel drive.

His feet tilted up higher than his head and the pace of the scuttling feet under him slowed—they were mounting an incline.

Damp night air struck his face; he heard the breeze

sighing in the leaves, accompanied by a full comple-
ment of crickets, with an owl and maybe a curlew providing the harmony.

He was dropped unceremoniously; the blindfold was
whipped from his eyes.

"Hey!" he protested "What do you think I am, a
sack of potatoes?"

He could hear a stream gurgling off to his left.

"Tha'rt free now, Rod Gallowglass," Puck's voice
husked in his ear. "May God be with you!" And the elf
bounded away.

Rod sat up, flexing his limbs to make them realize
they could move gain. He looked about.

It was a moonlit forest glade, with a silver stream
trickling past on the left. The trees were bright steel
trunk and tinsel leaf, and black shadow among the
trunks.

One of the shadows moved.

It stepped forward, a tall figure in a dark, hooded
monk's robe.

Rod scrambled to his feet.

The figure moved slowly toward Rod, halted ten feet
away, and threw back the hood.

Wild, disordered hair over a long, thin face, with
hollows under the cheekbones and caves for eye sockets, with two burning coals at their backs—and the
whole face twisted, curdled with bitterness.

The voice was flat and thin, almost a hiss. "Are you,
then, so tired of life that you come to a werewolf's
cage?"

Rod stared. "Werewolf!"

Well, why not! If elves were a basic assumption. . . .

Then Rod frowned. "Cage?" He looked around.
"Looks like the great outdoors to me."

"There is a wall of magic around this grove," hissed

the werewolf. " 'Tis a prison the Wee Folk have made me—and they do not feed me in my proper fashion."

"Oh?" Rod looked at the werewolf out of the corner of his eye. "What's your proper fashion?"

"Red meat." The werewolf grinned, showing a mouthful of canines. "Raw, red meat, and blood for my wine."

Something with lots of cold little feet ran down Rod's spine.

"Make peace with your God," said the werewolf, "for your hour has come."

Fur appeared on the backs of his hands, and his fingernails grew, curving outward. Forehead and cheeks sprouted fur; nose, mouth, and chin slipped together and bulged, tapering outward to a muzzle. His ears moved upward to the top of his head and stretched into points.

He flung off the dark cloak; his whole body was silvery fur, his legs had become haunches.

He dropped to all fours. His upper arms shortened and his forearms lengthened; his hands had become paws. A tail sprouted and grew into a long, silvery plume.

The silver wolf crouched close to the earth, snarling, growling low in its throat, and sprang.

Rod whirled aside, but the wolf managed to change course in mid-air just enough; its teeth ripped Rod's forearm from elbow to wrist.

The wolf landed and spun about with a howl of joy. It crouched, tongue lolling out, then it sprang again.

Rod ducked, dropping to one knee, but the wolf checked itself in mid-leap and fell on top of him. Its hindlegs clawed at his chest; the great jaws fumbled for a hold on his spine.

Rod surged to his feet, bowing forward and shoving

against the wolf's belly with all his strength. The wolf went flying, but its claws had raked Rod's back open.

The wolf landed on its back, hard, and howled with the pain. It scrambled to its feet and stalked around Rod in a circle, growling with blood-lust.

Rod pivoted, keeping his face toward the wolf. How do you handle a werewolf? Fess would know, but Fess was still out of order.

The wolf snarled and leaped for Rod's throat.

Rod crouched low and lunged with his hand stiffened. His fingers caught the wolf right in the solar plexus.

Rod leaped back, falling into a crouch. The wolf clawed at the ground, struggling to regain its breath as life poured back into its nerves. Rod circled around it, widdershins for luck.

How do you fight a werewolf?

Wolfbane, obviously.

But Rod couldn't tell wolfbane from poison ivy without a botany text.

The wolf dragged in a long, grating breath and rose into a crouch. It snarled and began to prowl, widdershins around Rod, watching for an opening.

So much for widdershins, Rod thought, and reversed direction, circling clockwise in an attempt to get behind the wolf.

The wolf sprang.

Rod pivoted aside and let fly a right jab at the wolf's jaw; but the wolf caught his fist in its teeth.

Rod bellowed with pain and kicked the beast in the belly. Fang went down for a breather again, freeing Rod's hand as the toothy jaws gaped for air.

Silver bullets. But chemical sidearms had been out of vogue for thousands of years, and the DDT had gone off the silver standard quite a while before.

A crucifix. Rod made a firm resolution to take up religion. He needed a hobby, anyway.

His furry friend had meanwhile pulled itself back together. Haunches tensed, it sprang.

Rod sidestepped, but the wolf had apparently counted on his so doing. It landed full on his chest, slavering jaws snapping for Rod's jugular vein.

Rod fell on his back. He pulled up his legs, planted his feet in the wolf's belly, and shoved, catapulting the canine clear of his corpus. The wolf fell hard and squirmed, getting its feet under its body.

What else didn't werewolves like?

Garlic.

Rod circled around the wolf, fumbling in his purse for the garlic sausage left over from dinner.

The wolf spread its jaws wide and hacked a cough.

Rod munched a mouthful of sausage.

The wolf came to its feet with an ugly, very determined growl. It tensed and sprang.

Rod caught the beast under the forelegs, staggering back under the weight of its body, and breathed full in its face. He dropped the wolf and sprang away.

The wolf rolled, spitting and coughing, drew in a shuddering gasp, and collapsed.

Its form stretched, relaxed, and slowly stretched again—and a tall, lean wiry man lay naked, face down, in the grass, unconscious body heaving with great panting breaths.

Rod sank to his knees. Saved by garlic sausage!

Grass whispered by his knee; he looked into the smiling eyes of Robin Goodfellow.

"Return with us if you will, Rod Gallowglass, for our paths are yours, to walk at your pleasure, now."

Rod smiled wearily. "He might have killed me," he said, with a nod at the unconscious werewolf.

Puck shook his head. "We looked on, and would

have prevented death to either of you; and as for your wounds, why! we shall quickly have them mended."

Rod rose, shaking his head in disbelief.

"Then, too," said Puck, "we knew you to be a warlock of such potency that you could defeat him . . . if you were a white warlock."

"Oh?" Rod raised an eyebrow. "What if I wasn't? What if I was black?"

"Why, then," Puck said, grinning, "you would have leagued with him against us, and sought to fight loose of the prison."

"Um." Rod gnawed at his lower lip. "Wouldn't that have put you in a rather delicate position?"

"Nay." Puck grinned again. "The magic of a score of elves has never yet been equaled by two warlocks."

"I see." Rod rubbed his chin. "Hedged your bets, didn't you? But you couldn't let me know, of course. As long as I was in the dark, fighting the werewolf proved I was one of the good guys?"

"Partly."

"Oh? What's the other part?"

"Why, Rod Gallowglass, there were several times when you had rendered the werewolf helpless, but you did not kill him."

"And that shows I've got a good heart."

"That," Puck agreed, "and also that you are sure enough of your own power that you dare be merciful. And *there* is proof that you are white, but greater proof that you are a warlock."

Rod squeezed his eyes shut. With exaggerated patience, he said, "Of course, it *might* just be that I'm a trained fighter."

"It might," Puck agreed, "but it was by sorcery that you overcame him."

Rod took a deep breath. "Look," he said carefully, "I am not a warlock. I have never been a warlock. I never want to be a warlock. I'm just a mercenary soldier who happens to know a few tricks."

"Assuredly, Master Warlock," said Puck cheerfully. "Will you come back to the cavern? We shall guide you forth to your inn."

"Oh, all right," Rod grumbled.

But he turned to look at the miserable collection of bone and sinew that was the sleeping werewolf, lying in the center of the glade.

"Master Gallowglass?" Puck's voice was puzzled, disturbed. "What troubles you?"

Rod shook his head, coming out of his reverie. "Nothing," he said, turning away. "Just wondering."

"What of, warlock?"

"They used to call me a lone wolf when I was a schoolboy . . . Never mind. Which way did you say the cavern was?"

The stars wheeled toward dawn as Rod stumbled, footsore and weary, across the inn-yard and into the stable.

A single candle-lantern lit the row of stalls, serving only to deepen the shadows.

Rod flung an arm across Fess's back to steady himself, his other hand groping across the robot's withers till he found the enlarged vertebra that was the reset switch. He pressed; the steel body stirred under its horsehair camouflage. The velvet black head lifted, shook twice, turned to look back over its shoulder, great brown eyes focusing on Rod. The robot was silent a moment; then the voice behind Rod's ear spoke with a touch of reproach:

"You have left me inactive a long time, Rod. I have no aftereffects from the seizure."

"Sorry, old iron." Rod kept his arms across the

horse's back; his legs felt a trifle wobbly. "I was on my way to reset you when I got clobbered."

"Clobbered!" Fess's voice writhed with shame. "While I slept! May my casing lie forever corroding on the junkpile! May my germanium be consigned to the Converter for reclamation! May my—"

"Oh, stow it!" Rod growled. "It wasn't your fault." He stepped away from the horse, straightening his shoulders. "I wasn't in any real danger, anyway. Just a busy night, that's all."

"How so, Rod?"

Rod started to answer, then changed his mind. "I'll tell you in the morning, Fess."

"I have reoriented my circuits to accept the discrepancies between accepted theory and actual occurrence, Rod. You may confide in me without fear of overload."

Rod shook his head and turned to stumble out of the stall. "In the morning, Fess. You might be able to believe it right now, but I'm not sure I could."

Rod sat down to a whopping breakfast, but he was on a starvation diet compared to Big Tom. The man was surrounded by unbelievable stacks of food.

Some of it was familiar to Rod—the eggs, pancakes, and ham. The 'cakes had a subtly alien flavor, though, and the eggs had three inch yolks. There was some sort of grain on any human-inhabited planet, usually a descendant of Terran cereals; but the soil of another planet sometimes produced weird variations in the grain. There was always some sort of domesticated fowl; but more often than not it was a local life-form. Hogs, of course, were ubiquitous; they were found on Terran planets even more consistently than dogs. Rod sometimes wondered about his species.

The food was all digestible, of course, and probably nourishing: genetic drift couldn't change human metabolism all that much. But trace elements were another matter; Rod swallowed an all-pupose pill just to be on the safe side.

Big Tom noticed it. "What was that, master?"

Rod forced a smile. "Just a minor spell. Don't let it worry you, Big Tom."

Tom stared, then looked down at his plate, muttering a quick prayer under his breath. He attacked the pancakes with a shaking fork.

The big man started to speak, but his voice cracked. He cleared his throat and tried again.

"What doth the new day bring, good master?"

"A trip to the castle," said Rod. "We'll see if the Queen's in the market for a new soldier."

Tom wailed a protest. "A Queen's sojer! Nay, master, that's no trade for a honest man!"

Rod cocked an eyebrow. "Are you trying to tell me that one of us might be honest?"

Big Tom shut up.

The landlord had a spare horse, or so he suddenly remembered when Rod rested a hand on the hilt of his dagger. It was an old, swaybacked gray gelding with a slightly longer neck and smaller ears than the Terran-standard animal. That was bad, since it would call a certain amount of attention to Fess; but then, the great black horse wasn't exactly inconspicuous anyway.

The church bells were ringing as they rode out of the inn-yard, Rod on Fess and Tom on the equine antique. The sound of the bells reminded Tom of the early hour; he began to grumble at masters who kept unreasonable hours.

But his gripes trailed off as they mounted the slope above the town, where they could look out to the horizon and see the east pregnant with the morning sun.

Tom took a deep breath of the dawn and grinned back over his shoulder at Rod. "Eh, master! 'Twill be a fine day!"

"And a chill one," said Rod, turning up his collar, for the wind was at his back.

"Aye, aye! Did I not say 'twould be fine?"

"I don't quite share your enthusiasm for low thermometer readings," Rod growled. "Look alive, Tom; we're almost to the castle."

"Stand and declare yourselves!" cried the sentry on the drawbridge.

"Oh, ye gods!" Rod rolled his eyes upward.

"Your name and your concern at the Queen's castle."

"Overdoing it a bit, aren't you?" Rod eyed the sentry sidewise.

The footman's mouth turned down sharply at the corners. "None of your mouthings," he barked. "I'm a Queen's man, and you'll speak with respect."

"Not likely," said Rod, smiling benignly. "My name is Rod Gallowglass."

"Gallowglass?" The sentry frowned. "Your time is wasted; the Queen already has a fool."

"From the look of you, I'd say she has many." Rod grunted. "My trade is soldier, and my manservant's, too. Call the master-at-arms, and let him enroll me."

The sentry glowered. "Enlisting in the Queen's army is not so easily done as that."

"Why, how now!" Rod scowled. "Must I prove I'm a soldier?" He dismounted, swinging out of the saddle to land just a yard from the sentry.

"If you're a soldier, you're a poor one," the sentry said with a sneer, "or you'd not leave your horse untethered."

Rod threw him a saccharine smile and called out,

"Fess, back up four feet, take a half step to the left, come forward four and a half feet, then stand till I call you."

The sentry stared, mouth gaping open, as Fess executed the maneuver with machine-like precision.

"I'm a soldier," said Rod, "and a good one."

The sentry's mouth opened and closed like a fish's. His eyes bulged slightly as they flicked over Rod's lean frame, the black-gloved hand on the pommel of the sword.

"You see," Rod explained, "I might have need of my horse. It's easier to let him come to me."

His right hand jumped out in a feint. The soldier grunted with surprise and stepped back as Rod's foot snaked out to catch him behind the ankle. The sentry went down in a clatter of tinware.

Rod twisted the pike from the sentry's hands as he fell and threw it back under the portcullis.

"Now," he said, "let's try it again, shall we?"

"Well done, oh! Well done, my master!" Big Tom pounded his nag's withers, grinning from ear to ear.

The sentry staggered to his feet, shouting, "A rescue! A rescue!"

"Oh, no!" Rod dropped his forehead into his palm. "Oh, no!"—shaking his head.

He leaned back against Fess' shoulder and folded his arms. Three guardsmen came running up, pikes at the ready. The leader looked from Rod to the sentry, back to Rod, then back to the sentry. He frowned. "What need for a rescue?"

The sentry fluttered a hand in Rod's general direction. "This man . . ."

"Yes?" Rod smiled.

"Why, he knocked me down, that's what he did, and took my pike from me!"

"I wouldn't brag, if I were you," Rod murmured.

Big Tom bent low over his saddlebow, convulsed with silent laughter.

"Is that the truth of it, man?" The leader glowered at Rod.

"True." Rod bowed his head.

"Well, then!" The leader straightened, planting his fists on his hips and scowling.

"Well, what?" Rod raised an eyebrow.

The sergeant was beginning to get flustered. "Well, what's your reason?"

"I wish to enlist in the Queen's army. This man-at-arms indicated I should prove myself."

The sergeant looked from the flabbergasted sentry to Rod, and nodded.

"You'll have your chance," he said. "Come."

The chance consisted of a hulking sergeant equipped with a broadsword and buckler.

"Will you not take a buckler, man?" growled the old knight who was Master of the Guard.

"No thanks." Rod slipped his dagger from its sheath. "This will do me quite well."

"Naught but a poniard and a wisp of a sword 'gainst broadsword and buckler!" Sir Maris shook his head sadly. "You must truly wish to die young!"

Rod's eyes widened in surprise. "Thank you," he said. "I haven't been told I looked young since I was thirteen."

"Well, cross your swords," Sir Maris sighed. Rod and the sergeant complied; Sir Maris limped forward, his own broadsword coming up to separate their blades.

The sergeant's broadsword swung up for a full-armed chop. Rod took advantage of the moment's delay to feint once at the sergeant's belly. The buckler dropped down to catch the sword-tip, and Rod's blade leaped over the sergeant's arm to rip the cloth over his heart.

"Hold!" cried Sir Maris, and the sergeant's broadsword paused in mid-chop. He dropped his buckler, staring about him. "Wot 'appened?"

"Had this Gallowglass not fought in sport alone," said Sir Maris, "thou wert a dead man this day, Sergeant Hapweed."

He scowled at Rod, puzzled. "Who would ha' thought to use a sword's point?"

"Shall we have at it again?" Rod's blade whined through the air and slapped against his leg.

Sir Maris studied Rod's face, his brow furrowing.

"Nay," he said, lifting his head. "I'll warrant you're a swordsman."

"Aye," muttered Big Tom, and Sir Maris glanced over at him; but the big man was only beaming with pride.

The Master of the Guard turned and caught up a quarterstaff. "Here!" He tossed it to Rod. "We'll try you with this."

Rod sheathed his dagger and caught the staff by the middle. He slipped his sword into its scabbard.

The big sergent was practicing quick one-two-three blows with his quarterstaff.

"Have at it!" Sir Maris called, and the big sergeant stepped forward, knees bent, quarterstaff on guard. Rod followed suit.

Then he was in the middle of an oaken rain, blows from the sergeant's staff drubbing about his head and shoulders, seeking an opening, a half second drop of Rod's guard.

Rod set his jaw and matched the sergeant's pace, catching the blows as quick as they came—just barely. His stomach sank as he realized he was on the defensive.

He blocked a swing at his shin, caught the rebound toward his head, swung the lower end of his staff to catch the answering blow at his belly—but the blow never came. It had been a feint.

Frantically, he tried to recover to guard his head, but the sergeant had gained his half second opening. Rod saw the heavy oak staff swinging at him out of the corner of his eye.

He sank back, rolling with the blow. It cracked on his skull like a thunderclap. The room darkened, filled with dancing motes of light; there was a roaring in Rod's ears.

He gave ground, blocking the sergeant's blows by sheer reflex, and heard the onlooking soldiers yell with triumph.

Won't do at all, Rod's thoughts whirled. He'd been trained at quarterstaff; but he hadn't had a bout in a year, whereas the sergeant had all the skill of a devout hobbyist. It was just a game to him, probably, as the swordplay had been to Rod. The sergeant was in the driver's seat, and he knew it.

There was one chance. Rod leaped back, his hands slipping to the middle of the staff. It began to turn end-over-end, twirling like a baton.

Rod set his jaw and put some muscle into it. His staff leaped into a whirling, whining blur.

It was French single-stick play, *le moulinet.* The sergeant probably knew it as well as Rod; but chances were he wasn't any better practiced at it than Rod was. It was rather exotic form, unless you were French. And with a name like Sergeant Hapweed . . .

Sir Maris and Co. gaped. The sergeant stepped back, startled. Then a wariness came into his face, and his staff jumped into a whirl.

So he knew the style. But he wasn't a master; in fact, Rod had the advantage. The sergeant's staff was a blur, but a quiet blur. Rod's staff was doing a very nice imitation of a buzz saw. He had the edge on the sergeant in angular velocity, and consequent greater striking power.

Sergeant Hapweed knew it too; the muscles of his neck knotted as he tried to speed up his wing.

Now! Rod leaped forward. His staff snapped out of its whirl, swinging down counter to the rotation of the sergeant's.

The sticks met with the crack of a rifle and a shudder that jarred Rod's back teeth. He recovered a half second ahead of the sergeant and brought his staff crashing down on the sergeant's in two quick blows, knocking the other's staff out of his hands.

Rod straightened, drawing a deep breath and letting the tension flow out of him as he grounded the butt of his staff.

The sergeant stared at his hands, numb.

Rod reached out and tapped the man's temple gently with the tip of his staff. "Bang! You're dead."

"Hold!" cried Sir Maris, making things official. Rod grounded his staff again, and leaned on it.

Sir Maris scowled at Rod, eyes bright under bushy eyebrows.

Rod gave him a tight smile.

Sir Maris nodded slowly. "Shall I try you with a longbow?"

Rod shrugged, bluffing. With a crossbow, maybe. But a longbow . . .

A deep, skirling laugh rolled from the rafters. The Master of the Guard and all his men jumped. Big Tom fell on his knees, arms flung up to protect his head.

Rod's head snapped out, eyes searching for the source of the laugh.

On one of the great oaken beams crossing the hall sat a dwarf, drumming his heels against the wood. His head was as large as Rod's, his shoulders broader, his arms and legs as thick as Rod's. He looked as though someone had taken a big, normal man and edited out three feet here and there.

He was barrel-chested, broad-shouldered, and bull-necked. The shaggy black head seemed strangely large for such a truncated body. Black, curly hair hung down to the point of the jaw and the nape of the neck; bushy black eyebrows jutted out from a flat, sloping forehead. The eyes were large coal-black, and, at the moment, creased with mirth. They were separated by a hawk-beak nose under which thick, fleshy lips grinned through a bushy black beard, jutting forward at the chin. Square, even teeth gleamed white through the beard.

Someone had tried to cram a giant into a nail-keg, and had almost succeeded.

"Longbow!" he cried in a booming, bass voice. "Nay, I'll wager he's as fair a shot as the county ram in springtime!"

Sir Maris glowered up at the dwarf. "A plague on you and your stealthy ways, Brom O'Berin! Is there not enough salt in my hair already, but you must whiten it all with your pranks?"

"Stealthy ways!" cried the dwarf. "Forsooth! Had you some pride in your calling, Sir Maris, you would thank me for showing you your own lack of vigilance!"

"Brom?" muttered Rod, staring "O'Berin?"

The dwarf turned to Rod, glowering. "Black Brom O'Berin, aye!"

"That's, uh, a combo of Dutch, Irish, and Russian, if I've got it right."

"What words of nonsense are these?" growled the dwarf.

"Nothing." Rod looked away, shaking his head. "I should have seen it coming. I should expect something else, on this crazy—uh . . . in Gramarye?"

The dwarf grinned, mischief in his eyes. "Nay,

unless I mistake me, that hath the sound of a slur on the great land of Gramarye!''

"No, no! I didn't . . . I mean . . ." Rod paused, remembering that apologies were unbecoming for a fighting man in this culture.

He straightened, chin lifting. "All right," he said, "it was an insult, if you want it that way."

The dwarf gave a howl of glee and jumped to his feet on the rafter.

"You must fight him now, Gallowglass," Sir Maris rumbled, "and you shall need every bit of your skill."

Rod stared at the Master of the Guard. Could the man be serious? A dwarf, give Rod a hard fight?

The dwarf chuckled deep in his throat and slipped off the beam. It was a twelve foot drop to the stone floor, more than three times Brom's height, but he hit the floor lightly, seeming almost to bounce, and wound up in a wrestler's crouch. He straightened and paced toward Rod, chuckling mischief.

There was a roar behind Rod, and Big Tom blundered forward. " 'Tis a trap, master!" he bellowed. "Witchcraft in this land, and he is the worst witch of all! None has ever beaten Black Brom! Yet I shall—"

Every soldier in the room descended on Big Tom in a shouting chaos of anger and outrage.

Rod stood a moment in shock. Then he dropped his staff and waded into the melee, hands flashing out in karate punches and chops. Soldiers dropped to the floor.

"*Hold!*" thundered Brom's voice.

Silence gelled.

Brom had somehow gotten up on the rafters again.

"My thanks, lads," the miniature Hercules growled. "But the big fellow meant no harm; let him go."

"No harm!" yelped half a dozen outraged voices.

Brom took a deep breath and sighed out, "Aye, no harm. He meant only defense of his master. And this Gallowglass meant only defense of his manservant. Stand away from them now; they're both blameless."

The soldiers reluctantly obeyed.

Rod slapped Tom on the shoulder and murmured, "Thanks, Big Tom. And don't worry about me; that Dutch Irishman is only a man, like you and me. And if he's a man, I can beat him."

The dwarf must have had very keen ears, for he bellowed, "Oh, can you, now? We'll see to that, my bawcock!"

"Eh, master!" Big Tom moaned, rolling his eyes. "You know not what you speak of. That elf is the devil's black own!"

"A warlock?" Rod snorted. "There ain't no such beasts."

Sir Maris stepped back among his men, ice-eyed and glowering. "Harm a hair of his head, and we'll flay you alive!"

"No fear," Brom O'Berin chuckled. "No fear, Gallowglass. Try all that you may to harm me. Be assured, you shall fail. Now look to yourself."

He jumped on the rafter, bellowed *"Now!"*

Rod dropped into a crouch, hands drawn back to chop.

Brom stood on the beam, fists on hips, great head nodding. "Aye, hold yourself ready. But"—his eyes lit with a malicious gleam; he chuckled—"Brom O'Berin is not a light man." He leaped from the rafter feet-first, straight at Rod's head.

Rod stepped back, startled at the suddenness of the dwarf's attack. Reflex took over; his hand swung up, palm upward, to catch Brom's heels and flip them up.

Then, expecting the dwarf to land flat on his back on the granite floor, Rod jumped forward to catch; but

Brom spun through a somersault and landed bouncing on his feet.

He slapped Rod's hands away with a quick swipe. "A courtly gesture," he rumbled, "but a foolish one; your guard is down. Save gentleness for those who need it, man Gallowglass."

Rod stepped back, on guard again, and looked at the little man with dawning respect. "Seems I underestimated you, Master O'Berin."

"Call me not master!" the dwarf bellowed. "I'm no man's master; I'm naught but the Queen's fool!"

Rod nodded, slowly. "A fool."

He beckoned with both arms, and a savage grin. "Well enough then, wise fool."

Brom stood his ground a moment, measuring Rod with a scowl. He grunted, mouth snapping into a tight smile, and nodded.

He sprang, flipped in mid-air, feet heading straight for Rod's chin.

Rod swung a hand up to catch Brom's heels again, muttering, "I'd've thought you'd learn."

He shoved the dwarf's feet high; but this time Brom flipped his head up under Rod's chin. He had a very solid head.

Rod rolled with the punch, wrapping his arms tightly around Brom O'Berin's body in the process.

The dwarf shook with merriment. "How now?" he chortled. "Now that you've got me, what shall you do with me?"

Rod paused, panting.

It was a good question. If he relaxed his grip for a moment, he could be sure Brom would twist a kick into his belly. He could drop the little man, or throw him; but Brom had a tendency to bounce and would probably slam right into Rod's chin on the rebound.

Well, when in doubt, pin first and think later. Rod

dropped to the floor, shoving Brom's body out at right angles to his own, catching the dwarf's knee and neck for a cradle hold.

But Brom moved just a little bit faster. His right arm snaked around Rod's left; he caught Rod's elbow in a vise-like grip and pulled.

Rod's back arched with the pain of the elbow lock. He now had a simple choice: let go with his left hand, or black out from pain.

Decisions, decisions!

Rod took a chance on his stamina; he tightened his hold on Brom's neck.

Brom grunted surprise. "Another man would have yelped his pain and leaped away from me, man Gallowglass."

Brom's knee doubled back; his foot shoved against Rod's chest, slid up under the chin, and kept on pushing.

Rod made a strangling noise; fire lanced the back of his neck as vertebrae ground together. The room darkened, filled with points of colored light.

"You must let hold of me now, Gallowglass," Brom murmured, "ere sight fails, and you sleep."

Did the damn half-pint *always* have to be right?

Rod tried a furious gurgle by way of reply; but the room *was* dimming at an alarmingly rapid rate, the points of light were becoming pinwheels, and a fast exit seemed indicated.

He dropped his hold, shoved against the floor with his arms, and came weaving to his feet, with a throaty chuckle filling his ears.

For Brom had kept his hold on Rod's arm and had wrapped his other hand in the throat of Rod's doublet, his weight dragging Rod back toward the floor.

Brom's feet touched the ground; he shoved, throwing Rod back.

Rod staggered, overbalanced, and fell, but habit took over again. He tucked in his chin, slapped the floor with his forearms, breaking his fall.

Brom howled with glee at seeing Rod still conscious, and leaped.

Rod caught what little breath remained to him and snapped in his feet. He caught Brom right in the stomach, grabbed a flailing arm, and shoved, letting the arm go.

Brom flipped head over heels, sailed twenty feet past Rod, and landed on the stone flags with a grunt of surprise. He landed on his feet, of course, and spun about with a bellow of laughter. "Very neat, lad, very neat! But not enough . . ."

Rod was on his feet again, panting and shaking his head. Brom hopped toward him, then sprang.

Rod ducked low, in a vain hope that Brom might be capable of missing once; but the little man's long arm lashed out to catch Rod across the throat, stumpy body swinging around to settle between Rod's shoulders.

One foot pressed into the small of Rod's back, both arms pulled back against the base of his throat.

Rod gurgled, coming to his feet and bending backward under Brom's pull. He seized the dwarf's forearms, then bowed forward quickly, yanking Brom's arms.

Brom snapped over Rod's head and somersaulted away. He crowed as his feet his the floor.

"Bravely done, lad! Bravely done!"

He turned about, the glint of mischief still in his eyes. "But I grow weary of this game. Let us be done with it."

"Tr-try," Rod panted.

Brom hunched forward, his long arms flailing out, slapping at Rod's guard.

He grabbed for Rod's knee. Rod dropped his right

hand to block Brom's attempt, then threw his left about Brom's shoulders, trying to shove him forward to lose his balance; but the dwarf's hands seemed to have gotten tangled in Rod's collar again.

Rod straightened, trying to throw Brom off, hands chopping at the little man's elbows; Brom's grip only tightened.

The dwarf kicked out, throwing all his weight forward. Rod stumbled, saw the floor coming up at him.

Brom leaped past him, catching Rod's foot on the way. Rod did a bellywhopper on the stone floor, but he slapped out with his forearms and kept his head from hitting.

He tried to rise but someone had tied a millstone across his shoulders. A snake coiled under his left arm and pressed against the back of his neck.

Rod tried to roll to break the half nelson, but a vise closed on his right wrist and drew it up into a hammerlock.

"Yield, lad," Brom's voice husked in his ear. "Yield, for you cannot be rid of me now."

He shoved Rod's arm higher in the hammerlock to emphasize his point. Rod ground his teeth against the pain.

He struggled to his feet somehow, tried to shake the little man off. But Brom's feet were locked around his waist.

"Nay," the dwarf muttered, "I told you you'd not be rid of me."

Rod shook himself like a terrier, but Brom held on like a bulldog. For a moment, Rod considered falling on his back to crush Brom under him. It was galling to be beaten by a man one-third your size. He discarded the idea quickly, though; there were many times in this bout where Brom could have played equally shabby tricks on Rod.

So Brom had a strong sense of fair play; and Rod was damned if he'd come off as smaller than a dwarf.

Brom's voice was a burr in his ear. "Will you not yield, man?" And Rod gasped as his right hand tried to touch the nape of his neck.

Then Brom shoved hard on Rod's neck, forcing his chin down to touch his collarbone. Rod staggered, lurched forward, and threw out a leg to keep himself from falling. The muscles across his back and neck screamed at the torture; his right arm begged him to give in. His diaphragm folded in on itself, stubbornly refusing to pull in another breath of air. His windpipe crooked into a kink, and his lungs called for air. In a weird, detached moment he noted that night seemed to have fallen all of a sudden; and, stranger yet, the stars were tumbling . . .

Water splashed cold on his face. The mouth of a bottle thrust between his lips, feeling as large as a cartwheel. Liquid trickled over his tongue and down to his belly, where it exploded into fire.

He shook his head, and noticed that there was cold stone under his back. Now, what the hell was he doing, trying to sleep on a stone floor?

Voices echoed in his head. He opened his eyes, saw a round face with great brown eyes framed in shaggy black hair and beard, peering down at him.

The head swam away, and gray stone blocks reeled about him. He gasped, stared at the glint of light from a spearhead, and the room slowly steadied.

A voice thundered in his ear. "He is a miracle, Sir Maris! He made me sweat!"

A massive arm cradled Rod's head and shoulders, lifting them from the stone. Big Tom's great round face swam into view, brows knit with concern.

"Be you well, master?"

Rod grunted something, waving a hand and nodding.

Then the shaggy head was there, too, a shaggy head with a chimpanzee's body, and a hand heavy with muscle clasped his.

"Well fought, lad," rumbled Brom O'Berin. "I've not had such a bout since I came to my manhood."

Rod gripped the dwarf's hand and tried to grin.

Then Sir Maris' scarred, white-bearded face bowed over him, his old hand clasping Rod's upper arm, lifting him to his feet. "Come, lad, stand tall! For you're a man of the Queen's army now!"

"Queen's army!" boomed Brom, somehow up on the rafters again. The room rocked with his laughter. "Nay, Sir Maris I claim this lad! 'Tis the Queen's own bodyguard for him!"

"No, dammit, Big Tom! Get away from me with that thing!"

"But, master!" Tom chased after him, holding up the breastplate. "You must wear *some* armor!"

"Give me one good reason why," Rod growled.

"Why, to turn away arrows and swords, master!"

"Swords I can turn easily enough with my own. Arrows I can duck. And against crossbow quarrels, it won't do a damn bit of good anyway! No, Big Tom! All it'll do is slow me down."

The guard room door groaned on its hinges, boomed shut. Brom O'Berin stood watching them, fists on his hips, a silver glimmer draped over one shoulder. "How is this, Rod Gallowglass? Will you not wear the Queen's livery?"

"I'll wear livery when you do, you motley manikin!"

The dwarf grinned, teeth flashing white through the wilderness of beard. "A touch, a distinct touch! But

I'm not a Guardsman, Rod Gallowglass; I'm a fool, and motley is fool's livery. Come, soldier, into your colors!"

"Oh, I'll wear the Queen's colors well enough. Fact is, I'm kinda partial to purple and silver. Only thing I've got against them is that they're livery; but I'll wear 'em. But, dammit, Brom, I absolutely refuse to have anything to do with that damn sweatbox you call armor!"

The dwarf's face sobered; he nodded slowly, his eyes holding Rod's. "Oh, aye. I had thought you to be of such persuasion."

The silver cloth flew jingling from his shoulder, slapped against Rod's chest. Rod caught it, held it up, inspected it with a frown.

"Will you wear a mail shirt, Rod Gallowglass?"

"I'd as soon wear a hair shirt," Rod growled; but he wriggled into the iron vest. "Good fit," he muttered, and gave the mail shirt a baleful eye; but his chest expanded and his shoulders came back, almost as though he were strutting.

His glance stabbed out at Brom O'Berin. "How is this, Brom? How come you'll let me get away without a breastplate? Out of uniform, aren't I?"

"Not so," Brom rumbled, "for the armor is hidden under the livery. And you are the only man of the guard who would not wish plate armor."

Rod looked at the little man out of the corner of his eye. "How'd you know I didn't want the breastplate?"

Brom chuckled, deep in his beard. "Why, I've fought you, Rod Gallowglass, and 'twas well you fought me, in my own manner!" His smile disappeared. "Nay, you'd no sooner wear armor than I would."

Rod scowled, studying the great bearded face. "You don't quite trust me yet, do you?"

Brom smiled, a tight grimace of irony. "Rod Gallowglass, there's no man I trust, and I regard any Queen's Guard with suspicion till he has given his life to save hers."

Rod nodded. "And how many is that?"

Brom's eyes burned into his. "Seven," he said. "In the last year, seven Guards have I come to trust."

Rod jerked the left side of his mouth into a hard smile.

He caught up the silver-on-purple doublet, shrugged into it. "So if you really come to think highly of me, you may let me taste the Queen's food to see if it's poisoned."

"Nay," Brom growled. "That pleasure is mine, mine to me alone."

Rod was silent a moment, looking into the little man's eyes.

"Well," he said, and turned away to buckle on the purple cloak. "I notice you're still alive."

Brom nodded. "Though 'tis several times I've been ill—ill for fair, my lad. But I seem to have the knack of telling poison by taste; I need not wait for death's proof."

He grinned, and strode across the floor to slap at Rod's iron-clad belly. "But come, there's no cause to be glum! All you'll have to face is swords, and perhaps now and again a crossbow, so be of good cheer."

"Oh, I'm just trembling with eagerness," Rod muttered.

Brom pivoted, headed for the door. "But now to the Queen's council chamber! Come, I'll show you your station."

He spun, arm pointing at Big Tom. "You there, man Tom! Back to the barracks with you; your master will call you at need."

Tom looked to Rod for confirmation; Rod nodded.

Brom slammed the door open and strode through. Rod shook his head, smiling, and followed.

The Queen's council chamber was a large, round room, mostly filled with a great round table twenty feet in diameter. There were ponderous doors at the south, east, and west points of the compass; the north point was taken up by a yawning fireplace, crackling with a small bonfire.

The walls were hung with gaudy tapestries and rich furs. A great shield blazoned with the royal arms hung over the fireplace. The ceiling arched concave, almost a dome, crossed by great curving beams.

The table was polished walnut. Around it sat the twelve Great Lords of the realm: the Duke Di Medici, the Earl of Romanoff, the Duke of Gloucester, the Prince Borgia, the Earl Marshall, Duke Stewart, the Duke of Bourbon, the Prince Hapsburg, Earl Tudor, the Baronet of Ruddigore, the Duke of Savoy, and the great grizzled old Duke of Loguire.

All were there, Rod saw, listening to a herald read their names from a scroll—all except the Queen, Catharine Plantagenet. Mulling over the list of names the elite of the Emigrés had chosen for themselves, Rod decided that they had been not only romantics, but also genuine crackpots. Plantagenet forsooth!

Next to each of the great lords sat a slight, wiry, wizened little man, an old man; each had an almost emaciated face, with burning blue eyes, and a few wisps of hair brushed flat over a leathery skull.

Councillors? Rod wondered. Strange that they all looked so much alike. . . .

All sat in massive, ornately carved, dark-wood chairs. A larger, gilded chair stood vacant at the east point of the table.

A drum rolled, a trumpet sneezed, and the lords and councillors rose to their feet.

The great double leaves of the east door boomed wide, and Catharine stepped into the chamber.

Rod was stationed at the side of the west door; he had an excellent view, one which gave his heart pause.

A cloud of silver hair about a finely chiseled, pouting face; great blue eyes and rosebud lips; and a slender child's body, budding breasts and kitten hips under clinging silk, molded tighter to her by the wide belt of her girdle, a Y from hips to floor.

She sat in the vacant chair, hands gripping the arm rests, back braced stiff against the gilded wood.

Brom O'Berin hopped up onto a stool at her right. Directly across from her, at the west point of the table, sat the Duke Loguire. His councillor leaned close, whispering. The Duke shushed him impatiently.

Brom O'Berin nodded to a herald.

"The Queen's Grand Council is met," the herald cried. "The high and great of the land of Gramarye are gathered. Let all among them who seek redress of wrongs petition now the Queen, in the presence of their peers."

Silence filled the room.

The Duke of Bourbon stirred uneasily and coughed.

Brom's head swiveled to the man. "My lord of Bourbon," he rumbled, "will you address the Queen?"

Slowly, the Duke rose. His doublet was blazoned with fleurs-de-lis, but his hair and moustache were blond.

"Your Majesty," said the Duke, bowing gravely to the Queen, "and my brother lords." He nodded his head toward the table in general, then lifted his chin, straightening his shoulders. "I must protest," he growled.

Catharine tilted her back so that she gave the impres-

sion of looking down her nose at the tall nobleman.
"What must you protest, my lord?"

The Duke of Bourbon looked down at the walnut
tabletop. "Since our ancestors came from beyond the
stars, the peasants have been subject to their lords; and
the lords have been subject to the Great Lords. The
Great Lords, in their turn, are subject to the King . . .
the Queen," he amended, with a slight bow to
Catharine.

Her lips pressed into a tight, thin line, but she took
the slight with good grace.

"This," the Duke resumed, "is the natural order of
mankind, that each man be subject to the man above
him; that justice and order be the concern of the lord;
within his demesne, he is, and should be, the law,
subject, of course, to the Queen."

Again the polite nod to Catharine, and again, she
accepted the slight; but her hands pinched the arms of
the chair so tightly the knuckles turned white.

"Yet now your Majesty would overturn this great
and lasting order, and force upon us judges of your own
appointing to dispense justice within our demesnes,
judges subject only to yourself. This, though it be
contrary to the wisdom of your father, noble Queen,
and his father before him, and all your ancestors from
the beginning of your line. If I may speak plainly, I find
it almost a mockery of your great and noble forebears;
and, speaking for myself, I cannot abide this peasant
underling of yours, who thinks to lord it over me in my
own manor!"

He finished almost in a shout, glaring red-faced at
the Queen.

"Are you done?" asked Catharine in a tone she'd
been keeping in cold storage for just such an occasion.

Slowly, the Duke of Bourbon bowed his head. "I
am." He sat.

Catharine closed her eyes a moment, then looked to Brom O'Berin and nodded, almost imperceptibly.

Brom stood. "Do any speak in support of my lord of Bourbon?" A young man with fiery red hair came to his feet. "I agree with all that my lord of Bourbon has said. I will add, moreover, that the Queen might do well to consider the question of the corruptibility of her appointed judges; for a man without lands or means, and no family name to uphold, might easily be tempted to sell his justice."

"If they do," Catharine snapped, "they shall be hanged from the highest gallows; and the men they have wronged shall serve for their executioners."

She was silent for the space of three breaths, eyes locked with the young nobleman's; then Brom O'Berin growled, "Our thanks to the noble Duke of Savoy."

The young man bowed, and sat.

"Who else will speak in favor of my lords of Bourbon and Savoy?"

One by one, the other ten lords rose to second the Duke of Bourbon. The Queen's Grand Council was unanimously against her.

Catharine held her eyes closed a moment; her lips pressed tight. She looked up to sweep the table with a glare. "My lords, I am deeply grieved to find you all so much opposed to the Queen's justice." She gave them a brittle smile. "I thank you for your *honest* council. Yet I am constant in my purpose; my judges shall remain on your estates."

The noblemen stirred in their seats, muttering to one another in low, husky voices. They seemed to comprise one large, restless animal, growling.

The old Duke of Loguire rose slowly, and leaned heavily on the table. "My Queen," he rumbled, "consider: even kings may fault in judgment, and you are young in statecraft yet. It is known that many minds together may come to clearer knowledge than one mind alone; and here are gathered with you twelve men of most ancient and honorable lineage, of families grown hoary in statecraft; old men of old families; and, it is to be hoped, wise with the weight of their years. Will you persist in your course, when so many are so sure that you are wrong?''

Catharine's face was pale, almost dead white. Her eyes were burning. ''I will,'' she said quietly.

The Lord Loguire held her eyes for a long moment, then slowly sat.

Catharine surveyed the faces around her, taking time to look deep into each pair of eyes.

Then, lifting her chin, she said, ''My judges will remain on your estates, my lords. As to their corruptibility, you will find them almost saintly in their disregard for money, wine, and . . . comforts. They care for one thing only, and that is justice.''

She paused to let her words sink in; and Rod noted tha there were several beet-red faces among the great lords. At a rough guess, he decided, justice had not been quite as pure as it might have been on some of their estates.

The Duke Loguire did not have a red face. The only emotion Rod could read in him was grief.

''This whole matter of the judges is, however, secondary to the purpose for which I have called you here today.'' Catharine smiled, with more than a hint of malice.

Heads jerked up in alarm, all around the board. Brom O'Berin looked more shocked than any. Apparently Catharine had not consulted with her Prime Councillor; even Brom was due for a surprise.

Each lord bent his head for a quick, whispered conference with his councillor; and the looks of alarm on their faces deepened into sullen anger.

"On each of your estates," said Catharine, "there is a monastery. You have been accustomed to appointing the priests for the parishes of your demesnes from your own monasteries."

She looked down at the tabletop for a moment, then lifted her head again. "Here in this castle I am gathering the best theologians of all the monasteries. You shall choose young brothers from your monks, one for each of your parishes, and send them here to me, to be trained by my monks. If in any case I do not approve of your choice in young men, I shall send them back to you, and demand others in their places. When they have finished their studies and taken their Orders, I shall return them to you, to be your parish priests."

The lords slammed to their feet, shouting and gesturing, fists thudding on the table.

Catharine's voice crackled into the uproar. "Enough! Be still!"

Slowly, one by one, the Great Lords fell into sullen silence and sank back into their seats, glaring.

But their councillors' faces seemed lit with a suppressed joy; their eyes were burning, and each face held a smile just short of a grin.

"I have spoken," Catharine said, voice and eyes both chill. "It shall be done."

Trembling, the old Lord Loguire rose. "Will your Majesty not—"

"I will not."

Brom O'Berin cleared his throat. "If your Majesty will permit—"

"I will not."

Silence sat over the council chamber. Once again, Catharine surveyed the faces of her lords and their councillors.

Then, turning to her left, she bowed her head. "My Lord Loguire."

The old nobleman rose, his jaw clamped tight under the grizzled beard, his liver-spotted fist palsied with barely-held anger.

He drew back the great, gilded chair, and Catharine rose. He stepped back to his place. Catharine turned away, and the great oak doors were thrown wide. Guardsmen fell in before and behind her.

She paused in the doorway, and turned. "Consider, my lords," she said, "and consent; for you cannot stand against me."

The great doors slammed behind her.

The council chamber burst into pandemonium.

"Oh, come off it! It's the classic pattern, right down to the last look of outrage!"

His day's duty done, Rod was riding Fess back to the inn, bent on picking up a little gossip and a lot of beer. Big Tom was tending the home fires at the Royal Castle, with orders to keep his ears open for juicy tidbits of information.

"I disagree, Rod. It's the classic pattern with something added."

"Bull! It's a simple, premature attempt at centralization of authority. She's trying to unify Gramarye under one law and one ruler, instead of twelve near-independent dukedoms. This business with the judges is that, and nothing more. Five'll get you ten some of those dukes have been playing god on their estates, forcing half the women to sleep with them and overtaxing everybody and anything else that occurred to them. Catharine's a reformer, that's all; she's trying to cure all the evils she can find by making herself the only law in Gramarye—and she won't make it. The noblemen just won't stand for it. She might have gotten away with the judges; but this business with the priests'll bring on a rebellion for sure. Priests have more influence over the people than any other officials in this kind of society. If she makes them responsible to her, and only her, she's really pulling the noblemen's teeth, and they know it. And they won't give up without a fight."

"So far, I'll agree with you," the robot said. "So far, it is the classic pattern, closely resembling the attempt of the English King John to centralize his nation before such a project could succeed."

"Yes." Rod nodded. "And we can hope that, like King John's noblemen, the great dukes will insist on a Magna Carta."

"But . . ."

Rod assumed a look of martyr-like patience. "But what, Fess?"

"But there is a foreign element: a group of councillors to the Great Lords, a group that seems to be very cohesive."

Rod frowned. "Well, yes. There is that."

"And from what you tell me of the scene after Catharine left . . ."

"Yii!" Rod shuddered. "It was just as though she'd thrown down a gauntlet, and all the dukes were out to see who'd get the honor of taking it up. The girl might know some elementary political science, but she sure doesn't know any diplomacy! She was just daring them to fight her!"

"Yes, and the councillors were egging them on very nicely—each one councilling his lord not to fight, because he was too weak . . . and then telling them that if he must fight, he'd better ally with the other lords, because each was too weak to stand alone. Expert use of reverse psychology. One would almost think the councillors were out to eliminate central authority completely."

"Yes . . ." Rod frowned, musing. "That's not quite normal to this kind of society, is it, Fess?"

"No, Rod. The theory of anarchy does not usually arise until the culture has attained a much higher degree of technology."

Rod chewed at his lip. "Outside influence, maybe?"

"Perhaps. And that brings us to the popular totalitarian movement: another anomaly. No, Rod, this is not the classic pattern."

"No, dammit. We've got three groups contending for power: the peasants, the dukes and their councillors, and the Queen and whoever supports her. That support seems to be limited to Brom O'Berin at the moment."

"Totalitarians, anarchists, and the Queen in the middle," Fess murmured. "Which one do *you* support, Rod?"

"Catharine, dammit!" Rod grinned. "I'm out to plant the seeds of democracy; and it looks like the only chance to do that is to engineer a constitutional monarchy."

"I might be mistaken," Fess murmured, "But I do believe you're delighted to find you must support her."

Around them the few lights were dimmed by the night mist, a wall of fog thirty feet away. Rod rode alone through a world of smoke; Fess's hooves rang strangely weird in the echoing silence.

A long yell split the night, followed by the slapping clash of swords. "A rescue, a rescue!" a young voice cried.

Rod froze, hand on the pommel of his sword; then he dug his heels into Fess's metal sides, and the great black horse sprang toward the ruckus.

A torch smoldered red through the fog at the mouth of an alley. There, under its smoky light, one man battled three, his back against the wall.

Rod bellowed and landed horse and all in the middle of the melee. He laid about him with the flat of his sword, howling like an Indian studying to be a Confederate soldier. He yanked the dagger from the small of his back, just in time to catch a rapier coming at him from his left. His own sword swung in an arc over his head and clashed against steel as his opponent caught the blow.

Then steel points were jabbing up at him like sawgrass. Rod was forced back on the defensive, swatting the blades aside.

But the intended victim let loose a yell that would have shamed a banshee and waded in from the rear.

All at once the three swords fell away, their owners pelting down the alley. Rod sat a moment dazed; then he yelled, and Fess sprang after the retreating figures.

But they gained the dark at the end of the alley; and when Rod caught up, the stones were empty. It was a dead end; they had gone through one of the shadowed, evil-smelling doorways.

Their would-be victim came running up behind, looked about, and panted.

"Gone, and no use to seek them further. They'll be five leagues away in as many minutes."

Rod swore and slapped his sword back into its scabbard. He winced, and touched his forearm gingerly; one of the rapier-points had slashed through his doublet and sliced his skin.

He turned to the stranger. "You all right?"

The young man nodded, sheathing his sword.

Rod looked down into an open, snub-nosed, blue-eyed face with a grin that flashed white through the fog. The cheekbones were high, and the eyes large and wide, with a look of innocence. Blond hair was cropped round in a bowl cut. It was a young, inexperienced, very handsome face—Rod felt a surge of resentment.

He swung down from his horse. The top of the youth's head was about on a level with Rod's eyes; but what the boy lacked in height, he made up in bulk. A barrel chest swelled into bull shoulders, a good six inches wider than Rod's. The arms would have looked more appropriate on a bear or gorilla; and the legs were too small tree trunks, rammed into narrow hips.

He wore a leather jerkin over a white shirt, a wide black belt, hose, and high, soft boots.

He frowned, seeing the blood on Rod's sleeve. "You're hurt."

Rod snorted. "A scratch," he said, and fumbled in Fess's saddlebag for an antiseptic bandage. He wound the bandage around his forearm, threw the youth a hard grin. "You can pay the tailor bill, though."

The boy nodded, blue eyes sober. "That will I gladly; for they would have cut my heart out, had it not been for your timely rescue. Tuan McReady stands in your debt."

Rod looked him up and down, nodding slowly. A good kid, he thought.

He held out his hand. "Rod Gallowglass, at your service; and there's no debt involved. Always glad to help one against three."

"Ah, but debt there is!" said the boy, clasping Rod's hand with a grip like a sentimental vise. "You must, at the least, let me buy you a tankard of ale!"

Rod shrugged. "Why not? I was on my way to an inn just now, anyway; come on along!"

To his surprise, Tuan hesitated. "By your leave, good Master Gallowglass . . . there is only one house in this town where I am welcomed. All others have known my custom of old, and"—the round face suddenly broke into a grin—"my manner of living does not please the peaceful and proper."

Rod grimaced, nodding. *"Post jocundum juventutem.* Well, one inn's as good as another, I guess."

The route to Tuan's inn was somewhat out of keeping with his well-bred looks. They dogged down two dark alleys, wriggled through a weathered brick wall, and came out in a wide, moonlit courtyard that had been elegant in its day. That day must have been a century or two in the past. The remains of a fountain burbled in the center of cracked flagstones, sending up a stench redolent of primitive plumbing. Weeds, themselves in a state of dire poverty, poked through the paving everywhere. The brick of the walls was cracked and split, the mortar crumbling. Heaps of garbage lay by the walls and in the corners, with stray mounds of refuse here and there about the yard.

The inn itself was a rotting granite block with tumbledown eaves. The overhanging second story was propped up with roughhewn timbers, not to be trusted due to the infirmities of age. The windows were boarded over, the boards split, moldy, and fungoid. The massive oak door was the only sound piece of wood in sight, and even it was sagging.

"Ah, they tolerate your behavior here?" Rod asked, surveying the stagnant courtyard as Tuan knocked on the door with the hilt of his dagger.

"Tolerate, yes," said Tuan, "though even their hospitality is sometimes strained."

Rod felt a chill between his shoulder blades and wondered just what kind of mild-mannered youth he'd run into.

Tuan knocked again. Rod wondered that he expected an answer; not a gleam of light showed through the sagging window boards. By the look of it, the place must be totally deserted.

But the door began to move, and groaned that it was going on strike for an oil break, till it was open just wide enough to admit the two men.

"Your host," said Tuan cheerily, "The Mocker."

A gnarled, hunched, dessicated travesty of a human

being peered around the door, making gobbling sounds in its throat. One ear was cauliflower, and the other was gone; a few strands of greasy hair straggled over a scabby skull. The nose was bulbous, the smouth a slash in a mass of warts, the eye malevolent, gleaming slits. It was dressed in a collection of tatters and patches that might once have laid claim to being a doublet and hose, sagging badly on the scarecrow figure.

The troll scurried away into the foul-smelling dark of its lair. Tuan strode through the door, following. Rod took a deep breath, squared his shoulders, and looked back over his shoulder to make sure Fess was still standing there, by the fountain, head lowered in a good imitation of a horse grazing. For a moment, Rod envied the robot his ability to cut off his olfactory receptors.

Then, lifting his chin, he followed Tuan into the inn.

The door ground shut behind him; there was a scurrying sound as the Mocker ran ahead to open another door.

This one opened easily, slammed back against the wall, flooding them with a blaze of torchlight and gales of coarse, bawdy laughter. Rod stared.

They stepped through the door, and Rod looked about him. It was a great common room, with four roaring open fires and score upon score of torches bracketed along the walls. Roasting meat hung over the fires; waiters wove their way through the crowd with tankards of ale and wine from two huge, flowing kegs that dominated the far side of the room.

The clientele were the lees of the city. Their clothes were crusted, patched castoffs. Their bodies bore the marks of primitive justice: this one was missing an ear, that one an eye. Their faces were disfigured and scarred by disease. Yet here in their own den they roared merrily; all of them grinned, though malice glinted in their eyes as they looked at Rod.

But the malice faded, was transmuted into something almost like worship, as they looked at young Tuan.

"It is said," and the boy smiled, "that there is no honor among thieves; but there is at least kinship here, among the beggars of Gramarye. Welcome, Rod Gallowglass, to the House of Clovis."

The hair at the base of Rod's skull prickled. He remembered the torchlight mob he had seen on the waterfront the night before.

His eyes widened; he stared at Tuan. He couldn't be. He couldn't be.

Oh, but he could. Yes, he could.

Tuan McReady was the young rabble-rouser who'd been haranguing the mob to march on the castle.

This apple-cheeked, wholesome youth was top rat in the local sewer.

The crowd broke into a raucous, cheering clamor, welcoming their Galahad. Tuan grinned and waved. A slight flush crept up from his collar. He seemed almost embarrassed by the reception.

He led Rod to a dark corner at the back of the hall. He hadn't said a word to the Mocker, but two steaming mugs of mulled wine thumped down on the table almost as they sat. The landlord scuttled away without pay.

Rod watched him go, one eyebrow lifted in cynicism. He turned to Tuan. "You don't use money here?"

"None." Tuan smiled. "All who come to the House of Clovis bring what little money they have. It is put into a common chest, and meat and wine given out to all according to their needs."

"And a place to sleep, I suppose?"

"Aye, and clothing. It is poor fare by a gentleman's standards; but it is great wealth to these my poor brethren."

Rod studied Tuan's face and decided the boy might have meant it when he said brethren.

He sat back and crossed his legs. "Would you call yourself a religious man?"

"I?" Tuan tried to choke back a laugh and almost succeeded. "Oh, nay! Would that I were; but I have not seen the inside of a church for three score and more Sundays!"

So, Rod noted, his motive for helping the poor probably wasn't too hypocritical, whatever else it might be.

He looked into his mug. "So you feed and clothe all these people out of the pennies they bring you, eh?"

"Nay, that is but a beginning. But with that much earnest proof of our good intentions, our noble Queen found us worthy of a livelihood."

Rod stared. "You mean the Queen is putting the lot of you on the dole?"

Tuan grinned with mischief. "Aye, though she knows not whom she aids. She knows not the House of Clovis by name, knows only that she gives the good Brom O'Berin moneys to care for her poor."

"And Brom gives it to you."

"Aye. And for his part, he is grateful that there are fewer thievings and murders among the dark alleys."

Rod nodded. "Very shrewd. And this whole setup is your idea, is it?"

"Oh, nay! 'Twas the Mocker who thought of it; but none would give ear to him."

Rod stared. "The Mocker? You mean that twisted fugitive from the late show is boss of this operation?"

Tuan frowned, shaking his head. "Men will not follow him, friend Gallowglass; there is nothing of governance in him. He is host, keeping the inn, doling out goods as they are needed — a steward, and only a steward, but a good one. You will find him a sharper clerk than any; aye, even the Queen's Lord Exchequer.''

"I see, just a steward." *But also the man who holds the pocketbook,* Rod added mentally. *The brains of the outfit, too. Tuan might know how to make people do what he wanted; but did he know what he wanted?*

Yes, of course he did. Hadn't the Mocker told him? Which made the Mocker the local political economist, and probably Tuan's speech-writer.

Rod leaned back, rubbing his chin. "And you manage to keep them in this decadent luxury with only the alms the beggars bring in? Plus the Queen's shilling, of course."

Tuan grinned sheepishly and leaned forward, nodding. " 'Tis not easy done, friend Gallowglass. These beggars are loath to let any man rule them. It is tedious labor, cajoling, threatening, flattering—a man grows a-weary of it. Yet it is well worth the doing."

Rod nodded. "It would take a man with no false pride, and less false humility, and one who could see into his fellow's heart."

Tuan blushed.

"Such a man," said Rod, "could make himself king of the beggars."

But Tuan shook his head, eyes closed. "No, there is no king here, friend Gallowglass. A lord of the manor, perhaps, but naught more."

"You don't want to be king?"

Tuan's shoulders shrugged with a snort of laughter. "The beggars would not hear of it!"

"That wasn't what I asked."

Tuan's eyes locked with Rod's, the smile fading from the boyish face. Then Tuan caught Rod's meaning, and his eyes hardened. "Nay!" he spat. "I do not seek the throne."

"Then why are you trying to lead the beggars against the Queen?" Rod rapped out.

The smile eased across Tuan's face again; he sat back, looking very satisfied with himself. "Ah, you know of my plotting! Then may I ask of you outright, friend Rod, will you join with us when we march on the castle?"

Rod felt his face setting like plaster. His eyes locked with Tuan's again; his voice was very calm. "Why me?"

"We shall have need of as many friends in the Queen's Guard as we may have. . . ."

"You must already have quite a few," Rod murmured, "if you know already that I joined the Queen's Guard today."

Tuan's grin widened; his eyelids drooped.

A stray fact clicked into place in Rod's mind.

"If I were to search through this hall," he said carefully, "would I find the three men who attacked you tonight?"

Tuan nodded, eyes dancing.

"A put-up job," Rod said, nodding with him. "A small performance, arranged solely for my benefit, with the single purpose of maneuvering me in here for a recruiting lecture. You *do* know how to manage people, Tuan McReady."

Tuan blushed, and looked down.

"But what if I don't want to join you, Tuan McReady? Will I leave the House of Clovis alive this night?"

Tuan's head came up, eyes boring into Rod's.

"Only," he said, "if you are an excellent swordsman, and a warlock to boot."

Rod nodded slowly, the events of the past two days whirling through his mind. For a moment, he was tempted to join; he had no doubt that he could maneuver himself into the throne after the revolution.

But no; what Tuan said was true. It took a man with an inborn gift of mass hypnotism to control the beggars. Rod might take the throne, but the beggars—and the Mocker, and whoever was behind him—would not let him keep it.

No, the power structure had to stay the way it was; a constitutional monarchy was the only hope for democracy on this planet.

Then, too, there was Catharine. . . .

Then the jarring note in the score of events caught Rod's ear. He was hung up on Catharine, probably; she was the Dream.

But he had liked Tuan at first sight. How could he like them both if they were really working against one another?

Of course, all Tuan's forthright charm might be an act, but somehow Rod doubted it.

No. If Tuan had really wanted the throne, he could have wooed Catharine, and could have won her—Rod had no doubt about that.

So Tuan was supporting the Queen. How he figured his demagoguery could help her, Rod couldn't figure, but somehow it made sense that Tuan believed he was.

Then why the elaborate plot to get Rod into the House of Clovis?

To test Rod, of course; to find out if he was to be trusted next to the Queen.

Which made sense, if this kid had dealings with Brom O'Berin. It would be just like Brom to try to drum up popular support for the Queen in just this way—but why the propaganda for a march on the castle?

Tuan probably had an answer to that one, and speaking of answers, it was about time Rod came up with one.

He gave Tuan a savage grin and rose, with his hand on his sword. "No thanks. I'll take my chances with swordcraft and sorcery."

Tuan's eyes lit with joy; he caught Rod's arm. "Well spoken, friend Gallowglass! I had hoped you would answer thus. Now sit, and hear the truth of my plot."

Rod shook his hand off. "Draw," he said between his teeth.

"Nay, nay! I would not draw 'gainst a friend. I have played a low trick on you, but you must not hold anger; 'twas for a good purpose. But sit, and I shall tell you."

"I've heard all I want." Rod started to draw his sword.

Tuan caught Rod's forearm again, and this time his hand wouldn't shake off. Rod looked into Tuan's eyes, jaw tightened and arm muscles straining; but slowly and steadily, his sword was forced back into its scabbard.

"Sit," said Tuan, and he forced Rod back into his chair as easily as though Rod had been a child.

"Now hear my plot." Tuan let go of Rod's arm and smiled, as warmly as though nothing had happened. "The Queen gives us money, and the beggars know that she gives it; but the taking of a gift raises only burning anger in the taker. If we would win friends for the Queen, we must find a way to transmute this anger to gratitude."

Rod nodded, frowning.

"Thus we must make the Queen's shilling something other than a gift."

"And you found a way to do it."

"Not I," Tuan confessed, "but the Mocker. 'When is a gift not a gift?' he riddled me, and answered, 'Why, when 'tis a right.' "

Tuan leaned back, spreading his hands. "And there you have it, so easily done. The beggars shall march to the castle and cry to the Queen that she owes them bread and meat, because it is their right. And she will give it to them, and they will be grateful."

Rod smiled, rubbing his chin. "Very shrewd," he said, nodding, but to himself he added: *If it works. But it won't; people who have money enjoy giving for charity, but they won't give a cent if you tell them they must. And how grateful will the beggars be when she refuses them, and calls out the army to drive them away?*

And even if she did yield to their demands, what then? What about the sense of power it would give them? Beggars, forcing a Queen's hand! They wouldn't stop at bread and meat; no, they'd be back with more demands in a week, with or without Tuan.

Oh, yes, it was a very shrewd plan; and Tuan had been sucked into it beautifully. The Mocker couldn't lose; and neither could the off-planet totalitarians who were behind him.

But Tuan meant well. His intentions fairly gleamed. He was a little weak on political theory; but his intentions were fine.

Rod raised his mug for a deep draught, then stared into it, watching the swirl of the heated wine. "Yet some say that the House of Clovis would pull Catharine off her throne."

"Nay, nay!" Tuan stared, appalled. "I love the Queen!"

Rod studied the boy's sincere, open face and made his own interpretation of the statement.

He looked back into his mug. "So do I," he said, with more truth than he liked. "But even so, I'd have to admit she's, shall we say, not acting wisely."

Tuan heaved a great sigh and clasped his hands.

"That is true, most true. She means so well, but she does so badly."

Have you looked in a mirror lately, Mr. Kettle? Rod wondered. Aloud, he said, "Why, how is that?"

Tuan smiled sadly. "She seeks to undo in a day what ages of her grandsires have wrought. There is much evil in this kingdom, that I will gladly admit. But a pile of manure is not moved with one swing of a shovel."

"True," Rod admitted, "and the saltpeter under it can be explosive."

"The great lords do not see that she is casting out devils," Tuan went on. "They see only that she seeks to fill this land with one voice, and only one—and that hers."

"Well"—Rod lifted his mug, face bleak with resignation—"here's to her; let's hope she makes it."

"An' you think it possible," said Tuan, "tha'rt a greater fool than I; and I am known far and wide as a most exceptional fool."

Rod lowered the mug untasted. "Are you speaking from a general conviction, or do you have some particulars in mind?"

Tuan set one forefinger against the other. "A throne rests on two legs: *primus,* the noblemen, who are affronted by anything new, and therefore oppose the Queen."

"Thanks," said Rod with a bittersweet smile, "for letting me in on the secret."

"Left to themselves," said Tuan, "the nobles might abide her for love of her father; but there are the councillors."

"Yes." Rod caught his lower lip between his teeth. "I take it the lords do whatever their councillors tell them?"

"Or what they tell the lords *not* to do, which comes

to the same thing. And the councillors speak with one voice—Durer's.''

"Durer?'' Rod scowled. ''Who's he?''

''Councillor to my Lord Loguire.'' Tuan's mouth twisted, bitter. ''He hath some influence with Loguire, which is a miracle; for Loguire is a most stubborn man. Thus, while Loguire lives, Catharine may stand. But when Loguire dies, Catharine falls; for Loguire's heir hates the Queen.''

''Heir?'' Rod raised an eyebrow. ''Loguire has a son?''

''Two,'' said Tuan with a tight smile. ''The younger is a fool, who loves his best enemy; and the elder is a hothead, who loves Durer's flattery. Thus, what Durer will say, Anselm Loguire will do.''

Rod raised his mug. ''Let us wish the Loguire long life.''

''Aye,'' said Tuan, fervently. ''For Anselm hath an ancient grievance against the Queen.''

Rod frowned. ''What grievance?''

''I know not.'' Tuan's face sagged till he looked like a bloodhound with sinus trouble. ''I know not.''

Rod sat back, resting one hand on the hilt of his sword. ''So he and Durer both want the Queen's downfall. And the other nobles'll follow their lead—if old Loguire dies. So much for one leg of the throne. What's the other one?''

''*Secundus*,'' said Tuan, with a Cub Scout salute, ''the people: peasants, tradesmen, and merchants. They love her for this newfound easing of their sorrows; but they fear her for her witches.''

''Ah. Yes. Her . . . witches.'' Rod scowled, managing to look sharp-eyed and competent while his brain reeled. *Witches as a political element?!*

''For ages,'' said Tuan, ''the witches have been put

to the torture till they forswore the Devil, or have undergone the trial of water or, failing all else, been burned at the stake.''

For a moment, Rod felt a stab of compassion for generations of espers.

''But the Queen harbors them now; and it is rumored by some that she is herself a witch.''

Rod managed to shake off his mental fog long enough to croak, ''I take it this doesn't exactly inspire the people with unflagging zeal for the Queen and her cause.''

Tuan bit his lip. ''Let us say that they are unsure. . . .''

''Scared as hell,'' Rod translated. ''But I notice you didn't include the beggars as part of the people.''

Tuan shook his head. ''Nay, they are apart, frowned and spat upon by all. Yet of this flawed timber, I hope to carve a third leg for the Queen's throne.''

Rod digested the words, studying Tuan's face.

He sat back in his chair, lifted his mug. ''You just may have what the Queen needs, there.'' He drank. Lowering the mug, he said, ''I suppose the councillors are doing everything they can to deepen the people's fear?''

Tuan shook his head, brow wrinkled in puzzlement. ''Nay, they do nothing of the sort. Almost, one would think, they do not know the people live.'' He frowned into his mug, sloshing the wine about inside. ''Yet there is little need to tell the people they must fear.''

''They know it all too well already?''

''Aye, for they have seen that all the Queen's witches cannot keep the banshee off her roof.''

Rod frowned, puzzled. ''So let it wear a groove in the battlements if it wants to! It's not doing any harm, is it?''

Tuan looked up, surprised. "Dost not know the meaning of the banshee, Rod Gallowglass?"

Rod's stomach sank; nothing like displaying your ignorance of local legends when you're trying to be inconspicuous.

"When the banshee appears on the roof," said Tuan, "someone in the house will die. And each time the banshee has walked the battlements, Catharine hath escaped death by a hair."

"Oh?" Rod's eyebrows lifted. "Dagger? Falling tiles? Poison?"

"Poison."

Rod sat back, rubbing his chin. "Poison: the aristocrat's weapon; the poor can't afford it. Who among the great lords hates Catharine that much?"

"Why, none!" Tuan stared, appalled. "Not one among them would stoop to poison, Rod Gallowglass; 'twould be devoid of honor."

"Honor still counts for something here, eh?" Seeing the scandalized look on Tuan's face, Rod hurried on. "That lets out the noblemen; but someone on their side's up to tricks. Wouldn't be the councillors, would it?"

Understanding and wary anger rose in Tuan's eyes. He sat back, nodding.

"But what do they gain by her death?" Rod frowned. "Unless one of them wants to crown his lordling and be the King's Councillor. . . ."

Tuan nodded. "Mayhap all wish that, friend Gallowglass."

Rod had a sudden vision of Gramarye carved up into twelve petty kingdoms, constantly warring against one another, each run by a warlord who was ruled by his councillor. Japanese usurpation, the man behind the throne, and anarchy.

Anarchy.

There was an outside force at work in Gramarye, agents with a higher technology and sophisticated political philosophies at work. The great nobles were slowly being divided, and the people were being set against the nobility, by means of the House of Clovis. The twelve petty kingdoms would be broken down to warring counties, and the counties to parishes, and so on until real anarchy prevailed.

The councillors were the outside force, carefully engineering a state of anarchy. But why?

Why could wait for later. What mattered now was that skulduggery was afoot, and it sat next to the Lord Loguire; its name was Durer.

And his top-priority goal was Catharine's death.

The castle loomed up black against the sky as Rod rode back, but the drawbridge and portcullis were a blaze of torchlight. Fess's hooves thudded hollow on the drawbridge. A blob of shadow detached itself from the larger shadow of the gate, a shadow that reached up to clamp a hand on Rod's shin.

"Hold, Rod Gallowglass!"

Rod looked down and smiled, nodding. "Well met, Brom O'Berin."

"Mayhap," said the dwarf, searching Rod's face. "Thou must come before the Queen for this night's work, Rod Gallowglass."

Rod was still wondering how Brom could have known where he'd been as they came to the Queen's audience chamber. Brom had a spy in the House of Clovis, of course; but how could the word have gotten back to Brom so fast?

The door was massive, oak, iron-studded, and draped with velvet, the green and gold of the Queen's house. Brom ran a practiced eye over the two sentries, checking to see that all leather was polished and all metal gleaming. Rod gave them a nod; their faces turned to wood. Was he under suspicion of high treason?

At Brom's nod, one Guardsman struck the door backhanded, three slow heavy knocks, then threw it wide. Rod followed Brom into the room. The door boomed shut behind them.

The room was small but high-ceilinged, paneled in dark wood, lit only by four great candles that stood on a velvet-draped table in the center of the room, and by a small fire on the tiled hearth. A rich carpet covered the stone floor; tapestries hung on the walls. A huge book-case filled the wall at the far end of th room.

Two heavy carved armchairs stood at either side of the fireplace; two more were drawn up at the table. Catharine sat in one of these, head bent over a large old leather-bound book. Five or six more lay open on the table about her. Her blond hair fell unbound about her shoulders, contrasting with the dark russet of her gown.

She lifted her head; her eyes met Rod's. "Wel-come." Her voice was a gentle, slightly husky con-tralto, so different from the crisp soprano of the council chamber that Rod wondered, for a moment, if it could be the same woman.

But the eyes were wary, arrogant. It was Catharine, all right.

But the heavy crown lay on the table beside her, and she seemed smaller, somehow.

"Hast been to the House of Clovis?" she demanded. Her eyes read like a subpoena.

Rod showed his teeth in a mock-grin and inclined his head in a nod.

" 'Tis even as you said, my Queen." Brom's voice had a grim overtone. "Though how you knew—"

"—is not your affair, Brom O'Berin." She threw

the dwarf a glare; Brom smiled gently, bowed his head.

"How?" Rod snorted. "Why, spies of course. A very excellent spy service, to get the word back to her so fast."

"Nay." Brom frowned, puzzled. "Our spies are few enough, for loyalty is rare in this dark age; and we keep no spies at all at the House of Clovis."

"No spies," Catharine agreed, "and yet I know that thou hast had words with Tuan of the beggars this day."

Her voice softened; her eyes were almost gentle as she looked at the dwarf. "Brom . . . ?"

The dwarf smiled, bowed his head, and turned to the door. He struck the wood with the heel of his hand. The door swung open; Brom turned with one foot on the threshold, and a malevolent glare stabbed at Rod from under the bushy eyebrows; then the door slammed behind him.

Catharine rose, glided to the fireplace. She stood staring at the flames, hands clasped at her waist. Her shoulders sagged; and for a moment, she looked so small and forlorn—and so beautiful, with the firelight streaming up like a mist about her face and shoulders—that Rod's throat tightened in an old, familiar way.

Then her shoulders straightened, and her head snapped around toward him. "You are not what you seem, Rod Gallowglass."

Rod stared.

Catharine's hand strayed to her neck, playing with a locket at her throat.

Rod cleared his throat, a trifle nervously. "Here I am, just a simple blank-shield soldier, just carrying out my orders and taking my pay, and three times in thirty hours I get accused of being something mysterious."

"Then I must needs think that it is true." Catharine's mouth twisted in a mocking smile.

She sat in one of the great oaken chairs, grasping the arms tightly, and studied Rod for a few moments.

"What are you, Rod Gallowglass?"

Rod spread his arms in a shrug, trying to look the picture of offended innocence. "A blank shield, my Queen! A soldier of fortune, no more!"

" 'No more,' " Catharine mimicked, malice in her eyes. "What is your profession, Rod Gallowglass?"

Rod scowled, beginning to feel like the rodent half of a game of cat-and-mouse. "A soldier, my Queen."

"This is your avocation," she said, "your pleasure and your game. Tell me now your profession."

The woman was A) uncanny; and B) a bitch, Rod decided. Trouble was, she was a beautiful bitch, and Rod had a weakness.

His brain raced; he discarded several lies and chose the most obvious and least plausible.

"My profession is the preserving of your Majesty's life."

"Indeed!" Catharine mocked him with her eyes. "And who hath trained you to that profession? Who is so loyal to me that he would send you?"

Suddenly, Rod saw through the mocking and the belligerence. It was all a mask, a shield; behind it lay a very frightened, very lonely little girl, one who wanted someone to trust, craved someone to trust. But there had been too many betrayals; she couldn't let herself trust any more.

He looked into her eyes, giving her his gentlest, most sincere gaze, and said in his best couch-side manner, "I call no man master, my Queen. It is myself who has sent me, out of love for Catharine the Queen and loyalty to the nation of Gramarye."

Something desperate flickered in her eyes; her hands clutched at the chair arms. "Love," she murmured.

Then the mockery was back in her eyes. "Yes, love—for Catharine *the Queen*."

She looked away, into the fire. "Be that as it may. But I think you are in most comely truth a friend—though why I believe that, I cannot say."

"Oh, you may be sure that I am!" Rod smiled. "You knew that I was at the House of Clovis, though you couldn't say how, and you were right about that."

"Be still!" she snapped. Then slowly her eyes lifted to his. "And what affairs took you to the House of Clovis this night?"

Was she a mind reader, maybe?

Rod scratched along his jaw; the bone-conduction microphone would pick up the sound. . . .

"There's some confusion *Fess*tering in my mind," he said. "How did you know I was at the House of Clovis?"

"Here, Rod," a voice murmured behind his ear.

Catharine gave him a look that fairly dripped with contempt. "Why, I knew you spoke with Tuan Loguire. Then where could you be but the House of Clovis?"

Very neat—only how had she known he was with Tuan . . . Loguire?

Loguire!

Rod stared. "Excuse me, but—uh—did you say Tuan *Loguire?*"

Catharine frowned.

"I thought his name was, uh—McReady."

Catharine almost laughed. "Oh, nay! He is the second son of Milord Loguire! Did you not know?"

Second son! Then Tuan was himself the man he had been condemning for a fool!

And his big brother was the man who had "an

ancient grievance 'gainst the Queen,'' and was a major threat to the throne.

"No," said Rod, "I did not know."

Fess' voice murmured, "Data indicate existence of excellent intelligence system."

Rod groaned mentally. Robots were a great help!

He pursed his lips, staring at Catharine. "You say you have no spies in the House of Clovis," he said, "and if I assume that you speak the truth, then that means . . ."

He left the sentence hanging; Fess would fill in the blank.

There was a moment of silence; then a loud hum behind Rod's ear, ended in a sharp click.

Rod cursed mentally. If Catharine had no spies, she logically couldn't have known what she did know. He'd given Fess another paradox, and the robot's circuits had overloaded. Epileptic robots could be very inconvenient.

Catharine glared at him. "Of a certainty, I speak truth!"

"Oh, I never doubted!" Rod held up a hand. "But you *are* a ruler, and you were reared to it; one of the first lessons you must have learned was lying with a straight face."

Catharine's face froze; then, slowly, she bent her head, looking down at her hands. When she looked up, her face was drawn; the mask had been stripped away, and her eyes were haunted. "Once again, my knowledge was true," she murmured. "You know more than soldiering, Rod Gallowglass."

Rod nodded heavily. He'd made another slip; blank-shield soldiers don't know politics.

"Then tell me," she murmured, "how you came to the House of Clovis, this night."

"My Queen," Rod said gravely, "one man was set

upon by three, in an alley. I helped him out; he took me to the House of Clovis to tell me his thanks with a glass of wine. That is how I came to meet Tuan Loguire.''

Her brows drew together in an anxious little frown. ''If I might but credit your words with truth,'' she murmured.

She rose and went to the fireplace. All at once, her shoulders slumped, her head bowed forward. ''I shall need all my friends in this hour that comes upon us,'' she murmured, voice husky, ''and I think thou art the truest of my friends, though I cannot say why.''

She raised her head to look at him, and he saw with a shock that her eyes swam with tears. ''There are still some to guard me,'' she said, her voice so low he could scarcely hear; but her eyes shone through the tears, and an invisible band tightened around Rod's chest. His throat tightened, too; his eyes were burning.

She turned away, biting her clenched fist. After a moment, she spoke again, her voice trembling. ''The time shall come soon when each of the Great Lords shall declare himself for or against me; and I think they will be few who ride to my standard.''

She turned, came toward him again, eyes alight and a shy, trembling smile on her lips. Rod rose to meet her, staring, fascinated, heart pounding in his ears.

She stopped just before him, one hand touching the locket at her throat again, and whispered, ''Will you stand by my side in that day, Rod Gallowglass?''

Rod nodded awkwardly and garbled out something affirmative. At that particular moment, his answer would probably have been the same if she'd requested his soul.

Then, suddenly, she was in his arms, lithe and squirming, and her lips were moist and full on his own.

Some timeless while later, she lowered her head and moved reluctantly away, holding to his arms as if to steady herself. "Nay, but I am a weak woman," she murmured, exultant. "Go now, Rod Gallowglass, with the thanks of a queen."

She said something else, but Rod didn't quite follow it; and, somehow, he was on the other side of the door, walking down a wide, cold, torchlit corridor.

He stopped, shook himself, made a brave try at collecting his wits, and went on down the hall with a step that was none too firm.

Whatever else you might think of her political abilities, the gal sure knew how to bind a man to her service. . . .

He stumbled and caught himself; his stumbling block shoved a hand against his hip to steady him.

"Nay, mind thy great feet," grumbled Brom O'Berin, "ere thou trip headlong and foul the paving."

The dwarf studied Rod's eyes anxiously; he found whatever he was looking for someplace between iris and cornea, and nodded, satisfied.

He reached up to grab Rod's sleeve and turned away, guiding him down the hall.

"What had you from Catharine, Rod Gallowglass?"

"Had from her?" Rod frowned, eyes unfocused. "Well, she took my pledge of loyalty . . ."

"Ah!" Brom nodded, as though in commiseration. "What more could you ask, Rod Gallowglass?"

Rod gave his head a quick shake, eyes opening wide. What the hell more could he ask, anyway? What in heaven's name had he expected? And what, in the seventh smile of Cerebus, was he getting moon-eyed for?

His jaw tightened, sullen anger rising in him. This bitch was nothing to him—just a pawn in the Great Game, a tool that might be used to establish a democracy. And what the hell was he getting angry about? He had no right to that, either. . . .

Hell! He needed a little objective analysis! "Fess!"

He meant it as a mutter, but it came out as a shout. Brom O'Berin scowled up at him. "What is a fess?"

"An unreliable gear train with a slipped cam," Rod improvised. Where the hell was that damn robot, anyway?

Then he remembered. Fess had had a seizure.

But Brom had stopped, and was studying Rod's face with his ultra-suspicious look. "What are these words, Rod Gallowglass? What is a gear train? And what is a cam?"

Rod pressed his lips together and mentally recited the books of the Bible. *Careful, boy, careful! You're at the brink! You'll blow the whole bit!*

He met Brom's eyes. "A gear train is the pack mule a knight uses to carry his armor and weapons," he growled, "and a cam is a half-witted squire."

Brom scowled, puzzled. "Half-witted?"

"Well, some kind of an eccentric. In my case, it all adds up to a horse."

"A horse?" Brom stared, completely at sea.

"Yes. My horse, Fess. The sum and total of my worldly goods and supporting personnel. Also the only soul—well, consciousness, anyway—that I can tell my troubles to."

Brom caught at the last phrase and held to it with all the vigor of a drowning man. His eyes softened; he smiled gently. "You are of us now, Rod Gallowglass, of we few who stand by the Queen."

Rod saw the sympathy in Brom's eyes and wondered what bound the deformed little man to Catharine's service—and suddenly hated Catharine again for being the kind of bitch that enjoyed using men.

He set off down the hall, striding long. Brom marched double-time to keep up with him.

"Unless I miss in my judgment of a man," Rod

growled through his teeth, "the Queen has another friend in the House of Clovis; yet she calls him her enemy. Why is that, Brom? Is it just because he's the son of her enemy the Duke of Loguire?"

Brom stopped him with a hand on his hip and looked up into Rod's eyes with a half-smile. "Not enemy, Rod Gallowglass, but one that she loves well: her uncle, blood-kin, who gave her sanctuary and cared for her five years while her father tamed the rebel Northern lordlings."

Rod raised his head slowly, keeping his eyes on Brom O'Berin's. "She chooses strange ways to show her love."

Brom nodded. "Aye, most truly strange, yet doubt not she loves them, both the Duke and his son Tuan."

He held Rod's eyes a moment, not speaking.

He turned away, pacing slowly down the hall. Rod watched him a moment, then followed.

"It is a long tale, and a snarled one," Brom murmured as Rod caught up with him. "And the end and beginning and core of it is Tuan Loguire."

"The beggar king?"

"Aye." Brom nodded heavily. "The lord of the House of Clovis."

"And one who loves the Queen."

"Oh, aye!" Brom threw his head back, rolling his eyes upward. "One who loves her right well, be certain; he will tell you as much!"

"But you don't believe him?"

Brom locked his hands behind his back and stamped as he walked, head bowed. "He is either truthful, Rod Gallowglass, or a most excellent liar; and if he lies, he has learned the way of it right quick. He was trained only in truth, in the house of his father. Yet he is lord of the House of Clovis, of they who claim the ruler should be chosen as the ancient King Clovis was, or as they say he was—by the acclamation of those whom he rules.''

''Well, they've warped history a little bit there,''
Rod muttered. ''But I take it their plans calls for pulling
Catharine off her throne?''

''Aye; and how can I then believe him when he says
that he loves her?'' Brom shook his head sadly. ''He is
a most worthy young man, high-minded and honest;
and a troubador who will sing you the beauties of
milady's eyetooth as quick as he will twist the sword
from your hands with his rapier. He was always a
gentleman withal, and in him was nothing of decep-
tion.''

''Sounds like you knew him pretty well.''

''Oh, aye! I did, most surely I did ! But do I know
him now?'' Brom heaved a sigh, shaking his head.
''They met when she was but seven years
of age, and he but eight, at the keep of Milord Loguire in the South, where her father had sent her for
safety. There two children met and frolicked and
played—under my eye, for I was ever a-watch over
them. They were the only two of their age in the whole
of the castle, and''—he smiled, and gave a bitter
laugh—''I was a miracle, a grown man who was smaller than they.''

Brom smiled, throwing his head back, looking past
the stones of the hall into the years that were dead.
''They were so innocent then, Rod Gallowglass! So
innocent, aye, and so happy! And he worshiped her; he
would pluck the flowers for her crown, though the
gardener scolded him. Did the sun chasten her? He
would put up a canopy of leaves! Had she broken
milady's crystal goblet? He would claim the fault for
his own!'

''Spoiled her rotten,'' Rod muttered.

''Aye; but he was not the first to play Tom Fool for

her; for even then, she was a most beautiful princess, Rod Gallowglass.

"Yet over their happiness stood a dark, brooding shadow, a lad of fourteen, heir to the keep and estates. Anselm Loguire. He would look down from the tower, watch them at play in their garden, his face twisted and knotted all sour; and he alone in the land hated Catharine Plantagenet—why, no man can say."

"And he still hates her?"

"Aye; and let us therefore wish my lord of Loguire long life.

"For near to five years Anselm's hatred did fester; but then at long last he did stand triumphant. For the lords of the North were subdued, and her father called for her to be brought again to his side, here in his castle. And then did they vow, Tuan and Catharine, she at eleven and he twelve, that they would never forget, that she would wait till he came for her."

Brom shook his great shaggy head sadly. "He came for her. He came for her, a lad of nineteen, a golden prince riding out of the South on a great white charger—broad-shouldered, golden-haired and handsome, with muscles that would thicken any woman's tongue and make it cleave to her palate. A troubador, with a harp on his back and a sword by his side, and a thousand extravagant praises for her beauty. And his laugh was as clear, his heart as open, and his temper as frolicsome as when he was twelve."

He smiled up at Rod. "She was eighteen, Rod Gallowglass, and her life had been as still and smooth as a summer stream. Eighteen, and ripe for a husband, and her head filled with the giddy gossamer dreams that a girl learns from ballads and books."

He peered sharply, but his voice was gentle, echoing strangely in the emptiness of his years. "Was there never a dream of a princess for you, Rod Gallow-glass?"

Rod glared at him and swallowed, hard. "Go on," he said.

Brom turned away, shrugging. "What need to say it? She loved him, of course; what woman would not? He knew not what a woman was for, and I'll swear it, and neither did she; but it may be that together, they learned; you may be sure that they had golden chances."

He shook his head, scowling. "If 'twas so, 'twas the crown of the last days of her youth; for it was that spring that her father died, and the scepter was set in her hands."

He fell still, measuring the hall with his stride, and was silent so long that Rod felt the need to say something.

"Here is no matter for hating, Brom O'Berin."

"Oh, aye! But hear the end of the tale, for only when the crown was on her head did Catharine come to see that Tuan was a second son; that he thus inherited his family's honor, but no more. She swore then that he loved her not, that he coveted only her throne. She would not have him; but in wrath and scorn she sent him away—without due cause, it seemed, though only they two could know the truth of that. She banished him to the Wild Lands with a price on his head, to dwell midst the beast-men and elves, or to die."

He fell silent again.

Rod prodded him. "And Milord Loguire rose up in wrath?"

"Aye," grated Brom, "and all his liegemen with him, and half the nobles of the kingdom besides. If Tuan failed in his courting, wrath and scorn were his due, quoth Loguire; but banishment comes only for treason.

"And was it not reason, Catharine answered hotly, to conspire for the crown?

"Then Loguire stood tall in cold pride and declared that Tuan had sought only the love of Catharine; but his words rang hollow, for he whom the Queen marries must reign; and this Catharine told him.

"Then did Loguire speak in sorrow, that his son was no traitor but only a fool, a fool to be courting a silly, spoiled child; and then would Catharine have cried 'Treason!' again, had I not prevented her."

"And yet you say she loves them, Loguire and Tuan?"

"Aye; why else such harshness?"

Brom lapsed into silence again. Rod cleared his throat and said, "Tuan doesn't seem to have stayed banished too well. . . ."

"Aye." Brom's mouth drew back at the corners. "The fool would be near her, he swore, though his head should be forfeit. But with a price on his life, he must live like a murderer or thief."

Rod smiled sourly. "And, somewhere, he got hold of the idea that the beggars would cause less trouble if someone took care of them."

Brom nodded. "And thus the beggars became somewhat a power; but Tuan swears he will throw all his forces to guard the Queen's back. He professes that he still doth love her; that he will love her though she hew off his head."

"And she, of course," Rod mused, "claims there isn't a reason in the world why he shouldn't hate her."

"And in that she is right; yet I think Tuan loves her."

They had come to the guard room door; Rod put a hand on the latch and smiled down at Brom O'Berin, smiled and shook his head sadly. "Brainless," he said. "The pair of them."

"And most tender loving enemies they are," Brom

smiled, with a touch of exasperation. "And here is your lodging; good night."

Brom turned on his heel and stalked off.

Rod looked after him, shaking his head and cursing himself silently. "Fool that I am," he murmured; "I thought he stood by her because he was in love with her. Oh, well, Fess makes mistakes too. . . ."

The great candle in the barracks was burned down to a stub. Time in Gramarye was kept by huge candles banded in red and white, six rings of red and six white. One candle was lit at dawn, the other twelve hours later.

According to this candle, it was three A.M. Rod's eyelids suddenly felt very heavy. The seemed down-right leaden when he remembered that an hour on Gramarye was roughly equal to an hour and twenty minutes Galyctic Standard.

He staggered toward his bunk and tripped. The object underfoot gave a muffled grunt; Rod had forgotten that Big Tom would be sleeping at the foot of the bed, on the floor.

The big man sat up, yawning and scratching. He looked up and saw Rod. "Oh, gode'en, master! What's the time?"

"Ninth hour of the night," Rod said softy. "Go back to sleep, Big Tom. I didn't mean to wake you."

" 'S what I'm here for, master." He shook his head to clear it of sleep.

Which was somewhat strange, Rod suddenly realized, since the man's eyes had been wide awake. A synapse flicked in Rod's brain, and he was wide awake and wary, once again the subversive agent.

So, to keep from arousing Big Tom's suspicions, he tried to appear even more sleepy than he had been.

"It was a great night, Big Tom," he mumbled, and fell face forward into his bunk. He hoped Big Tom would leave matters as they were and go back to sleep; but he heard a deep, warm chuckle from the foot of the bed, and Big Tom started pulling off Rod's boots.

"A bit of folly in you, hadn't you, master?" he muttered. "Aye, and a wench or two under your belt, I'll warrant."

"Wake me at the lighting of the candle," Rod mumbled into his pillow. "I'm to wait on the Queen at breakfast."

"Aye, master." Big Tom worried loose the other boot and lay down, chuckling.

Rod waited till Tom began to snore again, then propped himself up on his elbows and looked back over his shoulder. Generally, the big oaf seemed thoroughly loyal and superbly stupid; but there were times when Rod wondered . . .

He let his head slump down onto the pillow, closed his eyes, and willed himself to sleep.

Unfortunately, the mind-over-matter bit wasn't working tonight. All his senses seemed boosted past maximum. He would've sworn he could feel every thread in the pillow under his cheek, could hear the mouse gnawing at the baseboard, the frog croaking in the moat, the festive laughter wafted on the breeze.

His eyelids snapped open. Festive laughter?

He rolled out of bed and went to the high slit window. Who the hell was partying at this hour of the night?

The moon stood behind the castellated north tower; silhouettes flitted across its face, youthful figures in a three-dimensional dance; and some of them seemed to be riding on broomsticks.

Witches. In the north tower. . . .

Rod climbed the worn stone steps of the tower, toiling up the spiral. The granite walls seemed to crowd closer and closer the higher he went. He reminded himself that, having been declared a warlock by the elves—unreasonable little bastards!—he qualified for membership in this group.

But his stomach didn't get the message; it was still suing for a Dramamine. His mouth was bone-dry. Sure, the elves approved of him; but had they gotten the word to the witches?

All the old tales of his childhood came flooding back, liberally interspersed with chunks of the witch scenes from Macbeth. Now that he stopped to think about it, he couldn't remember one single instance of a philanthropic witch, except Glinda the Good, and you couldn't really call her a witch.

One thing in his favor: these witches seemed happy enough. The music floating down the stairwell was an old Irish jig, and it was salted with laughter, buoyant and youthful.

The wall glowed with torchlight ahead of him. He turned the last curve of the spiral and came into the great tower room.

A round, or rather globular, dance was in progress, a sort of three-dimensional *hora*. Through the clouds of torchsmoke he could make out couples dancing on the walls, the ceiling, in mid-air, and occasionally on the floor. Here and there were knots of chattering, giggling people. Their clothes were bright to the point of—well, hell, they were downright gaudy. Most of them held mugs, filled from a great cask near the stairwell.

They were all young, teenagers. He couldn't spot a single face that looked old enough to vote.

He paused on the threshold, possessed of a distinct feeling that he didn't belong. He felt like the chaperon at a high school prom—a necessary evil.

The youngster tapping the keg saw Rod and grinned. "Hail!" he cried. "You are laggard in coming." A full tankard slapped into Rod's hand.

"I didn't know I was coming," Rod muttered.

"Be assured that we did." The youth grinned. "Molly foresaw it; but she said you would be here half an hour agone."

"Sorry." Rod's eyes were a trifle glazed. "Ran into a couple delays . . ."

"Eh, think naught of it. 'Twas her miscalling, not yours; the wine, no doubt. Yet we have expected you since you set foot in the castle; the elves told us last night you were a warlock."

Rod's mind snapped clear. "Baloney! I'm no more a warlock than you . . . I mean . . ."

"Oh, thou art a warlock." The boy nodded sagely. "A warlock, and a most puissant one. Did you not come in a falling star?"

"That's science, not magic! And I'm not a warlock!"

The youth smiled roguishly. "Knowing or not, thou'rt most surely a warlock." He saluted Rod with the mug. "And therefore one of us."

"Uh . . . well, thanks." Rod returned the salute and took a draft from the mug. It was mulled wine, hot and spicy.

He looked around the room, trying to grow accustomed to the constant clamor and the flagrant violations of Newton's Laws.

His eyes lit on a couple seated under one of the windows, deep in conversation, which is to say, she was talking and he was listening. She was a looker, fairly bursting her bodice; he was thin and intent, eyes burning as he watched her.

Rod smiled cynically and wondered about the boy's motives for such steadfast devotion.

The girl gasped and spun around to glare outraged at Rod.

Rod's mouth sagged open. Then he began to stammer an apology; but before it reached his lips, the girl smiled, mollified, bowed her head graciously at him, and turned back to her one-man audience.

Rod's mouth sagged again. Then he reached out, groping for the tapster's arm, his eyes fixed on the girl.

The boy threw an arm around his shoulders, his voice worried. "What troubles thee, friend?"

"That—that girl," Rod stammered. "Can she read my mind?"

"Oh, aye! We all can, somewhat; though she is better than most."

Rod put a hand to his head to stop it from spinning. Telepaths. A whole room full of them. There were supposed to be about ten proven telepaths in the whole of the known galaxy.

He looked up again. It was a mutation, or genetic drift, or something.

He drew himself up and cleared his throat. "Say, pal . . . uh, what's your name, anyway?"

"Ay de mi!" The boy struck his forehead with the heel of his hand. "A pox upon my lacking courtesy. I am Tobias, Master Gallowglass; and thou must needs meet us all."

He whirled Rod away toward the nearest group.

"But—but I just wanted to ask—"

"This is Nell, this is Andreyev, this Brian, this Dorothy . . ."

A half hour and fifty-three introductions later, Rod collapsed on a wooden bench. He swung his tankard up and swallowed the dregs. "Now," he said, slamming it down on his knee, "we're both drained."

"Ah, let me fetch you another!" Toby snatched the mug from his hand and flew away.

Literally.

Rod watched him drift across the room, ten feet off the floor, and shook his head. He was beyond astonishment now.

It seemed what he had on his hands was a budding colony of espers—levitative, precognitive, and telepathic.

But if they could all teleport, how come the girls all rode broomsticks?

Toby appeared at Rod's elbow, with a slight *poof!* of displaced air. Rod goggled at him, then accepted the refilled mug. "Uh, thanks. Say, you can, uh, levitate *and* teleport?"

"Pardon?" Toby frowned, not understanding.

"You can-uh-fly? And, uh-wish yourself from one place to another?"

"Oh, aye!" Toby grinned. "We all can do that."

"What? Fly?"

"Nay; we all can wish ourselves to places that we know. All the boys can fly; the girls cannot."

Sex-linked gene, Rod thought. Aloud, he said, "That's why they ride broomsticks?"

"Aye. Theirs is the power to make lifeless objects do their bidding. We males cannot."

Aha! Another linkage. Telekinesis went with the Y-chromosomes, levitation with the X.

But they could all teleport. And read minds.

A priceless colony of espers. And, if their lives were anything like those of the rare telepaths outside the planet . . .

"And the common people hate you for this?"

Toby's young face sobered to the point of gloom. "Aye, and the nobles too. They say we are leagued with the Devil. 'Twas the trial by water, or a most thorough roasting for us, till our good Queen Catharine came to reign.'' Turning away, he shouted, ''Ho, Bridget!''

A young girl, thirteen at the most, spun away from her dance partner and appeared at Toby's side.

''Friend Gallowglass would know how the people do like us,'' Toby informed her.

All the joy went out of the child's face; her eyes went wide and round; she caught her lower lip between her teeth.

She unbuttoned the back of her blouse from neck to bodice and turned away. Her back was a crisscross of scars, a webbing of welts—the sign of the cat-o'-nine-tails.

She turned back to Rod as Toby buttoned her blouse again, her eyes still round and tragic. ''That,'' she whispered, ''for naught but suspicion; and I but a child of ten years at the time.''

Rod's stomach tried to turn itself inside out and climb out through his esophagus. He reprimanded it sternly, and it sank back to its ordinary place in the alimentary tract. Bile soured the back of Rod's tongue.

Bridgett spun and disappeared; a nano-second later she was back with her partner, giddy and exuberant again.

Rod frowned after her, brooding.

''So you may see,'' said Toby, ''that we are most truly grateful to our good Queen.''

''She did away with the fire and/or water bit?''

''Oh, she revoked the law; but the witch-burnings went on, in secret. There was only one way to protect us, and that she chose: to give sanctuary to any of us who would come here and claim it.''

Rod nodded, slowly. ''She's not without wisdom, after all.''

His eyes wandered back to Bridgett where she danced on the ceiling.

"What troubles you, friend Gallowglass?"

"She doesn't hate them," Rod growled. "She has every reason in the world to hate the normal folk, but she doesn't."

Toby shook his head, smiling warmly. "Not she, nor any of us. All who come to shelter in the Queen's Coven swear first to live by Christ's Law."

Slowly, Rod turned to look at him. "I see," he said after a moment. "A coven of white witches."

Toby nodded.

"Are all the witches of Gramarye white?"

"Shame to say it, they are not. Some there are who, embittered through greater suffering than ours—the loss of an ear or an eye, or a loved one, or all—have hidden themselves away in the Wild Lands of the mountains, and there pursue their vengeance on all mankind."

Rod's mouth pulled back into a thin, grim line, turned down at the corners.

"They number scarce more than a score," Toby went on. "There are three in the prime of life; all the rest are withered crones and shrunken men."

"The fairy-tale witches," Rod growled.

"Of a truth, they are; and their works are noised about just sufficient to cover report of any good works that we may deal."

"So there are two kinds of witches in Gramarye: the old and evil ones, up in the mountains; and the young white ones in the Queen's castle."

Toby shook his head and smiled, his eyes lighting once again. "Nay, there are near threescore white witches beside us, who would not trust to the Queen's promise of sanctuary. They are thirty and forty years aged, good folk all, but slow indeed to be trusting."

Understanding struck with all the power of Revelation. Rod leaned back, his mouth forming a silent O; then nodding rapidly, he leaned forward and said, *"That's* why you're all so young! Only the witches who still had some trust and recklessness left in them took the Queen's invitation! So she got a flock of teenagers!"

Toby grinned from ear to ear, nodding quick with excitement.

"So the mature witches," Rod went on, "are very good people, but they're also very cautious!"

Toby nodded. His face sobered a trifle. "There are one or two among them who had daring enough to come here. There was the wisest witch of all, from the South. She grows old now. Why, she must be fair near to thirty!"

That line caught Rod right in the middle of a drink. He choked, swallowed, gagged, coughed, wheezed, and wiped at his eyes.

"Is aught wrong, friend Gallowglass?" Toby inquired with the kind of solicitousness usually reserved for the octogenarian.

"Oh, nothing," Rod gasped. "Just a little confusion between the esophagus and the trachea. Have to expect a few quirks in us old folk, you know. Why didn't this wise witch stay?"

Toby smiled, fairly oozing understanding and kindness. "Ah, she said that we made her feel too much her age, and went back to the South. If thou shouldst come to trouble there, but call out her name, Gwendylon, and thou'lt right quick have more help than thou needst."

"I'll remember that," Rod promised, and immediately forgot as he had a sudden vision of himself calling a woman for help. He almost went into another coughing fit, but he didn't dare laugh; he remembered how sensitive he'd been in his teens.

He took another swig of the wine to wash down his laughter and pointed the mug at Toby. "Just one more question, now: why is the Queen protecting you?"

Toby stared. "Didst thou not know?"

"Know I didst not." Rod smiled sweetly.

"Why, she is herself a witch, good friend Gallowglass!"

Rod's smile faded. "Hum." He scratched the tip of his nose. "I'd heard rumors to that effect. They're true, eh?"

"Most true. A witch unschooled, but a witch nonetheless."

Rod raised an eyebrow. "Unschooled?"

"Aye. Our gifts need a stretching and exercising, a training and schooling, to come to their full. Catharine is a witch born, but unschooled. She can hear thoughts, but not at any time that she wishes, and not clearly."

"Hm. What else can she do?"

"Naught that we know of. She can but hear thoughts."

"So she's sort of got a minimum union requirement." Rod scratched in back of his ear. "Kind of handy talent for a Queen. She'd know everything that goes on in her castle."

Toby shook his head. "Canst hear five speak all at once, friend Gallowglass? And listen to them all the hours of the day? And still be able to speak what they spoke?"

Rod frowned and rubbed his chin.

"Canst repeat even one conversation?" Toby smiled indulgently and shook his head. "Of course thou can'st not—and neither can our Queen."

"She could write them down. . . ."

"Aye; but remember, she is unschooled; and it needs high training of an excellent good gift to make words of thoughts."

"Hold on." Rod's hand went up, palm out. "You mean you don't hear thoughts as words?"

"Nay, nay. An instant's thought suffices for a book of words, friend Gallowglass. Must you needs put words to your thoughts in order to have them?"

Rod nodded. "I see. Quantum thought mechanics."

"Strange . . ." murmured a voice. Looking up, Rod found himself the center of a fair-sized group of young witches and warlocks who had apparently drifted over to get in on an ineresting conversation.

He looked at the one who had spoken, a burly young warlock, and smiled with a touch of sarcasm. "What's strange?" He wondered what the kid's name was.

The boy grinned. "Martin is my name." He paused to chuckle at Rod's startled look; he still hadn't gotten used to the mind-reading. "And what is strange is that you, a warlock, should not know the ins and outs of hearing thoughts.

"Aye." Toby nodded. "You are the only warlock we have known, friend Gallowglass, that cannot hear thoughts."

"Uh, yes." Rod ran a hand over the stubble on his cheek. "Well, as I mentioned a little earlier, I'm not really a warlock. You see . . ."

He was cut off by a unanimous burst of laughter. He sighed, and resigned himself to his reputation.

He reverted to his former line of questioning. "I take it some of you can hear thoughts as words."

"Oh, aye," said Toby, wiping his eyes. "We have one." He turned to the ring of listeners. "Is Aldis here?"

A buxom, pretty sweet-sixteen elbowed her way through to the front rank. "Who shall I listen to for you, sir?"

A spark arced across a gap in Rod's mind. A malicious gleam came into his eyes. "Durer. The councillor to Milord Loguire."

Aldis folded her hands in her lap, settled herelf, sitting very straight. She stared at Rod; her eyes lost focus. Then she began to speak in a high-pitched nasal monotone.

"As you will, milord. Yet I cannot help but wonder, are you *truly* loyal?"

Her voice dropped two octaves in pitch but kept the monotonous quality. "Knave! Have you the gall to insult me to me face?"

"Nay, milord!" the high voice answered hurriedly. "I do not insult you; I do but question the wisdom of your actions."

Durer, Rod thought. The high voice was Durer, practicing his vocation—the care and manipulation of the Duke Loguire.

"Remember, milord, she is but a child. Is it kindness to a child to let her have her willful way? Or is it kindness to spank her when she needs it?"

There was a silence for a moment; then the deeper voice of the Lord Loguire answered, "There is some measure of truth in what you say. Certain, there is something of the wanton child in her taking up the power to appoint the priests."

"Why," murmured the high voice, " 'tis an act against tradition, milord, and against the wisdom of men far older than herself. 'Tis in bitter truth the act of a rebellious child."

"Mayhap," Loguire rumbled. "Yet she is the Queen, and the Queen's Law shall be obeyed."

"Even should the Queen make evil laws, milord?"

"Her actions are not evil, Durer." The deep voice took on an ominous quality. "Reckless, perhaps, and thoughtless, and ill-considered; for the good they bring today may bring havoc down upon our heads tomorrow. Foolish laws, perhaps; but evil, no.''

The high voice sighed. ''Mayhap, milord. Yet she threatens the honor of her noblemen. Is that not evil?''

''Why,'' rumbled Loguire, ''how is this? She has been haughty, aye, taking to herself greater airs than ever a Queen may own to, mayhap; but she has never yet done aught that could be construed as insult.''

''Aye, milord, not yet.''

''Why, what do you mean?''

''The day shall come, milord.''

''What day is that, Durer?''

''When she shall put the peasants before the noblemen, milord.''

''Have done with your treasonous words!'' Loguire roared. ''On your knees, slight man, and thank your God that I leave you with your head!''

Rod stared at Aldis' face, still not recovered from the shock of hearing two disembodied male voices coming from the mouth of a pretty girl.

Slowly, her eyes focused again. She let out a long breath and smiled up at him. ''Did you hear, friend Gallowglass?''

Rod nodded.

She spread her hands, shrugging. ''I cannot recall a word of what I said.''

''Don't let it worry you, I remember it all.'' Rod rubbed the stubble on his chin. ''You were acting as a channel, a medium in the purest sense of the word.''

He threw his head back, drained his mug, and tossed it to one of the young warlocks. The youth caught the tankard, disappeared, and reappeared. He handed the tankard, brimming full, to Rod, who shook his head in mock despair.

He leaned back and sipped at the wine, looking up at the young faces around him, smiling and fairly glowing with the knowledge of their power.

"Have you ever done this before?" he asked, with a wave of the mug that took them all in. "Listened to skull sessions like that one, I mean."

"Only of the Queen's enemies," Aldis answered with a toss of her head. "We often listen to Durer."

"Oh?" Rod raised an eyebrow. "Learn anything?"

Aldis nodded. "He is much concerned with the peasants of late."

Rod was very still for a moment. Then he leaned forward, elbows on his knees. "What's his interest in the peasants?"

Toby grinned knowingly. "Hark now to his latest exploit! He hath brooded trouble 'twixt two serfs on the Queen's own estate. A young peasant wished to marry an old farmer's daughter, and the old man said nay. And the youth would've thrown up his hands in despair and let himself waste away with a broken heart."

"But Durer stepped in."

"Aye. He was after the young one night and day; for knowledge of the boy's suit spread throughout all the villages, and saw to it that the rumor was told with one question appended: Could the youth be a man who would let a doddard idiot rob him of the girl he loved?"

Rod nodded. "And the other peasants started throwing that up to the kid."

"Most certainly. Taunts and jeers and mocking— and the lad stole the girl away by night and got her with child."

Rod pursed his lips. "I imagine Papa was a trifle perturbed."

Toby nodded. "He hauled the boy before the village priest and demanded the lad be hanged for a rapist."

"And the priest said . . . ?"

"That it was love, not rape, and the fitting punishment was marriage, not hanging."

Rod grinned. "Bet the two kids were real sad about that."

"Their grief was so great it set them to dancing." Toby chuckled. "And the old man gave a heavy sigh, and would have judged it the wisdom of God, and blessed them."

"And Durer stepped in again."

"Most certainly. He was up before the Queen, when she was at table before all her lords and her ladies, crying that the Queen must prove the justice of her new order by declaring herself what was just in this case; for were these not peasants on the Queen's own estates?"

Rod grinned and slapped his thigh. "She must have been ready to spit in his eye!"

"Oh, you know not the Queen!" Toby rolled his eyes up toward the ceiling. "She would most cheerfully have slipped a knife 'twixt his ribs. But the challenge must needs be answered; she must needs hear the case herself, when next she held General Court."

"General Court?" Rod scowled. "What the hell is that?"

"One hour each month the Queen opens her court to all in her realm who wish her ear; and peasants, nobility, and clergy come to her Great Hall. Mostly the great lords but look on while the petty nobility and peasantry bring forth their grievances. And with the great ones watching, you may be sure the grievances brought up are petty indeed."

"Like this case." Rod nodded. "When's this next General Court?"

"Tomorrow," said Toby, "and I think the great lords shall have their tame clergy and peasantry protest the Queen's new judges and priests. The lords shall lodge their protest first, of course; and the other, more common folk shall be echoing them.''

Rod nodded. "Put the whole matter on public record. But what does Durer hope to gain by bringing in this seduction case?''

Toby shrugged. "That, only Durer may know.''

Rod leaned back, frowning, and pulled at his mug. He studied the young faces around him and scratched at the base of his skull. "Sounds to me like this is information the Queen would like to have. Why don't you tell her?''

The faces sobered. Toby bit his lip and looked down at the floor.

Rod scowled. "Why don't you tell her, Toby?''

"We have tried, friend Gallowglass!'' The boy looked up at Rod in mute appeal. "We have tried; yet she would not hear us!''

Rod's face turned to wood. "How's that again?''

Toby spread his hands in helplessness. "The page we sent to her returned to tell us that we should be thankful for the protection she accorded us, and not be so ingracious and insolent as to seek to meddle in her governing.''

Rod jerked his head in tight, quick nods, mouth drawn back in grim agreement. "Yeah, that sounds like Catharine.''

"Mayhap," one of the boys murmured thoughtfully, "it is all to the best; for she hath cares enough without warnings of doom from us.''

Rod grinned without humor. "Yeah. Between the noblemen and the beggars, she's got more than enough worries to keep her busy.''

Toby nodded, eyes wide and serious. "Aye, she hath troubles sufficient, between the councillors, the House of Clovis, and the banshee on her roof. She hath great cause to be most afeard.''

"Yes." Rod's voice was tight, rasping. "Yes, she hath good cause; and I think that she is thoroughly afeard."

Big Tom must have been a very light sleeper; he sat up on his pallet as Rod came tiptoeing up to his bunk.

"Art well, master?" he whispered in a rasping voice that had about as much secrecy as a bullfrog in rut.

Rod stopped and frowned down at his manservant. "Yes, very well. Why shouldn't I be?"

Big Tom smiled sheepishly. "Thou hast small use for sleep," he muttered. "I had thought it might be a fever."

"No." Rod smiled with relief, shaking his head. He pushed past Big Tom. "It's not a fever."

"What is it, then?"

Rod fell backward onto the bed, cupping his hands under his head. "Did you ever hear of a game called cricket, Tom?"

"Cricket?" Tom scowled. "'Tis a chirping creature on the hearth, master."

"Yeah, but it's also the name of a game. The center of the game is a wicket, see, and one team tries to knock down the wicket by throwing a ball at it. The other team tries to protect the wicket by knocking the ball away with a paddle."

"Strange," Big Tom murmured, eyes wide with wonder. "A most strange manner of game, master."

"Yes," Rod agreed, "but it gets worse. The teams trade sides, you see, and the team that was attacking the wicket before is defending it now." He looked down over his toes at Tom's round beehive face.

"Nay," the big man muttered, shaking his head in confusion. "What is the point to it all, master?"

Rod stretched, let his body snap back to relaxation.

"The point is that no matter who wins, it's going to be hard on the wicket."

"Aye!" Big Tom nodded vigorously. "Most certain true, master."

"Now, I get the feeling that there's a colossal game of cricket going on around here; only there's three teams in the game: the councillors, the beggars . . ."

"The House of Clovis," Tom muttered.

Rod's eyebrows went up in surprise. "Yes, the House of Clovis. And, of course, the Queen."

"Then, who," asked Big Tom, "is the wicket?"

"Me." Rod rolled over on his side, thumped the pillow with his fist, and lowered his head onto it with a blissful sigh. "And now I am going to sleep. Good night."

"Master Gallowglass," piped a page's voice.

Rod closed his eyes and prayed for strength. "Yes, page?"

"You are called to wait upon the Queen at her breakfast, Master Gallowglass."

Rod forced an eyelid open and peered out the window; the sky was rosy with dawn.

He squeezed his eyes shut and counted to ten, almost dozing off in the process. He drew in a sigh that would have filled a bottomless pit, swung his legs over the side of the bed, and sat up. "Well, no rest for the wicket. What'd I do with my damn uniform, Tom?"

Rod had to admit that Catharine Plantagenet had a good dramatic instinct and, moreover, knew how to use it on her court. The guards were at their stations in the dining hall before sunrise. The lords and ladies who were privileged— or, more accurately, cursed—to share the Queen's dawn breakfast arrived right after the cock's crow. Not till they were all assembled, and all waiting some time eyeing the breakfast meats, did Catharine make her entrance.

And she definitely made an entrance, even at that hour. The doors of the hall were thrown wide, revealing Catharine standing in a pool of torchlight. Six buglers blew a fanfare, at which all the lords and ladies rose and Rod winced (pitch was more or less a matter of taste in that culture).

Then Catharine stepped into the hall, head high and shoulders back. She paced a quarter way around the wall to the great gilded chair at the head of the table. The Duke of Loguire stepped forth and pulled the chair back. Catharine sat, with the grace and lightness of a feather. Loguire sat at her right hand, and the rest of the company followed suit. Catharine picked up her two-tined fork, and the company fell to, while liveried stewards invaded from the four corners of the hall with great platters of bacon and sausage, pickled herring, white rolls, and tureens of tea and soup.

Each platter was brought first to Brom O'Berin, where he sat at the Queen's left hand. Brom took a sample of each platter, ate a morsel of it, and placed the remainder on a plate before him. Then the huge platters were placed on the table. By this time Brom, finding himself still alive, passed the filled plate to Catharine.

The company fell to with gusto, and Rod's stomach reminded him that all that had hit his digestive tract that night had been spiced wine.

Catharine picked daintily at her food with the original bird-like appetite. Rumor had it that she ate just before the formal meal in the privacy of her apartments. Even so, she was so thin that Rod found it in himself to doubt the rumor.

The stewards wove in and out with flagons of wine and huge meat pies.

Rod was stationed at the east door; he thus had a good

view of Catharine, where she sat at the north end of the table, Milord Loguire at her right hand, Durer, at Loguire's right hand, and the back of Brom O'Berin's head.

Durer leaned over and murmured something to his lord. Loguire waved a hand impatiently and nodded. He tore the meat off a chop with one bite, chewed, swallowed, and washed it down with a draft of wine. As he lowered the cup to the table, he turned to Catharine and rumbled, ''Your Majesty, I am concerned.''

Catharine gave him the cold eye. "We are all concerned, Milord Loguire. We must bear with our cares as well as we may.''

Loguire's lips pressed tight together, his mouth almost becoming lost between moustache and beard. ''My care,'' he said, ''is for your own person, and for the welfare of your kingdom.''

Catharine turned back to her plate, cutting a morsel of pork with great care. ''I must hope that the welfare of my person would indeed affect the welfare of my kingdom.''

Loguire's neck was growing red; but he pushed on obstinately. ''I am glad that your Majesty sees that a threat to your welfare is a threat to this kingdom.''

The skin furrowed between Catharine's eyebrows; she frowned at Loguire. ''Indeed I do.''

''Knowing that the Queen's life is threatened, the people grow uneasy.''

Catharine put down her fork and sat back in her chair. Her voice was mild, even sweet. ''Is my life, then, threatened, milord?''

''It would seem so,'' Loguire murmured carefully. ''For the banshee was upon your roof again last night.''

Rod's ears pricked up.

Catharine's lips turned in, pressed between her teeth;

her eyes closed. Silence fell around the table. Brom O'Berin's voice rumbled into the sudden quiet. "The banshee hath often been seen upon her Majesty's battlements; yet still she lives."

"Be still!" Catharine snapped at him. Her shoulders straightened; she leaned forward to take up her goblet. "I do not wish to hear of the banshee." She drained the goblet, then held it out to the side. "Steward, more wine!"

Durer was out of his seat and at the Queen's elbow in an instant. Plucking the goblet from her hand, he turned to the steward who had come running up. He held the goblet up while the steward filled it from his ewer and the court stared; such courtesy to the Queen was, from Durer, somewhat unusual.

He swung back to the Queen, dropping to one knee and holding up the goblet. Catharine stared, then slowly accepted it. "I thank you, Durer; yet must I confess that I had not expected such courtliness from you."

Durer's eyes glinted. He rose with a mocking smile and bowed very low. "Drink deep in health, my Queen."

But Rod was a trifle less trusting than Catharine; moreover, he had seen Durer pass his left hand over the goblet just before the steward poured.

He left his post and caught the goblet just as Catharine raised it to her lips. She stared at him, face paling, rage rising in her eyes. "I did not summon you, sirrah."

"Your Majesty's pardon." Rod unclipped his dagger from his belt, shook the blade out onto the table, and filled the conical sheath with wine. Thank Heaven he'd taken the precaution of resetting Fess before he went on duty!

He held up the silver horn and said, "I con*Fess*, with

apologies to your Majesty, that I cannot *analyze* my actions; it is only that I fear for your Majesty's life.''

But all Catharine's anger had vanished in fascination at Rod's action. ''What,'' she said, pointing to the silver horn, ''is that?''

''Unicorn's horn,'' Rod answered, and looked up to see Durer's eyes, burning with rage at him.

''Analysis complete,'' murmured the voice behind his ear. ''Substance poisonous to human metabolism.''

Rod smiled grimly and pressed the knob at the apex of the horn with his little finger.

The ''unicorn's horn'' turned purple.

A gasp of horror went up from the whole court; for they all knew the legend, that a unicorn's horn will turn purple if poison is placed in it.

Catharine turned pale; she clenched her fists to conceal their trembling.

Loguire's hand balled into a huge fist; his eyes narrowed as he glared at Durer. ''Slight man, if any part of this treachery was yours . . .''

''Milord, you saw.'' Durer's voice crackled. ''I but held the cup.''

But his burning eyes were fixed on Rod's, seeming to suggest that Rod could save himself a lot of trouble and agony if he would just drink the wine right there and then.

Rod was assigned as one of the four guards who would escort Catharine from her apartments to the Great Hall for the General Court. The four of them waited outside her chambers till the door opened, and Brom O'Berin stepped out, preceding the Queen. Two soldiers fell in before the Queen and behind Brom; Rod and another Guardsman fell in behind her.

They moved down the corridor slowly, matching their pace to Catharine's; and the Queen, draped in a heavy fur cloak and weighed down by the great gold crown, moved very slowly. Somehow, she contrived to look stately rather than clumsy.

As they drew near the Great Hall, a slight, emaciated, velvet-clad figure came scurrying up—Durer.

"Your pardon," he said, bowing three times. "but I must speak with your Majesty." His lips were pressed tight, anger in his eyes.

Catharine stopped and drew herself up to her haughtiest.

Chip on her shoulder as large as a two-by-four, Rod thought.

"Speak, then," she said, looking down her nose at the cringing little man before her; "but speak quickly, sirrah."

Durer's eyes flared at the word of contempt; "sir-rah" was a term reserved for peasants.

He managed to keep his manner respectful, though. "Your Majesty, I beg you to brook no delay in hearing the Great Lords' petition, for they are most greatly overwrought."

Catharine frowned. "Why should I delay?"

Durer bit his lip, looking away.

Catharine's eyes kindled in anger. "Speak, sirrah," she snapped. "Or do you mean to imply that the Queen fears to hear her noblemen?"

"Your Majesty . . ." Durer spoke with great reluc-tance; then the words came in a rush. "I had heard there were two peasants to be heard in Court today . . ."

"There are." Catharine's mouth hardened. " 'Tis the case you recommended to me, Durer."

The little man's eye shot a malevolent gleam at her; then he was all fawning humility again. "I had thought . . . I had heard . . . I had feared . . ."

"What hast thou feared?"

"Your Majesty hath been most concerned for your peasants of late. . . ." Durer hesitated, then stumbled on. "I had feared . . . that your Majesty might . . . perhaps . . ."

Catharine's eyes hardened. "That I might hear these two peasants before I gave ear to the petitions of my noblemen?"

"Your Majesty must not!" Durer dropped to his knees, hands clasped in supplication. "Thou must not risk offense of the Great Lords today! Fear for thy very life if thou—"

"Sirrah, do you call me coward?"

Rod closed his eyes; his heart sank.

"Your Majesty," cried Durer, "I meant but to—"

"Enough!" Catharine turned away, spurning the meager form of the councillor. Brom O'Berin and the Guardsmen moved with her. The great oaken doors swung open before them.

Rod risked a glance back over his shoulder.

Durer's face was contorted with malevolent glee; his eyes glittered with triumph.

The best way to get a teenager to do something is to tell her not to. . . .

Brom led the Queen's entourage into a great vaulted room, lighted by a row of clerestory windows on each side. Fifty feet above, the roof-beam ran through the hall like a spine, with oaken ribs running down to the granite walls. Two great wrought-iron chandeliers hung from the ceiling, with candles burning in the sconces.

They had come in onto a raised dais, ten feet above the floor of the hall. A huge gilded throne rose before them.

Brom led them in a swing around the lip of the dais to the throne. There the Guardsmen lined up on either side, and Catharine mounted the last half-step to stand slender and proud before the throne, gazing out over the multitude gathered below.

The multitude looked like a sampling of the population. They filled the great hall, from the steps of the dais to the triple doors at the far end of the hall.

In the first rank were the twelve great nobles, seated in wooden hourglass-shaped chairs in a semicircle twelve feet out from the steps of the throne.

Behind them stood forty or fifty aging men in brown, gray, or dark gree robes with velvet collars and small, square, felt hats. Chains of silver or gold hung down over their ample bellies. Burghers, Rod guessed—local officials, merchants, guildmasters—the bourgeoisie.

Beyond them were the black, cowled robes of the clergy; and beyond them were the dun-colored, patched clothing of the peasantry, most of whom, Rod felt moderately certain, had been sent up from the castle kitchen so that the Great Court would have representatives of all classes.

But in the center of the peasants stood four soldiers in green and gold—the Queen's colors—and between them stood two peasants, one young and one old, both looking awed and scared almost to the point of panic, caps twisting in their horny hands. The oldster had a long, grizzled beard; the youngster was clean-shaven. Both wore dun-colored smocks of coarse cloth; more of the same material was bound to their legs, to serve as trousers. A priest stood by them, looking almost as much out of place as they did.

All eyes were on the Queen. Catharine was very much aware of it; she stood a little taller, and held her pose until the hall was completely quiet. Then she sat, slowly, and Brom sank cross-legged at her feet. Pike-butts thudded on stone as Rod and the other three Guardsmen stood to rest, pikes slanting outward at twenty degrees.

Brom's voice boomed out over the hall. "Who comes before the Queen this day?"

A herald stepped forward with a roll of parchment and read off a list of twenty petitions. The first was that of the twelve noblemen; the last was Durer's two peasants.

Catharine's hands tightened on the arms of the throne. She spoke in a high, clear voice. "Our Lord hath said that the humble shall be exalted, the last shall be first; therefore let us first her the testimony of these two peasants."

There was a moment's shocked silence; old Lord Loguire was on his feet bellowing.

"Testimony! Have you such great need of their testimony that you must set these clods of earth before the highest of your nobles?"

"My lord," Catharine snapped, "you forget your place in my court."

"Nay, it is you who forget! You who forget respect and tradition, and all the law that you learned at your father's knee!"

The old lord drew himself up, glaring. "Never," he rumbled, "would the old king have disgraced his liegemen so!"

"Open thine eyes, old man!" Catharine's voice was chill and arrogant. "I would my father still lived; but he is dead, and I reign now."

"Reign!" Loguire's lips twisted in a sour grimace. "'Tis not a reign, but a tyranny!"

The hall fell silent, shocked. Then a whisper began and grew: "Treason! TreasontreasontreasonTreason!"

Brom O'Berin rose, trembling. "Now, Milord Loguire, must thou kneel and ask pardon of milady the Queen, or be adjudged forever a traitor to the throne."

Loguire's face turned to stone, he drew himself up, back straightening, chin lifting; but before he could answer, Catherine spoke in a tight, quavering voice.

"There shall be no forgiveness asked, nor none given. Thou, Milord Loguire, in consideration of insults offered our Royal Person, art henceforth banished from our Court and Presence, to come near us nevermore."

Slowly, the old Duke's eyes met the Queen's. "How then, child," he murmured, and Rod saw with a shock that there were tears in the corners of the old man's eyes. "Child, wilt thou serve the father as thou hast served the son?"

Catharine's face went dead white; she half rose from her throne.

"Hie thee from this place, Milord Loguire!" Brom's voice shook with rage. "Hie thee from this place, or I shall hound thee hence!"

The Duke's gaze slowly lowered to Brom. "Hound me? Aye, for thou art most surely our gentle Queen's watchdog!" He raised his eyes to Catharine again. "Lady, lady! I had hoped to grace thee with a greyhound ere I died."

Catharine sat again, drawing herself up proudly. "I have a mastiff, milord; and let my enemies beware!"

The old man nodded slowly, his grieving eyes never leaving her face. "Thou wilt, then, call me enemy. . . ."

Catharine tilted her chin a little higher.

Loguire's eyes hardened; the grief was swept from his face by cold pride.

He spun on his heel, stalking down the length of the great hall. A lane through the crowd opened before him. The Guardsmen at either side of the great central door snapped to attention and threw the portals open.

The Duke stopped short under the lintel and pivoted

to look back over the throng at Catharine. His heavy old voice filled the hall one last time.

And his voice was somehow gentle, almost kindly.

"Yet take this of me, Catharine, whom once I called my niece—thou shalt not fear the armies of Loguire while I live."

He stood motionless a moment, holding Catharine's eyes.

Then he swung about, cape swirling, and was gone.

The court was silent for the space of three breaths; then, as a man, the eleven remaining Great Lords rose and filed down the lane to the great central door, and followed Loguire into exile.

"So how did she decide the case of the two peasants?" Fess asked.

Rod was riding the robot horse on the slope outside the castle, "for exercise," or so he had told the stableboy. Actually, he needed Fess's advice as to What It All Meant.

"Oh," he answered, "she upheld the parish priest's decisions: the fitting punishment for the kid was marriage. The old man didn't like that too well, but Catharine had an ace up her sleeve—the kid would have to support his father-in-law in his old age. The old man grinned at that, and the kid walked out looking like he wasn't quite so sure he'd come out on top after all."

"An excellent decision," Fess murmured. "Perhaps the young lady should seek a career in jurisprudence."

"Anything, so long as it keeps her out of politics. . . . Glorious sunsets on this planet."

They were riding into the setting sun; the dying globe painted the sky russet and gold halfway around the horizon and nearly to the zenith.

"Yes," the robot supplied, "the excellence of the

sunsets is due to the density of the atmosphere, which is nearly one point five Terra-normal. At this latitude, however, due to the inclination of the planet's axis, which is—"

"Yes, yes, I wrote it all down in the logbook when we landed. Have the grace to let it rest in peace. . . . I notice the sun's rays turn almost blood-red . . ."

"Appropriate," Fess murmured.

"Hmm, yes. That brings us back to the point, doesn't it? What's this about another assassination coming up?"

"Not an assassination, Rod—an attempt."

"All right, an attempt. Pardon my denotations, and get on with it."

Fess paused a moment to set up the readout for a pre-fabricated report.

"The political situation on the island of Gramarye is comprised of three definite factions, one Royalist and two Anti-Royalist. The Royalist faction consists of the Queen, her chief councillor—one Brom O'Berin—the clergy, the Royal Army, the Queen's Bodyguard, and a group of espers known by the local term 'witches.' "

"How about the judges?"

"As I was about to say, the civil servants may also be included in the Royalist faction, with the exception of those officials whose corruption leaves them opposed to the Queen's reforms."

"Hmm, yes. I'd forgotten that hitch. Anybody else on the Plantagenet side?"

"Yes, a subspecies of Homo sapiens characterized by extreme dwarfism and referred to by the local term 'elves.' "

"Well, they sure don't seem to be against her, anyway," Rod murmured.

"The Anti-Royalist factions are significantly *not* united by their common opposition to the Throne. The first of these factions is the aristocracy, led by twelve dukes and earls, who are in turn led by the Duke Loguire. It is worth noting that the aristocrats are unanimous in their opposition to the Queen. Such unanimity among the aristocrats of a feudal culture is totally without precedent, and must therefore be regarded as an anomaly.''

"And just where did this strange united front come from?''

"The unanimity may be attributed to the presence of a group termed the councillors, each member of which serves in an advisory capacity to one of th twelve great lords. The physical coherence of this group indicates—''

Rod jerked his head around, staring at the robot horse's ears. "How's that again?''

"Each of the councillors is physically characterized by a stooped posture, extreme leanness, sparse cranial hair, pale skin, and a general apperance of advanced age.''

Rod pursed his lips. "Ve-ry interesting! I hadn't caught any significance in that.''

"Such a physical appearance is characteristic of an extremely advanced technological society, in which the problems of longevity, metabolic adjustment, and exposure to ultraviolet have been controlled.''

"Modern medicine and a barroom pallor.'' Rod nodded. "But how do you account for the hunched-over posture?''

"We may assume that is a part of the obsequious manner employed by this group. The extremeness of this behavior would seem to indicate that it is not natural to the men in question.''

"Finagle's Law of Reversal.'' Rod nodded. "Go on.''

"The goal of the Royalist faction is to increase the

power of the central authority. The goal of the councillors seems to be the elimination of the central authority, which will result in that form of political organization known as warlordism.''

"Which," said Rod, "is a kind of anarchy."

"Precisely; and we must therefore entertain the possibility that the councillors may pursue the pattern of political breakdown from warlordism through parochialism to the possible goal of total anarchy.''

"And that's why they're out to kill Catharine.''

"An accurate observation; any chance to eliminate the central authority will be taken.''

"Which means she's in danger. Let's get back to the castle.''

He pulled on the reins, but Fess refused to turn. "She is not in danger, Rod, not yet. The mythos of this culture requires that preliminary to a death, an apparition known as a banshee must be seen on the roof of the dwelling. And the banshee cannot appear until nightfall.''

Rod looked up at the sky. It was twilight; there was still some of the sunset's glow around the horizon.

"All right, Fess. You've got fifteen minutes, maybe a half-hour.''

"The evidence of the councillor's origin in a high-technology society,'' the robot droned on, "indicates that the group derives from off-planet, since the only culture on the planet is that of Catharine's realm, which is characterized by a medieval technology. The other Anti-Royalist faction also bears indications of off-planet origin.''

"I think I've heard that before,'' Rod mused. "Run through it again, will you?''

"Certainly. The second Anti-Royalist faction is known as the House of Clovis, a name deriving from the supposedly elective process of choosing ancient kings. The rank and file of the House of Clovis consists of beggars, thieves, and other criminals and outcasts. The titular leader is a banished nobleman, Tuan Loguire.''

"Hold it a moment," said Rod. *"Titular* leader?''

"Yes," said Fess. "The superficial structure of the House of Clovis would seem to verge on the mob; bur further analysis discloses a tightly-knit sub-organization, one function of which is the procurement of nourishment and clothing for the members of the House.''

"But that's what Tuan's doing!''

"Is it? Who supplies the necessities of life at the House of Clovis, Rod?''

"Well, Tuan gives the money to the innkeeper, that twisted little monkey they call the Mocker.''

"Precisely.''

"So you're saying," Rod said slowly, "that the Mocker is using Tuan as a fund-raiser and figurehead, while the Mocker is the real boss.''

"That," said Fess, "is what the data would seem to indicate. What is the Mocker's physical appearance, Rod?''

"Repulsive.''

"And how did he earn his nickname of 'the Mocker'?''

"Well, he's supposed to be a sort of Man of a Thousand Faces. . . .''

"But what is his basic physical appearance, Rod?''

"Uh . . .'' Rod threw his head back, eyes shut, visualizing the Mocker. "I'd say about five foot ten, hunched over all the time like he had curvature of the spine, slight build—very slight, looks like he eats maybe two hundred calories a day—not much hair

. . ." His eyes snapped open. "Hey! He looks like one of the councillors!"

"And is therefore presumably from a high-technology society," Fess agreed, "and therefore also from off-planet. This contention is reinforced by his political philosphy, as indicated in Tuan Loguire's speeches to the rabble. . . ."

"So Tuan is also the mouthpiece," Rod mused. "But of course; he never could have thought up proletarian totalitarianism by himself."

"It is also worth noting that the Mocker is the only member of the House of Clovis of this particular physical type."

"Ye-e-e-s!" Rod nodded, rubbing his chin. "He's playing a lone game. All his staff are locals trained to back him up."

"His long-range goal," said Fess, "may be assumed to be the establishment of a dictatorship. Consequently, he would wish someone on the throne whom he could control."

"Tuan."

"Precisely. But he must first eliminate Catharine."

"So the councillors and House of Clovis are both out for Catharine's blood."

"True; yet there is no indication that they have joined forces. If anything, they would seem to be mutually opposed."

"Duplication of effort—very inefficient. But, Fess, what're they doing here?"

"We may assume that they derive from two opposed societies, both of which wish to control some commodity which may be found on Gramarye."

Rod frowned. "I haven't heard of any rare minerals aroundabout . . ."

"I had in mind human resources, Rod."

Rod's eyes widened. "The espers! Of course! They're here because of the witches!"

"Or the elves," Fess reminded.

Rod frowned. "What would they want with the elves?"

"I have no hypothesis available; yet the logical possibility must be entertained."

Rod snorted, "All right, you stick with the logical possibility, and I'll stand by the witches. Anyone who could corner the market on telepaths could control the galaxy. Hey!" He stared, appalled. "They probably *could* control the galaxy."

"The stakes," Fess murmured, "are high."

"I'll have mine . . ." Rod began; but he was cut off by a ululating, soaring wail that grated like nails on glass.

Fess swung about; Rod looked back at the castle.

A dim shape glowed on the battlements, just below the east tower. Like a fox fire or a will o' the wisp. It must have been huge; Rod could make out detail even at this distance. It was dressed in the rags and tatters of a shroud, through which Rod could see the body of a voluptuous woman; but the head was a rabbit's, and the muzzle held pointed teeth.

The banshee began to wail again, a low moan that rose to a keening cry, then stabbed up the scale to a shriek, a shriek that held, and held, and held till Rod's ears were ready to break.

"Fess," he gasped, "what do you see?"

"A banshee, Rod."

Rod rode down, ran into, through and over five pairs of sentries en route to the Queen's chambers. But there, at her doors, he met an insurmountable roadblock about two feet high—Brom O'Berin, standing with feet set wide and arms akimbo.

"Thou hast been long in coming," the little man growled. His face was beet-red with anger, but fear haunted the backs of his eyes.

"I came as fast as I could," Rod panted. "Is she in danger?"

Brom grunted. "Aye, in danger, though there is as yet no sign of it. Thou must stand watch at her bedside this night, warlock."

Rod stiffened. "I," he said, "am not a warlock. I am a simple soldier-of-fortune who happens to know a little science."

Brom tossed his head impatiently. "This is a poor time to bandy words. Call yourself what you will, cook, carpenter, or mason, thou hast still warlock's powers. But we waste time."

He rapped back-handed on the door; it swung in, and a sentry stepped out. He saluted and stood aside.

Brom smiled grimly and went through the door. "Still don't trust me behind your back, eh?"

"Nearly," said Brom.

"That's what I said."

The sentry entered behind them and closed the door.

The room was large, with four shuttered slit windows on one side. The floor was covered with fur rugs; the walls were hung with silk, velvet, and tapestries. A fire crackled on a small hearth.

Catharine sat in a huge four-poster bed, covered to the waist with quilts and furs. Her unbound hair flowed down over the shoulders of a velvet, ermine-trimmed dressing gown. She was surrounded by a gaggle of ladies-in-waiting, several serving-girls, and two pages.

Rod knelt at her bedside. "Your Majesty's pardon for my tardiness!"

She gave him a frosty glance. "I had not known you were called." She turned away.

Rod frowned, looked her over.

She sat back against eight or ten fluffy satin pillows; her eyelids drooped in languid pleasure; there was a half-smile on her lips. She was enjoying the one spot of real luxury in her day.

She might be in mortal danger, but she sure didn't know about it. Brom had been keeping secrets again.

She held out a hand to one of her ladies; the woman gave her a steaming goblet of wine. Catharine brought it to her lips with a graceful flourish.

"Whoa!" Rod jumped to his feet, intercepted the goblet on its way to her lips, and plucked it away with his left hand while his right brought out his "unicorn's horn."

Catharine stared, amazed; then her eyes narrowed, her face reddened. "Sirrah, what means this?"

But Rod was staring at the "unicorn's horn" dagger-sheath; Fess's voice spoke behind his ear: "Substance with the analysis unit is toxic to human metabolism."

But Rod hadn't poured the wine into the horn yet. There was nothing in it.

Except air.

Rod pressed the stud that turned the horn purple.

Catharine stared in horror as the violet flush crept over the surface of the dagger-sheath.

"Sirrah," she gasped, "what means this?"

"Poison air," Rod snapped. She shoved the goblet at a servant-girl and looked about the room. Something in here was emitting poison gas.

The fireplace.

Rod crossed to the hearth and held the horn upside-down over the flames; but the color of the sheath dimmed to lavender.

"Not there," Rod spun about, coming to his feet. He paced about the room, holding the horn before him like a candle. It stayed lavender.

He frowned, scratched at the base of his skull. What would be the best place to put a poison-gas cartridge?

As close to the Queen as possible, of course.

He turned, moving slowly to the four-poster. As he came to Catharine's side, the horn's color darkened to violet.

Catharine stared at the horn in fascination and horror.

Rod knelt, slowly. The horn's color darkened to purple and began to shade toward black.

Rod threw up the bedskirts and looked under the four-poster. There before him, on the stone floor, steamed a warming-pan.

Rod grabbed the long handle and yanked the pan out. He inverted the horn over one of the holes in the cover—if his memory was correct, warming-pans didn't usually have holes. . . .

The horn turned dead black.

He looked up at Catharine. She had the knuckles of one hand jammed between her teeth, biting them to keep from screaming.

Rod turned, holding the pan out to the sentry. "Take this," he said, "and fling it into the moat."

The sentry dropped his pike, took the warming-pan, and rushed out, holding it at arm's length.

Rod turned slowly back to Catharine. "We have cheated the banshee again, my Queen."

Catharine's hand trembled as she took it away from her mouth. Then her lips clamped shut, her eyes squeezed tight, little fists clenched so hard the knuckles were white.

Then her eyes opened, slowly; there was a wild light in them, and a faint smile crept over her lips. "Master Gallowglass, stay by me. All else, remove yourselves!"

Rod swallowed and felt his joints liquefy. She was,

at that moment, the most beautiful woman he had ever seen.

The Guardsmen, ladies, and pages were already in motion, heading for an incipient traffic jam at the door.

Brom bawled orders, and the jam failed to develop. In thirty seconds, the room was clear, except for Rod, the Queen, and Brom O'Berin.

"Brom," Catharine snapped, eyes locked on Rod's face. Her teeth were beginning to show through her smile. "Brom O'Berin, do you leave us also."

Brom stared a moment, outraged; then his shoulders slumped, and he bowed heavily. "I will, my Queen."

The door closed quietly behind him.

Slowly, Catharine lay back against the pillows. She stretched with a luxurious, liquid grace. One hand snaked out to clasp Rod's. Her hand was very soft.

"It is twice now you have given me my life, Master Gallowglass." Her voice was a velvet purr.

"My—my privilege, my Queen." Rod cursed himself, he was gawking like an adolescent with a copy of *Fanny Hill*.

Catharine frowned prettily, tucking her chin in and touching a forefinger to her lips.

Then she smiled, rolled over onto her side. The velvet gown fell open. Apparently it was the custom to sleep nude.

Remember, boy, Rod told himself, *you're just a traveling salesman. You'll wake up in the morning and be on your way. You're here to peddle democracy, not to court a Queen. Not fair to take advantage of her if you're not going to be here to take advantage of it. . . . Did that make sense?*

Catharine was toying with a pendant that hung from her neck. Her teeth were worrying her lower lip. She looked him over like a cat sizing up a canary.

"Blank-shield soldiers," she murmured, "have a certain repute . . ."

Her lips were moist, and very full.

Rod felt his lips moving, heard his own voice stammering, "As—as my Queen seeks to reform the ills of her land, I . . . hope to reform the reputation of soldiers. I would do . . . only good to your Majesty."

For a moment, it seemed Catherine's very blood must have stopped, so still she lay.

Then her eyes hardened, and the silence in the room stretched very, very thin.

She sat up, gathering her dressing gown about her. "Thou art much to be commended, Master Gallowglass. I am indeed fortunate to have such loyal servitors about me."

It was much to her credit, under the circumstances, Rod thought, that there was only a faint tone of mockery to her voice.

Her eyes met his again. "Accept the Queen's thanks for the saving of her life."

Rod dropped to one knee.

"I am indeed fortunate," Catharine went on, "to be so loyally served. You have given me my life; and I think that few soldiers would have given me safe deliverance, as you have done."

Rod flinched.

She smiled, her eyes glittering malice and satisfaction for just a moment.

Then her eyes dropped to her hands. "Leave me now, for I shall have a trying day tomorrow, and must make good use of the night, for sleeping."

"As the Queen wishes," Rod answered, pokerfaced. He rose and turned away, his belly boiling with anger—at himself. It wasn't her fault he was a fool.

He closed the door behind him, then spun and

slammed his fist against the rough stone of the entry-way wall. The nerves in his fist screamed agony.

He turned back to the hall, forearm laced with pain—and there stood Brom O'Berin, face beet-red, trembling.

"Well, shall I kneel to thee? Art thou our next king?"

The anger in Rod's belly shot up, heading for Brom O'Berin. Rod clamped his jaws shut to hold it back. He glared at Brom, eyes narrowing. "I have better use for my time, Brom O'Berin, than to rob the royal cradle."

Brom stared at him, the blood and fury draining out of his face. " 'Tis true," he murmured, nodding. "By all the saints, I do believe 'tis true! For I can see in thy face that thou art filled with Furies, screaming madness at thy manhood!"

Rod squeezed his eyes shut. His jaw tightened till it felt as if a molar must break.

Something had to break. Something had to give, somewhere.

Somewhere, far away, he heard Brom O'Berin saying, "This one hath a message for thee, from the witches in the tower. . . ."

Rod forced his eyes open, stared down at Brom.

Brom was looking down and to his left. Following his gaze Rod saw an elf sitting tailor-fashion by Brom's foot. Puck.

Rod straightened his shoulders. Smother the anger; vent it later. If the witches had sent word, it was probably vital.

"Well, spill it," he said. "What word from the witches?"

But Puck only shook his head and murmured, "Lord, what fools these mortals be!"

He skipped aside a split second before Rod's fist

slammed into the wall where he'd been sitting.

Rod howled with pain, and spun. He saw Puck and lunged again.

But "Softly" said Puck, and a huge chartreuse-and-shock-pink filled the hall, a full-size, regulation, fire-breathing dragon, rearing back on its hind feet and bellowing flame at Rod.

Rod goggled. Then he grinned, baring his teeth in savage joy.

The dragon belched fire as it struck. Rod ducked under the flames and came up under the monster's head. His fingers closed on the scaly neck, thumbs probing for the carotid arteries.

The dragon flung its head up and snapped its neck like a whip. Rod held on grimly, held on and held on while the dragon battered him against the granite walls. His head slapped stone and he yelled with pain, stars and darkness before his eyes, but he tightened his grip.

The great neck bowed, and the huge talons of the hind feet raked at Rod's belly, splitting him from collarbone to thigh. Blood fountained out, and Rod felt himself reeling into blackness; but he held on, determined to take the dragon with him into death.

Yeah, death, he thought, amazed, and was outraged that he should die over a puny fit of anger, anger over a slip of a bitch of a girl.

Well, at least he'd have a mount in the land of the dead. As darkness sucked him down, he felt the great head drooping, bobbing lower and lower, following him down to death. . . .

His feet felt solid ground and, for a miracle, his legs held him up. Light misted through the dark around him, misted and gathered and grew, and he saw the beast lying dead at his feet.

The darkness ebbed away from the dragon; light

showed Rod granite walls and brocade hangings; and the castle hall swam about him, reeled, and steadied.

At his feet, the dragon's colors faded. Its outlines blurred and shimmered, and the beast was gone; there was only clean gray stone beneath Rod's feet.

He looked down at his chest and belly; his doublet was whole, not even wrinkled. Not a trace of blood, not a scratch on him.

He squeezed an elbow, expecting the pain of bruises; there was none.

His head was clear, without the ghost of even an ache.

Slowly, he raised his eyes to Puck.

The elf looked back, eyes wide and mournful. Amazingly, he wasn't smiling.

Rod covered his face with his hands, then looked up again. "Enchantment?"

Puck nodded.

Rod looked away. "Thanks."

"Thou hadst need of it," Puck answered.

Rod squared his shoulders and breathed deeply. "You had a message for me?"

Puck nodded again. "Thou art summoned to a meeting of the Coven."

Rod frowned, shaking his head. "But I'm not a member."

Brom O'Berin chuckled like a diesel turning over. "Nay, thou art of them, for thou art a warlock."

Rod opened his mouth to answer, thought better of it, and closed his jaws with a snap. He threw up his hands in resignation. "Okay, have it your own way. I'm a warlock. Just don't expect me to believe it."

"Well, thou wilt, at least, no longer deny it." Toby filled Rod's mug with the hot, mulled wine. "We ha' known thou wert a warlock even before we had set eyes on thee.''

Rod sipped at the wine and looked about him. If he'd thought it was a party last night, his naïveté had been showing. That had just been a *kaffeeklatsch*. This time the kids were really whooping it up.

He turned back to Toby, bellowing to hear his own voice. ''Don't get me wrong; I don't mean to be a cold blanket, but what's the occasion? How come all the celebrating?''

''Why, our Queen lives!'' yelled Toby. ''And thou art hero of the night! Thou hast banished the banshee!''

''Hero . . .'' Rod echoed, a wry smile twisting his face. He lifted his mug and took, a long, long draft.

Suddenly he swung the mug down, spluttering and coughing.

''What ails thee?'' Toby asked, concerned. He pounded Rod on the back till the older man wheezed, gasping.

''Leave off,'' he said, holding up a hand, ''I'm okay. I just thought of something, that's all?''

''What is thy thought?''

''That banshee ain't real.''

Toby stared. ''What dost thou say?''

Rod clamped a hand on the back of Toby's neck and pulled the boy's ear down to his own level.

''Look,'' he yelled, ''the banshee only appears before someone dies, right?''

''Aye,'' said Toby, puzzled.

''Before someone *dies*,'' Rod repeated, ''not every time someone's just in *danger* of death. And the Queen's still alive!''

Toby pulled back, staring at Rod.

Rod smiled, eyes dancing. ''It's only supposed to show up when death's inevitable.''

He turned, looked out over the great tower room.

The witches were dancing on the walls, the ceiling, occasionally the floor, and in mid-air, with a fine disregard for gravity. They were twisting through gyrations that would have given a snake triple lumbago.

Rod looked back at Toby, lifted an eyebrow. "Doesn't look much like a funeral."

Toby frowned; then his face split into a grin. "I think thou hast not seen a Gramarye wake," he yelled. "Still, thou art aright; we dance this night for Life, not Death."

Rod grinned savagely, took another pull from his mug, and wiped his lips with the back of his hand. "Now, if it's a fake, and it is, the next question is, who put it there?"

Toby's jaw dropped open. He stared.

"Get me Aldis," Rod shouted.

Toby closed his mouth, gulped, and nodded. He closed his eyes; a moment later, Aldis swooped down and brought her broomstick in for a two-point landing.

"What dost thou wish?" she panted. She was blushing, face lit with excitement and joy. The sight of her gave Rod a sudden pang of mourning for his own lost youth.

He leaned forward. "See if you can tune in on Durer, Loguire's chief councillor."

She nodded, closed her eyes. After a few moments she opened them again, staring at Rod in fear.

"They are much wroth," she reported, "that the Queen did not die. But they are more wroth in that they know not who put the banshee on the roof of the castle this night."

Rod nodded, lips pressed into a tight, thin line. He took a last draft from his mug and rose, turning away toward the stairwell.

Toby reached up, catching his sleeve. "Where dost thou go?"

"To the battlements," Rod called back. "Where else would you look for a banshee?"

Th night breeze cut chill through his clothes as he stepped out onto the battlements. The moon, over his shoulder, sent his shadow pacing before him.

The battlements stretched out before him like a great gap-toothed row of incisors.

"Fess," Rod called softly.

"Here, Rod," murmured the voice back of his ear.

"Does this banshee seem to be fonder of one stretch of battlements than another?"

"Yes, Rod. During the period in which we have been in Gramarye, the banshee has appeared under the east tower."

"Always?"

"To judge by an inadequate sample, yes."

Rod turned to his left, strolling east. "Well, you go on collecting an adequate sample while I do something about it."

"Yes, Rod," said the robot, somehow managing a tone of martyred patience.

Rod looked out over the battlements at the town, nestled below them at the foot of the great hill that served as the foundation for the castle. A long, white road wound up from the town to the drawbridge, with here and there the outpost of a low, rambling inn.

And down there below, in the rotting heart of the town, like some great basalt gravestone, stood the House of Clovis.

A stumbling, a scrabbling behind him. Rod snapped about into a wrestler's crouch, dagger a bite of moon-light in his hand.

Big Tom stumbled out of the winding stairway, with something draped across his arm. He stood, looking about him with wide-white-rimmed eyes, heaving hoarse gusts of air into his lungs.

He turned, saw Rod, and came running, his face flooded with relief. "Eh, master, thou'rt still whole!"

Rod relaxed and straightened up, sliding the dagger back into its sheath. "Of course I'm whole! What're *you* doing here, Big Tom?"

The big man stopped, the grin wavering on his face. He looked down at the cold stones, shuffling his feet. " 'Ell, master, I had heard . . .I . . .well . . ." He looked up; the words came in a rush: "Tha must not go again' the banshee; but if thou'lt go, thou'lt not go alone."

Rod studied the big man's face for a long moment, wondering where this deep devotion had come from.

Then he smiled gently. "Your knees have turned to jelly at the mere thought of the monster, but you still won't let me go alone."

He clapped Tom on the shoulder, grinning. "Well, then, come along, Big Tom; and I'm downright glad of your company, I don't mind telling you."

Tom grinned and looked down at the stones again. It was hard to be sure in the moonlight, but Rod thought there was a faint blush creeping up from the big man's collar.

He turned and set out toward the tower. Tom plodded along by his side. " 'Ere now, master, thou'lt grow a-cold," and Tom flung the cloak he had been carrying over his arm around Rod's shoulder.

A warm, friendly gesture, Rod thought as he thanked Big Tom. He was touched that the clumsy ape should be worried about him—but he was also aware that the cloak hampered his knife hand, and was pretty sure Big Tom was aware of it, too.

"Art not afraid, master?"

Rod frowned, considering the question. "Well, no, not really. After all, the banshee's never been known to hurt anybody. It's just, well, a forecast, you know? Herald of Death and all that."

"Still, 'tis a marvel thou'rt not afeard. Wilt thou not even walk in the shadows by the wall, master?"

Rod frowned and looked at the shadows along the battlements. "No, I'll take the center of the way when I can. I'd always rather walk-tall in the sunlight than skulk in the shadows at the side of the road."

Big Tom was silent a moment, his eyes on the shadows.

"Yet," he said, "of necessity, a man must go through the shadows at one time or other, master."

With a shock, Rod realized Tom had picked up the allegory. Illiterate peasant, *sure!*

He nodded, looking so serious it was almost comic. "Yes, Big Tom. There's times when he has to choose one side of the road or the other. But for myself, I only stay on the sidelines as long as I have to. I prefer the light." He grinned. "Good protection against spirits."

"Spirits!" Tom snorted. He quickly threw Rod a half-hearted grin.

He turned away, frowning. "Still, master, I do much marvel that you will take the middle road; for there may a man be attacked from both sides. And, more to the point, he cannot say that he has chosen either the right or the left."

"No," Rod agreed, "but he can say that he has chosen the middle. And as to attack, well, if the road is well-built, the center is highest; the pavement slopes away to right and left, and the shoulder is soft and may give way beneath you. A man in the middle can see where his enemies are coming from; and it's firm footing. The sides of the road are treacherous. Sure it's an exposed position. That's why not too many have the courage to walk it.''

They walked a moment in silence; then Rod said, ''Did you ever hear of a dialectical materialism, Tom?''

''How . . . ?'' The big man's head jerked up in surprise, almost shock. He recovered, scowling and shaking his head fervently, and muttering, ''No, no, master, no, never, never!''

Sure, Big Tom, Rod thought. Aloud, he said, ''It's a Terran philsophy, Big Tom. Its origins are lost in the Dark Ages, but some men still hold by it.''

''What is Terran?'' the big man growled.

''A dream,'' Rod sighed, ''and a myth.''

''Are you one man who lives by it, master?''

Rod looked up, startled. ''What? The dream of Terra?''

''No, this dialec—what magic didst thou term it?''

''What, dialectical materialism?'' Rod grinned. ''No, but I find some of its concepts very handy, like the idea of a synthesis. Do you know what a synthesis is, Tom?''

''Nay, master.'' Tom shook his head, eyes round in wonder.

The wonder, at least, was probably real. The last thing Big Tom could have looked for was Rod to start quoting a totalitarian philsophy.

''It's the middle way,'' Rod said. ''The right-hand side of the road is the thesis, and the left-hand side is the antithesis. Combine them, and you get a synthesis.''

''Aye,'' Big Tom nodded.

Pretty quick thinking for a dumb peasant, Rod noted. He went on, ''The thesis and antithesis are both partly false; so you throw away the false parts, combine the true parts—take the best of both of them—call the result a synthesis, and you've got the truth. See?''

Tom's eyes took on a guarded look. He began to see where Rod was going.

"And the synthesis is the middle of the road. And, being true, it's naturally uncomfortable.''

He looked up; the east tower loomed over them. They stood in its shadow. "Well, enough philosophizing. Let's get to work.''

"Pray Heaven the banshee come not upon us!'' Big Tom moaned.

"Don't worry; it only shows up once a day, in the evening, to predict death within twenty-four hours,'' Rod said. "It's not due again till tomorrow evening.''

There was a sudden scrabbling in the shadows. Big Tom leaped back, a knife suddenly in his hand. "The banshee!''

Rod's blade was out too, his eyes probing the shadows. They locked with two fiery dots at the base of the tower wall.

Rod stepped out in a crouch, knife flickering back and forth from left hand to right. "Declare youself,'' he chanted, "or die.''

A squeal and a skitter, and a huge rat dashed away past him, to lose itself in the shadows near the inner wall.

Big Tom almost collapsed with a sigh. "Saints preserve us! 'Twas only a rat.''

"Yes.'' Rod tried to hide the trembling of his own hands as his knife went back to its sheath. "There seem to be a lot of rats in the walls of this castle.''

Big Tom straightened again, wary and on his guard.

"But I saw something as that rat ran by me . . .'' Rod's voice trailed away as he knelt by the outer wall, running his hands lightly over the stone. "There!''

"What is it, master?" Big Tom's garlic breath fanned Rod's cheek.

Rod took the big man's hand and set it against his find. Tom drew in a shuddering breath and yanked his hand away.

" 'Tis cold," his voice quavered, "cold and square, and—it bit me!"

"Bit you?" Rod frowned and ran his fingers over the metal box. He felt the stab of a mild electric shock and jerked his fingers away. Whoever had wired this gadget must have been the rankest of amateurs. It wasn't even grounded properly.

The box was easy to see once you knew where to look for it. It was white metal, about eight inches on a side, two inches deep, recessed so that its front and top were flush with the stone, halfway between two of the crennelations.

But come to think of it, that faulty grounding might have been intentional, to keep people from tampering.

Rod drew his dagger, glad of the insulation provided by the leather hilt. Carefully, he pried open the front of the box.

He could make out the silvery worm-trails of the printed circuit and the flat, square pillbox of the solid-state components—but the whole layout couldn't have been larger than his thumbnail!

His scalp prickled uneasily. Whoever had built this rig knew a little more about molecular circuitry than the engineers back home.

But why such a big box for such a small unit?

Well, the rest of the box was filled with some beautifully-machined apparatus with which Rod was totally unfamiliar.

He looked at the top of the box; there was a round, transparent circle set in the center. Rod frowned. He'd never run into anything quite like this before. At a guess, the circuitry was part of a remote-control system, and the machined parts were—what?

"Master, what is it?"

"I don't know," Rod muttered, "but I have a sneaking suspicion it's got something to do with the banshee."

He probed the mechanism with his dagger, trying to find a moving part. He felt sublimely reckless; the gadget could very easily have a destruct circuit capable of blowing this whole section of the battlements halfway back to Sol.

The probing point found something; the machine clicked and began to hum, almost subsonic.

"Away, master!" Big Tom shouted. " 'Tis accursed!"

But Rod stayed where he was, hand frozen for fear the knife-point would lose whatever contact it had closed.

Smoke billowed out of the transparent circle, shooting ten feet into the air, then falling back. In less than a minute, a small localized cloud had formed.

A second machine clicked, somewhere in front of Rod, and a shaft of light stabbed upward from the outer wall, toward Rod but over his head, shooting into the smoke-cloud. The shaft of light spread into a fan.

Big Tom wailed in terror. "The banshee! Flee, master, for your life!"

Looking up, Rod saw the banshee towering ten feet above him. It seemed he could almost smell the rotting, tattered shrouds that covered the voluptuous woman's body.

The rabbit mouth opened, showing long, pointed teeth. A hidden loudspeaker hummed into life; the apparition was about to start its wailing.

Rod lifted his dagger a quarter of an inch; the fan of

light blacked out, the hiss of the mechanical smoke-pot died.

The wind murmured over the battlements, dispelling the last of the smoke-cloud.

Rod knelt immobile, still staring upward; then, shaking himself, he picked up the front of the box and forced it back into place.

"Master," whispered Big Tom, "what was it?"

"A spell," Rod answered, "and the banshee it called up was a sham."

He stood, drumming his fingers on the stone.

He struck his fist against the wall. "No help for it. Come on, Big Tom, hold my ankles."

He lay face-downward between the two great granite blocks, his knees above the smoke-pot machine.

"What, master?"

"Hold my ankles," Rod snapped. "I've got to take a look at the outside of the wall. And you've got to keep me from falling into the moat."

Tom didn't answer.

"Come on, come on!" Rod looked back over his shoulder. "We haven't got all night."

Big Tom came forward slowly, a huge, hulking shape in the shadow. His great hands clamped on Rod's ankles.

Rod inched forward until his head was clear of the stone.

There, just under his chin, was a small, square box with a short snout: a miniaturized projecter, shooting a prerecorded banshee into the cloud of smoke, giving the illusion of three dimensions—a very compact projecter and removable screen, all susceptible to remote control.

From where?

Rod craned his neck. All he could see was gray stone.

"Hold tight, Big Tom." He inched forward, hoping he'd guessed right about the big peasant.

He stopped crawling when he felt the granite lip of the battlements pressing his belt buckle. His upper body jutted free beyond the castle wall, with nothing underneath but air, and, a long way down, the moat.

He looked down.

Mm, yes, that *was* a long way, wasn't it? Now, just what would happen if he'd judged Big Tom wrong? If, contrary to expectation, the big lug let go of Rod's ankles?

Well, if that happened, Fess would sent a report back to SCENT headquarters, and they'd send out another agent. No need to worry.

Tom's hoarse, labored breathing sounded very loud behind him.

Get it over with quick, boy. Rod scanned the wall under him.

There it was, just under the projector, a deep, silver-lined cup recessed into the wall—a hyperbolic antenna.

Why a hyperbolic? he wondered.

So that the radio impulse that turned the projection machines on could be very, very small, impossible to detect outside the straight line between the transmitting and receiving antennas.

So, if you want to find the transmitting antenna, just sight along the axis of the receiving dish.

And, looking along that line and allowing for parallax, he found himself staring straight at the rotting basalt pile of the House of Clovis.

For a moment, he just stared, dumbfounded. So it hadn't been the councillors after all.

Then he remembered Durer's poison attempt at breakfast, and amended his earlier guess: it hadn't been the councillors *all* the time.

And, come to think of it, that warming-pan trick

would have been much easier for a servant to pull than for a councillor.

He was jarred out of his musing rather abruptly; Big Tom's hands were trembling on his ankles.

Hell, I don't weigh that much, he thought; but he wriggled backward while he thought.

He thought he hard a sigh of relief as Big Tom hauled him in.

Rod rose and turned. Sweat streamed down Big Tom's face; his complexion looked very much like dirty dishwater, and his lower lip still trembled as he sucked in a noisy deep breath.

Rod looked into the big man's eyes for a long moment, without saying anything.

Then he murmured, "Thanks."

Tom held Rod's eyes a moment longer, then turned away.

Rod fell into step beside him.

They were halfway back to the stairwell before Big Tom said, "And dost thou know who hath sent this enchantment, master?"

Rod nodded. "The House of Clovis."

Their boots echoed hollow on the stone.

"Why hast thou not destroyed it?"

Rod shrugged. "It's a good warning that the Queen's in danger."

"Then who wilt thou tell of it?"

Rod looked up at the stars. "My horse," he said slowly.

"Horse?" Big Tom frowned.

"Yes, my horse. And no one else, until I've figured out just where Tuan Loguire stands—for the Queen or against her."

"Ah." Big Tom seemed to think that was explanation enough.

Rod boosted his estimate of Big Tom's status. Apparently the man knew what was going on, more thoroughly than Rod did.

Big Tom was silent till they came to the stairwell.

"Thou wast not a hair's breadth from Death this night, master."

"Oh, I don't think so." Rod folded his arms and leaned against the wall. "That was just a fake banshee; it couldn't have hurt us. And even as it was, I knew the spell that got rid of it."

"I was not speaking of the banshee, master."

"I know." Rod looked straight into Tom's eyes.

Then he turned and started down the stairs.

He'd gone six steps before he realized Big Tom hadn't followed.

He looked back over his shoulder. Tom was staring at him, mouth slack with shock.

Then the mouth closed, the face froze. "Thou didst know thy danger, master?"

"I did."

Tom nodded, very slowly. Then he looked down to the stairs and came down.

"Master," he said after the first landing, "thou'rt either the bravest man or the greatest fool that ever I met."

"Probably both," said Rod, keeping his eyes on the torchlit steps.

"Thou shouldst have slain me when first thou guessed." Tom's voice had an edge.

Rod shook his head, wordless.

"Why not?" Tom barked.

Rod let his head loll back. He sighed. "Long ago, Tom, and far away—Lord, how far away!"

" 'Tis no time for fairy tales!"

"This isn't a fairy tale. It's a legend—who knows? Maybe true. A king named Hideyoshi ruled a land called Japan; and the greatest duke in the land was named Ieyayasu.'

"And the duke wished to be king."

"I see you know the basic techniques. But Hideyoshi did *not* want to kill Ieyayasu."

"He was a fool," Tom growled.

"No, he needed Ieyayasu's support. So he invited Ieyayasu to take a walk in the garden with him, just the two of them, alone."

Tom stopped, turned to look down at Rod. His eyes glittered in the torchlight. "And they fought."

Rod shook his head. "Hideyoshi said he was getting old and weak, and asked Ieyayasu to carry his sword for him."

Tom stared.

Then his tongue flicked out over his lips. He swallowed and nodded. "Aye. What happened?"

"Nothing. They talked a while, and then Ieyayasu gave Hideyoshi his sword again, and they went back to the castle."

"And?"

"And Ieyayasu was loyal until the old man died."

Big Tom's eyes were hooded; he could have been carved from wood.

He nodded, mouth tightening. "A calculated risk."

"Pretty high-falutin' language for a peasant."

Tom snarled and turned away. Rod stood a moment, looking after him. Then he smiled and followed.

They were almost back to the guard room when Tom laid a hand on Rod's shoulder. Rod turned to face him.

"What are you?" Tom growled.

Rod smiled with one side of his mouth. "You mean who do I work for? Only myself, Big Tom."

"Nay." Tom shook his head. "I'll not believe that. But 'twas not what I asked."

Rod raised an eyebrow. "Oh?"

"Oh. I mean what are you, you, yourself, what manner of man?"

Rod frowned. "Nothing so strange about me."

"Aye, there is. Thou wilt not kill a peasant out of hand."

Rod stared. "Oh?" He pursed his lips. "That's out of the ordinary?"

"Most surely. And thou'lt fight for a manservant. And trust him. And speak with him, more than commands. What arr thou, Rod Gallowglass?"

Rod shook his head and spread his hands in bewilderment. He laughed once, hollow. "A man. Just a man."

Tom eyed him for a long moment.

"Thou art," he said. "I am answered."

He turned away to the guard room door, flung it open.

"Master Gallowglass," said the page, "the Queen summons you."

One of life's greatest and least expensive treasures is false dawn. The world lies waiting for the sun, lit by a glowing sky, chill and fresh, filled with rippling bird song.

Big Tom took one long, deep breath of the morning air, filling his lungs with the innocence he had never known. "Eh, master!" he called back over his shoulder, "this is the world for a man!"

Rod answered with a feeble smile as Tom turned away, to ride on ahead of Rod, singing jubilantly and with gusto, though somewhat off-key.

Rod, unfortunately, was in no condition to appreciate the aesthetic qualities of the dawn, having had about three hours of sleep in the last forty-eight hours.

Then, too, there was Catharine.

The interview had been short and sour. She'd received him in her audience chamber, and had kept her eyes on the fire, not once looking at him. Her face had been cold, lips drawn tight against her teeth.

"I fear for my Uncle Loguire," she had said. "There are men about him who would rejoice to see his eldest son become the Duke."

Rod had answered in the same stiff, formal tone. "If he dies, you lose your strongest friend among the lords."

"I lose one who is dear to me," she snapped. "I care not for friendship among the lords; but I care greatly for my uncle."

And that, Rod reflected, was probably true—to her credit as a woman, and her detriment as a ruler.

"Do you," she resumed, "ride south this day to Loguire's demesne; and do you see that none bring harm to him."

And that, aside from a very formal leavetaking, had been that. Hell hath no stupidity like a woman scorned, Rod thought; she was sending her most competent bodyguard as far away as she could.

"Fess?"

"Yes, Rod?" The horse turned its head to look back at its rider.

"Fess, I am without a doubt the prize booby ever hatched."

"You are a great man, Rod, from a line of great men."

"Oh yeah, I'm *so* great! Here I am, supposed to be turning this kingdom into a constitutional monarchy; and while I'm jauntily wandering southward, the councillors are tearing apart any possibility of a constitution, while the House of Clovis is on the verge of killing off the monarch!

"And here I ride south, with a manservant who

would probably gleefully slip a knife between my ribs if his sense of duty got the upper hand over his conscience for half a minute.

"And what have I accomplished? I've established that the place is filled with ghosts, elves, witches, and a lot of other monsters that can't possibly exist; I've given you five or six seizures; and to top it all off, a beautiful woman propositioned me, and I refused! Oh, I'm so great it's unbelievable! If I were just a little bit more efficient, I'd have managed to botch the whole thing by now! Fess, wouldn't I be better off if I just gave up?"

The robot began to sing softly.

"I am a man of constant sorrow,
I've seen trouble all my days. . . ."

"Oh, shut up."

PART TWO

THE WITCH OF LOW ESTATE

Dawn found them in the midst of hayfields, half-mown and dew-laden. Rod looked about him from the top of the rise, looking down on rolling farmland and tidy hedges, with here and there a clump of trees, dark against the rising sun.

"Big Tom!"

Tom turned in the saddle and looked back, then reined in his horse when he saw Rod had halted.

"Breakfast!" Rod called, dismounting. He led Fess off the road to a rock outcrop beneath a thicket of gorse. Tom shrugged and turned his mount.

Rod had the fire laid and kindled by the time Big Tom had hobbled his pony and turned it to graze. The big man stared in amazement as Rod unlimbered a frying pan and coffeepot, then turned away, shaking his head in wonder, and dried a place to sit on a log further down the slope. He sniffed at the scent of frying ham, sighed, and took out a pack of hardtack.

Rod looked up, frowning, and saw Big Tom sitting in wet grass with a biscuit and a skin of ale. He scowled and shouted.

"Hey!"

The shout caught Big Tom in mid-swig; he choked, spluttered, and looked up.

"Eh, master?"

"My food not good enough for you?"

Big Tom stared, open-mouthed.

"Come, on, come on!" Rod waved an arm impatiently. "And bring those biscuits with you; they'll go good fried in hamfat."

Big Tom opened and closed his mouth a few times, then nodded vaguely and stood up.

The water was boiling; Rod pried the lid off the coffeepot and threw in a handful of grounds. He looked up as Big Tom came to the fire, brow furrowed, staring.

Rod's mouth turned down at the corner. "Well, what're you looking at? Never saw a campfire before?"

"Thou bid me eat with my master!"

Rod scowled. "Is that some major miracle? Here, give a drag of that ale-skin, will you? That road gets dusty."

Tom nodded, eyes still fixed on Rod's, and held out the skin. Rod took a swig, looked up, and frowned. "What's the matter? Never saw a man take a drink? What am I, some alien monster?"

Tom's mouth closed; his eyes turned dark and brooding.

Then he grinned, laughed, and sat down on a rock. "Nay, master, nay. Thou'rt a rare good man, and that only. Nay, only that!"

Rod frowned. "Why, what's so rare about me?"

Tom threw two cakes of hardtack into the frying pan and looked up, grinning. "In this country, master, a gentleman does not take food with his servant."

"Oh, that!" Rod waved the objection away. "It's just you and me out here on the road, Big Tom. I don't have to put up with that nonsense."

"Aye," Big Tom chuckled. "A most wonderous rare man, as I said."

"And a fool, eh?" Rod served up two slices of ham on wooden saucers. "Guess we eat with our knives, Tom. Dig in."

They ate in silence, Rod scowling at his plate, Tom leaning back and looking out over the countryside.

They were at the head of a small valley, filled now

with the morning mist, a trap for small sunbeams. The sun lurked over the hedges, and the mist was golden.

Tom grinned as he chewed and jerked his thumb toward the valley. " 'Tis the end of the rainbow, master."

"Hm?" Rod jerked his head up. He smiled sourly; it was, after all, more of a pot of gold then he'd had any right to expect.

Tom gave a rumbling belch and picked at his teeth with his dagger. "A golden mist, master, and mayhap golden girls within it."

Rod swallowed quickly and objected. "Oh, no! No tomcatting on the side of this trip, Big Tom! We've got to get down to the South and get down there fast!"

"Eh, master!" Tom wailed in shocked protest, "what harm another hour or four, eh? Besides"—he sat forward and poked Rod in the ribs, grinning—"I'll wager thou'lt outdo me. What lasses may not a warlock have, mm? . . . Eh, what's the matter?"

Rod wheezed and pounded his chest. "Just a piece of hardtack having an argument with my gullet. Tom, for the umpteenth penultimate unprintable time, I am *not* a warlock!"

"Oh, aye, master, to be sure!" Big Tom said with a broad-lipped grin. "And thou mayst be certain thou'rt as poor a liar as thou art an executioner."

Rod frowned. "I haven't killed a man the whole time I've been here!"

"Aye, and this is my meaning."

"Oh." Rod turned and looked out over the fields. "Well, you might as well add lover to that list of things I'm not good at, Tom."

The big man sat forward, frowning, searching Rod's face. "In truth, I think he doth mean it!"

"Be sure that I doth."

Tom sat back, studying his master and tossing his dagger, catching it alternately by the hilt and the point. "Aye, thou speakest aright of thy knowledge." He sat forward, looking into Rod's eyes. "And therefore shall I dare to advise thee."

Rod grinned and gave him a hollow laugh. "All right, advise me. Tell me how it's done."

"Nay." Tom held up a palm. "That much I am sure that you knowest. But it is these farm girls against which I must caution thee, master."

"Oh?"

"Aye. They are—" Tom's face broke into a grin. "Oh, they are excellent, master, though simple. But"—he frowned again—"never give them a trace of a hope."

Rod frowned too. "Why not?"

" 'Twill be thy undoing. Thou mayst love them well, master, once—but once only. Then must thou leave them, right quickly, and never look back."

"Why? I'll be turned into a pillar of salt?"

"Nay, thou'lt be turned into a husband. For once given the merest shred of hope, master, these farm girls will stick tighter than leeches, and thou'lt never be rid of them."

Rod snorted. "I should have a chance to worry about it! Come on, drink up your coffee and mount up."

They doused the fire and packed up, and rode down into the red-gold mist.

They had gone perhaps three hundred yards when a long-drawn alto voice hailed them.

Rod looked up, tensed and wary.

Two big peasant girls stood with pitchforks at the base of a haystack in one of the fields, laughing and waving.

Big Tom's eyes locked on them with an almost-audible click. "Eh, master! Pretty little mopsies, are they not?"

They were pretty, Rod had to admit—though certainly anything but little. They were both full-hipped and high-breasted, wearing loose low-cut blouses and full skirts, their hair tied in kerchiefs. Their skirts were girded up to their knees, to keep them from the dew on the hay.

They beckoned, their laughter a mocking challenge. One of them set her hands on her hips and executed a slow bump-and-grind.

Big Tom sucked his breath in, his eyes fairly bulging. "Eh, now, master," he pleaded, "are we in so much of a hurry as all that?"

Rod sighed, rolling his eyes up, and shook his head. "Well, I'd hate to see them suffering from neglect, Big Tom. Go ahead."

Tom kicked his horse with a yelp of joy, leaped the ditch, and galloped full tilt into the field. He was out of the saddle before the horse slowed past a trot, catching a girl in each arm, lifting them off the ground and whirling them about.

Rod shook his head slowly, saluted Big Tom and his playmates, and turned away to find a neighboring haystack where he could catnap in peace.

"Rod," said the quiet voice behind his ear.

"Yes, Fess?"

"Your conducts disturbs me, Rod. It's not natural for a healthy young male."

"It's not the first time someone's told me that, Fess. But I'm methodical; I can't keep two girls on my mind at once."

He found another haystack just over the next hedge. Rod parked in the shadow and unbridled Fess, who began to crop at the hay, to keep up appearances. Rod remounted and jumped from the horse's back to the top of the haystack and wallowed down into the soft, fragrant hay with a blissful sigh. The pungent smell of new-mown hay filled his head, taking him back to his boyhood in the field of his father's manor, during haying time; a *real* Eden, without any soft, nubile problems to run around creating havoc. Just robots. . . .

He watched the gilt-edged clouds drifting across the turquoise sky, not realizing when he dozed off.

He came wide awake and stayed very still, wondering what had wakened him. He ran through the catalog of sensations that were apt to start the alarm clock ringing in his subconscious.

Somebody was near.

His eyes snapped open, every muscle in his body tensed to fight.

He was looking into a very low-cut bodice.

He raised his eyes from the pleasant pastoral view, a task which required no small amount of willpower, and saw two large sea-green eyes looking into his. They were long-lashed, moist, and looked worried.

Their surroundings came into focus: arched eyebrows, a snub nose sprinkled with freckles, a very wide mouth with full, red lips, all set in a roundish face framed in long, flowing red hair.

The full red lips were pouting, the eyes were troubled.

Rod smiled, yawned, and stretched. "Good morning."

The pouting lips relaxed into a half-smile. "Good morning, fine gentleman."

She was sitting beside him, propped on one hand, looking into his eyes.

"Why do you sleep here alone, sir, when nearby a woman awaits your call?"

It felt as though someone had just poured bitters into Rod's circulatory system; a thrill, and not completely a pleasant one, flooded through him.

He smiled, trying to make it warm. "I thank you, lass, but I'm not feeling gamesome today."

She smiled, but there was still a frown between her eyes. "I thank you for your gentleness, sir; but I scarce can credit your words."

"Why?" Rod frowned. "Is it so impossible that a man shouldn't want a frolic?"

The girl gave a forlorn half of a laugh. "Oh, it might be, milord, but scarce is it likely. Not even with a peasant, and even less with a lord."

"I'm not a lord."

"A gentleman, then. That, surely, thou art. And therefore, surely, thou wouldst never lack interest."

"Oh?" Rod raised an eyebrow. "Why?"

She smiled, sadly. "Why, milord, a peasant might fear forced marriage; but a lord, never."

Rod frowned again and studied the girl's face. He judged her to be a little younger than himself, about twenty-nine or thirty.

And for a peasant girl in this kind of society to be unmarried at thirty . . .

He threw out an arm. "Come here to me, lass."

There was hope, for a moment, in the girl's eyes; but it faded quickly, was replaced by resignation. She fell into the hay beside him with a sigh, rolling onto her side to pillow her head on his shoulder.

Hope, Rod mused, very conscious of her breasts and hips against the side of his body. *Hope to be tumbled, and thrown away. . . .*

He shuddered; and the girl raised her head, concerned. "Art chilled, milord?"

He turned to her and smiled, a sudden wave of gratitude and tenderness surging up to clog his throat.

He clasped her tight against him, closing his eyes to better savor the touch of her body against his own. An aroma filled his head, not rose-oil or lilac, but simply the salt-sweet scent of a woman.

A pain was ebbing away inside him, he realized, faintly surprised, a pain that he had not known was there till it began to leave him.

She clung to him, fists clenched in the cloth of his doublet, face pressed into the angle of his neck and shoulder.

Then, gradually, he began to relax again, his embrace loosening. He lay very still, letting the focus of his mind widen, open him again to the world around him; faint in the distance he heard birdsong, and the gossip of the wind through the hedges and trees. Somewhere near his head, a cricket chirped in the hay.

Her embrace had loosened with his; her arms and head lay leaden on him now.

He kept his eyes closed, the sun beating down on the lids; he lay in crimson light, "seeing" the world with his ears.

There was a rustle, and her body rose away from his; she had sat up now. She would be looking down at him, hurt aching in her eyes, lower lip trembling, a tear on her cheek.

Pity welled up in him, pity for her and, close behind it, anger at himself; it wasn't her fault that all he wanted just now was peace, not romance.

He opened his eyes, rolling onto his side and frowning up at her.

But there was no hurt in her eyes—only a grave, deep acceptance, and concern.

She raised her fingertips to his cheek, shyly, not quite touching the skin. He caught it, nestling the palm against the line of his jaw, and was amazed at how small her hand was in his own.

He closed his eyes, pressing her hand tighter.

A cow lowed far away; the wind chuckled in the grain.

Her voice was low, and very gentle. "Milord, use me as you will. I ask no more."

I ask no more. . . . Love, she must have love, if only for a minute, even if desertion came hard on its heels; even if looking back, she must know that it was lust, and not love. Even if it brought only sorrow and pain, she must have love.

He looked into her eyes; they held tears.

He closed his eyes again, and Catharine's face was before him, and Tuan's face next to hers. A part of him stood back, aloof, and contemplated the faces; it remarked on how well they looked together, the beautiful princess and the gallant young knight.

Then his own face came up next to Tuan's, and, *compare*, the aloof part of him murmured, *compare*.

Rod's hands tightened, and he heard the peasant girl give a little cry of startled pain.

He let go his grip, and looked up at her; and Catharine's face swam next to hers.

He looked on the two of them, the one bent on using him, the other bent on being used by him, and anger suddenly burned in a band across his chest, anger at Catharine for her self-righteousness and determination to bend her world to her will; and at the peasant girl for her mute acceptance and deep resignation, for the depth of her warmth and her gentleness. The band of anger across his chest tightened and tightened, anger at himself for the animal in him, as his fingers bit into her shoulders, and he drew her down in the hay. She gasped with the pain, crying out softly till his lips struck hers, crushing and biting and bruising, his fingers clamped on the points of her jaw, forcing her mouth open and his tongue stabbed hard under hers. His hand groped over her body, fingers jabbing deep into the flesh, lower and lower, gnawing and mauling.

Then her nails dug into his back as her whole body knotted in one spasm of pain. Then she went loose, and her chest heaved under him in one great sob.

Half his anger sublimed into nothingness; the other half turned about and lanced into him, piercing something within him that loosed a tide of remorse.

He rolled to the side, taking his weight off her. His lips were suddenly gentle, warm and pleading; his hands were gentle, caressing slowly, soothingly.

She drew in breath, her body tensing again. *Fool*, the detached voice within him sneered, *Fool! You only hurt her the more!*

Ready to turn away from her in shame, he looked up into her eyes . . . and saw the longing burning naked there, craving and demanding, pulling him down into the maelstrom within her. Her lips parted, moist and full and warm, tugging and yielding, pulling him down and down, into blind, light-flooded depths where there was no sight nor hearing, but only touch upon touch.

Rod levered himself up on one elbow and looked down at the girl, lying naked beside him with only his cloak for a rather inadequate coverlet. It clung to her contours, and Rod let his eyes wander over them, drinking in the sight of her, fixing every feature of her body in his mind. It was a picture he did not want to lose.

He caressed her, gently, very tenderly. She smiled, murmured, closing her eyes and letting her head roll to the side.

Then her eyes opened again; she looked at him sidelong, her lips heavy and languid.

"You have emerald eyes," Rod whispered.

She stretched luxuriously, her smile a little smug,

wrapped her arms around his neck, and hauled him down to her, her kisses slow, almost drowsy, and lasting.

Rod looked into her eyes, feeling enormously contented and very much at peace with the world. Hell, the world could go hang!

He raised himself up again, his eyes upon her; then, slowly, he looked away and about them, and the blue of the sky arching overhead . . . and a mound of clothing to each side.

He looked down again; there was nothing in his world now except her, and he found, vaguely surprised, that he rather liked it that way. The peace within him was vast; he felt completely filled, completely satisfied with the world, with life, at one with them and with God—and with her most of all.

He let his hand linger over the cloaked curve of her breast. She closed her eyes, murmuring; then, as his hand stilled, she looked up at him again. Her smile faded to a ghost; concern stole into her eyes.

She started to say something, stopped, and said instead, almost warily, "Are you well, lord?"

He smiled, his eyes very sober; then he closed them and nodded, slowly.

"Yes. I am very well."

He bent to kiss her again—slowly, almost carefully—then lifted away. "Yes, I am well, most strangely well, more than I have ever been."

The smile lit her face again, briefly; then she turned her eyes away, looking down at her body, then up at him again, her eyes touched with fear.

He clasped her in his arms and rolled onto his back. Her body stiffened a moment, then relaxed; she gave a little cry, half sob and half sigh, and burrowed her head into the hollow of his shoulder and was still.

He looked down at the glory of her hair spread out

over his chest. He smiled lazily and let his eyes drift shut.

"Rod." Fess's voice whispered behind his ear, and the world came flooding in again.

Rod tensed, and clicked his teeth once in acknowledgment.

"Big Tom is dressed again, and coming toward your haystack."

Rod sat bolt upright, squinted up at the sun; it was almost to the meridian. Time and distance nagged him again.

"Well, back to the world of the living," he growled, and reached out for his clothes.

"Milord?"

She was smiling regretfully, but her eyes were tight with hurt—a hurt which faded into the deep acceptance and resignation even as he watched.

"The memory of this time will be dear to me, lord," she whispered, clasping the cloak to her breast, her eyes widening.

It was a forlorn plea for reassurance, a reassurance he could not honestly give, for he would never see her again.

It came to him then that she was expecting refusal of any reassurance, expecting him to lash out at her for her temerity in implying that she had some worth, that she was worthy of thanks.

She knew her plea would bring hurt, yet she pled; for a woman lives on love, and this was a woman near thirty in a land where girls married at fifteen. She had already accepted that there was to be no lasting love in her life; she must subsist on the few crumbs she could gather.

His heart went out to her, somewhat impelled by the jab of self-reproach.

So, of course, he told her one of the lies that men tell

women only to comfort them, and later realize to be very true.

He kissed her and said, ''This was not Life, lass, it was what living is for.''

And later, when he mounted his horse and turned back to look at her, with Big Tom beside him waving a cheery farewell to his wench, Rod looked into the girl's eyes again and saw the desperation, the touch of panic at his leaving, the silent, frantic plea for a shred of hope.

A shred, Tom had said, would be too much, but Rod would probably never see this girl again. Not even a spark of hope—just a glimmer. Could that do any hurt?

''Tell me your name, lass.''

Only a spark, but it flared in her eyes to a bonfire. ''Gwendylon am I called, lord.''

And when they had rounded a turn in the road and the girls were lost to sight beyond the hill behind them, Tom sighed and said, ''Thou hast done too much, master. Thou shalt never be rid of her now.''

There was this to be said for a roll in the hay: it had sapped enough of Big Tom's vitality so that he wasn't singing any more. Probably still humming, to be sure; but he was riding far enough ahead so Rod couldn't hear him.

Rod rode in silence, unable to rid his mind of flaming hair and emerald eyes. So he cursed at the vision, under his breath; but it seemed to his aloof self that the cursing lacked something—vehemence, perhaps. Certainly sincerity. It was, his aloof self accused, a very half-hearted attempt at malediction.

Rod had to admit it was. He was still feeling very much at one with creation. At the moment, he couldn't have been angry with his executioner. . . . And that worried him.

"Fess."

"Yes, Rod?" The voice seemed a little more inside his head than usual.

"Fess, I don't feel right."

The robot paused; then, "How *do* you feel, Rod?"

There was something about the way Fess had said that . . . Rod glanced sharply at the pseudo-horse head. "Fess, are you laughing at me?"

"Laughing?"

"Yes, laughing. You heard me. Chuckling in your beard."

"This body is not equipped with a beard."

"Cut the comedy and answer the question."

With something like a sigh, the robot said, "Rod, I must remind you that I am only a machine. I am incapable of emotions. . . . I was merely noting discrepancies, Rod."

"Oh, *were* you!" Rod growled. "What discrepancies, may I ask?"

"In this instance, the discrepancy between what a man really is and what he wishes to believe of himself."

Rod's upper lip turned under and pressed against his teeth. "Just what do I wish to believe?"

"That you are not emotionally dependent upon this peasant woman."

"Her name is Gwendylon."

"With Gwendylon. With any woman, for that matter. You wish to believe that you are emotionally independent, that you no longer enjoy what you call 'being in love.' "

"I enjoy love very much, thank you!"

"That is a very different thing," the robot murmured, "than being in love."

"Damn it, I wasn't taking about *making* love!"

"Neither was I."

Rod's lips pressed into a thin white line. "You're talking about emotional intoxication. And if that's what you mean—no, I am not in love. I have no desire to be in love. And if I have any say in the matter, I will never be in love again!"

"Precisely what I said you wished to believe," mused the robot.

Rod ground his teeth and waited for the surge of anger to pass. "Now what's the truth about me?"

"That you are in love."

"Damn it, a man's either in love, or he's not, and he damn well knows which."

"Agreed; but he may not be willing to admit it."

"Look," Rod snapped, "I've been in love before, and I know what it's like. It's . . . well . . ."

"Go on," the robot prodded.

"Well, it's like"—Rod lifted his head and looked out at the countryside—"you know the world's there, and you know it's real; but you don't give a damn, 'cause you know for a certainty that you're the center of the world, the most important thing in it."

"Have you felt that way recently?" Fess murmured.

"Well . . . yes, damn it." Rod's mouth twisted.

"With Catharine?"

Rod stared, and glared at the back of the horse's head. "How the hell would *you* know?" His eyes narrowed.

"Logic, Rod." The robot's voice had a touch of smugness. "Only logic. And how did you feel while you were with Gwendylon?"

"Oh . . ." Rod threw his shoulders back, stretching. "Great, Fess. Better than I ever have. The world's clearer, and the day's younger. I feel so healthy and clearheaded I can't believe it. It's just the opposite to how I feel when I'm in love, but I like it."

Rod frowned at the back of Fess's head. "Well?"

The robot plodded on, not answering.

"Cat got your tongue?"

"I am not equipped with a tongue, Rod."

"Don't change the subject."

The horse was silent a moment longer; then, "I was mistaken, Rod. You love, and are loved—but you are not in love."

Rod frowned down at the roadway. "Why not, Fess?"

The robot made a sound like a sigh. "How do the two women differ, Rod?"

"Well . . ." Rod chewed at the inside of his cheek. "Gwendylon's human. I mean, she's just an ordinary, everyday woman, like I'm an ordinary man."

"But Catharine is more?"

"Oh, she's the kind of woman I tend to put on a pedestal . . . something to be worshiped, not courted . . ."

"And not loved?" the robot mused. "Rod, of the two women, which is the better human being?"

"Uh . . . Gwendylon."

"The prosecution," said the robot-horse, "rests."

The demesne of the Loguires was a great, broad plain between the mountains and the sea. The low, rolling mountains stood at the north and east; beach curved in a wide semi-circle in the south; a sheer, hundred foot high cliff face towered in the northwest. The ocean battered at its seaward side; a waterfall poured over the other face into the valley. A long, old river twisted over the plain to the sea.

The plain itself was a patchwork of fields, with here and there a cluster of peasant huts—Loguire's people.

Tom and Rod stood at the verge of one of the mountain forests, where the road from the North fell away to the plain.

Rod turned his head slowly, surveying the demesne. "And where," he said, "is the castle?"

"Why, back of the waterfall, master."

Rod's head jerked around, staring at Tom; then he followed the road with his eyes.

It wound across the plain to the foot of the waterfall; there, where the cliff met the plain, a great gate was carved in the rock, complete with portcullis and a drawbridge over the natural moat formed by an oxbow of the river. The lords of Loguire had honeycombed the cliff for their home.

An exclamation point formed between Rod's eyebrows as they drew together. "Is that a dike to either side of the drawbridge, Big Tom?"

"Aye, master; and there are said to be charges of gunpowder within it."

Rod nodded, slowly. "And the land before the portcullis gate sinks down. So if unwelcome callers come knocking, you blow up the dike, and your front door gets covered with thirty feet of water. Very neat. Then you just sit and wait out the seige. The waterfall gives you plenty of fresh water, so your only worry is food."

"There are said to be gardens within the keep," Big Tom supplied helpfully.

Rod shook his head in silent respect. "So you're completely defended, and stocked for a ten years' siege. This place ever been taken, Tom?"

The big man shook his head. "Never, master." He grinned.

"Wonder if the old boy who built this place was maybe a little bit paranoid. . . . Don't suppose they'd have room in that place for a couple of weary travelers, do you?"

Big Tom pursed his lips. "Aye, master, if they were noblemen. The hospitality of the Loguires is famed.

But for the likes of me, and even yourself, who are no more than a squire, master, that hospitality lies in the cottages.''

The sun winked. Rod scowled and peered into the sky. ''There's that damn bird again. Doesn't it know we're too big for lunch?'' He unlimbered his crossbow and cranked it back to cocked.

''Nay, master.'' Big Tom put out a hand. ''You've lost four bolts on it already.

''I just don't like anything airborne following me, Tom. They're not always what they seem.'' Tom's brow furrowed at the cryptic statement. Rod tucked the stock into his shoulder. ''Besides, I've taken one shot a day at it for the last four days; it's getting to be a habit.''

The bow hummed, and the quarrel leaped upward; but the bird sailed up faster. The bolt passed through the place where the bird had been, rose another fifty feet, hit the top of its arc, and began to fall. The bird, fifty feet higher, watched it sink.

Big Tom raised an eyebrow, his mouth quirked up on one side. ''You'll never strike it, master. The fowl knows the meaning of a crossbow.''

''You'd almost think it does.'' Rod slung the bow over his shoulder. ''What kind of country is that, with elves under every tree and hawks in the sky shadowing you?''

'' 'Tis not a hawk, master,'' Big Tom reproved. '' 'Tis an osprey.''

Rod shook his head. ''It started following us the second day out. What would a fish hawk be doing that far inland?''

''Myself, I cannot say. Thou might ask it, though, master.''

''And I wouldn't really be all that surprised if it answered,'' Rod mused. ''Well, it isn't doing us any harm, I suppose, and we've got bigger problems at the moment. We came here to get into that castle. Do you sing, Big Tom?''

Tom did a double take. "Sing, master?"

"Yeah, sing. Or play the bagpipes, or something."

Tom tugged at his lip, frowning. "I can make some manner of noise on a shepherd's flute, and the half dead might put the word *music* to it. But what folly is this, master?"

"Fool's folly." Rod unstrapped a saddlebag and took out a small harp. "As of now, we're minstrels. Let's hope the cliffdwellers are a little short on music at the moment." He pulled an alto recorder out of the saddlebag and gave it to Tom. "I hope that's enough like your shepherd's flute to do some good."

"Aye, master, very like it. But—"

"Oh, don't worry, they'll let us in. Folks this far away from the capital tend to be out of touch; they're hungry for news and new songs, and minstrels carry both. Do you know "Eddystone Light'?"

"Nay, master."

"Too bad; that's one that alwasy goes over well in a seaport town. Well, no matter, I can teach it to you as we go."

They set off down the road, singing in accidentals unknown to any human mode or scale. This fish hawk screamed and sheered off.

"Bring ye news from the North?" the sentry had asked eagerly; and Rod, recollecting that minstrels were the closest medieval equivalent to journalists, had replied in the affirmative.

Now he and Tom stood before a gathering of twenty-eight noblemen, their wives and attendants, ranging in age from pretty teenage serving maids to the ninety year old Earl of Vallenderie, all with the same eager, hungry glint in their eyes, and Rod without a scrap of news to tell them.

Well, no matter; he'd make it up as he went along. He wouldn't be the first journalist who'd done it.

The crusty old Duke of Loguire sat in a great oaken chair in the midst of the company; he didn't seem to recognize Rod. But Durer did; he stood hunched over Loguire's left shoulder, eyes twisting hate at Rod. But it would have done him no good to expose Rod, and he knew it; Loguire still loved his niece, though he was at odds with her. He would have honored Rod for saving Catharine's life.

It was Loguire who voiced the question for all his people; and Rod, reflecting that the Duke had very personal reasons for wanting news of the House of Clovis, had replied that as yet, all was quiet in the North. Oh, one heard talk and saw signs of the House; but that was talk, and talk only—so far.

Then he and Tom swung into a foot-stamping rendition of "Eddystone Light." The gathering stood in astounded silence a moment; then grins broke out, and hands started clapping the rhythm.

Encouraged, Big Tom picked up both the tempo and the volume; Rod struggled to match him while he scanned the faces of the audience.

The old Duke was trying to look sternly disapproving, and not succeeding too well. A tall young man of about Rod's age stood behind the old man's right shoulder, a grin coming to his lips and a gleam to his eye as he listened to the song, displacing a grimace of discontent, self-pity, and bitterness. The elder son, Rod guessed, with a host of weaknesses Durer could prey upon.

It was easy to pick out Loguire's vassal lords; all were richly dressed, and accompanied by an even more

richly-dressed wire scarecrow of a man: the councillors, Durer's boys.

Rod felt strangely certain that anything Durer pro-
posed would have the unanimous approval of all the
Southern lords, with only Loguire dissenting.

And Loguire, of course, had one more vote than all
the vassal lords put together. Rod remembered
Loguire's unsolicited promise to Catharine: "No harm
shall come to the Queen while I live. . . ."

"While I live. . . ."

The performance was literally a howling success;
Rod had managed to keep it on a ribald rather than a
political level, walking the thin line between the risqué
and the pornographic. The audience had loved it, Rod
decided that the tin ear must be a genetic dominant in
Gramarye. He'd noticed, too, that the eyes of all the
serving girls had been riveted to himself and Big Tom;
he was still trying to understand why. It didn't seem to
have done Big Tom's ego any harm, though.

But now and again, one of the councillors had asked
a question that could not be put off; and when Rod had
answered with rumors that the House of Clovis would
rise against the Crown, a frantic, acid joy had burned in
their eyes.

That, at least, he understood. The important thing
about a revolution is that it begin; you can always take
control of it later.

That he understood; but now, with the singing done,
as he was going to the loft which had been temporarily
assigned to Tom and himself, he was still pondering the
look on the faces of the serving maids. When they had
looked at Tom, he'd been quite sure what it was; he
expected to find the loft fully occupied by the time he
arrived, since Big Tom had gone on ahead.

But that look couldn't mean the same thing when

applied to himself—unless the occupation of minstrel carried a great deal more prestige than he'd thought.

So, all in all, he was even more confused but not too surprised when one of the servant girls intercepted him with a cup of wine.

"Salve for a parched throat, Master Minstrel," she murmured, her eyes shining as she held the cup out to him.

He looked at her out of the corner of his eye and reluctantly accepted the cup; no call for bad manners, was there?

"And," she murmured as she drank, "warmth for your bed, if you will."

Rod choked and spluttered, lowered the cup, glaring at her; then he looked her up and down quickly. She was full-bodied and high-breasted, with a wide- full-lipped mouth—very like Gwendylon, in some ways. . . .

Suddenly suspicious, Rod looked more sharply; but no, this girl's eyes were tilted upward at the outer corners, and her nose was long and straight, not snub. Besides, her hair and eyes were black.

He smiled wryly and drank off the rest of the cup and returned it to her. "Thank you, lass, right deeply."

It was indicative, he thought, that she had come to him instead of Big Tom. Tom was certainly the more appealing chunk of man; but Rod was obviously the one who had the status. A bitch like any of them, he thought: she doesn't give a damn for who the man is, just as long as *what* he is is a station higher than hers.

"I thank you," he said again, "but I have been long on the road, and am like to swoon from my weariness." A very pretty speech, he thought; and go ahead, let her think less of my manhood for it. At least she'll leave me alone.

The serving maid lowered her eyes, biting her lip.

"As you will, good master." And she turned away, leaving Rod staring after her.

Well, that hadn't taken much refusing. Come to think of it, he was a little indignant . . . but had there been just a hint of triumph in her eyes, a shard of rejoicing?

Rod went on his way, wondering if perhaps he hadn't inadvertently stepped into the pages of a Machiavellian textbook.

The door to the loft was closed, as Rod had guessed; a muffled feminine squeal, followed by Tom's bass laugh, further confirmed his guess.

So he shrugged philosophically, settled his harp over his shoulder, and turned back down the long, winding staircase. He could put the time to good use, anyway. The castle had so obviously been built by a paranoid that he was certain there had to be secret passages.

He sauntered down the main corridor, whistling. The granite walls were painted ocher, ornamented with standing suits of armor and here and there a tapestry. Some of the tapestries were huge, reaching from floor to ceiling; Rod noted their locations carefully in his mind. They could very easily conceal the mouths of passageways.

Twelve sub-corridors intersected the main hall at right angles. As he came near the seventh, he noticed that his footsteps seemed to have acquired an echo—a very curious echo, that took two steps for each one of his. He stopped to look at a tapestry; the echo took two more steps and stopped. Looking out of the corner of his eye, Rod caught a glimpse of one of the wizened, richly-dressed scarecrows; he thought he recognized Durer, but it was hard to tell by peripheral vision.

He turned away and swaggered on down the hall, humming "Me and My Shadow." The echo started again.

Now, Rod was mildly gregarious; he didn't really mind company. But it was a safe bet that he wasn't going to learn very much with Durer on his tail with a saltshaker. Ergo, he had to figure some way to lose his emaciated companion. This would not be easy, since Durer almost surely knew the castle very thoroughly, while Rod knew it not at all.

But the ninth cross-corridor seemed as though it would do nicely for the purpose—it was unlit. Strange, Rod mused; the other halls had all had a torch every several paces. But this was as dark as Carlsbad before the tourists came; it also had a thick carpet of dust, with not a single footprint in evidence. Cobwebs hung thick from the ceiling; trickles of moisture ran down the walls, watering patches of moss.

But the darkness was the main feature. He would leave a nice trail in the dust, but the darkness offered a chance of ducking into a room or side-hall; also, Durer couldn't very well pretend he just happened to be going the same way.

Rod turned into the corridor, sneezing in the cloud of dust he kicked up, and heard a sudden scurrying behind him. A claw grabbed his shoulder; he turned to face the little man, ready to swing.

Yes, it was Durer, glaring at Rod with his usual look of hate and suspicion. "What seek you in there?" he croaked.

Rod brushed the bony hand off his shoulder and leaned back against the wall. "Nothing in particular; just looking around. I don't have much of anything to do at the moment, unless you'd like a song?"

"Damn your caterwauling!" Durer snapped. "And you may leave off your pretense of minstrelsy; I know you for what you are."

"Oh?" Rod raised an eyebrow. "How'd you know I'm not really a minstrel?"

"I heard you sing. Now off to your chamber, if you've no business elsewhere!"

Rod scratched his nose. "Ah—about that chamber," he said delicately. "My companion seems to have found, uh, a better use for it than sleeping. So I'm, ah, sort of locked out, if you follow me."

"Corruption!" the councillor hissed.

"No, I suspect Big Tom goes about it in a very healthy manner. And since I have no place to stay at the moment, I thought none would mind my wandering about."

Durer glared at him, a look like a laser beam. Then, very reluctantly, he backed off a pace or two.

"True," he said. "There are no secrets here for you to pry out."

Rod managed to limit his laughter to a mild convulsion in the depths of his belly.

"But did you not know," the scarecrow continued, "that this is the haunted quarter?"

Rod's eyebrows shot up. "You don't say." He tugged at his lower lip, eyeing Durer judiciously. "You seem to know the castle pretty well."

Durer's eyes snapped like a high-voltage arc. "Any in this castle could tell you that. But I am Durer, councilor to the Duke of Loguire! It is my place to know the castle well—as it is *not* yours!"

But Rod had turned away, looking down the dark hallway. "You know," he mused, "I've never seen a ghost before. . . ."

"None have, and lived to tell of it! To enter there is the act of a fool!"

Rod turned, smiling cheerfully. "Well, I'm qualified. Besides, a meeting with a ghost would make a good ballad."

The little man stared; then a contemptuous smile twisted into his face. He began to chuckle, sounding strangely like ball bearings rolling over corrugated iron. "Go then, fool! I should have seen 'twould be no matter whether you went there or not.''

Rod grinned, shrugged, and stepped into the black corridor.

"A moment!" Durer called.

Rod sighed and turned. "What do you want now?"

"Before you go to your death," said Durer, his eyes feverishly bright, "tell me: what are you?"

A chill ran down Rod's back. The little man had seen through his cover.

He leaned against the wall, radiating boredom. "A minstrel, of course. What else would I be?

"Nay, fool! Do you think me so blind? You are a spy!"

Rod's hand crept to his dagger-hilt. It was balanced for throwing.

"A spy from the House of Clovis!" Durer howled.

Rod's hand relaxed; he let out a breath that he hadn't known he'd been holding. "Guess again, little man."

Durer scowled. "Not from the House? But then . . . Nay, you are their spy! Even now you will not admit to it!"

A synapse spat in Rod's brain.

He leaned back against the wall, folding his arms, grinning. "Why, what interest have you in the House of Clovis, good councillor? And why would Clovis wish to know of your doings here?"

"Nay!" Durer hissed, his eyes widening. "Fool, do you think I would answer such . . . Aie! Curse my old mind, not to have thought it! You are a spy from the Queen!"

Rod stepped away from the wall, loosening the dagger in its sheath. He didn't particularly care if Durer knew Catharine had sent him; but he did want an answer. "I asked you a question," he said mildly.

Terror welled up in the little man's eyes. He leaped back against the far wall. "Hold! At my call a score of soldiers come!"

Rod gave him a look that was somewhere between a sneer and a smile. "That won't do you much good if you're dead by the time they get here." He gestured toward the dark corridor. "Also, I'd probably be gone by the time they arrive."

The little man stared, horrified, and began to tremble.

But the little bastard had guts, Rod had to give him that. His voice broke like a cicada in autumn, but he kept talking.

"It might be . . . it just might be that it is even as you say, that you are not of Clovis! And if you come from the Queen, why, then, you are welcome among us!"

Rod half-turned his head, giving the little man a measuring, sidewise look.

"I will tell all that you wish to know!" The councillor's hands came up in pathetic eagerness. A strange light came into his eyes. "Aye, all will I tell you, even to the day that we march on the Queen's capital! Then you may tell her, and she can march south to meet us halfway! Even this will I tell you!"

He leaped forward, hands clawing. "Only come out from the hallway! If you come from the Queen, I would not have you die!"

Rod's face turned to stone. "No. You've got something hidden in there, and I've got a strange notion it might be more important than the date set for your rebellion. I think I'll just have a look." He turned back into the dusty hallway.

Durer ran after him a few steps, almost wailing. "No, no! You must carry word North! Come away, you fool!"

Rod kept walking.

Behind him, the little man screeched in anger. ''Go, then, to your death! There is no need for you! I will take word to the North myself! Die, like the fool that you are!''

His shrill, hysterical laughter echoed and slapped from the walls, beating into Rod's ears as he strode into the moldering, lightless depths of the Castle Loguire.

He turned a corner, and the laugh died away. The faint torchlight from the main hall died with it; here the darkness was complete.

Rod walked through it, chewing at the inside of his cheek. Obviously, the little man really expected him to die . . . which was strange, since he had tried to keep Rod from going in. Which meant he'd really wanted Rod to carry word of the rebellion back to Catharine. But why did he want to doublecross the rebels?

Unless it was a triple-cross, somehow. . . .

Then, too, he obviously had something hidden back in these corridors, and might be afraid Rod would find it and somehow manage to come out alive.

However, he expected Rod to die, which meant automated defenses surrounding Durer's Big Secret. . . .

Unless, of course . . .

Rod stopped, suddenly realizing he didn't know the way out. He had a hazy recollection of having turned several corners while he'd been pondering; but he couldn't remember which corners, or how many, or which way he'd turned.

He noticed that his voice shook just a trifle when he murmured ''Fess.''

''Yes, Rod,'' the calm voice behind his ear answered instantly. It was vastly reassuring.

''Fess, I'm in the haunted part of the castle.''

"Haunted?"

"It has that reputation, yes."

There was a pause; then the robot said, "Rod, an analysis of your voice patterns indicates mild fear. Surely you do not believe in ghosts."

"No, I don't. But I just remembered, Fess—I didn't believe in elves, either. Or banshees. Or—"

"Elves," Fess replied evenly, "are a myth."

"Uh, Fess . . ."

"Yes, Rod?"

"I've seen quite a few elves since we landed."

"A *fait accompli*," the robot admitted reluctantly, "which I am constrained to acknowledge. I have not as yet sufficient data to explain the seeming conflict with known principles."

"You're as bad as a Catholic," Rod growled. "But at least it doesn't give you fits any more?"

"No-o-o." The robot was thoughtful. "The initial datum caused an overload; but that datum has since been assimilated."

"As long as you're sure there's a rational explanation."

"Precisely."

"So you're capable of handling the practical matters?"

"Quite capable."

"Because you're sure you'll be able to fit it into the Laws of Science eventually."

"Very perceptive, Rod."

"Sounds like a Jesuit," Rod growled. "But the practical matter at hand is that I *am* scared. And for a very good reason. Fess . . ."

"Yes, Rod?"

"If elves can exist on this crazy planet, why not ghosts?"

There was another pause; then Fess admitted, "There is no evidence that would directly contradict the hypothesis."

A moan, so deep that Rod could hardly hear it, and so loud that he winced in pain, shook the walls of the hallway.

Rod gasped. "What was *that?*"

"A complex wave-pattern of low frequency and high amplitude," Fess answered obligingly.

"Thank you, Dr. Slipcam. *What caused it?*"

"There is as yet insufficient data for—"

The moan came again, and a wraith of mist with hollow black eyes and a black circle of mouth swooped straight at Rod's head, starting as a pinpoint far down the hall and towering over him a second later.

Rod screamed and plastered himself against the wall. Fear knotted his belly, fear slackened his limbs, fear jellied his brain and squeezed at his heart.

Another moan sounded, a half-step above the first; Rod jerked his head to his right. Another ghost loomed over him.

A third moan, and Rod's eyes slapped up; a third specter towered before him.

Three ghosts, towering high about him, ringing him in against the stone wall. Their mouths formed great, lightless O's, cold bony fingers reaching out for him.

Through the moiling panic of his brain fought a single thought: *Fess didn't believe in ghosts.*

"Ghosts!" Rod screamed. "Ghosts, Fess, ghosts!"

"Ghosts," droned the robot, "are immaterial, even if they did exist. They are manifestations of neither energy nor matter, incapable of causing damage to a material being."

"Tell *them!* Tell *them!*" Rod shrieked.

The hand around his heart tightened. He gasped and coughed. Something was mashing his lungs, a steel

band around his chest, tightening, tightening. . . .
Fear was a physical thing, a looming presence, armed
and hating. Fear could paralyze, fear could kill . . .

"Rod, cover your ears."

Rod tried to obey the robot's order, and couldn't.
"Fess!" he screamed. "Fess, I can't *move!*"

A loud, raucous buzz shook his skull, blotting out the
moans. It modulated into monotone words: "C-O-
V-E-R Y-O-U-R E-A-R-S."

And the fear was gone, vanished—or almost gone, at
least; reduced to the cold, familiar lump in the pit of the
belly. Rod could move again, as easily as he ever had.
He put his fingers in his ears. The buzz stopped, and he
could hear the ghosts again, their moans dulled and
distant through his fingers. The fear rose into his throat
again, but it was no longer paralyzing.

"Can you hear them, Rod?"

"Yeah, but it's not so bad now. What'd you do,
Fess?"

"Nothing, Rod. Their moans have a harmonic frequency in the subsonic range, capable of inducing fear
in members of your species."

"Oh."

"The fear-inducing tone is a beat frequency produced by the simultaneous emission of subsonic har-
monics incorporated in the three moans."

"So it takes three of them to scare me?"

"Correct, Rod."

"And they're not really scaring me, just making me
feel scared?"

"Again, correct."

"Well, that's a relief. For a minute there I was afraid
I'd all of a sudden turned into a full-blown coward."

"All men fear, Rod."

"Yeah, but only a coward lets it stop him."

"That is a redundant statement, Rod."

"Oh, the hell with theory! Pardon me while I put it into practice."

Rod stepped away from the wall, forcing himself to move. He kept walking, right through the ghost in front of him. The moans suddenly ceased; then, with a howl of despair, the ghosts disappeared.

"They're gone," Rod croaked.

"Of course, Rod. Once you have demonstrated their inability to control you, they begin to fear you."

"Ye-e-es," Rod breathed. He set his feet wide apart, jammed his fists on his hips, flung his head back, and grinned. "Okay, spooks! Any doubts about who's boss?"

He stood, listening to the echoes of his voice die away among the empty corridors. A loud voice could be pretty impressive in here.

A mournful, sepulchral voice answered him out of thin air, moaning. "Leave us, mortal. Leave us to the peace of our graves. We harm no one here, in our cold, old halls."

"No one except the people who come in here," Rod snapped. "Them you kill, as you would have killed me, through weight of fear alone."

"Few," mourned the ghost. "Very, very few, mortal man. Only madmen, and fools."

"If you have killed one man here in your halls, you have killed one too many!' Rod rapped back.

"Would you not slay, Man, in defense of your home?"

Rod snorted. "What right have you to these halls?"

Suddenly the ghost was there, towering over him. "I once was Horatio, first Duke Loguire!" it thundered in anger. "I it was built this keep! Have I no right to a poor, cold quarter of its halls?"

Fear lanced Rod's belly; he took a step back, then set

his teeth and stepped forward again. "You got a point there," he admitted. "And possession *is* nine-tenths of the law. But how many did you have to kill to gain possession?"

"None." The ghost sounded very unhappy about it. "All fled in fear."

Rod nodded, revising his estimate of the ghost. Apparently Horatio didn't kill if he could help it. Probably delighted when it became necessary, though. . . .

"I mean you no harm, Horatio." He grinned suddenly, sardonically. "What harm could I do you, even if I wanted to?"

The ghost's head snapped up, empty eyes staring into Rod's. "You know not, mortal?"

"A ghost," Fess's voice said hurriedly behind Rod's ear, "like all supernatural creatures, can be hurt by cold iron or silver, or any medium of good conductivity, though gold is usually regarded as too expensive for such uses."

The ghost loomed larger over Rod, advancing on him.

Rod stepped back, his dagger at the ready. "Hold it right there," he snapped. "Cold iron, remember?"

"Then, too," Fess murmured, "you do know the secret of their power. You could bring in an army with earplugs."

"Then, too," said Rod, "I *do* know the secret of your power. I could bring in an army with earplugs."

The ghost halted, the corners of its mouth turning down. "I had thought thou hadst said thou knew not."

"I do now. One step backward, if you please."

The ghost reluctantly retreated, groaning, "What phantom stands at your side to advise you?"

Rod's teeth bared in a grin. "A black horse, made of

cold iron. It's in the castle stables, but it can talk to me from there."

"A pouka," Horatio growled, "a spirit horse, and one who is a traitor to the world of ghosts."

"No." Rod shook his head grimly. "It's not a spirit at all. I said it was made of cold iron, didn't I?"

The ghost shook its head decisively. "No such thing could exist."

Rod sighed. "There are more things in Heaven and Earth, Horatio, than are dreamt of in your philosophy. But that's beside the point. All that matters to you is that I don't mean any harm here. I'm just looking for something. I'll find it and go. Okay?"

"You are master. Why dost thou ask?" the ghost said bitterly.

"Courtesy," Rod explained. Then a vagrant and vague possibility crossed his mind. "Oh, by the way, I'm a minstrel. . . ."

The ghost's mouth dropped open; then it surged forward, hands grasping hungrily. "Music! Oh, sweet strains of melody! But play for us, Man, and we are thine to command!"

"Hold on a second." Rod held up a hand. "You built these halls, Horatio Loguire, and therefore do I ask of you the boon that I may walk these halls in peace. Grant me this, and I will play for you."

"You may walk, you may walk where you will!" the ghost quavered. "Only play for us, Man!"

Very neat, Rod thought. As good a job of face-saving as he'd ever done. After all, no sense making enemies if you can help it.

He looked up, started, and stared in shock. He was ringed by a solid wall of ghosts, three deep at least, all staring like a starving man in a spaghetti factory.

He swallowed hard and swung his harp around with a

silent prayer of thanks that he hadn't been able to leave it in the sleeping-loft.

He touched the strings, and a groan of ecstasy swept through the ghosts like the murmur of distant funeral bells on the midnight wind.

It then occurred to Rod that he was in an excellent bargaining position. "Uh, Lord Horatio, for *two* songs, will you tell me where the secret passages are?"

"Aye, aye!" the ghost fairly shrieked. "The castle is thine, my demesne, all that I have! The kingdom, if thou wish it! Only play for us, Man! For ten hundreds of years we have heard not a strain of Man's music! But play, and the whole world is thine!"

His fingers started plucking then, and the ghosts shivered like a schoolgirl getting her first kiss.

He gave them "Greensleeves," and "The Drunken Sailor," they being the oldest songs he knew. From there he went on to "The Ghost's High Noon," and "The Unfortunate Miss Bailey." He was about to swing into "Ghost Riders in the Sky" when it occurred to him that ghosts might not particularly like songs about ghosts. After all, mortals told spook stories for escapism; and by that yardstick, specters should want songs about humdrum, ordinary, everyday life, something peaceful and comforting, memories of green pastures and babbling brooks, and the lowing herd winding slowly o'er the lee.

So he went through as much of Beethoven's Sixth as he could remember, which was not easy on an Irish harp.

The last strains died away among the hollow halls. The ghosts were silent a moment; then a satiated, regretful sigh passed through them.

Horatio Loguire's great voice spoke quietly at Rod's

elbow. "In truth, a most fair roundelay." Then, very carefully: "Let us have another, Man."

Rod shook his head with a sorrowful smile. "The hours of the night crowd down upon us, my lord, and I have much that I must do ere daybreak. Another night I shall return and play for you again; but for this night, I must away."

"Indeed," Horatio nodded, with another mournful sigh. "Well, you have dealt fairly with us, Man, and shown us courtesy without constraint to it. And shall we, for hospitality, be beholden to a guest? Nay; but come within, and I will show you doors to the pathways within the walls of this keep, and tell you of their twists and turnings."

All the ghosts but Horatio disappeared, with the sound of mouse feet running through the autumn leaves. Horatio turned abruptly and fled away before Rod, who dashed after him.

Rod counted his running steps; after fifty, the ghost made a right-angle turn with a fine disregard for inertia and passed through a doorway. Rod made a manful attempt at the inertialess turn, and got away with only a slight skid.

The ghost's voice took on the booming echo of the cavernlike room. "This was a cavern indeed, ready-made by God, lo, many centuries before I came. Loath to begrudge His gifts, I took it for my great banquet hall." The room seethed with the voices of a thousand serpent-echos as the patriarch ghost heaved a vast sigh. "Boisterous and many were the feastings held within this great hall, Man. Beauteous the maidens and valiant the knights." His voice lifted, exulting. "Brilliant with light and music was my banquet hall in that lost day, the tales and sagas older and more vital than the singing of this latter world. Wine flushed the faces of my court, and life beat high through the veins of their temples, filling their ears with its drumming call!

"The call of life . . ." The spirit's voice faded; its echoes died away among the cold cavern stones, till the great hall stood silent in its enduring midnight.

Somewhere a drop of water fell, shattering the silence into a hundred echoes.

"Gone now, o Man," mourned the ghost. "Gone and dead, while threescore of the sons of my blood have ruled these marches in my stead, and come home to me here in my halls. Gone, all my bold comrades, all my willing maidens—gone, and dust beneath our feet."

Rod's shoulders tightened as though a chill wind had touched him between the shoulder blades. He tried to stand a little more lightly in the dust carpet of the old banquet hall.

"And now!" The ghost's voice hardened in sullen anger. "Now others rule these halls, a race of jackals, hyenas who blaspheme my old comrades by walking in the forms of men."

Rod's ears pricked up. "Uh, how's that again, my lord?" Somebody's stolen this hall from you?"

"Twisted, stunted men!" grated the wraith. "A race of base, ignoble cowards—and the lord of them all stands as councillor to a scion of my line, the Lord Duke Loguire!"

"Durer," Rod breathed.

"Calls he himself by that name" growled the ghost. "Then well is he named, for his heart is hard, and his soul is brittle.

"But mark you, Man," and the ghost turned his cavern eyes on Rod, and the base of Rod's scalp seemed to lift a little away from his skull, for embers burned at the backs of the specter's eyes.

"Mark you well," it intoned, stretching forth a

hand, forefinger spearing at Rod, "that the hard and brittle steel will break at one strong blow of iron forged. And so may these evil parodies of humankind be broken by a man that you may call a man!"

The ghost's hand dropped. His shoulders sagged, his head bowed forward. "If," he mourned, "if any live in this dark day who may call themselves men in truth. . . ."

Rod's eyes broke away from the ghost and wandered slowly about the great chamber. There was only blackness, close and thick. He blinked and shook his head, trying to rid himself of the feeling that the darkness was pressing against his eyeballs.

"My Lord Loguire," he began, stopped, and said again, "My Lord Loguire, I may be your lump of iron—I've been called things like that before, anyway. But if I am to break the councillors, I must know as much about them as I can. Therefore tell me: what work do they do within these halls?"

"Witchcraft," growled the ghost, "black witchcraft! Though the manner of it I scarce could tell . . ."

"Well, tell me what you can," Rod prodded. "Anything you can spare will be gratefully appreciated."

"Thou speakest like the parish priest a-tithing," the ghost snorted. "Naetheless, I will tell thee what I can. Know, then, Man, that these twisted men have builded themselves a great altar here, of a shining metal, it is not steel, nor silver or gold, nor any metal that I wot of—here in the center of my hall, where once my courtiers danced!"

"Oh." Rod pursed his lips. "Uh, what worship do they make before this altar?"

"What worship?" The ghost's head lifted. "Why, I would warrant, 'tis a sacrifice of themselves; for they step within that evil artifice, and then are gone; then lo!

there they are again, and come forth whole! I can only think they must have given of their life's blood to the dark demon within that shining altar, for they come forth gaunt and shaken, Indeed,'' he mused, ''why otherwise would they be shriveled, little men?''

An uneasy prickle began at the base of Rod's skull and worked its way down his neck to spread out across his shoulders. "I must see this artifice, my lord." He fumbled at his dagger. "Let us have some light!"

"Nay!" The shriek tore at Rod's eardrums. The ghost pulsed, shrinking and growing, its outline wavering, like a candle-flame.

"Would you destroy me, Man, and send me screaming to a darker realm than this?"

Rod massaged the back of his neck, trying to loosen the muscles that had cramped themselves together at the ghost's shriek. "Forgive me, Lord Loguire; I had forgotten, My torch will rest darkened; but you must, then, lead me to this strange altar, that I may see it with my hands."

"Would you worship there, then?" The hollow eyes deepened ominously.

"No, my lord; but I would know this thing, that I may bring it down in the fullness of time."

The ghost was silent a moment; then it nodded gravely, and glided ahead. "Come."

Rod stumbled forward, hands outstretched, in the ghost's wake, till his palms came up against something hard and cold.

"Beware, Man," rumbled the ghost, "for here lie dark powers."

Hand over hand, Rod felt his way slowly along the metal, glinting softly in the ghost's faint luminescence. Then his right hand fell on nothingness. He groped, found it was a corner, wished the ghost gave off just a little more light, and groped until he had located the outline of a door, or rather a doorway, seven feet high by three wide.

"What lies within, my lord?" he whispered.

"It is a coffin," the ghost moaned; "a metal coffin without a lid, standing on end, and you have found its open side."

Rod wondered what would happen if he stepped into the cubicle; but for some strange reason, he lacked the experimental urge of the true scientist.

He groped across the doorway. A circle pressed into his palm, a circle protruding slightly from the face of the metal block.

Running his fingers over the area to the right of the doorway, he discovered a full array of circles, oblongs, and buttons. The area within their outlines was smoother and less cold than the metal around them— glass, he decided, or plastic. He had found a control panel.

"My Lord Loguire," he called softly, "come here to me now, I beg of you, for I must have light."

The ghost drifted up beside him; and, by the light of its cold radiance, Rod made out a set of meters, a vernier dial, and a set of color-coded buttons.

The ghost's voice was gentle, almost sympathetic. "Why do you tremble, Man?"

"It's cold," Rod snapped. "Milord Loguire, I'm afraid I have to agree with your opinion of this monstrosity. I don't know what it is, but it ain't pretty."

The ghost rumbled agreement. "And that which is evil to look upon must be doubly so in its action."

"Well, I'm not so sure about that as a basic principle," Rod demurred, "but it might apply in this case. Milord, pay no heed to my mumblings in the next small while; I must, ah, recite an incantation against the malice of this, ah, engine.''

He switched to the patois of the galactic deckhand while the ghost scowled in perplexity. ''Fess, you there?''

''Yes, Rod.''

''Have you been listening in?''

''Certainly, Rod.''

''Um. Well, then, uh, this thing's a hunk of metal, rectangular, about, uh, twenty feet long by, say, ten high, and maybe ten wide. Got a little cubicle cut into the front, just about the size of a coffin.''

''Appropriate,'' the robot murmured.

''No kibitzing on the job, please. It's white metal with a dull finish, and colder than hell, right now, anyway. Set of controls next to the cubicle—a long strip-meter with a scale and a slider.''

''How is the scale calibrated, Rod?''

''Looks like logarithms, Fess. Arabic numerals. The zero's about three-quarters of the way from left end. Left side of the scale is marked to ten thousand. The right-hand side goes up to, uh, 2,385. Sound like anything you've heard of?''

There was a pause; then the robot answered, ''Filed for analysis. Proceed with the description.''

Rod ground his teeth; apparently the huge gizmo was as much of an unknown to Fess as it was to himself.

''There's a dial with a knob in the middle of it, just to the right of the strip-meter. Reference point at the top, twelve o'clock, negative number to the left, positive to the right. At least, I assume they're numbers. The thing just to the right of the reference point looks something like a French curve, or maybe a paranoid sine wave. Then there's a shape like an upside-down pear. Then there's a pair of circles with a line lying across them.

The last one is a question mark lying on its side; then there's infinity in the six o'clock position. Left-hand side is the same way, only all the symbols are marked with a negative sign.''

The robot hummed for a moment; Rod recognized the tune: "Sempre Libera" from *La Traviata*. Fess was enjoying himself.

"Filed for analysis and reference, Rod. Proceed with description.''

"You don't recognize 'em either, huh?''

"They are totally without precedence in the discipline of mathematics, Rod. But if there is any logic to their derivation, I will decipher them. Proceed.''

"Well, there're seven buttons set flush with the surface, in a row just under the strip-meter, color-coded. Colors are—uh—hey, it's the spectrum!''

"So I feared,'' the robot murmured. "Use of the spectrum in color-coding would indicate arbitrary assignation of values. There is no anomaly in the color sequence?''

"Well, the paint's iridescent . . .''

"Not quite what I meant by anomaly. Well, it is filed. Proceed.''

"Nothing. That's all.''

"All? Only three controls?''

"That's all.''

The robot was silent a moment.

"What do you make of it, Fess?''

"Well . . .'' the robot's voice was hestitant. "The control system appears to be designed for the layman, Rod. . . .''

"Why? Because it's so simple?''

"Precisely. Beyond that, there is insufficient data for—''

"Oh, make a guess, damn it! Make a wild guess!''

"Rod, guesswork is not within the capabilities of a cybernetic mechanism, involving as it does an exercise of the intuitive—"

"So extrapolate from available data, already!"

He heard *La Traviata*, as it might have been sung by a wistful audio generator; then Fess said, "The irregularity of the figure 2,385 would seem to indicate the number of a year, Rod, due to its juxtaposition with the figure ten thousand."

"Uh, how's that again?"

"The figure ten thousand," Fess lectured, "has many probable referents, one of which is the period of recorded human history."

"Now, wait a minute, Fess. Written history doesn't go back beyond 2000 B.C.; even I know that."

"And a miracle it is, Rod, considering your resistance to instruction from your earliest ages."

"All right, all right! I was a bad little boy who didn't do his homework! I'm sorry! I repent! Just get on with the extrapolation, will ya?"

He heard the burring of serially closing relays that always reminded him of a chuckle; then Fess said, "Human history prior to the development of written language may be said to have been recorded in the legends and mythology of the vocal tradition, in works such as *The Epic of Gilgamesh*. The period included by such works may be estimated as having begun nearly four thousand years B.C. This figure, added to the present date, gives us the figure 9,432, which is a sufficiently close approximation to the figure ten thousand to be included as a referent."

"Hmm." Rod gnawed his upper lip. "Well, when you look at it that way, I suppose 2,385 could be a date. But what does that mean?"

"Why, the inference is obvious, Rod."

"So I'm a microcephalic idiot. Spell it out."

The robot hesitated. "The accuracy of the inference has a very low probability rating. . . ."

"I asked for guesswork, didn't I? Come on, out with it."

"The artifact, Rod, would by this theory be a vehicle for chronical travel."

Rod stared at the strip-meter. "You mean it's a time machine?"

The slider was shoved all the way to the right, resting over the figure 2,385.

"Rod, you must bear in mind that the theory's probability index—"

"A time machine!" Rod's brain whirled. "Then the little bastards came out of the future!"

"Rod, I have cautioned you before about your tendency to accord an unproved hypothesis the weight of a conviction."

Rod gave his head a quick shake. "Oh, don't worry, Fess. It's just a guess, probably wrong. I'm keeping that in mind."

He turned away from the control panel, eyes glowing. "A time machine! Whaddaya know!"

He became aware of the faint glow to his left again. Horatio Loguire towered over him, brooding.

"What witchcraft is it, Man?"

Rod frowned, turning back toward the machine. "Strange, my lord, both dark and strange. I have some knowledge of the various, ah, magics; but this is one with which I have no acquaintance."

"What then will you do?"

Rod scowled at the floor, looked up with a bleak smile. "Sleep. And ponder what I have seen."

"And when will you destroy this plaything of Satan?"

"When I am sure," murmured Rod, turning back to look at the machine again; "sure that this is the plague, and not the cure, of this benighted world."

Loguire's eyebrows drew together as his scowl deepened. He seemed almost to swell, looming taller and wider, dwarfing the man before him. Rod had the insane feeling that an ancient locomotive was roaring down on him.

The voice was distant thunder. "I charge you, then, with the exorcising of this demon altar and the rending of its ragtag priests."

The old boy, Rod decided, had definitely slipped a cog.

The ghost's sword flashed out of its scabbard; involuntarily, Rod fell back into defense stance. Then he straightened, cursing himself; a spectral sword could scarcely hurt him.

The sword floated before him, point downward, a glittering cruciform ghost-light.

"Swear now upon the hilt of this my sword, that you shall not rest until you have purged this land of corruption in the seats of power, that you shall exorcise this dark altar and all its minions, and more: that you shall never till you die desert this Isle of Gramarye in the hour of its peril."

Awe slacked Rod's jaw; he stared wide-eyed at the sudden power and majesty of the ghost. An alien, formless dread crept into his belly. The hairs at the nape of his neck lifted with a chill of nameless apprehension.

He shrank back. "My lord, this scarce is necessary. I love the Isle of Gramarye; I would never—"

"Lay your hand upon this hilt and swear!" The words were terse and stern.

Rod fairly cowered, well aware that the oath would bind him to the planet for life. "My lord, are you asking me to take a loyalty oath? I am insulted that you should doubt my—"

"Swear!" the ghost thundered. "Swear! Swear!"

"Art there, old mole?" Rod muttered under his breath, but it didn't work; he had never felt less funny.

He stared at the glowing hilt and the stern face beyond it, fascinated. Almost against his will, he took one step forward, then another; he watched his hand as it closed itself around the hilt. His palm felt nothing within it, no pressure of solid metal; but the air within his fist was so cold it paralyzed the knuckles.

"Now swear to me and mine!" Horatio rumbled.

"Oh, well, Rod thought, *it's only words. Besides, I'm an agnostic, aren't I?*

"I . . . swear," he said reluctantly, fairly forcing out the words. Then inspiration glimmered in his brain, and he added easily, "And I further swear that I will not rest until the Queen and all her subjects with one voice shall rule again."

He took his hand from the sword, rather pleased with himself. That additional clause gave him a clear track to the goal of his mission, whether or not Horatio counted democracy among the perils of Gramarye.

The ghost frowned. "Strange," he grumbled, "a most strange oath. Yet from the heart, I cannot doubt, and binding to you."

Of course, Rod admitted to himself, the oath still bound him to Gramarye; but he would bridge that gulf when he came to it.

The sword glided back to its scabbard. The ghost turned away, his voice trailing over his shoulder. "Follow now, and I shall show you to the halls within these halls."

Rod followed until they came to the wall. The ghost pointed a long, bony finger. "Grope until you find a stone that yields to your hand."

Rod reached for the stone the ghost pointed to, and pushed, leaning all his weight against it. The stone groaned and grudgingly gave way, sliding back into the wall. As it fell back, a door ground open with the protest of hinges that were long overdue for an oil break. Cold, dank air fanned Rod's cheek.

"Leave me now," said the ghost, tall and regal beside him, "and go to your duty. Yet remember, Man, your oath; and be assured that if ever you should lay it aside, the first Duke Loguire shall ever stand beside your bed until at last you yield to fear."

"Definitely a comforting thought," Rod mused. He groped his way down the moss-grown steps, humming "You'll Never Walk Alone."

This time, the door to the loft was open, and Tom's deep earthquake snores echoed in the rocky chamber.

Rod paused in the doorway, chewing at his lip. He went back into the hall, pulled a torch from its bracket, and thrust it ahead of him into the room, peering in cautiously, just to be sure there was no one trying to rearouse Tom with a paternity suit in mind.

The wavering light of the torch disclosed the stocky peasant's slumbering form, his cape thrown over his body from the rib cage down. One ursine arm was curled comfortably about the soft, rounded body of a blonde, covered (or uncovered) to the same degree by the cape. Her small, firm breasts were pressed against Tom's side; her head rested on his shoulder, long hair flung in a glorious disarray over her shoulders. One sun-browned arm was flung possessively across the big man's beer-keg chest.

Rod frowned, and stepped over for a closer look. The face was slender, the nose tilted, mouth small, with a smug little smile of content.

It was obviously not the brunette who had accosted

Rod in the hallway earlier. He grunted in surprise; so the wench hadn't gone after the servant when she was refused by the master.

Of course, it might be just that she hadn't moved fast enough. . . . But no, Big Tom would've been glad to accommodate both.

He replaced the torch, came back to the loft with a nod of grudging admiration at Big Tom, and without bothering to pull off his doublet, dropped into the heap of hay that served for a bed. It brought back fond memories. He yawned, cushioned his head on his forearm, and drifted slowly toward sleep.

"Man Gallowglass!"

The voice boomed in the little room. Rod jerked bolt upright; the girl screamed, and Big Tom swore.

A ghost towered before them, glowing cold in the dark.

Rod came to his feet, flicking a glance at Tom and the girl. She cowered in abject terror against the bearhide of his chest. Tom's face had already settled into surly (and probably frightened) defiance.

Rod switched his eyes to the ghost, standing tall above him in plate armor, its face incredibly long and thin. The sword at its hip was a rapier; it was not Horatio Loguire.

Rod reminded himself that he was boss, a fact he had almost forgotten. He repaid the hollow gaze with the haughtiest look he could manage. "What sty were you raised in," he snapped, "that you come before a gentleman with such ill ceremony?"

The cavern eyes widened, the ghost's jaw dropping down inside its mouth. It stared at Rod, taken aback.

The mortal pressed his advantage. "Speak, and with courtesy, or I'll dance on your bones!"

The ghost fairly cringed; Rod had struck pay dirt. Apparently there was some sort of ectoplasmic link between a ghost and its mortal remains. He made a mental note to track down the graves of all relevant ghosts.

"Your pardon, milord," the ghost stammered. "I meant no offense; I only—"

Rod cut him off. "Now that you have disturbed my rest, you may as well speak. What brings you to me?"

"You are summoned—"

Rod interrupted him off again. "None summon me."

"Your pardon, lord." The ghost bowed. "Milord Loguire requests your presence."

Rod glared a moment longer, then caught up his harp with a sigh. "Well, he who deals with spirits must deal at odd hours." He cocked his head. *"Horatio* Loguire?"

"The same, my lord."

The servant girl gasped.

Rod winced; he had forgotten his audience. His reputation would be all over the castle by noon.

"Well," he said, shouldering his harp, "lead on."

The ghost bowed once more, then turned toward the wall, stretching out a hand.

"Hold it," Rod snapped. Better to leave the secret passages secret. "Go ye to Milord Loguire and tell him I shall come to him presently. You forget that I cannot walk through walls, like yourself."

The ghost turned, frowning. "But, my lord . . ."

"Go to Milord Loguire!" Rod stormed.

The ghost shrank away. "As you will, my lord," it mumbled hastily, and winked out.

In the sudden darkness, the girl let out her breath in a long, sobbing sigh; and, "How now, master," said Big Tom, his voice very calm, with only a trace of wonder, "do you traffic with spirits now?"

"I do," said Rod, and flung the door open, wondering where Tom had picked up a word like "traffic."

He turned to look at the couple in the light from the doorway, his eyes narrowed and piercing. "If word of this passes beyond this room, there shall be uneasy beds and midnight guest for the both of you."

Big Tom's eyes narrowed, but the girl's widened in alarm.

Good, thought Rod, *I've threatened her income. Now I can be sure she'll keep quiet.*

He spun on his heel, pulling the door shut behind him. Big Tom would console her, of course, and his master's control over ghosts wouldn't exactly hurt his standing with her.

And, of course, she'd keep her mouth shut.

Which was just as well. For a man who didn't believe in magic, Rod already had altogether too much of a name as a warlock.

He prowled along the hall till he found an empty chamber with access to the hidden tunnel. The granite blocks of one wall had been carved into a bas-relief of an orange flute being burned at the stake; apparently the Loguires took their adopted Irish name rather seriously. Rod found the one coal in the pile of faggots that was cut a little deeper than the rest, and threw all his weight against it, pushing it to his right. The ancient machinery gave a deep-throated grumble, and a trapdoor pivoted up from the stone flags of the floor.

Rod felt for the steps with his toes, reached up for the great iron ring set in the underside of the trapdoor, and pulled it shut as he went down the stairs.

He emerged from the massive door in the great hall with the dark altar. His phantom guide was there before him, waiting.

The ghost bowed. "If you would be so good as to

follow me, master . . ." It turned away, drifting toward the archway into the corridor.

Rod followed, muttering, "A little lighter on the sarcasm there."

They came out into the corridor; and, off to his right, Rod saw the fox-firelight of a cluster of ghosts. They were motionless, their heads bent, looking at something on the floor in the center of their circle. Rod heard a very mortal, and very terrified, whimper.

Horatio looked up at Rod's approach. He glided apart from the knot of ghosts, his cadaverous face knotted with anger.

"My Lord Loguire!" Rod bowed his most courtly, straightened. "Why do you summon me?"

The ghost's brow smoothed a little, somewhat mollified. "Man Gallowglass," it growled, "wherefore did you not tell me you had come accompanied into our halls?"

"Accompanied?" Rod's eyebrows lifted. "Oh, was I, now?"

Loguire's frown deepened again, puzzled. "In truth, there was one who followed after you, as I found upon my outgoing from the chamber with the strange device."

"Excelsior," Rod murmured.

"*Gesundheit,*" said Loguire. "If we are to have a continual passage of mortals here, I shall have to see to the heating of these halls. But anon: I found your servant, as I have said, directly without the chamber."

"Servant?" Rod frowned. "How do you know it was a servant?"

"It was listening at the door. And we may know that it is yours, for when we advanced upon it, it cried your name."

"Oh." Rod scratched at the base of his skull, frowning. "It did, did it?"

"Aye; else would we have slain it. And therefore did I send to you to claim it."

Loguire stepped aside; the circle of ghosts parted, and Rod stepped up. By the cold light of the ghosts, he saw a huddle of misery trying to push itself into the wall. The face was turned away from him. Long black hair flowed down over the shoulders. It wore white blouse, full skirt, and black bodice. The last was very well filled.

"My Lord Loguire," Rod began; his voice cracked; he tried again. "My Lord Loguire, this is scarcely an 'it.' " Then, in the gentlest voice he could manage, "Look at me, wench."

The girl's head jerked up staring, lips parted. Joy and relief flooded her face. "My lord!"

Then her arms were about his neck, so tight he had to fight for breath; and her body was pressed tight against him, head burrowing into his shoulder, her whole frame trembling with sobs. "My lord, O my lord!"

"My Lord!" Rod echoed, prying at her shoulder to get clearance for his larynx.

He recognized her, of course. It was the servant girl who had propositioned him earlier in the evening.

"There, there, now, lass, it's all right," he murmured, rubbing her back. The room seemed to reel about him; he picked out a fixed point of light and stared at it.

It turned out to be Horatio Loguire, face contorted by a touch of disgust. "Take her out from my halls, Man. They are damp enough of their own."

Rod was just noticing how nicely the peasant girl fitted in his arms. He closed his eyes, savoring the warmth and closeness of her. He nodded. "Aye, my lord, that I shall. There, there, now, lass, you mustn't cry." He pulled a handkerchief from his cuff and dabbed at her cheeks with it. "No more tears, there's a darling, you're raising the humidity, and Horatio's got arthritis, if he can just remember where he put his bones—there, that's right.''

Her head lay against his chest, sniffling. Her eyes closed, her face relaxed; it almost seemed she was asleep. Rod was swept with a sudden wave of tenderness, aided and abetted by a feeling of towering strength contributed by his protective instinct, and silently cursed the adhesive effect of a damsel in distress.

He looked up into the brooding, empty eyes of the Loguire.

"Thou'rt ensnared, Man."

"Who, me?" Rod scowled and thumped his throat in the carotid region. "Fire seven times tried this."

"And found it wanting," Loguire agreed, "and seven times tried *that* judgment is. Take her from my halls, Man."

Rod threw him one last look of defiance and turned to the girl. "Come lass," he murmured, "we must go out from this place now."

He swung her up into his arms. She stirred, murmured petulantly, and burrowed her head tight into his shoulder again, her arms tight about his neck.

Babies and women, Rod thought, exasperated; *they're worse than quicksand.*

"My lord," he said to Loguire, "will you lead me? You may understand that I am somewhat turned about. . . ."

"Aye," said the ghost, and turned away down the hall; but not before Rod had glimpsed a faint, phantom smile on the ghost's face. . . .

He came out into the torchlit corridor, where he had met Durer earlier. The little man was gone; apparently he had assumed the worst and gleefully gone his way.

Rod lowered the girl's feet to the floor. She murmured another little inarticulate protest, and pressed her head tighter against him.

Rod tightened his arms about her and brushed his cheek against her hair, drawing out the moment as long as he could.

Then he smiled sadly and lifted his hand to stroke along her jaw, tilting her chin up. The long-lashed eyes were still closed; the full red lips pursed and parted, just a little . . .

Rod steeled himself and said gently, "You must tell me now, lass. Why did you follow me?"

Her eyes flew open, widened in alarm. Then she bit her lip, bowing her head, and stood away from him, clenching her hands in the cloth of his doublet.

"You must tell me, lass," he repeated softly. "Who sent you to spy on me?"

Her head flew up, eyes wide in dismay. She shook her head. "None, my lord. None, only myself."

"Oh?" Rod smiled sadly. "Of your own doing, you followed me into the haunted quarter?"

She looked down again. "I did not fear the spirits, lord."

Rod pursed his lips in surprise. If it was so, she had uncommon courage for a serving maid. Her nerve hadn't broken till she actually saw the ghosts—and having experienced their moans himself, Rod could understand her breaking then.

Too, she might have followed him in hopes that he might reconsider his decision to sleep alone. Or maybe she'd thought she could help if he got into trouble. Rod smiled at that last thought. But he had to make sure.

"Still, you have not yet told me: why did you follow me?"

She bit her lip again, her face twisting. Rod waited, quietly.

Grudging every word, she said, "I—I feared for you, my lord."

Rod stared; then his mouth twisted into a wry smile. He shook his head, slowly. "You *feared* for me!"

"Aye!" Her head snapped up, eyes flashing. "I had no knowing you were a warlock, and . . . a man alone, in those halls . . ."

Her voice trailed off; her eyes dropped again.

Rod heaved a sigh and clasped her to him. She resisted a moment, then yielded.

"Lass, lass!" he murmured. "What could you have done to help me?"

"I—I have some small way with some spirits, lord." Her voice was muffled by the cloth of his tunic. "I had thought . . ."

Rod scowled. Was communication with the spirit world the norm on this kooky planet?

He rubbed her back gently, pressed his cheek against her hair. She could be lying, of course; but that would imply she was an excellent actress, and she seemed a little too ingenuous for that.

He sighed and tightened his arms about her. She murmured sulkily and pushed her hips against him.

Rod closed his eyes and wiped his mind of all but the touch of her body. She felt good, very good. Almost like that farm wench, Gwendylon . . .

His eyes snapped open. He stared into the torchlit dusk of the hall, picturing the two faces before him, side by side. Dye the hair black, tilt the eyes a little, straighten the nose . . .

She had felt him tense; she looked up at him. "What is it, my lord?"

The voice was a little higher-pitched, yes; but it had that same quality.

He looked down at her. The complexion was flawless, not a single freckle; but it didn't take that much technology to concoct a makeup base.

He pointed his forefinger between her eyes. "You," he said, "have been deceiving me." His finger came to rest on the tip of her nose.

There was a flicker of disappointment in her eyes; then she was all innocence. "Deceiving you, my lord? I—I know not . . ."

Rod flicked his finger; the tip of her nose came off. He smiled grimly, nodding. "Cornstarch and water. But you were wrong to straighten it; I like it much better with that little tilt at the end."

He rubbed his fingertip across the corner of her eye; the eye was no longer slanted, and there was a dark smudge on his finger. "Cornstarch and water, and black paint at the eye-fold. Flour mixed with a little burnt umber on the face, and henna in the hair."

The corners of her mouth tightened. Her face blushed with the heat of anger under the paint.

He shook his head, brow puckered. "But why, lass? Your face is so much more beautiful."

He allowed himself a shot of self-satisfaction as the anger in her face melted into tenderness and longing.

She lowered her eyes. "I—I could not leave you, lord."

He closed his eyes, grinding his teeth, and only by main force of will kept himself from squeezing her.

"But . . ." He stopped, and drew a long hissing breath. "But how did you follow me, lass?"

She looked up, eyes wide in innocence. "In the guise of an osprey, lord."

His eyes snapped open with a near-audible click. He stared. "A witch? You? But . . ."

"You will not despise me for it, lord?" she said anxiously. "You, who are a warlock?"

His eyes had lost focus. "Huh? Uh—warlock? He

shook his head, trying to clear it. "Uh, I mean . . .
No, of course I don't. I mean . . . well, some of my
best friends are . . . uh . . ."

"My lord?" She peered into his face. "Art thou
well?"

"Who, me? Of course not! No, wait a minute . . ."
He stopped and drew a very, very deep breath. "Now,
look. You're a witch. So. Big deal. I'm far more
interested in your beauty than your talents."

Embers there, in her eyes, ready to flame if he
breathed upon them.

He took another deep breath and called his hormones
to order. "Now. Let's get one thing straight."

She brushed up against him, breathing, "Aye, my
lord."

"No, no! I didn't mean *that!*" He took a step back,
hands coming up to hold her off. "Look. The only
reason you followed me here was because you were
afraid I'd get into trouble I couldn't handle, right?"

She paused, the glow dying in her eyes under a chill
flow of disappointment. She lowered her eyes. "Aye,
my lord."

The way she said it made him think she was leaving
an awful lot to implication; but he hurried on to the next
point.

"But now you know I'm a warlock. Right?"

"Aye, my lord." He could scarcely hear her.

"So you know I don't have to be afraid of anything,
right? So there's no reason to follow me any more,
right?"

"Nay, my lord!" Her face whipped up to him,
glaring; then her chin lifted a little higher, proud and
haughty and stubborn. "Still will I follow you, Rod
Gallowglass. There be spells in this world that you wot
not of."

And one of the most galling things about her, he

decided, was that she was always so damned *right*. In this crazy, topsy-turvy world, there probably were quite a few "spells" he couldn't even imagine.

But, on the other hand, there seemed to be a few that she didn't know, either. An amateur witch, most likely, and too old to join the union—she must be almost as old as Rod was. In fact, her "witchcraft" seemed to consist of cosmetic skill, the ability to go birdie (he hadn't quite figured that one out yet), and a degree of courage that was totally unexpected in a woman.

So she was right, she had good cause to worry about him, he would still be in danger—but so would she.

No. It wouldn't do any good to tell her she couldn't follow him—she would anyway. And he'd come out of it alive, like he always did, but she'd get murdered in a ditch somewhere along the way. Or maybe she'd handicap him enough so they'd both wind up dead.

His head moved from side to side, tightening into a quick shake. He couldn't let her get killed. He had to shake her somehow—and he knew just how.

His mouth quirked into a sour smile. "It's true, what they say about farm girls: give them a moment of kindness, and you'll never be rid of them. My dear, you have an excellent nuisance rating."

She gasped, stepped away from him, her face twisting into a grimace of pain, the back of her hand coming up to her lips. Her eyes flooded with tears; she bit on her hand, turned, and fled.

He stared at the floor, listening to her sobs fading, feeling the hollowness grow within him.

A fist thundered on the heavy oaken door. Rod struggled up out of the depths of sleep, floundering to sit up in the hay.

Big Tom and his wench lay still, eyes fixed on the door.

Rod grunted and levered himself to his feet. "Don't worry," he growled. "Ghosts don't knock."

"Ho, minstrel!" a gruff beery voice bellowed. "Come forth to my master!"

Rod struggled into his doublet and caught up his harp. He swung open the great oak door, shaking his head to clear the traces of his meager sleep. "You might at least try to be civil at this hour of the damn morning," he growled. "And just who the hell is your master?"

The heavy fist caught him under the ear, sent him sprawling against the wall. He fought down the instant impulse to break the man's neck.

Through a ringing, blurred haze he heard a deep, sadistic chuckle. "Mind how you speak to your betters, gleeman. 'Tis a good rule for a peasant."

Rod gathered himself, hands braced against the wall, and sized up his persecutor. It was a common foot soldier in leather and mail, both of which needed cleaning, as did the soldier himself. He might have been a commoner, but he had an uncommon case of B.O., and halitosis on top if it, possibly due to the rotting teeth he was exhibiting in a self-satisfied grin.

Rod sighed and straightened, deciding it might be better to play his part; in fact, he'd deserved the blow, for having dropped out of character. The jester in medieval society served as an emotional release, not only through entertainment, but also through providing an outlet for aggressions by becoming their object.

"All right," he said, "I'm schooled. Let's go."

The fist caught him beneath the jaw this time. As he rolled with the blow, he heard the gleeful voice growl, "Thou'rt not schooled enough. To address your betters with *master* is the rule."

Rod fought the anger down into a cold, calm, calculating rage and lunged, his hands chopping out in three quick blows.

"I've got a better rule for a soldier," he informed the crumpled heap at his feet. "First be sure who your betters are. Now take me to your master."

The master, as it turned out, was Loguire. Rod was ushered into a medium-sized room, high-ceilinged and hung with tapestries. Three tall, narrow windows, through which Rod saw sunlight, dawn-colored, broken by the shifting prism of the waterfall. The room was filled with its roaring. But the sound was muted; looking closer, Rod saw the windows were double-paned, and three feet deep. Somebody had remembered some of the old technology.

The walls were hung with tapestries; there was a heavy carpet underfoot. A great oval table took up the center of the chamber. At its head sat Loguire; at his right, his eldest son. Durer sat at his left. The other places were taken up by eight men who had a familiar look. Rod's eyes widened as he recognized them: the Duke Di Medici, the Earl of Romanoff, the Duke Bourbon, and the Prince Hapsburg, and their councillors.

After Loguire, they were the four most powerful of the Great Lords. And if these five were gathered together, might not the other seven be close by?

All were at breakfast, but none of them really seemed to realize they were eating. Take Anselm, there, Loguire's son—he ate like a machine, glaring at his plate, face set like a sculpture of cold fury.

His father sat with head bowed, hands pressed tight to the table before him.

At a guess, Rod decided, there had been a bit of a quarrel here, between father and son, and Loguire had won—but only by ordering his son to shut up.

And Rod had been called in to heal the breach. Oy! The things people expect of performers!

Durer's face was lit with a subterranean glow of vindictive joy; the other councillors had milder versions of the same look. Whatever had happened here had gone the way Durer wanted; in fact, he'd probably instigated it. The man was the perfect catalyst, Rod decided: he never got involved in the reactions he caused.

Loguire looked up at his son, mute appeal in the old, red-rimmed eyes. But Anselm gave him not so much as a glance, and Loguire's face firmed into flint.

Turning, the old man saw Rod. "Minstrel!" he barked. "Why stand you there idle? Give us merriment!"

Durer's head snapped around, his eyes locked on Rod. Alarm chased shock across his face, to be followed by distilled, murderous hate.

Rod smiled cheerfully, bowed, and touched his forelock in salute. Inwardly, he wondered what song could possibly burn away the tensions in this room. He strongly suspected the custom was to clear the air by beating the minstrel for failing to fulfill his assignment.

He began to play "Matty Groves," figuring his only chance lay in giving them something more gruesome than anything that could possibly have just taken place.

He held off on the words for a few minutes, though, to give him time to study the faces of the four lords. Their looks ranged from ruminative speculation to outright (though veiled) contempt, the last apparently directed at the old Duke. It would seem that Loguire had no virulent supporters here; the balance of opinion seemed to rest with his son.

"Minstrel!"

Rod looked up; it was Anselm who had spoken. The young man's face seemed to have soured so much it had curdled. "Have you a song for a lad made a fool by a woman, yet doubly a fool, still, to love her?"

"Ha' done!" Loguire snapped; but before Anselm could reply, Rod said, "Many, my lord, of a man still loving a woman who scored him; and in all of them, the lady comes back to him."

"Comes back!" Anselm spat. "Aye, she'd take him back—to hang him in shame at her castle gate!"

The old Duke drew himself to his feet, roaring, "Enough of your slander!"

"Slander!" Anselm's chair crashed over as he rose to meet his father. "And is it slander to say she has spit on the proud name of Loguire, aye, and not once but twice, and will do so again?"

"Nay!" He slammed his fist on the board, turning to rake the lords with his glare. "This vile wench shall learn that she dare not trample the honor of her peers! We must tear her from the seat of power and break her beneath us for ever and aye!"

Loguire's face reddened, his throat swelled with a rebuke; but before he could speak it, Rod murmured, "Nay, my lord, not so harsh. Not a defeat, but a discipline."

He was caught in a crossfire of laser-beam glares from Anselm and Durer; but Loguire boomed "Aye!" with a giant's joy and relief. "He speaks out of place, but his speaking is true! Our young Queen is headstrong; but so is a filly before it is bridled. She must learn her authority is not absolute, that there are checks upon her power; but she is the sovereign, and must not be torn down!"

Anselm made a gurgling sound, his face swollen red and his eyes starting forth from their sockets, choking with rage; then he managed to speak, fairly stuttering in his wrath.

"Nay, now! Now I say nay! A woman for a

sovereign? 'Tis a mockery! And a whoring, arrogant bitch of a—''

"Be still!" Loguire thundered, and even the four great lords shrank away from the savage power of his voice.

As for Anselm, he fairly cowered, staring appalled at the white-bearded giant before him, who almost seemed to swell and tower high as they watched.

Then, slowly, and with greater dignity than Rod had ever seen in a man, the true regal dignity that only comes unaware, Loguire resumed his seat, never taking his eyes from his son. "Retire to your chambers," he said in a cold, still voice. "We shall speak no more of this till the conclave at sunset."

Anselm somehow managed to summon the strength to lift his chin again, a gesture that somehow seemed pompous and ridiculous, and turned on his heel. As he stalked to the door, his eyes fell on Rod. Rage and humiliation boiled up in him, and he swung up his arm to favor the minstrel with a back-handed slap.

"Nay!" barked Loguire, and Anselm froze.

"This man," said the Duke, speaking in centimeters, "has spoken truth. I will not have him maltreated."

Anselm locked glares with his father; then his look faltered, and dropped. He turned away; the door slammed behind him.

"Minstrel," rumbled Loguire, "play!"

Rod let his fingers ramble through "The Old Man of Tor Tappan" while he reflected.

So there would be a council of war tonight, eh? And the main issue would apparently be constitutional monarchy versus warlordism, though only he and Durer might know it. Well, he knew which side he was on.

He looked again at the straight-backed old Duke, eating token bits of food, lips pressed tight under his flowing white beard, brow locked in a slight scowl, only the slightest hint of his grief showing in the deep, shadowed eyes.

Yes, Rod knew which side he was on.

They met in the great hall, large enough to act as a hangar for a good-sized spaceship, if the Gramarians had known what a spaceship was.

The stone floor was inlaid with Loguire's coat of arms. Great silver sconces supported torches every yard or so along the walls. The ceiling was concave and gilded, with an immense silver chandelier suspended from its center. There were no windows; but that made little difference, since night had fallen.

Loguire sat in a great carved chair at one end of the hall, bunting of his family's colors draped on the wall behind him. His chair was raised on a four foot dais, so that the standing lords must look up at him.

There were a good many of them, not only the twelve greats, but with them a host of counts, barons, and knights, their vassals.

And at each one's elbow stood, or rather hunched, a thin-faced, bony little man, with scant light hair lying close against his scalp.

Rod surveyed the hall; his lips pursed into a soundless whistle. He hadn't realized the councillors were so numerous. There were at least fifty, maybe seventy.

And there might be more outside his field of view. At the moment, he had literal tunnel-vision, and one-eyed at that. The torches that illuminated the hall sat in sconces that were held to the wall with three rough bolts.

But one of the sconces behind Loguire's throne was missing a bolt, and the stone behind it was bored through for an inch, then hollowed out to the depth and width of a man's head. The head, at the moment, was

Rod's, where he stood in the clammy darkness of a narrow passage behind the wall.

His peephole afford him an excellent view of the back of Loguire's head, and some nice over-the-shoulder shots of anyone addressing him.

His right hand rested on a lever; if he pushed it down—if it wasn't rusted tight—the stone before him *should* swing wide to make a handy door. From the looks on the faces of the lords confronting the Duke, it might be very handy.

The man immediately in front of the Duke was Anselm. Bourbon and Di Medici stood at either side of the young man. Durer, of course, stood at Loguire's left hand.

Loguire rose heavily. "We are met," he rumbled. "Here in this room is gathered all the noble blood of Gramarye, the true power of the land." He scanned the faces before him slowly, looking each of his brother Great Lords directly in the eye.

"We are met," he said again, "to decide on a fitting rebuke for Catharine the Queen."

The Duke of Bourbon stirred, unfolding his arms and setting his feet a little further apart. He was a great black bear of a man, with shaggy brows and a heap of beard on his chest.

His fists clenched, his mouth tightened. There was something furtive, sheepish, in his stance.

He glared at Loguire. "Nay, good Uncle, you have the wrong of it. We are met to say how we may pull her down, she who would trample upon the honor and the power of our nobles Houses."

Loguire stiffened, his eyes widening in outrage. "Nay!" he choked, "there is not cause enough . . ."

"Cause!" Bourbon straightened, his black beard jumping with his jaw. "She hath taxed our lands more heavily than ever in the traditions of our lore, and wasted the substance upon the filth and dirt of peasants; she sends her judge amongst us every month to hear complaints from all the manor; and now she will appoint her priests within our lands—and we have no cause? She robs us of our rightful rule within our own demesnes, and then upon this all insults us to our faces by hearing the petitions of besotted beggars ere she will bend her ear to ours!''

Di Medici had bent to listen to the slight man at his elbow; now he straightened, smiling faintly, and murmured, ''And was it custom, ever, for a monarch to receive petitions from his peasants within his own Great Hall?''

''Never!'' thundered Bourbon. ''But now our gentle monarch will place the rabble thus before us! And these, my *reverend* Duke, be but the greatest of her enormities, and the atrocities she hath wreaked upon the custom of the land. And this while she is but a child! What will she do, my lord, when she is grown!''

He paused for breath, then shook his head and growled, ''Nay, good coz! We must needs pull her down!''

''Aye,'' murmured Di Medici, and

''Aye,'' declared the other lords, and

''Aye'' rolled through the hall and swelled, till the word came full, clamoring from every throat, again and yet again.

''Aye!'' and ''Aye!'' and ''Aye!''

''Now I say *nay!*'' Loguire roared above them all.

The hall fell still. Loguire drew himself up to his full height and breadth, looking more a king than duke.

His voice was only a little calmer, falling like the toll of a battle tocsin. ''She is the sovereign. Capricious, aye, and arbitrary, hot and headstrong, aye. But these are faults of youth, of a child who must be taught that there are limits to her power. We must now show her those limits that she has exceeded. That may we do, and nothing more. Our cause does not admit of further action."

"A woman cannot rule wisely," murmured Di Medici's councillor, and Di Medici took it up: "My good and gentle cousin, God did not make Woman wise in ruling."

Bourbon took his cue. "Aye, good Uncle. Why will she give us not a king? Let her marry, if she doth wish this land well-governed."

Rod wondered if Bourbon was a disappointed suitor. There was something vaguely lecherous about him, and nothing at all romantic.

"The rule is hers by right!" Loguire rumbled. "Hers is the blood Plantagenet, the Crown of this land since its birth! What, good nephew, have you so easily forgotten the oath you swore in fealty to that good name?"

"Dynasties grow corrupt," muttered Bourbon's councillor, eyes gleaming.

"Aye!" Bourbon bellowed. "The blood Plantagenet has thinned and soured, *good* my lord!"

Ah, so! Rod thought. *He's not an uncle any more. . . .*

"Weakened sore, my lord!" Bourbon ranted. "Weakened till it can no longer sire a man, but only a woman, slip of a girl, with a woman's moods and whims, to reign! The bloodline of Plantagenet is worn and spent; we must have new blood now for our kings!"

"The blood of Bourbon?" Loguire lifted an eyebrow, his smile contemptuous.

Bourbon's face swelled red, eyes bulging. He had begun to splutter when Di Medici's voice interposed itself smoothly.

"Nay, good cousin, not the blood of Bourbon. What throneblood should we have but the noblest in all the South?"

Loguire stared, the blood draining out of his face in shock and horror. "I will not!" he hissed.

"Nay, my lord, and this we knew." Di Medici went oily on. "Yet must we have good blood, and a man of courage and decision, a man of youth who knows what must be done and will not hesitate to do it."

His voice rose. "What king should we have but Anselm, Loguire's son?"

Loguire's head jerked as though he had been slapped. He stared, his face paling to a waxen texture, taking on a grayish hue.

He reached behind him with a palsied hand, groping for his chair, and age draped heavy on his shoulders.

He lowered himself to the edge of the seat, leaning heavily on the arm. His vacant eyes sought out his son, then turned slowly from side to side.

"Villains!" he whispered. "Bloody, bawdy villains! And thus you steal my son . . ."

Anselm's chin was lifted in defiance, but guilt and fear had hollowed his eyes. "Nay, my lord, I was with them from the first."

Loguire's empty eyes sought him out again. "But thou, even thou . . ."

His voice strengthened. "But it is, thou more than any. Above all, it is thou!"

Durer now stepped forward, away from Loguire, to take his place by Anselm's side, his smile split into a grin of triumph.

Loguire's eyes gradually focused on him. Their eyes met, and held.

A slight rustle passed through the hall as all the councillors craned for a better view.

"Nay," Loguire whispered. "it was *thou*. . . ."

He straightened slowly. Then, deliberately and slowly, he looked each Great Lord in the eyes once more. His eyes turned back to Durer.

"You are all of one mind." His voice had gained strength; but it was the strength of bitterness and contempt. "The debate has been before this, has it not? For you are all agreed; each man among you has quarreled with his conscience and won over it."

His voice hardened even more. "What wasp has flown among you, to sting your souls to such accord?"

Durer's eyes snapped fire. His mouth broke open for retort; but Loguire cut him off.

"Thou! Thou from the star! Thou camest to me five years ago, and I, aged fool, thought 'Well and good'; and as thy bastard, cringing servants crept one by one into our households, still I rejoiced—poor, aged, doddering fool!"

He lifted his eyes to seek out Anselm's. "Anselm, who once I called my son, awake and hear! Beware the man who tastes thy meat, for he it is who best may poison it."

Rod suddenly realized how the meeting would end. The councillors couldn't risk leaving Loguire alive; the old man was still strong and vital, still indomitable. He just might be able to sway the lords to loyalty again. The chance was slight, but definite, and Durer couldn't afford it.

Anselm straightened his shoulders, his face set with rebellion. He clapped a hand to Durer's shoulder, not noticing that the little man's teeth grated as his jaws clamped shut.

"This man I trust," he stated in what might have been intended to be ringing tones. "He was with me from the first, and I welcome his wisdom—as I will welcome yours, if you are with us."

Loguire's eyes narrowed. "Nay," he spat. "Away

with you, false child, and your tongue of treachery! I had sooner die than join you."

"You shall have your preference," Durer snapped. "Name the manner of your dying."

Loguire glared, then threw himself to his full height in one lurching motion.

Anselm stared, then reddened. "Be—be still, Durer! He is—is a fool, aye, and a traitor to the land. But he is my father, and none shall touch him!"

Durer's eyebrow shot up. "You would harbor snakes within your bed, my lord? Naetheless, it is the wish of all the nobles, not yours alone, that must be done."

He raised his voice, shouting, "What say you, lords? Shall this man die?"

There was a moment's pause. Rod rested his hand on the door-lever; he had to get Loguire out of there. He could open the door and pull Loguire into the passage before anybody realized what was happening . . .

But could he close it before they came running? Probably not; there were just too many too close. And Durer, at least, would react very quickly.

If only the hinges and springs were in decent shape! But he had a notion they hadn't been too well maintained in the last few centuries.

A chorus of reluctant "Ayes" rolled through the great hall.

Durer turned to Loguire, bowing his head politely. "The verdict, my lord, is death."

He drew his poniard and started forward.

And the light went out.

Rod stood a moment in the total blackness, stunned. How . . . ?

Then he threw his weight on the lever. He jerked out his dagger as the stone slab groaned open. Act now, understand later.

The grating of the stone door broke the instant of shocked silence. Pandemonium struck as every voice in the hall started shouting—some in anger, some in distress, some calling for a porter to bring a torch.

The noise would be a good cover. Rod lunged out of the passage, groping blindly till he slammed into somebody's rib cage. The Somebody roared and lashed out at him. Rod ducked on general principles, felt the blow skim his hair. He flicked the button on the handle of his dagger and identified Somebody as the Duke Loguire in the flicker of light that stabbed up from the hilt.

A kindling-wood, twisting body struck into Rod with a howl of rage. Rod gasped and stumbled as steel bit into his shoulder. Apparently Durer had seen the flicker of light, too.

The dagger wrenched itself out of Rod's shoulder; he felt the warm welling flow out of the blood, and rolled away.

But the scarecrow was on him again. Rod groped, and by great good luck caught the man's knife-wrist.

But the little man was unbelievably strong. He forced Rod's arm down, down, and Rod felt the dagger's point prick his throat.

He tried to force his other hand up to help push the needle-point away. His shoulder screamed pain, but the hand wouldn't budge.

The dagger pricked a fraction of an inch deeper. Rod felt blood rise on his throat, and fear clawed its way up from his guts.

Total, numbing, paralyzing fear—and Rod heard a booming moan.

Durer gasped; the poniard clattered to the floor, and the weight rose off Rod's body.

The whole hall rang with a triple, very low moan, counterpointed with shrieks of terror.

Three huge white forms towered high in the blackness. At the tops were skeletal faces, their mouths rounded into O's: Horatio and two other erstwhile Lords Loguire, having the time of their afterlives.

Rod forced a shout out of his terror. "Fess! Sixty cycles!"

His head clamored with the raucous buzzing, and the fear evaporated. His light flicked again, found Loguire. Rod sprang, struck him in the midriff. The breath went out of the old lord in a *whoof!* and he doubled over Rod's shoulder—the good one, fortunately.

Rod turned and ran, stumbling, hoping he was headed in the right direction.

Behind him, Durer was shrieking, "Clap your hands to your ears, fools! Fools! Fools!"

Rod blundered about in the dark, Loguire's weight dragging heavier on his shoulder. He couldn't find the door! And now he heard staccato steps in short, quick bursts—Durer, trying to find Rod by blind chance. And now that he had his earplugs in, Durer would once again be a formidable enemy. Also, Rod couldn't fight with one shoulder shot and the other under Loguire.

Cold air fanned his cheek, and a dim white form brushed past him. "Follow!" boomed Horatio Loguire.

Rod followed.

He ran after Horatio, his good arm out like a broken-field runner. It didn't help; his wounded shoulder slammed against the stone of the doorway and spun him around with a wrench of pain. He gasped, almost dropping Loguire, and stumbled back against the wall of the narrow passage.

He leaned against the wall, breathing horsely.

"Quickly, Man!" boomed Horatio. "The slab! You must close it!"

Rod nodded, gasping, and groped for the lever, hoping Loguire would stay balanced on his shoulder.

His hand found rusty metal. He hauled upward; the door grated shut.

He stood hunched over, just breathing.

After a small eternity, Loguire began to struggle. Rod called up the energy to lower him to the floor. Then, still panting, he looked up at Horatio.

"Many thanks," he wheezed, "for this timely rescue."

Horatio waved away the thanks, coming dangerously close to a smile. "Why, Man, how could you fulfill your oath to me dead?"

"Oh, I dunno." Rod sagged against the wall. "You seem to manage all right. I'd love to know how you pulled the fuse on those torches."

"Pulled . . . the fuse?" Horatio frowned.

"You know, the trick with the lights."

The ghost's frown deepened. "Was that not your doing?"

Rod stared. Then he raised a hand, palm out. "Now, wait a minute. Wait a minute. Now. You thought I did it . . . and I thought you did it."

"Aye."

"But, you didn't do it?"

"Nay."

"And I didn't do it."

"It would seem not."

"Then"—Rod gulped—"who . . . ?"

"Who is this?" Loguire rumbled at Rod's elbow.

A beam of light stabbed through the peephole.

Horatio gave one moan of fear, and winked out.

Rod put his eye to the peephole. The torches were lit again. Durer was on the dais, stabbing the air about him with his dagger and screaming, "Where? Where?"

Rod lifted his head away from the peephole and smiled up at Loguire thinly. "I don't think we ought to stay to find out, my lord. Shall we go?"

He turned to go; but Loguire's fingers dug into his shoulder. Rod gasped. "Please, milord—would you mind—the other shoulder, please. . . ."

"What man was that?" Loguire growled.

"Man?" Rod looked about him. "What man?"

"Why, he who stood before us in white!"

"Oh." Rod scanned the old man's face. Apparently Loguire was still in shock, not quite yet ready to face reality, such as it was. "Uh, just a relative, milord."

"Your relative? Here?"

"No, milord. Yours." He turned away, groping down the passage.

After a moment, Loguire followed.

The light from the peephole fell off after a few yards. Rod groped his way, cursing; it would be pitch dark when they turned the corner to go down the narrow steps.

He turned the corner, fumbling out his dagger—and saw a ball of fox-fire before him. He stared, an eerie tingling nesting at the base of his neck; then, as his eyes adjusted to the dim glow, he made out a face and a body (it was impossible to see them as a unit, since each was worthy of independent study), one arm extended, with the fox-fire sitting on her palm. Her face was tense with worry.

"Gwendylon," he stated.

Her face flooded with relief and joy, but only for a moment; then the light of mischief was in her eyes.

She bobbed in a mock curtsy. "My lord."

"My Aunt Nanny!" he growled. "What the hell are you doing here?"

Her eyes widened in offended innocence. "I followed you, lord."

"No, no, no!" Rod squeezed his eyes shut. "That's

not in the script. You were supposed to hate me now. You were supposed to quit following me.''

"Never, lord.'' Her voice was very low.

He looked up to see if she was joking. No luck. Tom's line about farm girls ran through his mind.

"What,'' he said, nodding at the ball of fox-fire, "have you got there?''

"This?'' She glanced at the ball of light. "Only a little spell my mother taught me. 'Twill light us through this maze, lord.''

"Light,'' Rod agreed. "And may I ask how you killed the torches in the great hall?''

She started to answer, then frowned. '' 'Tis not quickly said, lord. Have we time?''

Rod studied her face with his lips pursed. "But it was you who did it?''

"Aye, lord.''

"Just another little spell that . . .''

''. . . my mother taught me, yes.'' She nodded brightly.

"Oka-a-a-y!'' He shrugged. "Why not? Let's go, babe.''

He started groping his way down the narrow stairs, wincing as his shoulder brushed the wall.

"My lord!'' Gwendylon gasped, her hand darting out to touch his shoulder. "You're hurt!''

He half-turned toward her, lurching against the wall, still groping for the stone; but the full, firm mound that his hand found was anything but granite.

He jerked his hand away. She stared at him a moment, surprised; then her lids drooped, she smiled lazily, and caught up his hand, pulling it toward her. "Milord, you need not—''

"Yegad!'' He pulled his hand away, shrinking back against the wall. She swayed toward him, lips parting.

"My dear lady . . . !"

"I ha' ne'er claimed that title," she murmured, her voice warm, rich, and husky. Her body pressed softly against him.

"Woman, please!" Rod made a valiant attempt to push his way into the stone. "I can't imagine a less aesthetic atmosphere."

"Neither time nor place matter to me, lord, when you are near," she breathed into his ear, and nibbled.

And I thought I had some lines, Rod told himself. "Look," he said, wriggling, "we don't have time, we don't have room . . ." He gasped and shivered as she caught just exactly the right spot. "Look, baby, just get us out of here, and I'm yours to command!"

She caught her breath and stood just far enough back to look up at him. "Truly, lord?"

"Well, uh . . ." Rod backpedaled furiously. "For twenty-four hours, anyway."

"That will do," she murmured smugly, with a similar quality in her smile.

He glowered down at her for a moment; then, "Take those canary feathers out of your mouth," he growled, "and get us out here!"

"Aye, lord!" She turned in a swirl of skirts and ran lightly down the mossy steps.

He watched her run for a moment, a gleam coming into his eye.

He caught up to her in three bounds and swung her around to face him.

She looked up in surprise, then turned on the sultry look again. "My lord, we must not delay. . . ."

"This won't take long," he answered, and pulled her hard against him. Her lips were moist and warm, and parted . . .

She gave a happy little sigh and pushed him away. "Well! And what was that for?"

"Promissory note." He grinned.

She giggled, then spun away, tugging him down the hall. "We must hurry!"

He freed his arm and watched her run.

A deep, warm chuckle sounded behind him.

Rod threw Loguire a look of disgust. "Dirty old man," he growled, and ran after Gwen.

The slimy stones of the passage slid by on either side, scarcely three inches from each shoulder. Up a flight of steps, turn, up another flight, the stones greasy and slippery with dripping water, seepage from the lake overhead. Patches of pale moss grew like sores on the walls. Old spiderwebs festooned the low ceiling.

At the top of the twelfth staircase, Rod heard water chuckling somewhere in the distance.

"The inlet to the lake," Gwendylon informed him. "We shall come out along its border." She glanced back over her shoulder. "Your shoulder, Lord Rod?"

"Oh, it'll wait," he growled.

"Doth it yet bleed?"

"No; the doublet seems to have stanched it. Be a hell of a cleaning bill though."

"Hmm." She turned away, hurrying. "'Twill hold till we come to the riverbank, then. Hurry, lords; we must be away ere they think to search in the stables."

Rod frowned. "Why? Are we coming out in the stableyard?"

"Nay, by the river; but when they look in the stables, they shall see that your black and the Duke's dun stallion have fled."

"You don't say!" He cleared his throat and spoke a little louder than necessary. "And where would my horse be?"

"By the riverbank, Rod," Fess's voice murmured, "with Big Tom and two real nags."

Gwendylon had started to answer, but Rod cut her off. "Yes, yes, they're by the riverbank, I know."

Gwen looked faintly surprised.

"But how," Rod went on, "did Big Tom know we'd be needing horses?"

She frowned at him a moment, then turned away. " 'Twas at my urging, lord. 'Twas but a thought, and could do little harm. I had a seeming they might be needed."

"A seeming," Rod echoed. Was she clairvoyant, too?

"Aye, lord, a seeming." She slowed suddenly. "Walk wary, lords." She stepped carefully over something lying in the passage.

Rod stopped and stared at it.

It was a miniature human skeleton, perhaps eighteen inches long; but the proportions were those of an adult, not a bably. It was green with mold.

He looked up at Gwendylon. "This has not been here so very long," he said. "What is it?"

"One of the Wee Folk, lord." Her mouth hardened. "There ha' been evil spells in this keep of late."

Rod looked up, surprised at the tone of her voice, ignoring Loguire's startled exclamation.

Her face was flint, set in a mold of bitterness. "Poor wee fellow," she murmured. "And we dare not stop to give him burial." She spun about and hurried on.

Rod stepped carefully over the tiny skeleton and followed.

"What manner of spell?" he asked as he caught up to her.

" 'Twas a sort of . . . singing . . . in the air, lord, though not for the ear, but the mind. If you or I tried to move against it, 'twould but stop us, like a wall. But it slew the Wee Folk."

Rod frowned. "A *singing*, you say?"

"Aye, lord. Yet not of the ear, as I told you."

A force field! But that was impossible. Ask any physicist, he'd tell you . . .

"How long ago?"

"It was cast five years agone, milord. It lasted no more than a month, for its master took no note of my stopping it, nor did he cast it again."

Rod stopped so fast Loguire stumbled into him. He stared at the gentle, very feminine form hurrying down the passage before him. Then he closed his mouth, swallowed, and followed.

A force field! And five years ago, that was when Durer had shown up. . . .

Rod thought again of the dial on the supposed time machine. Then he stared at Gwen's long, red hair, swinging with her steps.

And she had stopped it? A machine out of the future, and *she* had stopped it?

He looked at his farm girl with new respect.

"Uh, Gwen, dear . . ."

"Aye, my lord?" She looked back at him, with a look of pleased surprise and a faint blush.

He frowned. *What . . . ?* Oh. He'd called her "Gwen." Also "dear."

"Aye, my lord, exorcised it. But the Wee Folk would not come here more, and I too thought it wise."

Yes, Rod mused, *very wise*. Durer & Co. would not have taken kindly to diminutive spies, and could probably have devised some very unpleasant preventatives. He fastened his eyes on Gwendylon's retreating back, watching her absently; she was just full of surprises, this one. . . .

"We come near, lords!"

Rod jerked his head up and saw a point of dim light ahead. The ball of light in Gwen's hand flickered out.

A moment later, they stepped through the weath-

ered, weed-grown mouth of the tunnel into the moonlit
night. The river flowed by a few dozen yards away,
bordered with willow and cypress. The breeze was chill
after the dampness of the tunnel. Loguire shivered.

"Master!" came a soft, low cry, and Big Tom
stepped out of the riverbank shadows, leading three
horses.

Rod grabbed Gwendylon's hand and ran for the
horses . . . and was brought up sharp by a most un-
feminine jerk on his arm—fortunately, the good
one.

"Nay, my lord," she said firmly. "First we must see
to your arm."

"Which one," Rod grumped, swiveling his good
shoulder; it had developed a sudden ache. "Look, we
don't have time . . ."

"It will slow us in our ride soon or late," she said
sternly. "Better to tend it now, when it will take but a
moment."

Rod sighed and capitulated. He watched her run to
the riverbank with a connoisseur's interest and wondered what the strange, pleasant feeling inside him
was.

"She hath the right of it," growled Loguire, swinging Rod about to face him. "Clamp your teeth."

He unbuttoned Rod's doublet. Rod's nascent protest
was cut off by a gasp of agony as Loguire snapped the
doublet open, tearing the scab off in the process.

"Let it bleed freely a moment," Loguire growled,
jerking the doublet off the injured shoulder.

Then Gwendylon came up with a handful of some
sort of herb and a small wineskin—*trust Big Tom to
have one on him*, Rod thought—and perhaps five minutes later, Rod swung her onto Fess's saddle and leaped
up behind her. He dug his heels into Fess's sides.
Gwendylon started at the muted clang, and, as Fess

sprang out into a gallop, she twisted about to frown, puzzled, at Rod.

"That's why I call him Old Ironsides," Rod explained. "Just relax and lean back against me. It's going to be a long ride."

"But, my lord, I have no need to—"

"There're only three horses, Gwen. Somebody has to ride double. Don't worry, Fess won't even notice the difference."

"But my lord, I—"

"Hush. My Lord Loguire!" he called back over his shoulder. "Lead us, my lord; you know this land best."

Loguire nodded mutely and spurred the big bay; it speeded a little, and passed Rod. Rod followed him, listening to the drum of hooves from Tom's mount behind him.

"Believe me, my lord, there is no need for—"

"Time enough to talk later," Rod growled. "We're leaving a trail as clear as Polaris. We've got to get far enough away fast enough so it won't matter if they follow us."

Gwendylon sighed. "Look behind you, my lord."

Rod turned, and saw a crowd of at least a hundred elves lined along their trail with miniature brooms, sweeping away every trace of their passing—even straightening the grass the horses' hooves had flattened.

Rod squeezed his eyes shut. "No. Oh, no. Why me, Lord? Why me?"

He turned back to Gwendylon. "Gwen, did you call out these . . . Gwen!"

The saddle was empty. She was gone.

"Gwen!" he shouted, and sawed back on the reins.

"Really, Rod," protested the murmur in his mastoid, "I must ask that you attempt to control—"

"Gwendylon!" Rod yelled.

A cry like the mew of a seagull drifted down from the sky.

Rod looked up.

The osprey. The same one. He was willing to swear to it. Anyway, he was willing to swear.

The bird plummeted low and circled Rod's head, mewing urgently.

How the hell could she make a fish hawk sound so feminine?

The osprey shot away in front of him, skimming low over the ground after Loguire's horse.

Then it wheeled back, circled his head again, then lit out on the straightaway again.

"Yeah, yeah," Rod growled, "I get the message. I should quit holding up the party. Fess, follow that bird! Fess? Fess!"

The horse stood stiff-legged, head swinging between the fetlocks.

Oh, well, it had been a strain on Rod's neurology, too. He slapped at the reset button.

They rode the moon down, slowing to a trot after the first half-hour. Loguire was slumped in his saddle, almost too exhausted to stay on his horse, by the time the air freshened with dawn.

Rod, frankly, wasn't in much better shape. He reined in beside the Duke. "There're haystacks in that field over there, my lord. We must pause to rest. It will be dawn soon, and we dare not travel by day."

Loguire lifted his head, blinking. "Aye. Aye, most certain." He reined in his horse. Rod and Tom followed suit.

They broke through the hedge at the roadside and trotted for the nearest haystack. Rod dismounted and caught Loguire as he all but fell from his saddle. Big Tom unsaddled the horses and turned them out to the field with a slap on the rump as Rod half-led, half carried the old nobleman to the top of the haystack.

He lowered Loguire into the hay, stepped back, and murmured, "Fess."

"Yes, Rod."

"Get those nags far away from here, someplace where it's not too likely they'll be noticed, will you? And bring them back at sundown."

"I will, Rod."

Rod stood a moment, listening to the fading drum of hooves.

He looked down at Loguire; the old man was out cold: the strain, and the long night ride, to say nothing of how long it had been since he'd slept.

Rod pulled hay over the sleeping lord to hide him. Looking for Big Tom, he saw shins and feet disappearing into the side of the haystack. The saddles and bridles had already disappeared into the hay.

The feet were likewise removed from sight; then there was a protracted rustling, and Tom's ruddy face popped out of his burrow-hole. "Thou must take tha'self from sight right quickly, master. 'Twill be sunrise ere long, and the peasants mustn't see us."

"They won't come near this stack?"

"Nay. This field is far from the keep, so 'twill be some days yet ere they take in this hay."

Rod nodded. He threw up his hands and jumped, sliding down the side of the stack. He turned to see Tom's burrow fast closing. He grinned. "Good night, Big Tom."

"Good morn, master," answered the muffled voice within.

Rod chuckled, shaking his head, as he went to the

nearest other haystack. He climbed to the top, mashed the hay down into a bowl, and stretched out with a blissful sigh.

There was a soft mew, and the osprey dropped down beside him into the hay. It fell onto its side, its form fluxed and stretched, and Gwendylon was lying beside him.

She smiled mischievously and began to untie the strings of her bodice. "Twenty-four hours, my lord. Sunrise to sunrise. You ha' said you would obey my commands for so long."

"But—but—but . . ." Rod stared and swallowed as the bodice fell open and was thrown away. The blouse began to inch upward.

He swallowed again and stammered, "Bu-but somebody's got to keep watch!"

"Never fear," she murmured. The blouse went flying. "My friends shall do that."

"Your friends?" In a detached sort of way, Rod noted that in this culture the concept of the brassiere was not yet developed.

Gwendylon was, though.

"Aye, the Wee Folk." Skirt and slippers joined the discard pile with one smooth, sinuous motion.

The setting sun turned the straw blood-gold as Rod's head poked up out of the hay.

He looked around, sniffed the cool, fresh evening breeze, and expelled a sign of great satisfaction.

He felt immensely well.

He thrust the covering of hay aside with one sweep of his arm and reflected that it had been a busy day, as his eyes traveled slowly and lovingly over Gwen's curves.

He leaned forward and touched his lips to hers for a long, deep kiss. He felt her come awake beneath him.

He drew back; her eyes opened halfway. Her lips curved in a slow, sultry smile.

She stretched, slow and feline. Rod was surprised to feel his pulse quicken. His opinion of himself went up a notch.

His opinion of her was altogether too high already. With a twinge of alarm, Rod realized he was regretting that he was a traveling man. He also realized something was gnawing at the base of his conscience. She looked into his eyes and sobered. "What saddens you, lord?"

"Don't you ever worry about being used, Gwen?"

She smiled lazily. "Do you, lord?"

"Well, no . . ." Rod frowned at his palms. "But that's different. I mean, I'm a man."

"I would never ha' guessed," she murmured, biting his ear lobe in the process.

He grinned and twisted, trying to retaliate; but she wasn't done with his ear yet.

"Men are fools," she murmured between bites. "You are forever saying what is not instead of what is. Be done with the night, and live in the evening while you are in it."

She eyed him then through heavy lids with a somewhat proprietary joy, looking him up and down slowly.

Oh, well, Rod thought, *so much for my one attempt to be honorable* . . . "Kamere!" After all, there was only one way to wipe that smug smile off her face.

Big Tom chose just that moment to call, "Master! The sun has set, and we must away."

Rod let go of Gwen with a disgusted growl. "That boy has definitely the greatest sense of timing . . ." He started pulling on his hose. "Up and away, my dear!"

"Must we, lord?" she said, pouting.

"We must," he answered. "Duty calls—or at least Big Tom. Onward for the glory of France! or something like that. . . ."

Two nights of pushing the pace, alternating canter and walk, brought them back to the capital.

As they came to the bridge over the river that curved around the town, Rod was surprised to see two foot soldiers armed with pikes, torches flaring by their sides in the darkness of the seventh hour of night.

"I shall clear the way," Tom muttered, and spurred his horse ahead of Rod and Loguire. "Stand aside," he called to the guards, "for my masters wish to enter."

The pikes clashed as they crossed, barring the bridge. "Who are your masters?" retorted the one of them. "Be they rebels? Or Queen's men?"

"Rebels?" Tom frowned. "What ha' passed in the Queen's Town while we ha' been to the South?"

"The South?" The guard's eyes narrowed. " 'Tis the lords of the South that rebel."

"Aye, aye!" Big Tom waved the objection away impatiently. "We ha' been there on the Queen's affairs—spies, i' truth. We bear word that the lords of the South rise in revolt, and the name of the day that they march; but how has this news come here afore us?"

"What is this badinage?" snapped Loguire, riding up with Rod at his side. "Stand aside, sirrahs, that a man of noble blood may enter!"

Th guards' heads swiveled to stare up at Loguire; then both pikes jumped forward, their points scarce an inch from his chest. "Dismount and stand, Milord Duke of Loguire!" The first guard's voice was firm, but deferential. "We must hold you in arrest, on command of her Majesty the Queen."

And the other guard bawled, "Captain! Captain of the Guard!"

Loguire stared in disbelief. Rod nudged his way past

the lord and glared at the guard. "Name the crime for which the Queen holds Milord Loguire in arrest!"

The guard's eyes flicked from Loguire's face to Rod's, and back; then, dubiously, he answered, "Most high treason to the body and person of her Majesty the Queen."

Loguire's jaw sagged. Then his lips pressed thin and his brows beetled down, hiding his eyes in caves of shadow. His face seemed bloody in the torchlight.

"I am most sternly loyal to her Majesty the Queen!" he exploded. "Be done with your impertinence and stand aside!"

The sentry swallowed and stood his ground. "It is said Loguire leads the rebels, milord."

"Soldier." Rod spoke quietly, but with the tone of an old field sergeant.

The sentry's eyes jumped to him, but the pike didn't waver.

"You know me," and Rod's voice held the veiled threat of non-com authority.

It had more effect than all Loguire's lofty phrases. The soldier licked his lips and agreed, "Aye, master."

"Who am I?"

"You are Master Gallowglass, late of the Queen's Guard."

"*Still* of the Queen's Guard," Rod corrected, still softly. "Sent to the South a week agone, to guard Milord Loguire."

Loguire's head jerked up; his eyes blazed at Rod.

"We ha' known that you were gone," the soldier mumbled.

"And now you know why." Rod kept his voice under careful control, managing to imply that the Queen's Own Wrath would fall on the guard's miserable head if he disobeyed. "My Lord Loguire cries sanctuary from his kinswoman and suzerain, her Majesty the Queen. She would be wroth to hear him detained. Let us pass.''

The guard took a firmer hold on his pike, gulped, and thrust out his jaw stubbornly. ''The order ha' gone forth that Milord Loguire be held in arrest in the Queen's dungeon, good master. More than that I know not.''

''Dungeon!'' Loguire thundered, beet-red. ''Am I a tuppenny footpad, to be crooked from a hedgerow to a dungeon cell? Is it thus that the Queen would acknowledge her vassal? Nay, nay! The blood Plantagenet hath not ebbed so low! Knave, I'll hale thy lying tongue from thy head!''

His hand went to his dagger, and the soldier cowered back; but Rod's hand stayed the nobleman's

''Calm yourself, milord,'' he murmured, '' 'Tis Durer hath sent this word here before us. The Queen could not know of your loyalty.''

Loguire checked his temper with vast effort, subsiding into a sort of gurgling fury. Rod leaned over and whispered to Tom.

''Tom, can you find someplace to hide the old man where he'll be safe?''

''Aye, master,'' Tom frowned down at him. ''With his son. But why . . . ?''

''At the House of Clovis?''

''Aye, master. 'Twould take all the Queen's men, and great bombards, to hale them forth from the House.''

''I would have said a good strong wind would've done it,'' Rod muttered, ''but I guess it's the best we can do. So . . .''

''Speak so that all may hear!'' shouted a new voice.

''That had a familiar ring,'' Rod muttered, looking up.

Sir Maris strode forth between the two vastly relieved guardsmen. "Well done, Rod Gallowglass! Thou hast brought a most pernicious rebel to the safekeeping of our stronghold!"

Loguire's narrowed eyes stabbed hate at Rod.

"Do not speak among yourselves," Sir Maris went on; "I forbid it. And hearken well to my orders, for there are twelve good crossbowmen with their quarrels aimed at your hearts."

Loguire sat back in his saddle, tall and proud, his face composed in the granite of fatalism.

"Twelve?" Rod gave Sir Maris a one-sided mocking smile. "Only twelve quarrels, to kill the Loguire? Good Sir Maris, I must think you grow rash in your old age."

The granite mask cracked; Loguire darted a puzzled glance at Rod.

Rod dismounted and stepped out toward the bridge, away from the horses. He shook his head woefully. "Sir Maris, Sir Maris! My good Sir Maris, to think that—"

Suddenly he whirled, with a high, piercing cry, slapping at the horses' chests. "Turn and ride!" he shrieked. "Ride!"

Sir Maris and his men stood frozen with surprise as the horses reared, wheeled about, and sprang away. An instant later, twelve crossbow bolts bit the ground where they had been.

One archer had been a little quicker than his fellows; his bolt struck Fess's metal hindquarters with a clang and ricocheted off into the river.

There was an instant's shocked silence; then the whisper ran through the ranks, swelling with fear: Witch horse! Witch horse!"

"Cloud the trail, Fess," Rod murmured, and the

great black horse reared, pawing the air and screaming combat; then it wheeled away and was gone, lost in the night, hoofbeats drumming away.

Rod smiled grimly, sure that Fess's trail would cross and recross Tom and Loguire's till an Italian spaghetti cook wouldn't be able to unsnarl it.

He peered up into the sky. He couldn't see beyond the circle of torchlight, but he thought he heard a faint mewing.

He smiled, again, a little more sincerely this time. *Let Catharine try to imprison. Let her try.*

Then his smile settled and soured as he turned to face Sir Maris.

The old knight was struggling manfully to look angry; but the fear in his eyes blared as loud as a TV commercial. His voice quavered. "Rod Gallowglass, you have abetted the escape of a rebel."

Rod stood mute, eyes glittering.

Sir Maris swallowed hard and went on. "For high treason to the body and person of her Majesty Queen of all Gramarye, Rod Gallowglass, in arrest I must hold thee."

Rod inclined his head politely. "You may try."

The soldiers muttered fearfully and drew back. None wished to match arms with the warlock.

Sir Maris' eyes widened in alarm; then he spun and grabbed one of his soldiers by the arm. "You there! Soldier! Soldier!" he hissed. "Run ahead and bear word to the Queen. Say what transpires here."

The soldier bolted, overwhelmingly glad to lose out on the action.

Sir Maris turned back to Rod. "Thou must now come to judgment before the Queen, Master Gallowglass."

Oho! thought Rod. *I'm a master now, am I?*

"Wilt thou go to her freely?" said Sir Maris apprehensively, "Or must I compel thee?"

Rod fought to keep his shoulders from shaking with laughter at the dread in the old knight's voice. His reputation had decided advantages.

"I will come freely, Sir Maris," he said, stepping forward. "Shall we go?"

Sir Maris' eyes fairly glowed with gratitude.

Abruptly, he sobered. "I would not be in thy place for a castle and dukedom, Rod Gallowglass. Thou must needs now stand alone before our Queen's tongue."

"Well, yes," Rod agreed. "But then, I've got a few things to say to her too, now haven't I? Let us go then, Sir Maris."

Unfortunately, the march to the castle gave Rod time to mull over Catharine's latest churlish tricks; so by the time they came to the door to her chambers, Rod's jaw was clenched and shivering with rage.

And, equally unfortunately, there was a reception committee, consisting of two sentries, the soldier who had been sent ahead as messenger, and two pikes pointed right at Rod's midriff.

The procession halted. "And what," said Rod, with icy control, "is *this* supposed to mean?"

The messenger stammered an answer. "Th-the Queen forbids that the w-warlock be brought before her unch-chained."

"Oh." Rod pursed his lips for a moment, then gave the messenger a polite lift of the eyebrow. "I am to be chained?"

Th messenger nodded, on the verge of panic.

The pikes crashed as Rod knocked them away to each side. He grabbed the messenger by the scruff of the neck and threw him into the pack of Guardsmen as they surged forward. Then he lashed out with a kick that wrenched the crude metal hinges from their bolts.

The door crashed down, and he strode in over it, stepping hard.

Catharine, the Mayor of the Queen's Town, and Brom O'Berin shot to their feet from their chairs around a mapladen table.

Brom sprang to bar Rod's path. "What devil possesses you, Rod Gallowglass, that you . . ."

But Rod was already past him and still moving.

He swung to a stop before the table, glaring across at her, his eyes chips of dry ice.

Catharine stepped back, one hand coming to her throat, disconcerted and afraid.

Brom leaped to the tabletop, thundering, "What means this unseemly intrusion, Rod Gallowglass? Get thee hence, till the Queen shall summon thee!"

"I would prefer not to come before her Majesty in chain—" his words cold and clipped. "And I will not allow that a nobleman of the highest rank be clapped in a common, noisome dungeon with rats and thieves."

"*Thou* wilt not allow!" Catharine gasped, outraged; and, "Who art thou to allow or not allow?" roared Brom. "Thou hast not even gentle blood!"

"Then I must think that blood is opposed to action," Rod snapped.

He flung the table out of his way and advanced on the Queen. "I had thought you noble." The word was a sneer. "But now I see that you will turn against your very family, even to one near as nigh you as a father! Certes, if you would fight any of your nobles, you must needs fight a kinsman; but your very uncle? Fie, woman! Were he the foulest murderer, you had ought to receive him with courtesy and the honor due his station. Your finest chamber you should appoint his cell; 'tis but your duty to blood!"

He backed her up against the fireplace, glowering deep into her eyes. "Nay, were he but a murderer, no doubt you would receive him with all honor! But no, he has committed the heinous crime of objecting to your high-handed, arbitrary laws, and the further calumny of maintaining his honor against your calculated insults. He will insist on being accorded the respect due a man during the reign of a vindictive, childish, churlish chit of a girl who hath the title of a Queen but none of the graces, and for this he must needs be damned!"

"Fie, sirrah," she quavered, waxen pale, "that you would speak so to a lady!"

"Lady!" he snorted.

"A lady born!" It was a forlorn, desperate cry. "Will you, too, desert me? Will you speak with the tongue of Clovis?"

"I may speak like a peasant, but you act like one! And now I see why all desert you; for you would whip to scorn Loguire, who alone of all your lords is loyal!"

"Loyal!" she gasped. "He, who leads the rebels?"

"*Anselm* Loguire leads the rebels! For keeping faith with you, the old Duke is now deposed in favor of his son!"

He smiled bitterly as the horror and guilt dawned in her, then turned his back upon her and stepped away, giving her time to realize the breadth of her betrayal. He heard a long-drawn, shuddering breath behind him; Brom rushed past him to aid his Queen. He heard a chair creak as Brom made her sit.

Looking up, he saw the Lord Mayor staring past him wide-eyed. Rod cleared his throat; the burgher's eyes shifted to him. Rod jerked his head toward the door. The Mayor glanced back at the Queen, hesitating. Rod toyed with the hilt of his dagger. The Mayor saw, blanched, and fled.

Rod turned back to the stricken girl.

Brom, at her elbow, threw Rod a glance of withering hatred and growled, "Ha' done! Have you not cut deep enough?"

"Not yet." Rod's lips thinned. He stepped up to the Queen again, his voice cold. "This good nobleman, the Duke Loguire, your own uncle, out of love for you stood against the whole of your nobility, *even his own son!*" His voice crackled. Her eyes jerked up to him, filling with dread. "And it is your doing, by your high-handed lawmaking and utter lack of diplomacy, that Anselm turned against his father. He had two sons, and you have robbed him of both!"

She shook her head, faster and faster, lips shaping silent denials.

"Yet still he is loyal!" Rod murmured. "Still he is loyal, though they would have slain him for it—and damn near did!"

She stared in horror.

Rod tapped his shoulder. "This took the dagger that would have pierced his heart. And even at that, 'twas only by a miracle, and the help of one of the witches whom you scarce acknowledge, that I managed to bring him out alive!"

Brom's head snapped up, searching Rod's face for something. Rod frowned, and went on.

"But bring him out I did, at peril of my life, and brought him safely back. And what do I find? He is to be held a prisoner! And not even as befits a royal prisoner! No, not to be treated with due courtesy and deference, but as a common cutpurse, in a lightless, damp, dank dungeon!"

He paused for effect, rather proud of the last bit of alliteration.

But he had overdone it a bit; she rallied. Her chin came up, and she sniffled back some tears. "Before my laws, sirrah, all are equal!"

"Yes," Rod agreed, "but that should mean you treat a peasant like a lord, not that you treat a lord like a peasant!"

He leaned over her, his face an inch from hers. "Tell me, Queen: why is it that Catharine must treat all with contempt?"

It was a lie; she didn't treat all with contempt, just the noblemen; but anguish and sudden self-doubt showed in her eyes.

Still she tilted her chin a fraction of an inch higher, and declaimed, "I am the Queen, and all must bow to my power!"

"Oh, they bow, they bow! Until you slap them in the face; then they slap back!"

He turned away, glowering at the hearth. "And I can't say I blame them, when you deprive them of liberty."

Catharine stared. "Liberty? What talk is this, sirrah? I seek to give the serfs greater liberty!"

"Aye, so you seek." Rod smiled sourly. "But how do you go about giving it? You gather all ever more tightly unto you. You deprive them today, that you may give them more later!"

He slammed his fist onto the arm of her chair. "But later will never come, don't you see that? There is too much ill in the land, there will always be another evil to fight, and the Queen's word must be law unquestioned to command the army against the evil."

He drew his hand back slowly, eyes burning. "And so it will never come, the day that you set them free; in your land, none will have liberty, save the Queen."

He locked his hands behind his back and paced the room. "There is only just so much of it to go around, you know—this liberty. If one man is to have more, another must needs have less; for if one is to command, another must obey."

He held his hand before her, slowly tightening it into a fist. "So little by little, you steal it away, till your slightest whim is obeyed. You will have complete freedom, to do whatever you wish, but you alone will be free. There will be none of this liberty left over for your people. All, all, will be gathered unto Catharine."

His hand loosened and clasped her throat lightly. She stared and swallowed, pressing against the back of the chair.

"But a man cannot live without at least a little liberty," he said softly. "They must have it, or die." His hand tightened slowly. "They will rise up against you, made one by their common enemy—you. And then will squeeze their liberties out of you again, slowly, slowly."

Catharine tore at his hand, fighting for breath. Brom leaped to free her, But Rod loosed her first.

"They will hang you from your castle gates," he murmured, "and the nobles will rule in your stead; your work will all be undone. And of this you may be certain, for thus was it ever with tyrants."

Her head jerked up, hurt deep in her eyes. She gasped for breath to speak, shaking her head in ever harder denial.

"No, not I," she finally rasped. "Not that, no! Never a tyrant!"

"Always a tyrant," Rod corrected gently, "from your birth. Always a tyrant to those about you, though you never knew it till now."

He turned away, hands locked behind his back. "But now you know, and know also that you have none to blame but yourself for rebellion. You pushed them and pushed them, harder and harder, your nobles— for the good of your people, you said."

He looked back over his shoulder. "But was it not also to see which among them would dare say you nay? To see which among them were men?"

Contempt curdled her face. "Men!" The word was obscenity. "There are no men in Gramarye any more, only boys, content to be a woman's playpretties!"

He smiled, one-sided. "Oh, there be men still. Men in the South, and men in the House of Clovis—or one, at least, there. Men, my Queen, but gentle men, loving their Queen, and loath to strike at her."

Her lids lowered, the contempt playing over her lips in a smile. "It is as I have said: there are no men in Gramarye more."

"They are men," Rod answered, very quietly, "and they march north to prove it."

She stared.

Then slowly sat back. "Well, then, they march north, and I shall meet them on Breden Plain. Yet still there is none among them I would call man. Beasts, every one."

"Oh, you shall meet them." Rod gave her a syrupy, mocking smile. "And what shall you use for an army? And who will command it?"

"I will command," she replied hautily, "I and Brom. And there be five hundred of the Queen's Guard, and seven hundred of the Queen's Army, and threescore knights at my manors."

"Sixty knights!" Rod's lips tightened, pulling down at the corners. "Not even enough to give the Southern knights entertainment for one full charge! Sixty knights out of how many hundreds in your kingdom? And all the rest arrayed there against you! And twelve hundred footmen against the rebels's thousands!"

Her hands seized the arms of the chair in a spasm, to hide their trembling; fear drained her face of its color.

"We shall win, for the honor of Plantagenet or Gramarye, or die nobly."

"I have yet," Rod said tightly, "to see a noble death in battle. They're all just a little on the messy side."

"Be still!" she snapped, then closed her eyes and bowed her head, knuckles whitening on the chair arms.

She rose, proud and calm again, and Rod couldn't help a brief, admiring thought for her spunk.

She sat at the table, drew up parchment and quill, scribbled a moment, then folded the parchment and held it out to Rod. "Bear this to my Uncle Loguire," she said. " 'Tis a command that he appear here before me, and a warrant of safe-conduct; for I bethink me that I shall need all loyal to me by my side ere greatly long."

Rod took the parchment and crumpled it slowly in his fist.

He flung it into the fire without taking his eyes from Catharine. "You shall write a letter to the Duke, and I shall bear it," he said in an antarctic voice; "but in it you shall beg of him the courtesy of an audience."

Her back stiffened and her chin came up. Rod warmed his voice hastily, smiling. "Come, come, my Queen! You already have all the liberty; can you not expend a little in courtesy?"

His eyes darkened, the smile faded. "Or will you be swept by the sin of pride, and allow your liberty to become license?"

He stepped a little closer, towering over her. "Will your people pay the price of your pride, my Queen? Or will you?"

She glared back at him a moment, but something inside her was clamoring for attention. She dropped her eyes and sat quiet a moment, then turned to the table again and wrote.

She folded the letter, sealed it, and held it out to him.

He took it, bowed a little too deeply, with a click of the heels, and turned for the door.

He caught a quick scurry of movement along the baseboard out of the corner of his eye. He turned, saw a mouse duck under the tapestry, where it stayed very still.

Rod's jaw tightened. He crossed the room in two strides, lifted the tapestry.

The mouse looked up at him, its eyes very wide, very green, and very intelligent.

"I do not appreciate eavesdroppers," Rod said coldly.

The mouse flinched, but stared back defiantly.

Rod frowned at a sudden thought. Then his stern look melted. He picked the mouse up, gently, held it level with his eyes, with a tender look that did a very nice job of negating any image of dignity he might have built up.

He shook his head slowly. "You didn't really think I'd need help in here, did you?"

The mouse lowered its eyes, whiskers twitching a little.

"Certes," murmured Catharine, "methinks the man is possessed."

"Your Majesty," Brom said with a musing tone and a gleam in his eye, "may speak more truth than she knows."

The drawbridge echoed hollowly under Rod's striding feet. He ran lightly down the slope, away from the castle, and slipped into a copse of spruce.

"Fess," he called softly.

"Here, Rod." The great black steel horse came through the trees.

Rod smiled, slapped the metal side affectionately. "How the hell'd you know I'd come here?"

"Quite simply, Rod. An analysis of your behavior patterns, coupled with the fact that this grove is the closest to—"

"Skip it," Rod growled. "Big Tom took Loguire to the House of Clovis?"

"Affirmative, Rod."

Rod nodded. "Under the circumstances, it's probably the safest place for the Duke. What a comedown for a nobleman."

He swung into the saddle, then fumbled in his doublet and brought out the little mouse. It looked up at him apprehensively.

"Well," he sighed, "it doesn't seem to make any difference what I tell you to do; you're going to go right ahead and do whatever you want anyway."

The mouse lowered its eyes, trying to look guilty and ashamed; but its whiskers quivered with delight.

It rubbed its cheek against the skin of his palm.

"Affection will get you nowhere," Rod growled. "Now, listen. You go to the House Of Clovis; that's where I'm bound. That's an order."

The mouse looked up at him with wide, innocent eyes.

"And it's one order I can be sure you'll obey," Rod went on, "since it's what you were going to do anyway. But, look!" A note of anxiety crept into his voice. "Be careful, will ya?"

He brought his hand forward and kissed the mouse's nose, very gently.

The mouse leaped, wriggled with delight, dancing gleeful on his hand; as it danced, it reared up, its front paws stretching and broadening into wings. Its tail fanned out; feathers sprouted on its body; its nose blurred and became a beak, and a wren was dancing on Rod's hand.

Rod caught his breath. "Uh . . . yeah," he said

after a while. "That's just a little hard to take the first time I watch it happen. But don't worry, I'll get used to it."

The bird hopped from his hand, few once around his head, hovered in front of him, then sprang arrowing into the sky.

Rod looked after the wren, murmured, "Do you think she'll do what I tell her this time, Fess?"

"She will." There was a strange quality to the robot's voice.

Rod looked sidewise at the great black head. "Thought robots couldn't laugh."

"A misconception," Fess replied.

"Git." Rod knocked his heels against the steel sides. Fess leaped into his long, steel canter.

"What else could I do?" Rod growled.

"With that lady," Fess answered, "nothing. But have no regrets, Rod. It's excellent policy. Many kings have used it."

"Yes," Rod mused. "And after all, being obeyed is the important thing, isn't it?"

Fess galloped silently into the moonlit courtyard on rubber-padded hooves and stopped abruptly. Rod's chest slammed against the horse's neck.

"Whuff!" He slammed back into the saddle. "Ohhhh! My tailbone! Look, Fess, warn me before you pull a stunt like that, will ya? Inertia may be just a nuisance to you, but it hits me right where I live."

"Where is that, Rod?"

"Never mind," Rod growled, dismounting. "Suffice to say that I just learned why the cavalry used split saddles."

He crossed the courtyard, glancing at the moon as he went. It was low in the sky; dawn was not far off.

He pounded on the door. There was a rustle of

movement inside, then the door opened. The gnarled, bent figure of the Mocker stood before him.

"Aye, milord?" he said with a snaggle-toothed grin.

Wouldn't do to let him know that Rod knew he was the power behind the throne. Rod stepped in through the door, scarcely noticing the little man's presence. "Take me to the Lord Loguire, fellow."

"Certes, milord." The Mocker scurried around Rod and opened the inner door. Rod passed through it, pulling off his gauntlets . . . and stepped into the middle of a semicircle of beggars and thieves, standing three deep and armed with truncheons and knives.

They grinned, their eyes hungry; here and there one licked his lips.

Their faces were dirty and scarred, mutilated, and festering with sores; their clothes were threadbare, patched, torn; but their knives were remarkably well-kept.

Rod tucked his gloves into his belt, hands stiffening into karate swords, and turned to the Mocker. That worthy was now flanked by five or six prime samples of the lees of society.

"I come here in friendship." Rod's face was immobile.

"Do ye, now?" The Mocker grinned, exposing bleeding gums, and cackled. Suddenly his eyes gleamed with hate. "Declare yourself, lordling!"

Rod frowned. "Declare myself how?"

"For the noblemen, for the Queen, or for the House of Clovis!"

"Be done with your blathering!" Rod snapped. "I have small stomach for nonsense, and I'm beginning to feel very full. Take me to Loguire, *now!*"

"Oh, aye, that we shall. Yes, milord, at once, milord, straightaway." He rubbed his hands, chortling with glee. Then his glance darted over Rod's shoulder, and he nodded.

Rod started to turn, but something exploded on the back of his head. Stars reeled about him, then blackness.

Slowly, Rod became aware of pink light, pain, and a thousand discordant bass fiddles tuning up inside his head.

Slower yet, he became aware of something cold and slimy against his cheek. The pink light, he realized, was sunlight filtered through closed eyelids.

Th pain pulled itself in and concentrated in his head. He winced, then by heroic measures managed to open his eyes, and winced again.

Everything was blurred, out of focus, sunlight and blobs of color.

The slime under his cheek was moss, and the coldness beneath it was stone.

He shoved hard with his hands; the slimy surface swung away, left him reeling, leaning on his hands heavily, stomach churning.

He shook his head, flinched at the pain, and blinked several times. His lids rasped over gummy eyeballs, but slowly his vision cleared. He forced his eyes to focus on . . . the face of Tuan Loguire.

Tuan sat with his back against black, old stone. There were huge iron staples in the stone, and the chains that hung from them ran to manacles on Tuan's wrists and ankles. He sat in a heap of dirty, moldering straw, in the watery light of a weak sunbeam.

Tuan smiled with irony as heavy as the rusty chains on his body, and lifted a hand in greeting, chain jangling with the movement. "Welcome."

Rod turned his eyes away, looking about him. The old Duke sat against the next wall, chained beside his son. "Cold welcome, Rod Gallowglass," the old lord mumbled, face heavy and brooding. "It is scant safety your serving-man has brought me to."

Treachery! Rod should have known better than to trust Tom. "Big Tom, you . . . !"

"Here, master."

Rod looked, turning; Big Tom sat against the far wall, chained like the rest of them.

Tom smiled sadly, bent a reproachful, bloodhound-eyed look on his master. "I had thought you would free us, master. Yet here art thou, chained one amongst us."

Rod scowled, looked down at his wrist, A rusty, thick iron band circled it. It had mates on his ankle and other wrist.

He looked up at Tom, smiled, and raised his hand, giving the chain a shake. "Ever hear tell that stone walls don't make a prison?"

"Who spoke those words was a fool," said Tom bitterly, from the shadows.

Rod lifted his eyes to the small, barred window set high in the wall. It was the only light in the room, a chamber perhaps ten feet wide by fifteen long, with a ten foot high ceiling, all moss-grown, rotting stone, floored with moldering straw.

The only decoration was a skeleton, held together by mummified ligament, chained to the wall like themselves.

Rod eyed the silent partner warily. "Not such great housekeepers, are they? They could at least have lugged the bones into the nether room."

He turned to the window again. "Fess," he mumbled, low enough so the others couldn't make out the words. "Fess, where are you?"

"In the most filthy, broken-down stable I've ever seen," the robot answered, "along with five of the sorriest nags outside of a glue factory. I think we're supposed to be the cavalry of the House of Clovis, Rod.''

Rod chuckled softly. "Any mice with large green eyes running around, Fess?"

"No, Rod, but there is a wren perched on my head."

Rod grinned. "Ask her if she has any power over cold iron."

"How am I to speak with her, Rod?"

"Broadcast on human thought-wave frequency, of course! She's a telepath, you idiot savant!"

"Rod, I strongly resent the derogatory connotions of references to my abilities in areas in which I am not programmed to—"

"All right, all right, I'm sorry, I repent! You're a genius, a prodigy, an Einstein, an Urth! Just ask her, will you?"

There was a pause; then Rod heard a faint series of chirpings in the background.

"What's the chirping, Fess?"

"Gwendylon, Rod. She reacted significantly to the novel experience of telepathy with a horse."

"You mean she almost fell off her perch. But did she say anything?"

"Of course, Rod. She says that now she is certain you're a warlock."

Rod groaned and rolled his eyes up to the ceiling. "Look, get her back to business, will you? Can she get us out of these chains and cut the bars on our window?"

There was another pause; then Fess answered, "She says she has no power over cold iron, Rod, nor has any witch or elf that she knows. She suggests a blacksmith, but fears it is impractical."

"Genesis, Exodus, Leviticus . . . Well, tell her I'm glad she hasn't lost her sense of humor. And ask her how the hell she's going to get us out of here!"

"She says there is no need for hard language, Rod."

"You didn't have to transmit me literally, you bumblebrain!"

"And she thinks that the Prince of the Elves may be able to free you. She thinks he will come, but he is some short distance away, so it may be a while."

"I thought she said elves couldn't handle cold iron!"

There was another pause; then Fess said, "She says that the Prince of the Elves is not quite an elf, Rod, being but half of the Old Blood."

"Only half . . . Wait a minute!" Rod scowled. "You mean he's a half-breed between elf and mortal?"

"Precisely, Rod."

Rod tried to imagine how an eighteen-inch elf and a six-foot mortal could have a child; his brain reeled.

"She departs now, Rod, to summon him, and will return as quickly as she may, but will be a while. She bids you be of stout heart."

"If my heart were any stouter, it'd be positively obese! Give her my . . . No, just tell her I thank her, Fess."

He seemed to hear a faint sigh behind his ear, and the robot said, with a touch of resignation, "I'll tell her, Rod."

"Thanks, Fess. Stay lively."

Rod turned back to his prison. The Loguires were both plastered against the wall, looking at him strangely.

"He speaks to thin air," murmured Tuan. "Certes, the man is possessed!"

"Seems to me I've heard that before," Rod mused, "and the air in here is anything but thin."

"Still," muttered Loguire, " 'tis the act of one crazed!"

Big Tom rumbled a laugh. "Not so, my lords. This man speaks with spirits."

Rod smiled bleakly. "How come so cheerful all of a sudden, Big Tom?"

The big man stretched, chains clashing. "I had thought for a moment they had beaten you, master. Now I know 'twas fool thinking."

"Don't be so sure, Tom. Cold iron is a tough spell to break."

"Nay, master." Tom's eyelids drooped lazily. "Thou'lt find a way to it, I warrant."

He clasped his hands over his belly, leaned his head back against the wall.

Rod smiled as Tom began snoring. He looked at the Loguires and jerked his head toward Tom. "There's confidence for you. While I work things out, he takes a nap."

"Let us hope 'tis a faith warranted," said Tuan. He eyed Rod dubiously.

"Let's," Rod echoed grimly.

He nodded at the Duke. "Been renewing acquaintance?"

Loguire smiled. "I rejoice to see my son again, though I had lief it were more open welcome."

Tuan frowned at his hands. "It is sad news he hath brought me, Rod Gallowglass, most sad and sorrowful." He looked at Rod, bright anger in his face. "I had known my brother hateful and ambitious, but I had not thought he would sink into treason."

"Oh, don't be too hard on the poor boy." Rod leaned back against the wall, closing his eyes wearily. "Durer's got him spellbound. And if his magic came so close on the father, how could it fail on the son?"

"Aye," Tuan agreed darkly. "Myself had fallen like prey to the Mocker."

"Oh?" Rod opened one eye. "You've realized that, have you?"

"Oh, aye! A most excellent villain is that! He will

bow him most humbly before you, while his henchman is slitting your purse—and thus hath he served me!"

Rod pursed his lips. "He's the one who gave you the idea for organizing the beggars?"

"Aye." Tuan nodded heavily. "I had first thought only to provide them relief from hunger and chill; but his word in my ear made me think of an army, for defense of the Queen. And I had seen and heard in the South that which led me to think such an army might well be needed."

The old Duke made a choking sound.

"Pardon, my father," said Tuan, bowing his head, "but I knew even thou couldst not check them forever. But I had not thought"—and his voice hardened—"'twould be treason from Anselm."

Rod twisted, feeling decidedly uncomfortable. "Well, as I said, you shouldn't blame him too much. After all, he did try to keep Durer from killing your father."

He stretched his legs and crossed them. "So when the Mocker learned that the South was up in arms, he decided it was time to assert his rightful authority and overthrow the Queen. Right?"

"Aye." Tuan's lips tightened as though he had his first taste of straight vermouth. "When I spoke against, saying that 'twas our time to defend the Queen, he called me traitor, and"—he frowned, words coming very hard—"one of the beggars would ha' slain me. But the Mocker would not hear of it; no, he threw me here without food or fire."

He looked up at Rod, frowning. "Which is most truly strange, Rod Gallowglass. Would not you ha' thought he would ha' killed me himself?"

"No." Rod closed his eyes, shaking his head. "He needs somebody to be figurehead king after they've pulled down Catharine."

"Nay, not a king," Tuan said, brooding. "He cries that we shall ne'er have a king more, but only a sort of chieftain, raised by acclaim of the people."

" 'A sort of chieftain.' " Rod scowled. "What name does he call this chieftain by?"

"Dictator." Tuan chewed at the inside of his cheek. "A most strange title. There shall be no nobles or king, only the dictator. In all truth, most strange."

Rod's mouth tightened with sourness. "Not so strange as all that. But you don't mean to say the beggars think they can take the castle?"

"Nay, but it is known that the South is in arms, and Catharine was never one to be waiting till the battle was brought to her."

"Oh." Rod chewed that one over. "You mean the Mocker's pretty sure she'll march south to meet them?"

"Most assuredly. And the Mocker will march south behind her."

Rod nodded. "So when the armies join battle, the beggars will attack the royal forces from the rear."

"Ever their way," rumbled Loguire.

Tuan nodded agreement. "And caught between two forces, her armies will last scarce half an hour."

"And what does the Mocker propose to do about the councillors and noblemen after the battle's over? Durer means to make your brother king."

"So it would seem," Tuan agreed, "but the Mocker hath an answer to that, and to all the noblemen."

"Oh?" Rod raised an eyebrow.

"Aye, 'Tis a tube of metal fitted into a crossbow stock, nothing more; but it throws a ball of lead which can pierce the stoutest armor."

"And he means to put one of these into the hands of every man in the army?"

"Oh, nay." Tuan frowned. "He hath but the five of

them, one for himself, one for each of his three lieutenants, and one for his fourth lieutenant.'' Tuan jerked his head toward Tom's recumbent mountain form. ''But that one hath lately fallen into disfavor. He assures us the five tubes shall answer for the full force of noblemen and councillors.''

But Rod was staring at Tom. ''Big Tom?'' He gulped. ''A lieutenant?''

''Aye.'' Tuan frowned. ''Did you not know he was of Clovis?''

Tom opened one hound's eye and looked back at Rod.

Rod looked away, cleared his throat, and pursed his lips. ''Well, ah, that does explain a few things.''

He switched his eyes back to Tom. ''So you're part of the Inner Circle?''

Big Tom smiled sourly and held up one lumber forearm. The chain clashed and rattled. ''Was,'' he said.

''He stood against them,'' rumbled Loguire, ''stood against his fellows and this—how do you name him? The Mocker—stood against the Mocker and his three jackals when they commanded I be 'prisoned with my son. 'Nay,' quoth your man Tom, 'I must needs take him back to my master, where he will be aid to your plans.' 'The plans are changed,' quoth they, and would not hear of enlarging me; and then your man Tom, here, fought cheek by jowl at my side, and accounted for a most goodly number of them.'' This last was said in a tone of surprised respect.

Tom grinned, and Rod saw with a shock that one tooth was missing from the big man's smile. ''Thou art braw brawler tha'self,'' Tom chuckled. ''I ha' not thought gentlemen could fight so well without armor or sword.''

Rod peered into the shadows at Tom's end of the room and saw that the big man's eye was swollen and purple; also, there was a slash with a new scab across one lumpy cheek.

He sat back, smiling on one side of his face. "How many heads did you bash in, Big Tom?"

"Scarce a round score," Tom replied with disgust. "I had but this one stalwart gentleman to guard my back, and there were too many for us."

Rod grinned, wondering if Loguire knew just how deeply he had been complimented.

He stretched, yawned. "Well, that pretty well brings us up to date. Anybody got a poker deck?"

The two Loguires frowned, puzzled; but a flicker of recognition passed in Big Tom's eyes.

Rod smiled sourly at the big peasant, and Tom's face turned wooden. He stared back at Rod.

"Oh, come on now, Tom!" Rod snapped. "Your secret's official knowledge now. No more point to playing games, is there?"

Tom glowered at him; then slowly, his face livened again, to a brooding, meditative look.

He leaned back against the wall, half closing his eyes. "Aye, tha hast the right of it, as when hast thou not?"

With a sinking feeling, Rod began to realize that Big Tom saw him as more than just an employer, or a piece in the game.

"My lot is cast with thee now," said Tom, "whether I would have it or no; so wherefore should I dissemble?"

"Dissemble?" Rod cocked an eyebrow at his serving-man. "Pretty high-falutin' vocabulary for a simple peasant, Big Tom."

Tom waved a hand impatiently. "Be done with your

games! I am unmasked; do me the courtesy to take off your own.''

Rod froze.

Then, slowly, he smiled. ''You're quicker than the average ursine, Big Tom. How long have you known?''

The Loguires stared, totally lost.

Big Tom gave a short bark of laughter. ''Why, master, since first you used judo on me!''

''Ah.'' Rod's eyebrows lifted. ''From the first, then? So that's why you wangled the batman job.''

Tom smiled lazily.

''Under orders?''

Tom nodded.

Rod lowered his eyes, studying the chain on his wrist.

''What are you, master?''

''A warlock.'' Rod winced inside; but it was the best answer under the circumstances.

Big Tom spat. ''Games, master, games! 'Twas yourself said to be done with 'em! You are not of the councillors, else you would not ha' stolen the Lord Loguire away from them; and you are not of the House, or I would ha' known you of old. What are you, then?''

''A warlock,'' Rod repeated. ''A new player in the game, Big Tom, and one who stands squarely behind the Queen. X, the unknown factor in the councillors' and Clovis' equations, here by pure happenstance and coincidence.''

''Warruh!'' Big Tom spat again. ''I ha' small faith in happenstance, master. I ha' known that you back the Queen; may I ask who stands behind you?''

''Strange manner of talk,'' growled Loguire, angering, ''for a footman to his lord.''

Rod smiled bleakly. ''A most strange footman, my lord.''

"Aye, and a most strange lord," Tom snarled. "Who backs you, Rod Gallowglass?"

Rod studied the big man, then shrugged. The word would mean nothing to the Loguires, and Tom was on his side now anyway.

"SCENT," he answered.

Tom stared; then, almost whispering, he said, "I ha' thought the last of them were dead." He swallowed, bit his lip. "Eh, but tha'rt alive. Tha might be a ghost, but nay; tha'rt alive, or the witch would scarce be so fond of thee. I ha' heard ye were dispersed, after ye won; but nay, I ought to ha' known. 'Twas secret, and secret from all, mayhap; but thou lived."

"Won?" Rod frowned.

And was answered by a frown of even deeper perplexity from Tom.

Then the big man's face cleared. He grinned, rocking back against the wall, and roared laughter.

The Loguires stared from him to Rod, who spread his hands, shaking his head. They looked back at Tom, wiping his eyes and eking the remains of his laugh into chuckles. "Eh, eh, now I see it, aye, now, and fool that I was not to see it before. What age art thou, master?"

"Age?" Rod scowled. "Thirty-two. Why?"

"Nay, nay!" Tom shook his head impatiently. "What age are thou *from?*"

Rod's mouth formed a round, silent O as the light dawned. "It *was* a time machine!"

Big Tom's face froze as he realized the implications of Rod's answer.

"And," Rod pressed, "there's another one hidden in this building, isn't there?"

"Enough!" Big Tom snapped, and his eyes were very cold. "You know too much already, Rod Gallowglass."

Fear gathered in Rod's belly and crawled up his spine

as he saw chill, amoral murder come into the man's eyes.

"Big Tom." He cleared his throat, spoke in a swift, driving monotone. "Big Tom, your own kind have turned against you now. You owe them no allegiance; and the wrongs they said they'd fix, I can fix, too. Go back to them, and they'll kill you. I won't, you know that."

The annihilation ebbed from Tom's eyes, the huge body relaxed.

"Nay," Tom growled, "thou hast right again, though not in the way tha knowest. They ha' but bottled me up for now, till the great deeds are done; but they will hale me forth again, for I am too costly a man to discard so lightly. But tha'rt right they will slay me—in a year, two years, or five, when my office is done. And I do wish to live."

Rod raised an eyebrow skeptically. "They don't doubt your loyalty?"

Big Tom chuckled deeply. "They ha' no need to, master. I disagree only on means, not on goals. But I disagree, and for that, soon or late, they will slay me."

"Rod," said in a quiet voice that only he could hear.

Rod held up a hand. "Hold it! Late news on the Rialto!"

"Rod, the Prince of the Elves has arrived. He is leading a squad of elves toward your cell." There was a touch of laughter to the robot's voice.

"All right, what's so funny?" Rod muttered.

"You have a surprise in store, Rod."

Two gnarled, bent, white-bearded figures scurried up to the window. Rod frowned.

"Fess, those are gnomes, not elves."

"Gnomes? Oh, yes, metal-working elves. Purely semantics, Rod. They are still incapable of dealing with iron."

The gnomes pulled out a hammer and cold chisel with a faint bronze sheen, then stepped back and handed them to a larger, darker figure that blocked out the sunlight.

The Loguires, chained under the window, craned their necks backward to try to see as the first blow sounded.

Big Tom frowned. "There be something that pricks at my memory about that form at the window. Ah, for light, to see his face!"

Rod frowned. "What's so great about his face? Probably pretty ugly."

Tom gave a toothy grin. " 'Twould be excellent fine to tell my children, good master, if I should live long enough to sire them. No mortal has yet looked upon the faces of the royalty of the Elves, though they are said to be aged past believing. They are . . . uh . . . ah . . . mmmmmm!"

Tom's head lolled forward; he began to snore.

Two other snores answered him. Turning, Rod saw the Loguires, chins on their chests, sleeping blissfully.

Rod stared.

A metal bar dropped from the window and bounced on the floor. The ends were sheered through.

Rod whistled. This Prince of the Elves might be old, but he certainly wasn't languishing—not if he could still cut through inch-thick iron with nothing but a cold chisel and a mallet.

The third bar fell down. There was a scrabbling sound, and the squat, broad form shot through the window and leaped to the floor.

Rod stared, squeezed his eyes shut, and shook his head. Then he looked again, and understood why Tom and the Loguires had suddenly dozed off.

He swallowed, fought for composure, and smiled. "Well met, Brom O'Berin."

"At your service." The little man bowed, smiling maliciously. "I owe you a rap on the head, Master Gallowglass, for the way that you spoke to the Queen: a rap on the head, or great thanks, I know not which."

He turned to the window and called softly in a strange, fluid tongue. The cold chisel arced through the air and fell to his feet. He reached up and caught the hammer as it dropped.

"Now, then." He dropped to his knees and pressed Rod's forearm flat against the floor. "Stir not, or thou'lt have a gouge out of thy wristbone." He set the chisel against the first link of chain and tapped lightly with the hammer. The link fell off, sheared through. Brom grunted and moved to Rod's other side.

"Thou'lt wear bracelets when I've done," he grumbled, "but no chains. The manacles must wait till we're at the castle smithy."

"Uh . . . that's pretty hard bronze you've got there," Rod ventured, watching the chisel slide through the iron.

"Most hard," Brom agreed, attacking the ankle chains. "An old recipe, known long in my family."

"Uh . . . in your family?"

"Aye." Brom looked up. "There were elves in lost Greece, too, Rod Gallowglass. Didst thou not know?"

Rod didst not; but he didn't figure this was the time to mention it.

He stood up, free of the chains at least, and watched Brom cutting the others loose. The Prince of the Elves bit explained a lot about Brom: his size and bulk, for one thing.

"Never knew you were royalty, Brom."

"Hm?" Brom looked back over his shoulder. "I would have thought thou'd have guessed it. Why else am I named as I am?"

He turned back to his work. Rod frowned. Name?

What did that have to do with anything? Brom? O'Berin? He couldn't see the connection.

"There, the last," said Brom, cutting through Big Tom's foot shackle. "Do thou now lend me aid of thine shoulder, Master Gallowglass."

He jumped back out through the window. Rod got a shoulder in Tom's midriff and, staggering, somehow manhandled him over to the window as a rope flew through.

Rod tied it under Tom's arms, threw the loose end out, and called "Heave!"

He heard Brom grunt, and marveled again at the little man's muscles as Big Tom moved jerkily up the wall, still snoring happily.

What with the beerbelly and the muscles, and the minimal size of the window, Big Tom was a tight fit.

"Why don't you just wake him and let him shove himself out?" Rod grunted as he shoved at Tom's ample rear.

"I have no wish for my office to be known among mortals," came Brom's muffled reply.

The window now framed only Tom's sizable posterior and sequoia shanks. Rod eyed the former, weighing the merits of a well-placed kick, and decided against it.

"So, why'd you let me stay awake?" he grunted as he pushed.

"One amongst you must needs aid me with the others," answered Brom, but Rod had a notion that wasn't quite the whole story.

He left off the questions, however, until his cellmates were deposited on the ground outside the window. Tuan's shoulders had proved even more of an obstacle than Tom's belly; they had to back him up, feed his hands through in front of his head, while Rod wondered fleetingly about brachiator ancestry.

Then Brom hauled Rod out, muttering something about the fish being undersized these days. Rod snarled a return compliment as he gained his feet, then bowed double, putting his head on Brom's level.

"And what's that for?" Brom growled.

"For belting," Rod answered. "You owe me a rap on the head, remember?"

The dwarf chuckled, clapped him on the shoulder. "Nay, lad; you did only that which I should ha' done myself years ago; but I had never the heart. But come now, we must away."

Brom caught up Tuan's midsection. The gnomes took his shoulders and feet, and bore him away toward the ruined fountain in the center of the courtyard.

More gnomes materialized out of the stonework and tucked their shoulders under Big Tom.

Rod shook his head wonderingly, and stooped to sling Loguire over a shoulder.

Brom fumbled with a stone at the fountain's base and pulled it away to disclose the dark mouth of a small tunnel three feet in diameter.

Rod tapped Brom on the shoulder. "Wouldn't this be a little easier if we woke them first?"

Brom stared, scandalized; then his face darkened. "We go to Elfland, Master Gallowglass! And no mortal may journey there and remember it!"

"I have."

"Well, truth," Brom admitted, turning back to the Tuan problem, "but then thou'rt not so mortal as some. Thou'rt a warlock." He disappeared into the burrow.

Rod started to reply, then thought better of it. He contented himself with a few grunted remarks about discrimination and a report to the Human Rights Commission as he lugged Loguire into the tunnel.

Two gnomes started to swing the stone back into place, but Rod stopped them with an upraised hand.

"Fess," he murmured, looking at the stable, "we're on our way. Get out of that hole and meet me at the castle."

There was a moment's silence; then a crash and the sound of splintering wood came from the stables. The door crashed open, and the great black horse came trotting out into the morning sunlight, head held high, mane streaming.

Heads popped out of slit-windows in the inn as a bleary-eyed hostler came stumbling out of the stable in Fess's wake, screaming for the horse to stop.

"Come on, get moving!" Rod growled, but instead, Fess stopped and looked back over his shoulder at the hostler.

The youth came running up, shouting, one hand outstretched to grab Fess's bridle.

A great, blue electric spark crackled from Fess's hide to the youth's hand.

The hostler screamed and fell backward, nursing his hand and moaning as he rolled on the cobbles. Fess was off in a swirl and a clatter of hooves.

"Show-off," Rod growled as the horse disappeared.

"Not at all, Rod," came the horse's quiet answer. "Merely providing an instructive object lesson—at low amperage, it shook him up but didn't hurt him—and enhancing your reputation as a warlock."

Rod shook his head slowly. "As if it needed enhancing!"

"Why, Master Gallowglass," one of the gnomes chuckled in a voice strongly reminiscent of a rusty can opener, "wouldst thou have us believe thou'rt *not* a warlock?"

"Yes! Uh, that is, I uh . . ." Rod glanced back at the tunnel. "Warlock? Of course I'm a warlock! Till we get through Elfland, anyway. Shall we go, boys?"

Not so very much later, they sat around the fire in the Queen's council chamber. Catharine had apologized profusely to Loguire, pointedly ignoring Tuan the while; and the amenities over, reverted to type.

Tuan sat to the left of the fireplace, eyes fixed in brooding on the flames.

Catharine sat in the angle of the room, as far from Tuan as possible, with a heavy oak table and Brom O'Berin carefully interposed between.

". . . and that is full standing in the South, my Queen," said Loguire, gnarled hands twisting as he wound up his report, which had abounded in nuances of intrigue that Rod couldn't follow at all. "I am no longer duke; and the rebel lords march already."

Catharine stirred. "Thou shalt be Duke Loguire again," she stated coldly, "when we have beaten these traitors!"

Loguire smiled sadly. "They shall not be easily beaten, Catharine."

" 'Your Majesty'!" she snapped.

" 'Catharine'!" Rod barked.

She glared at him.

He glared back.

Catharine turned haughtily away. "What am I, Brom?"

" 'Your Majesty,' " Brom answered with the ghost of a smile. "But to your uncle, and to his son, your cousin, you must needs be Catharine."

Rod fought down a smile as Catharine sank back in her chair, staring aghast at Brom.

She composed herself, and gave Brom the best et tu, Brute? look in her repertoire. "I had thought you were for me, Brom O'Berin."

"Why, so I am," Brom smiled, "and so is this gyrfalcon, here"—he jerked a thumb toward Rod—"if you would but see it."

Catharine favored Rod with a cold glance. "A gyr-falcon, aye." Her voice hardened. "And what of the poppinjay?"

Tuan's head shot up as though he'd been slapped. He stared at her, appalled, eyes wide with hurt.

Then his mouth tightened, and a crease appeared between his eyebrows.

Some day, Rod thought, *she will push him just a little too far, and that may be the luckiest day of her life–if she lives through it.*

"I am for you," Tuan breathed. "Even now, Catharine my Queen."

She smiled, smug and contemptuous. "Aye, I had known you would be."

Oh, bitch! Rod thought, his fist tightening. *Bitch!*

Catharine noticed the silent motions of his lips.

She smiled archly. "What words do you mumble there, sirrah?"

"Oh, ah, just running through a breath-exercise my old voice-and-diction coach taught me." Rod leaned back against the wall, folding his arms. "But about the rebels, Queenie dear, just what do you propose to do about them?"

"We shall march south," she snapped, "and meet them on Breden Plain!"

"Nay!" Loguire bolted from his chair. "Their force is ten to our one, if not more!"

Catharine glared at her uncle, the corners of her mouth curled into tight little hooks. "We shall not stay to be found like a rat in a crevice!"

"Then," said Rod, "you will lose."

She looked down her nose at him (no mean trick, when she was seated and he was standing). "There is naught of dishonor in that, Master Gallowglass."

Rod struck his forehead and rolled his eyes up.

"What else ought I do?" she sneered. "Prepare for a siege?"

"Well, now that you mention it," said Rod, "yes."

"There is this, too," Tuan put in, his voice flat. "Who shall guard your back 'gainst the House of Clovis?"

Her lip curled. "Beggars!"

"Beggars and cutthroats," Rod reminded her. "With very sharp knives."

"Shall the Queen fear a beggar?" she snapped. "Nay! They are dust at my feet!"

"That which crawls in the dust at your feet is a snake," Brom rumbled, "and its fangs are sharpened, and poisonous."

She caught her lip between her teeth and lowered her eyes, uncertain; then she lifted her chin again, and glared at Tuan.

"So you have armed them against me, and beaten them into an army, ruled and ordered and forged them into a dagger for my back! Most bravely well done, King of Vagabonds!"

Rod's head snapped up. He stared. He turned his head slowly toward Tuan, a strange light in his eyes.

"I will march," said Catharine. "Will you march at my side, my Lord Loguire?"

The old lord bent his head slowly in affirmation. "You play the fool, Catharine, and will die; but I will die with you."

Her composure wavered for a moment; her eyes moistened.

She turned briskly to Brom. "And you, Brom O'Berin?"

The dwarf spread his hands. "Your father's watchdog, milady, and yours."

She smiled fondly.

Then her eyes snapped hard as she looked at Tuan. "Speak, Tuan Loguire."

The youth raised his eyes, very slowly, to the fires. "It is strange," he murmured, "at but twenty-two years of ago, to look back over so very short a time, and see so much folly."

Rod heard a choked gasp from Catharine.

Tuan slapped his thigh. "Well, then, 'tis done; and if I have lived in folly, I might as well die in it."

He turned, his eyes gentle, brooding. "I shall die with you, Catharine."

Her face was ashen. "Folly . . ." she whispered.

"He knows not what wisdom he speaks," Brom growled. He looked over Tuan's shoulder at Rod. "What say you to folly, Rod Gallowglass?"

Rod's eyes slowly focused on Brom's. " 'Wise fool, brave fool,' " he murmured.

Brom frowned. "How say you?"

"I say that we may yet live through this!" Rod grinned, eyes kindling. "Ho, King of the Vagabonds!" He slapped Tuan's shoulder. "If the Mocker and his henchmen were gone, could you sway the beggars to fight for the Queen?"

Tuan's face came alive again. "Aye, assuredly, were they gone!"

Rod's lips pulled back in a savage grin. "They shall be."

The moon was riding high when Rod, Tuan, and Tom darted from the shadow of the tottering wall to the shadow of the ruined fountain in the courtyard of the House of Clovis.

"Thou wouldst make most excellent burglars, thou," growled Big Tom. "I might ha' heard thee a league or three away."

It hadn't been easy to persuade Tom to come along. Of course, Rod had started on the wrong tack; he'd assumed Tom's loyalties to the proletarian idea had died when he was clapped into irons. He'd clapped Tom on the back, saying, "How'd you like a chance to get back at your friends?"

Tom had scowled. "Get back at 'em?"

"Yeah. They booted you out, didn't they? Threw you in the calaboose, didn't they? After your blood now, ain't they?"

Tom chuckled, "Nay, master, not by half! Eh, no! They'd ha' freed me when the trouble was done!"

"Oh." Rod scowled. "I see. Trained men are hard to come by."

Tom's face darkened. "Thou seest too quick for my liking."

"Well, be that as it may . . ." Rod slung an arm around the big man's shoulder, almost dislocating his arm in the process. "Uh, in that case . . . what did they lock you up for?"

Tom shrugged. "Disagreement."

"Ways and means, eh?"

"Aye. They held for attacking Queen and nobles both at one time, though 'twould mean dividing of forces."

"Sounds risky. What did you want to do?"

"Why, to bring down the noblemen and their councillors first, under guise of loyalty to the throne. Then we might slowly woo all the land to the House of Clovis, and, secured by the people, pull down the Queen and Brom O'Berin with two blows of a knife."

Rod swallowed and tried to remember that the man was on his side now. "Very neat." He slapped Tom on the back. "Spoken like a good little Bolshevik. How much does that way of doing things mean to you, Tom?"

Big Tom gave him a long, calculating look. "What price were you minded of, master?"

Rod grinned. "Shall we throw your four colleagues in the cell they'd reserved for you?"

" 'Twould be pleasant," said Tom slowly. "What comes after, master?"

"Why, then," said Rod, "the House of Clovis fights on the Queen's side, against the nobles. That gives you a better chance of beating the councillors and nobles; afterward, you can follow through with your own plan."

Tom nodded, slowly. "But will the beggars fight for the Queen?"

"That, we leave to Tuan Loguire."

Tom's face stretched into a huge grin. He threw back his head and roared, slapping Rod on the back.

Rod picked himself up off the floor, hearing Big Tom gasp between spasms of laughter, "Eh, I should ha' thought of it, master! Aye, that boy will charm them! You know not the powers of that silver tongue, master. The lad could make a leopard believe it had no spots!"

Rod held his peace, trying to remember if he'd seen a leopard on Gramarye, while he tried to rub the sore spot between his shoulders.

"Thou'll twist thine arm loose that way." Tom grinned. He turned Rod around and began to massage his back. "Thou knowest, master, if together we bring down the councillors, 'twill be thy head, alongside Brom's and the Queen's, that I'll next be a-chasing."

Rod closed his eyes, savoring the massage. "It oughta be a great fight. A little further to the left, Big Tom."

So now they stood in the shadows of the fountain with Tuan between them, planning assault on the moldering heap of stone that stood across a moon-filled expanse of courtyard.

Rod counted his pulse beats, wondering if his heart had really slowed that much, until Tom whispered, "No alarm. They ha' not seen us, good masters. Ready thyselves, now."

Tom gathered himself, looking like a diesel semi that had decided to turn cat-burglar.

"Now!" he growled, and ran.

They charged lightly, quietly, through the seeming glare of the moonlight to the welcoming shadow of the walls, then flattened themselves against the stone, hearts thudding, breath held as they strained their ears for some sound of alarm.

After a small eternity of three minutes, Big Tom loosed his breath in a great, gusty sigh.

"Eh, then, lads!" he hissed. "Come along, now."

They crept around the corner of the great dank stone pile. Big Tom splayed his fingers out wide, set his elbow at the corner of the wall, and marked the spot where his second finger ended. He put his other elbow against the mark.

"Big Tom!" Rod called in an agonized whisper, "we don't have time for—"

"Hsst!" Tuan's fingers clamped on Rod's shoulder. "Silence, I pray thee! He measures in cubits!"

Rod shut up, feeling rather foolish.

Tom made a few more measurements, which apparently resulted in his finding what he was looking for. He pulled a pry from the pouch at his belt and began to lever at the base of a three-foot block.

Rod stared, uncomprehending. It would take all night and most of the next day to dig the block out. What was Tom trying to do?

Tom gave a last pry, and caught the sheet of stone as it fell outward. It was perhaps an inch thick.

He laid the slab on the ground and looked up at his companions. His grin flashed chill in the moonlight. "I had thought I might have need of a bolthole one day," he whispered. "Gently now, lads."

He ducked head and arms through the hole, kicked off with his feet, and slithered through.

Rod swallowed hard and followed Tom. Tuan came through at his heels.

"All in?" Tom whispered as Tuan's feet stood hard to the floor, and the moonlight was cut off as Tom fitted the stone plug back into place.

"Light," he whispered. Rod cupped his hand over the hilt of his dagger and turned it on, letting a ray of light escape between two fingers. It was enough to see Big Tom grope up a worm-eaten panel from the floor and fit it back into place in the bolthole.

Tom straightened, grinning. "Now let them wonder at our coming. To work, masters."

He turned away. Rod followed, looking quickly about him.

They were in a large stone room that had once been paneled. The panels were crumbled and fallen away for the most part. The room held only cobwebs, rusty iron utensils, and long trestle tables, spongy now with rot.

" 'Twas a kitchen, once," Tom murmured. "They cook at the hearth in the common room, now. None ha' used this place for threescore years or more."

Rod shuddered. "What's a good kid like you doing in a place like this, Tom?"

Big Tom snorted.

"No, I mean it," said Rod urgently. "You can judge a god, an ideal, by the people who worship it, Tom."

"Be still!" Tom snapped.

"It's true, though, isn't it? The councillors are all rotten, we know that. And the Mocker and his buddies

are lice. You're the only good man in the bunch. Why
don't you—''

"Be still!'' Tom snarled, swinging about so suddenly that Rod blundered into him. Rod felt the huge,
hamlike hand grabbing a fistful of his doublet, right at
the throat, and smelled the beery, garlic reek of Tom's
breath as the man thrust his face close to Rod's.

"And what of the Queen?'' Tom hissed. "What says
she for her gods, eh?''

He let Rod go, with a shove that threw him back
against the wall, and turned away.

Rod collected himself and followed, but not before
he had caught a glimpse of Tuan's eyes, narrowed and
chill with hate, in the beam of the torch.

"We approach a corner,'' Tom muttered. "Dampen
the light.''

The torch winked out; a few moments later, Rod felt
the stone wall fall away under his left hand. He turned,
and saw a faint glow at the end of the blackened, short
hallway ahead.

Big Tom stopped, '' 'Tis a corner again, and a sentry
beyond. Walk wary, lads.''

He moved away again, stepping very carefully. Rod
followed, feeling Tuan's breath hot on the back of his
neck.

As they neared the corner, they heard a rhythm of
faint snores to their right, from the new hallway.

Big Tom flattened himself against the wall with a
wolfish grin. Rod followed suit . . . and drew away
with a gasp and a convulsive shudder.

Tom scowled at him, motioning for silence.

Rod looked at the wall and saw a thick blob of
grayish-white stuff fastened to the wall. It had brushed
the back of his neck, and he could say with authority
that the texture was flaccid, the touch cold and moist.

He looked at the obscene glop and shuddered gain.

" 'Tis but witch-moss, Rod Gallowglass," Tuan whispered in his ear.

Rod frowned. "Witch-moss?"

Tuan stared, incredulous. "Thou'rt a warlock, and knowest not witch-moss?"

Rod was saved from an answer by the cessation of the snores from around the corner.

The trio caught their collective breath and flattened themselves against the wall, Rod carefully avoiding the witch-moss. Tom glared at his sidekicks.

The moment of silence stretched out as thin as the content of a congressman's speech.

"Hold!" shouted a voice from around the corner.

Their muscles snapped tight in a spasm.

"Where do you go at this hour?" the sentry's voice snarled.

Dread clambered its way up Rod's spine.

A quaking, nasal voice answered the sentry. "Nay, I do but seek the jakes!"

The three men let their breath out in a long, silent sigh.

"*Sir*, when yer speak to a soldier!

"Sir," the whining voice echoed, surly.

"What was your reason for walking past curfew?" the sentry threatened in ominous tones.

"I do but seek the jakes, *sir*," the nasal voice whined.

The sentry chuckled, mollified. "And the jakes are near to the women's hall? Nay, I think not! Back to your pallet, scum! Your doxie's not for you this night!"

"But I—"

"Nay!" the guard snapped. "You do know the rule, fellow. Do you ask of the Mocker first." The voice became almost confidential. " 'Tain't so much as all that, chum. Like as not he'll give yer the paper says yer can do't, an' set yer a fit place an' time. He's free 'nough about it."

The nasal one hawked and spat.

"Come on, now," the guard growled. "Yer've but to ask of him."

"Aye," sneered the nasal voice, "and ask again every night that I'm wishin' to see her! Hell, 'twas the one thing in this world that came cheap!"

The guard's voice hardened again. "The Mocker's word is the law in this House, and my club'll remind you of it, if my word's not enough!"

There was a pause, then an angry, despairing snarl, and feet padded away.

There was silence again; after a while, the guard began to snore again.

Rod glanced at Tuan. The boy's face was dead white, lips pressed so tight the color'd gone out of them.

"I take it you didn't know anything about this?" Rod whispered.

"Nay," Tuan whispered back. "Once they'd set me by, they wasted no time. A guard at each hall, a writ ere two may share a bed—this is worse than the lords of the South!"

Tom's head jerked up. "Nay!" he snarled. " 'Tis but inconvenience. The gains to be got from it are well worth the price."

For his part, Rod agreed with Tuan. Police state, control over every facet of the people's lives—yes, the Mocker's Marxism was showing.

"What gains are worth *that* price?" Tuan snorted, raising his whisper a trifle.

"Why," growled Big Tom, at minimum bullfrog volume, "more food for all, more and better clothing, none poor and none starving."

"And all thanks to planned parenthood," Rod murmured, with an apprehensive glance at the corner.

"And how may this come?" asked Tuan, hiking his voice another notch and ignoring Rod's frantic signals. "From a writ of consent for a lovemaking? I cannot see how!"

Tom's lip twisted in scorn, and the bullfrog croaked louder. "Nay, you cannot! But the Mocker can!"

Tuan stared; then his jaw tightened, and his hand slipped to his dagger. "Do you place yourself and your kind above a nobleman, churl?"

"Uh, gentlemen," Rod whispered.

Big Tom tensed, grinning; his eyes danced mockery. "Blood will tell," he said, full voice.

Tuan's dagger leaped out as he sprang.

Tom lugged out his minor sword.

Rod threw out his hands, stiff-arming both of them at the collarbone. "Gentlemen, *gentle*men! I realize you both feel very strongly about the issues at hand; but it is my bounden duty to remind you that a sentry fully capable of bringing the wrath of the House down on our heads is dozing, and not too heavily either, just around the corner!"

"This is not to be borne, Rod Gallowglass!"

"Aye," chuckled Big Tom, "the truth was ever hard to bear."

Tuan lunged, trying to stab at Tom over Rod's head. Rod shoved back on the boy's collarbone and ducked as the knife arced past his head.

Tom chuckled softly. "There is a nobleman for you! A fool could see the reach is too great! Ever will he overreach himself, when he knows he must fail."

Rod eyed Tom sideways. "You're slipping, Big Tom. That was almost a compliment."

"Nay!" Tom hissed, his eyes fire. "To attempt the impossible is the act of a fool! The nobles are fools, and the roads to their utopias are paved with the bones of the peasants!''

Tuan spat. ''And what else are they—''

''Be still!'' Rod gave them both a shake. ''Could I possibly persuade you to overlook your obvious differences in favor of the common good for a moment?''

Tom straightened to his full height and looked down his nose at Tuan. *''Little* man,'' he crooned.

Rod let go of Tuan and swung on Big Tom, grabbing the big man's collar with both hands. Tom grinned and brought up a hamlike fist. ''Aye, *master?''*

''What's the utopia right now, Big Tom?'' Rod breathed.

Tom's grin faded to a frown. ''Why, that the people of Gramarye should rule their land for themselves.''

''Right!'' Rod let go of Tom's collar, patting the man's cheek. ''Bright boy! You get the silver star this week! And what do you have to do first?''

''Kill the councillors and noblemen!'' Tom grinned.

''Very good! A gold star for the boy! You'll make valedictorian yet, Big Tom! Now, if you *really* want to be a good boy, tell teacher what you have to do before that!''

Tom sobered. ''Jail the Mocker.''

''A-plus! And what comes before that?''

Big Tom knit his brown, confused. ''What?''

''Be quiet!'' Rod roared in his face, in a stage whisper. He spun on Tuan. ''Now! What do we do about that sentry?'' And to himself, he mumbled, ''Sheesh! I should maybe have brought a political convention in here!''

Tuan's chin jutted out stubbornly. ''Ere we go further, this fellow must acknowledge me lord!''

Tom took a breath for a fresh blast.

''Down, boy!'' Rod said hurriedly. ''High blood

pressure's bad for you! Is Tuan Loguire a nobleman born, Tom?''

"Aye," Tom grudged, "but that does not—"

"Is Loguire one of the greatest of the noble houses?"

"It is, but—"

"And your mother and father were peasants?''

"Yes, but that's not to say that—"

"And you have absolutely no wish to have been born a nobleman!"

"Never!" Tom hissed, eyes glowing. "May I be hanged from the highest gallows in Gramarye if ever I had wished that!"

"And you wouldn't want to be a nobleman if you could?"

"Master!" Big Tom pleaded, wounded to the core. "Hast so little regard for me that thou couldst think such of me?"

"No, I trust you, Big Tom," said Rod, patting his shoulder, "but Tuan has to be shown." He turned to the young nobleman. "You satisfied? He knows his place, doesn't he?"

"Aye." Tuan smiled like a fond father. "Fool I was to doubt him."

Understanding came into Tom's eyes as his mouth dropped open. His heavy hand closed on Rod's neck. "Why, thou lump of . . . !"

Rod reached up and squeezed Tom's elbow just at the funny bone. Tom let go, eyes starting from their sockets, mouth sagging in a cry of agony that he dared not voice.

"Now," said Rod briskly, "how do we get rid of that sentry?"

"Oh, thou scum!" Tom breathed. "Thou slimy patch of river-moss, thou mongrel son-of-a-democrat, thou!"

"Precisely," Rod agreed.

"Nay, but tell me," Tuan breathed in Rod's ear, eyes glowing. "What didst thou do to him? Thou didst but touch him and—"

"Uh . . . warlock trick," said Rod, falling back on the easiest, though most distasteful, excuse. He caught the back of Tuan's neck and jerked the youth's head down into the huddle with himself and Big Tom. "Now, how do we knock out that sentry?"

"There is but one way," murmured Tuan. "Wake him and fight him."

"And let him give the alarm?" Tom stared, horrified. "Nay, nay! Come catpaw behind him, and give him a blow o' the head!"

"That," said Tuan grimly, "lacks honor!"

Tom spat.

"Big Tom's plan is okay," said Rod, "except what happens if he wakes while we're sneaking up? And there's a very good chance of it; that lecherous beggar proved it for us!"

Tom shrugged. "Then a quick rush, and a hope. If we die, then we die."

"And the Queen dies with us," Rod growled. "No good."

Tom pulled out his short sword and balanced it on a finger. "I'll strike him in the throat with this blade at full fifty paces."

Tuan stared, appalled. "A man of your own men, sirrah!"

"One for the good of the cause." Tom shrugged. "What of it?"

Tuan's eyes froze. "That is worse than a stab in the back! We must needs give him lief to defend himself."

"Oh, aye!" Tom snorted. "Lief to defend himself, and to raise the whole House with his cries! Lief to . . ."

Rod clapped a hand over each mouth, glad that he hadn't brought three men with him. He hissed at Big Tom, "Be patient, will you? He's new to commando work!"

Tom sobered.

Tuan straightened, eyes icy.

Rod put his mouth next to Tom's ear and whispered, "Look, if you hadn't known he was an aristocrat, how would you have judged him?"

"A brave man, and a strong fighter," Tom admitted, "though foolish and young, with too many ideals."

Rod shook a finger at him. "Prejudice, Big Tom! Discrimination! I thought you believed in equality!"

"Well said," Tom growled reluctantly; "I'll bear him. But one more of his pious mouthings and . . ."

"If we get this job done fast, he won't have a chance to. Now, I've got an idea."

"Then why didst thou ask us?" growled Tom.

" 'Cause I didn't get my idea till you two started haggling. What we need is a compromise solution, right? Tuan won't stand for a knife in the back, or a knife while the guy's sleeping, or for killing a loyal retainer who might make good cannon fodder tomorrow. Right?"

"Aye," Tuan agreed.

"And Big Tom won't stand for him giving the alarm—and neither will I, for that matter: we're all good fighters, but just the three of us against the whole Houseful of cutthroats is straining the bonds of fantasy just a little bit far. So, Tom! If that sentry should come running around this corner all of a sudden, will you clobber him lightly?"

"Aye!" Tom grinned.

"*Lightly*, I said. Does that satisfy honor, Tuan?"

"Aye, since he faces us."

"Good! Now, if we could just get him to chase a mouse around this corner, we'd be all set."

"Aye," Tuan agreed, "but where's the mouse that would so nicely oblige us?"

"The master could make one," Tom growled.

"Make one?" Rod stared. "Sure if I had a machine shop and a . . ."

"Nay, nay!" Tuan grinned. "I know not those spells; but thou hast the witch-moss, and thou'rt a warlock! What more dost thou need?"

"Huh?" Rod swallowed. "Witches make things out of that stuff?"

"Aye, aye! Dost thou not know? Living things, small things—like mice!"

The missing piece in the puzzle of Gramarye clicked into place in Rod's mind. "Uh, say, how do they work that trick?"

"Why, they have but to look at a lump of the stuff, and it becomes what they wish it!"

Rod nodded slowly. "Very neat, ve-ry neat. The only hitch in the plan is, that's not my style of witch-craft."

Tuan sagged. "Thou craftest not witch-moss? Then how are we to . . . ? Still, 'tis most strange that thou shouldst not know of it."

"Not so," Tom dissented. "A very poor briefing bureau . . ."

"Oh, shut up!" Rod growled. "There are other ways to get a mouse." He cupped his hands around his mouth and called softly, "Gwen! Oh, Gwe-en!"

A spider dropped down on a thread right in front of his nose.

Rod jumped. "Ye cats! Don't *do* that, girl!"

"Vermin!" Tom hissed, and swung his hand back for a swat.

Rod poked him in the solar plexus. "Careful, there!

Squash a spider, and you get bad luck, you know—
namely, me!''

He cupped the spider in his hand and caressed it very
gently with a finger. ''Well, at least you didn't choose a
black widow. Prettiest spider I ever saw, come to think
of it.''

The spider danced on his hand.

''Listen, sweetheart, I need a mouse to bring me that
sentry. Can you handle it?''

The spider shape blurred, fluxed, and grew into a
mouse.

It jumped from his hand and dashed for the corner.

''Oh, no you don't!'' Rod sprang, cupped a hand
over it, then very carefully picked it up. ''Sorry,
sweetheart, you might get stepped on—and if anything
like that happened to you, I'd be totally crushed.''

He kissed its nose, and heard Tom gagging behind
him. The mouse wriggled in ecstasy.

''No,'' said Rod, running a fingertip over its back
and pinching the tail, ''you've got to make me one
instead, out of that blob of witch-moss. Think you can
handle it, pet?''

The mouse nodded, turned, and stared at the witch-
moss.

Slowly, the blob pulled itself in, extruded a tendril
into a tail, grew whiskers at the top end, changed color
to brown, and a mouse crept down off the wall.

Tom gulped and crossed himself.

Rod frowned. ''Thought you were an atheist.''

''Not at times like this, master.''

The witch-moss mouse scurried around the corner.

Big Tom lifted his dagger, holding it by the tip, the
heavy, weighted handle raised like a club.

The snores around the corner stopped with a grunt.

''Gahhh! Nibble on me, will ya, y' crawlin' fer-
leigh?''

The sentry's stool clattered over. He stamped twice, missed both times; then the waiting men heard running footsteps approaching.

Tom tensed himself.

The mouse streaked around the corner.

The sentry came right behind it, cursing. His feet slipped on the turn. He looked up, saw Tom, and had just time enough to begin to look horrified before Tom's knife-hilt caught him at the base of the skull with a very solid thunk.

Rod let out a sigh of relief. "At last!"

The sentry folded nicely into Tuan's waiting arms. The young nobleman looked at Rod, grinning.

"Who fights by the side of a warlock," he said, "wins."

"Still, it was a pretty ratty trick," said Rod sheepishly.

Tom winced and pulled a length of black thread from his pouch.

"Nay, that will not hold him," Tuan protested.

Tom's only answer was a grin.

"Fishline?" Rod lifted an eyebrow.

"Better," said Big Tom, kneeling, beginning to wrap up the sentry. "Braided synthetic spider silk."

"And we owe it all to you," said Rod, petting the mouse in his hand.

It wriggled its nose, then dove between the buttons on his doublet.

Rod stifled a snicker, cupped a hand over the lump on his belly. "Hey, watch it! That tickles!"

Tom had the sentry nicely cocooned, with a rag jammed in his mouth and held in place by a few twists of thread.

"Where shall we hide him?" Tuan whispered.

"There's nary a place close to hand," Tom muttered, tongue between his teeth as he tied a Gordion knot.

"Hey!" Rod clapped a cupped hand over a lump moving south of his belt buckle. "Cut that out!"

"There's a torch-sconce on this wall," said Tuan, pointing.

"The very thing," Tom growled. He heaved the inert sentry up, hooked one of the spider-thread loops over the sconce.

Rod shook his head. "Suppose someone comes by this way? We can't have him hanging around like that."

He reached in his doublet and hauled the mouse away from its exploratory tour of his thorax. "Listen, baby, you know what a dimensional warp is?"

The mouse rolled its eyes up and twitched its whiskers. Then it shook its head firmly.

"How about a uh, time-pocket?"

The mouse nodded eagerly; then the little rodent face twisted up in concentration . . . and the sentry disappeared.

Tuan goggled, mouth gaping open.

Big Tom pursed his lips, then said briskly, "Ah . . . yes! Well, let's get on with it, then."

Rod grinned, put the mouse on the floor, turned it around, gave it a pat on the backside.

"Get lost, you bewitching beast. But stay close; I might need you."

The mouse scampered off with a last squeak over her shoulder.

"The Mocker will be sleeping in what was Tuan's chamber, I doubt not," Tom muttered, "and his lieutenants, we may hope, will not be far off."

"May not one of them be wakeful?" whispered Tuan. "Or might one be set Master of the Watch?"

Tom turned slowly, eyeing Tuan with a strange look on his face. He raised an eyebrow at Rod. "A good man," he admitted, "and a good guess." Then, "Follow," and he turned away.

They were able to bypass the only other sentry between themselves and the common room.

The room itself, cavernous and slipshod as ever, was lit only by the smoky glow from the great fireplace, and a few smoldering torches. It was enough, however, to make out the great stone staircase that curved its way up the far wall with a grace that belied its worn treads and broken balustrade.

A gallery jutted out into the hall at the top of the stair. The doors opening off it gave onto private rooms.

A broad-shouldered, hatchet-faced man sat sprawled and snoring in a huge chair by the side of the vast fireplace. A sentry stood guard at the foot of the great staircase, blinking and yawning. Two more guards slouched at either side of the door in the center of the balcony.

"Here's a pretty mess," said Big Tom, ducking back into the hallway. "There's one more of them than there are of us, and they be so far between that two must surely take alarm as we disable two others."

"To say nothing of that wasteland of lighted floor that we have to cross to get to any of them," Rod added.

"We might creep up through the tables and stools," Tuan suggested, "and he at the foot of the stairs must surely nod himself asleep ere long."

"That takes care of the two on the ground floor," Rod agreed, "but how about the pair on the balcony?"

"To that," said Tuan, "I have some small skill at the shepherd's bow."

He drew out a patch of leather with two rawhide thongs wrapped about it.

"How didst thou learn the craft of that?" Tom growled as Tuan unwound the strings. " 'Tis a peasant's weapon, not a lordling's toy."

There was a touch of contempt in the glance Tuan threw Tom. "A knight must be schooled in all weapons, Big Tom."

Rod frowned. "I didn't know that was part of the standard code."

"It is not," Tuan admitted. "But 'tis my father's chivalry, and mine, as you shall see. Both yon knaves shall measure their length on cold stone ere they could know what has struck them."

"I don't doubt it," Rod agreed grimly. "Okay, let's go. I'll take the one by the fireplace."

"Thou'lt not," Big Tom corrected him. "Thou'lt take him by the stairway."

"Oh? Any particular reason?"

"Aye." Tom grinned wolfishly. "He in the great chair is the lieutenant that Tuan foresaw—and one among those who ha' jailed me. 'Tis my meat, master."

Rod looked at Tom's eyes and felt an eerie chill wind blow up along his spine.

"All right, butcher," he muttered. "Just remember, the lady's not for carving, yet."

" 'Let each man pile his dead according to his own taste and fashion,' " Tom quoted. "Go tend your corpses, master, and leave me to mine."

They dropped to their bellies and crawled, each to his own opponent.

To Rod, it was an eternity of table-legs and stool-feet, with plenty of dropped food scraps between, and the constant fear that one of the others might reach his station first and get bored.

There was a loud, echoing clunk.

Rod froze. One of the others had missed his footing.

There was a moment's silence; then a voice called, "What was that?" Then, "Eh, you there! Egbert! Rouse yourself, sot, and have a mind for the stairs you're guarding!"

"Eh? Wot? Wozzat?" muttered a bleary, nearer voice; and, "What fashes ye?" grumbled a deeper, petulant voice from the fireplace. "Must ye wake me for trifles?"

There was a pause; then the first voice said, with a note of obsequiousness, " 'Twas a noise, Captain, a sort of a knock 'mongst the tables."

"A knock, he says!" growled the captain. "A rat, mayhap, after the leavings, nowt more! Do ye wake me for that? Do it more, an' thou'lt hear a loud knock indeed, a blow on thy hollow head." Then the voice grumbled to itself, "A knock, i' faith! A damned knock!"

Then there was silence again, then a muted clang as one of the sentries shifted his weight uneasily.

Rod let out a sigh of relief, slow and silent.

He waited for the sentry to start snoring again.

Then he wormed his way forward again, till at last he lay quiet under the table nearest the stairway.

It seemed he lay there for a very long time.

There was a piercing whistle from the fireplace, and a clatter as Big Tom overturned a stool in his charge.

Rod sprang for his man.

Out of the corner of his eye, he saw Tuan leap upright, his sling a blurred arc; then Rod crashed into the sentry, fist slamming at the midriff, left hand squeezing the throat.

The man folded. Rod chopped at the base of the skull lightly, just under the iron cap, and the sentry went limp.

He looked up just in time to see a sentry on the

balcony sag to the floor. The other lay writhing on the stones, hands clasped at his throat.

Rod was up the stairs in five leaps. He landed a haymaker on the man's jaw. The man's eyes closed as he went under.

His larynx was pushed out of line. It was not a pretty sight.

But at that, he'd been lucky. If it had been a direct blow, his trachea would have been crushed.

His companion hadn't been so lucky. The pebble had crushed his forehead. Blood welled over his face and puddled to the floor.

"Forgive me, man," whispered Tuan, as he contemplated his handiwork. Rod had never seen the boy's face so grim.

"Fortunes of war, Tuan," he whispered.

"Aye," Tuan agreed, "and had he been my peer, I could dismiss it at that. But a man of my blood is intended to protect the peasants, not slay them."

Rod looked at the boy's brooding face and decided it was men like the Loguires who had given aristocracy what little justification it had had.

Tom had glanced once and turned away to bind the remaining man, his face thunderous.

There had been only the one casualty; the captain and stair-guard lay securely trussed with Tom's black thread.

Tom came up, glowering at Tuan. " 'Twas well done," he growled. "You took two of them out, and were able to spare the one; tha'rt braw fighter. And for the other, do not mourn him: thou couldst scarce take the time for better aim."

Tuan's face was blank in confusion. He couldn't rightly object to Tom's manner; yet it was disquieting to have a peasant offer him fatherly advice, and forgiveness.

Rod gave him an out. "You used to sleep there?" He jerked a thumb over his shoulder at the door the sentries had guarded.

He broke through Tuan's abstraction; the youth turned, looked, and nodded.

"Well, that's where the Mocker'll be, then." Rod looked up at Tom. "That captain downstairs was one of the Mocker's cadre?"

"Aye."

"That leaves two lieutenants, then. How's chances for one of them being in each of these rooms next to the Mocker's?" As Tom pulled at his lower lip and nodded, Rod went on: "One for each of us, then. You boys take the lieutenants. I'll take the Mocker."

He turned to the door. Big Tom's meaty hand fell on his shoulder.

"How now?" growled the big peasant. "How is the Mocker your meat, not mine?"

Rod grinned. "I'm the middleman, remember? Besides, what belt do you hold?"

"Brown," Tom admitted.

"And the Mocker?"

"Black," Tom answered reluctantly. "Fifth dan."

Rod nodded. "I'm black, eighth dan. You take the lieutenant."

Tuan frowned. "What is this talk of belts?"

"Just a jurisdictional dispute; don't worry about it." Rod turned to the center door.

Big Tom caught his arm again. "Master," and this time he sounded like he meant it. "When this is done, thou must teach me."

"Yeah, sure, anything. I'll get you a college degree, just let's get this over with, shall we?"

"I thank thee." Tom grinned. "But I've a doctorate already."

Rod did a double take, then stared at him. "In what?"

"Theology."

Rod nodded. "That figures. Say, you haven't come up with any new atheist theories, have you?"

"Master!" Tom protested, wounded. "How can one prove or disprove the existence of a non-material being by material data? 'Tis an innate contradiction of—"

"Gentlemen," said Tuan sarcastically, "I greatly dislike to interrupt so learned a discourse, but the Mocker awaits, and may shortly awake."

"Huh? Oh! Oh, yes!" Rod turned to the door. "See you in a few minutes, Big Tom."

"Aye, we must have further converse." Tom grinned and turned away to the right-hand door.

Rod eased his own door open, hands stiffened.

The door creaked. It groaned. It shrieked. It lodged formal protest.

Rod threw himself forward, having just time to realize that the Mocker had left his hinges carefully unoiled as a primitive but very effective burglar alarm, before the Mocker screamed "Bloody Murder!" and jumped from his bed, hands chopping.

Rod blocked an overhand blow and thrust for the solar plexus. His hand was skillfully rerouted, the Mocker's scream for help dinning in his ears.

Rod had just time to appreciate the humor of a black belt calling for help before he saw the kick smashing at his groin.

He leaped back, and the Mocker leaped after him. This time, the kick landed.

Rod rolled on the floor, curled around his agony.

He saw the foot aimed at his jaw and managed to turn his head aside just enough; the foot glanced off the side of his head.

He saw a shower of red asterisks, glowing against black, and shook his head frantically, trying to clear it.

Through the ringing in his ears, he heard another scream, suddenly cut off, then a thud; then Big Tom was bellowing, ''Thy sling, Tuan! There'll be guards to answer that scream!''

Then the big man was bending over him, face close. ''How bad art thou hurt, master?''

Rod had never known stale beer and onions could smell so good.

''I'm all right,'' he gasped. ''The blow landed a little off-center, thank heaven!''

''Canst thou stand?''

''In a minute. Gwen may be in for a temporary disappointment, though. How'd you do it, Big Tom?''

''Caught his foot on the upswing,'' Tom grinned, ''and threw him high. Then I got in an uppercut ere he landed.''

Rod stared. ''A what?''

''An uppercut. A haymaker.''

Rod rolled over, got his knees under him, shook his head in amazement. '' 'Uppercut takes out Black Belt.' Call the newspapers.''

There was a cry outside, choked off suddenly.

Rod's head snapped up, listening. Then he stumbled to his feet, hands still pressed to his groin, and all but fell out the door, ignoring Big Tom's solicitous protests.

Three more bodies lay on the stone floor of the common room.

Tuan stood at the balcony rail, sling stretched tight between his hands, jaw clamped shut, bleak dismay in his eyes.

''First the one came,'' he said in a monotone, ''then the other, then the third. The first two I dispatched ere they could cry; but on the third, I was tardy.'' Tuan turned back to the hall. After a moment, he said, slow and hard, "I do not like this killing."

Then his vision cleared.

"Huh." Rod nodded, gasping, as a brief spasm of nausea made him clutch at the railing. "No man worthy to be called a man does like it, Tuan. Don't let it worry you. It's war."

"Oh, I ha' slain before." Tuan's lips pressed thin. "But to slay men who three days agone drank my health . . .!"

Rod nodded, closing his eyes. "I know. But if you have any hope of being a king, Tuan, or even a good Duke, you've got to learn not to let it bother you."

He looked up at the boy. "Besides, remember—they'd have killed you if they could."

Tom came out on the balcony, carrying the trussed-up Mocker in his arms, like a baby.

He looked briefly at the common room; his face hardened. "More killing?"

He turned away, laying the Mocker carefully on the floor next to the prone bodies of his lieutenants, and sighed. "*Ay de mi!* But 'tis the times, and the fashion."

He bent to the work of binding up one of the lieutenants, a tall, emaciated skeleton of a man with a scar where he should have had an ear, a souvenir of royal justice.

Rod looked, and nodded; the Mocker had chosen his confederates well. They had cause for hating the monarch.

Rod slowly straightened, wincing at the pain.

Tuan glanced at him. "Thou ought to seat thyself and take rest, Rod Gallowglass."

Rod pulled in a sharp, quick breath and shook his head. "It's just pain. Hadn't we better cart these three down to the dungeon?"

A gleam sparked in Tuan's eye. "Nay. Bind them and keep them here; I have uses for them."

Rod frowned. "What do you mean, *uses?*"

Big Tom held up a hand. "Do not ask, master. If Tuan has need of them, let him have them. This lad knows his craft; I ha' ne'er seen, and but rarely heard, of any man who could so sway the mob."

He turned and leaped down the stairs, checked for heartbeats in the fallen men, bound up the one that still lived, and dragged them all under the balcony. Then he caught up the their lieutenant from the hearth, slung him over a shoulder.

"Tom!" Tuan called, and the big man looked up.

"Bring that horn that hangs o'er the mantle, and the drum beside it!" Tuan called.

Tom nodded and took down the battered, curled hunting horn from its nail and plucked one of the rude drums—nothing more than an empty cask with hide stretched over each end—from its place on the mantle.

Rod frowned, perplexed. "What do you want the drum and bugle for?"

Tuan grinned. "Canst play at the horn?"

"Well, I wouldn't exactly qualify for first chair in the Philharmonic, but . . ."

"Thou'lt do," said Tuan, eyes dancing.

Big Tom bounded back up the stairs with the Mocker's lieutenant over one shoulder and the trumpet and drum over the other.

He dropped the instruments and laid the bound man by his companions.

He straightened, fists on hips, grinning. "Halloa, my masters! What would you have us do with 'em, lordling?"

"Do thou take the drum," said Tuan, "and when I give the word, hang these four from the balcony rail, but not by their necks. 'Tis far more to our credit we've taken them living.''

Rod cocked an eyebrow. "Not that old wheeze about being powerful enough to be merciful?''

He didn't hear the answer, because Tom started pounding the drum. The tenor throbbing filled the room.

Rod caught up the horn.

Tuan grinned, jumped up on the rail, stood with feet wide apart and arms folded. "Summon them, Master Gallowglass,'' he shouted.

Rod set the mouthpiece to his lips and blew "Reveille.''

It sounded rather weird on a hunting horn, but it had its effect. Before he was halfway through with the second chorus, the hall had filled with beggars, muggers, lame, one-armed, thieves and cutpurses and murderers.

Their muttering, surf and wind before a storm, filled the hall as an undercurrent to the drum and horn. They were fresh-woken, bleary-eyed and fuzzy-brained, hurling a thousand incredulous questions at one another, shaken and cowed to see Tuan, whom they had jailed, standing tall and proud in the hall he'd been exiled from.

He should fear them; he should have feared to return; and if he had come back, it should have been as a thief in the night, skulking and secret.

Yet here he stood, free in their eyes, summoning them to him with bugle and drum—and where was the Mocker?

They were shaken, and more than a little afraid. Men who had never been taught how to think now faced the unthinkable.

Rod ended with a flourish, and flipped the trumpet

away from his lips, whirling it in a flashing circle to land belldown at his hip.

Big Tom gave the drum a last final boom.

Tuan held his hand out to Tom and began clicking his fingers very softly.

The drum spoke again, throbbing, insistent, but very soft.

Rod looked up at Tuan, who was grinning, arms akimbo, a royal elf come into his kingdom. He looked down at the audience, shaken and fearful, staring, mouths agape, at the lordly, commanding figure above them.

Rod had to admit it was a great way to open a speech.

Tuan flung up his arms, and the hall stilled, except for the low-pitched throb of Tom's drum.

"You cast me out!" Tuan shouted.

The mob shrank back on itself, muttering, fearful.

"Cast out, thrown to exile!" Tuan called. "You had turned your eyes from me, turned away from me, thought never to look upon me!"

The muttering grew, began to take a surly, desperate quality.

"Was I not banished?" Tuan called, then, "Be still!" he snapped.

And, miraculously, the room stilled.

He leveled an accusing forefinger at the crowd and growled, "Was I not banished?"

This time there werea few muttered "Ayes."

"Was I not?"

The mutter of "Ayes" grew.

"Was I not?"

"Aye!" rolled across the heads of the crowd.

"Did you not call me traitor?"

"Aye," the crowd growled again.

"Yet here I stand," Tuan cried, "strong and free, and master again of the House of Clovis!"

Nobody disputed it.

"And where are the real traitors, who would ha' seen you all torn to bits in hopeless battle? The traitors, who ha' turned this House to a jail in my absence? Where are they now, to dispute my mastership?"

He rested his hands on his hips while the crowd took up the question in its own ranks, and Tom quickly lashed ten feet of thread to the Mocker's bonds, lashing the other end to a railing-pillar. As the mutters of "Where?" and "The Mocker!" began to grow, he served the three lieutenants likewise.

Tuan let the mutters swell and grow; then, just as they hit their peak, he gave Tom the signal.

Tom and Rod threw the bound men over, where they hung two on each side of Tuan. The Mocker had regained consciousness; he began writhing and kicking at the end of his rope.

A shocked silence filled the hall.

Tuan grinned and folded his arms.

The crowd roared, like one huge, savage beast, and pressed forward. The front ranks began to jump at the dangling feet. Obscene epithets, cursing the Mocker and his men, blasted from the packed floor.

"Behold!" Tuan shouted, throwing up his arms, and the crowd fell silent. "Behold them, the traitors who once you called masters! Behold them, the traitors, the thieves who took from you all the liberty I had gained for you!"

Big Tom was grinning, eyes glowing and fixed on the young lord, swaying to the rhythm of the boy's words.

For, truly, the lad seemed twelve feet tall now.

"Were you not born without masters?" Tuan shouted.

"Aye!" the crowd roared at him.

"You were born to freedom!" Tuan bellowed. "The

freedom of outlawry and poverty, aye, but born free!''

Then, ''Were you not born wild?'' he fairly shrieked; and:

''Aye!'' the crowd shrieked in response, ''Aye, aye! *Aye!*''

''Did I steal your freedom from you?''

''Nay, nay!''

A twisted hunchback with a patch over his eye shouted, ''Nay, Tuan! You gave us more!''

The crowd clamored.

Tuan crossed his arms again, grinning, letting the acclamation run its course.

When it had just passed its peak, he threw up his arms again, and shouted. ''Did I tell you?''

Silence fell.

''Did I tell you that you must have my permission for a night's loving?''

''Nay!'' they roared back, both sexes united for a change.

''And never I will!''

They cheered.

Tuan grinned, and bowed his head in thanks, almost shyly.

''And yet!'' Tuan's voice dropped down low, surly, angry. He hunched forward, one fist clenched, shaking at the audience. ''When I came back to your halls this dark eventide, what did I find?'' His voice rose, building. ''You had let these base knaves steal away all I had given you!''

The crowd roared.

Tuan flicked his left hand: Tom struck the drum with a boom that cut the crowd short.

''Nay, more!'' Tuan cried. His forefinger jabbed out at the crowd, his eyes seeking hot individual faces. His voice was cold, now, and measured. ''I found that in your base cowardice you had let them steal from you even that liberty you were born with!''

The crowd murmured, frightened, unsure. The front ranks shrank back.

''Even your birthright you had let them steal from you!''

The murmuring was a wave of fright at the contempt in the silver tongue.

''You would let them take from you even bed-freedom!''

He flicked his hand; the drum boomed.

''And you call yourselves men!'' Tuan laughed, harsh and contemptuous.

The murmuring wave came back at him now, with sullen, protesting voices. ''We are men!'' someone cried, and the crowd took it up, ''We are men! We are men! We are men!''

''Aye!'' shrieked the eye-patched hunchback. ''But give us these dangling knaves who h' robbed us, Tuan, and we shall prove we are men! We shall rend them, shall flay them! We shall leave not an ounce of flesh to cling to their bones! We shall crack even their bones and hale out the marrow!''

The crowd howled in blood-lust.

Tuan straightened and folded his arms, smiling grimly. The crowd saw him; their roar subsided to a growl, with an undertone of guilt, then broke up into sullen lumps of murmurs, and stilled.

''Is this manhood?'' said Tuan, almost quietly. ''Nay!'' His arm snapped out, pointing, accusing. ''I ha' seen packs of dogs could do better!''

The muttering ran through the crowd, growing angrier, louder and louder.

''Careful, there!'' Rod called to Tuan. ''You'll have them tearing us apart next!''

"No fear," said Tuan, without taking his eyes from the crowd. "Yet let it work a while."

The muttering rose sharply. Here and there a man shouted, angry shouts, fists waved at Tuan where he stood on the balcony rail.

Tuan flung up his arms again, shouting, "But I say you are men!"

The crowd quieted, staring.

"There are others who slander you; but I call you men!" Then, looking from face to face: "And who will gainsay me?"

For a moment, they were quiet; then someone called, "None, Tuan!" and another answered, "None!"

"None!" called the several, and "None!" called the many, till "None!" roared the crowd.

"Will you prove you are men?" Tuan shouted.

"Aye!" the crowd bellowed.

"Will you fight?" Tuan howled, shaking a fist.

"Aye!" they cried, crowding closer with blood-thirst.

Tuan's hands shot out waist-high, palms down, fingers spread.

The crowd stilled.

His voice was hushed, chanting. "You were born to filth and the scabs of disease!"

"Aye," they muttered.

"You were born to the sweat of your joints, and the ache of your back in hard labor!"

"Aye!"

"You were born to the slack, empty belly and the want of a home!"

"Aye!"

"Who filled your bellies? Who gave you a roof for your head in this very house?"

"You did!"

"Who gave you a fortress?"

"You did!"

"Who?"

"You!"

"Tell me the name!"

"Tuan Loguire!" they shrieked.

"Aye!" Tuan's hands went out again; he stood crouched, eye afire.

"This was the misery I took from you. But who gave it to you at birth? Who is it has beaten you down, century upon century, from father to son, age upon age to the time of your remotest grandfathers?"

The crowd muttered, uncertain.

"The peasants?"

"Nay," the crowd answered.

"Was it the soldiers?"

"Aye!" they shouted, come to life again.

"And who rules the soldiers?"

"The nobles!"

Rod winced at the hate they packed into the word.

"Aye! 'Twas the nobles!" Tuan shouted, thrusting upward with his fist, and the crowd howled.

He let pandemonium reign for a few moments, then threw up his arms again.

Then his hands dropped down to belt-level again; he fell into the crouch.

"Who!" he demanded, and the drum throbbed behind him. "Who! Who alone of all the high-born took your part? Who gave you food when you cried for it, heard your petitions? Who sent judges among you, to give you justice instead of a nobleman's whim?"

His fist thrust upward with his whole body behind it, "The Queen!"

"The Queen!" they echoed him.

"She shut her ears to the noblemen, that she might hear your cries!"

"Aye!"

"She hath shed tears for you!"

"Aye!"

"Yet," cried the hunchback, "she cast you out, our Tuan Loguire!"

Tuan smiled sourly. "Did she? Or did she send me among you!" He threw up his arms, and they roared like an avalanche.

"It is the Queen who has given you your birthright again!"

"Aye!"

"Are you men?" Tuan shouted.

"We are!"

"Will you fight?"

"We will fight! We will fight!"

"Will you fight the noblemen?"

"Aye!"

"Will you fight for your Queen?"

"Aye!"

"Will you fight the noblemen for Catharine your Queen?"

"Aye! Ayeayeaye*aye!*"

Then the noise of the crowd covered all. The people leaped and shouted; men caught women and swung them about.

"Have you weapons?" Tuan shouted.

"Aye!" A thousand daggers leaped upward, gleaming.

"Catch up your packs, fill them with journeybread! Burst out of this house, through the south gate of the city! The Queen will give you food, give you tents! So run you all to the South, south along the great highway to Breden Plain, there to wait for the noblemen!

"Go do it!" he shouted. "Go now! For the Queen!"

"For the Queen!"

Tuan flipped his hand; the drum boomed loud and

fast. "Hunting call!" Tuan snapped in aside to Rod.

Rod flourished the trumpet to his lips and began the quick, bubbling notes.

"Go!" Tuan roared.

The people broke, to their rooms, to the armory. In ten minutes time they had caught up packs, staffs, and knives.

"It is done!" Tuan leaped down off the rail to the balcony floor. "They'll ha' run down to Breden Plain in two days!" He grinned, slapping Big Tom's shoulders. "We ha' done it, Tom!"

Tom roared his laughter and threw his arms about Tuan in a bear-hug.

"Whew!" Tuan gasped as Tom dropped him. He turned to Rod. "Do you, friend Gallowglass, tell the Queen, and see that the word of it goes out to her soldiers. Tell her to send meat, tents, and ale, and right quickly. And do you hurl these lackeys"—his thumb jerked at the Mocker and his lieutenants—"deep into the Queen's dungeon. Farewell!" And he was bounding and leaping down the stairs.

"Hey, wait a minute!" Rod shouted, running to the rail. "Where do you think you're going?"

"To Breden Plain!" Tuan shouted, stopping to look back up. "I must guard my people, or they'll strip the countryside worse than any plague of locusts could do, and kill themselves off in a fight o'er the spoils. Do you tell Catharine of my"—he paused; a shadow crossed his face—"loyalty."

Then he was gone, leading the mob that boiled out the great front doors of the house, running before them in a wild, madcap dance.

Rod and Tom exchanged one glance, then turned and ran for the stairs to the roof.

They watched from the rooftop as the chanting mob

poured out the south gate. Somehow, by means of the chant, Tuan had gotten them moving in good order, almost marching.

"Do you think he needs any help?" Rod murmured.

Tom threw back his head and guffawed. "Him, master? Nay, nay! Rather, help those who come up against him, with that army at his back!"

"But only one man, Tom! To lead two thousand misfits!"

"Canst doubt it, master, when thou hast seen his power? Or didst thou not see?"

"Oh, I saw." Rod nodded, light-headed. "There's more witchcraft in this land than I thought, Big Tom. Yes, I saw."

"Waken the Queen, and beg of her that she join us here in her audience chamber!" Brom snapped at a hastily-wakened lady-in-waiting. "Go!"

He slammed the door and turned to the fireplace, where Rod sat with a bleary-eyed Toby, rudely awakened after only an hour o sleep; the nightly party in the Witches' Tower had run a little late tonight. He held a steaming mug in his hand and a throb in his head.

"Assuredly," he muttered thickly, "we wish to aid the Queen in any manner we may; but what aid would we be in a battle?"

"Leave that to me." Rod smiled. "I'll find something for you to do. You just get the Queen's Witches down to Breden Plain by . . . uh . . ."

"Three days hence." Brom smiled. "We march at dawn, and will be three days in our journey."

Toby nodded, hazily. "We shall be there, my masters. And now, with your leave . . ."

He started to rise, gasped, and sank back in his chair, hand pressed to his head.

"Easy there, boy!" Rod grasped an elbow, steadying him. "First hangover?"

"Oh, nay!" Toby looked up, blinking watery eyes.

" 'Tis but the first time I've been wakeful when the drunk turned to the hangover. If you'll pardon me, masters . . ."

The air slammed at their eardrums as it rushed in to fill the space where Toby had been.

"Uh . . . yes," Rod said. He shook his head and eyed Brom. "Teleportative, too?"

Brom frowned. "Tele-what?"

"Uh . . ." Rod closed his eyes a moment, cursing the slip of the tongue. "I take it he's just gone back to bed."

"Aye."

"He can disappear from here and reappear there?"

"Quick as thought, aye."

Rod nodded. "That's what I thought. Well, it oughta come in handy."

"What wilt thou have them do, Rod Gallowglass?"

"Oh, I dunno." Rod waved his mug airily. "Conjure up feathers inside the Southern knights' armor, maybe. Or something like that, good for a joke. They'll just die laughing."

"Thou knowest not what thou'lt be having them do, yet thou would bring them?"

"Yeah, I'm beginning to think a little witchcraft can come in handy at times."

"Aye." Brom smiled covertly. "She hath saved your life twice over, hath she not?"

Rod swung about. "She? Who? She who, huh? What're you talking about?"

"Why, Gwendylon!" Brom's smile absorbed mischief.

"Oh, yes! Uh . . . you know of her?" Rod raised a

cautious eyebrow; then he smiled, relaxing. "No, of course you'd know of her. I forget; she's on pretty good terms with the elves.''

"Aye, I know of her.'' Brom's eyebrows pinched together. "Nay, but tell me,'' he said, almost anxiously, "didst thou love her?''

"Love her?'' Rod stared. "What the hell business is that of yours?''

Brom waved a hand impatiently. " 'Tis of concern to me; let it pass at that. Dost thou love her?''

"I won't let it pass at that!'' Rod drew himself up with a look of offended honor.

"I am Prince of the Elves!'' Brom snapped. "Might I not have concern for the most powerful witch in all Gramarye?''

Rod stared, appalled. "The most . . . *what?*''

Brom smiled sourly. "Thou didst not know? Aye, Rod Gallowglass. 'Tis a most puissant wench thou hast grappled with. Therefore, do you tell me: dost thou love her?''

"Well, uh, I, uh . . . I don't know!'' Rod sat, cradling his head in his hands. "I mean, uh, this is all so sudden, I, uh . . .''

"Nay, nay!'' Brom growled impatiently. "Surely thou must know if thou lovest!''

"Well, I mean, uh . . . well, no, I don't know! I mean, that's a subject that it's a little hard to be objective about, isn't it?''

"Thou dost not know?'' Thunderclouds gathered in Brom's face.

"No, damn it, I don't!''

"Why, thou fool of a puking babe, thou mock of a man! Dost thou not know thine own heart?''

"Well, uh, there's the aortic ventricle, and, uh . . .''

"Then how am I to know if thou lovest her?" Brom thundered.

"How the hell should *I* know?" Rod shouted. "Ask my horse!"

A quivering page thrust his head in, then came quivering into the room. "My lords, her Majesty the Queen!"

Brom and Rod swung about, bowed.

Catharine entered in a dressing gown of the royal purple her loosened hair a pale, disordered cloud around her head. She looked very tired, and scarcely wakened.

"Well, milords," she snapped, seating herself by the fire, "what great news is it makes you waken me at so slight an hour?"

Rod inclined his head toward the page. The boy paled, bowed, and left.

"The House of Clovis is up, into arms, and away," Rod informed her.

She stared, lips parting.

"They have boiled out of the south gate, and this very night run south toward Breden Plain."

Catharine's eyes closed; she sank back in her chair with a sigh. "May Heaven be praised!"

"And Tuan Loguire," Rod murmured.

Her eyes opened, staring. "Aye. And Tuan Loguire," she said reluctantly.

Rod turned away, running his hand over the mantle. "They must be sent food and drink, so that they will not strip the countryside as they pass. And a courier must ride ahead to tell soldiers to let them pass."

"Aye," she said grudgingly, "surely."

Her eyes wandered to the fire. "And yet it is strange, that they who have ever raised their voices in clamor against me, now should fight for me," she murmured.

Rod looked at her, his smile tight and ironic.

"Tuan . . ." she murmured.

Brom cleared his throat and stumped forward, hands locked behind his back. "And this very night," he growled, "have I spoken with the King of the Elves; all his legions are ours."

She was her old self again, smiling sourly. "Legions of elves, Brom O'Berin?"

"Oh, don't underestimate them." Rod rubbed the back of his head, remembering a clout on the skull and a prisoned werewolf. "And to top it off, we've got your own personal coven of witches . . ."

". . . and the most powerful witch in all Gramarye," Brom interjected.

"Uh, yes, and her," Rod agreed, with a shish-kebab glance at Brom. "All ready and eager to serve the only ruler in history who has protected witches."

Catharine's eyes had slowly widened as she listened; now her eyes took on a distant look, and wandered to the fire. "We will win," she murmured. "We will win!"

"Well, uh, with all due respect to your Majesty, uh, it might be a trifle more correct to say we stand an even chance."

Breden Plain was a delta, open to the south but closed on the north by the meeting of two rivers. A dense thicket of trees ran along each river, bordering the field. The field itself was tall grass and lavender.

Not that they could see much of it, Rod thought as he squatted by a campfire. A thick, chill mist covered the field; at least Rod, who had seen something of civilized smog, would have called it a mist; but Tuan, chafing his hands across the fire from Rod, shook his head and muttered, "A most dense and unclement fog, Master

Gallowglass! 'Twill weigh heavily on the spirit of the troops!''

Rod cocked an eyebrow at him and listened to the sounds of revelry drifting over the field from the beggars' pickets. The witches were at it, too; the usual party had started at noon today, out of respect for the weather.

His shoulders shrugged with a snort of laughter. ''Well, don't let it worry you, Tuan. The precog—uh, witches, say it'll be a beautiful, sunny day, tomorrow.''

''And St. George be praised, we will not have to fight until then!'' Tuan drew his cloak about him, shivering.

The latest word from Brom's miniature spies—whom Rod had immediately dubbed the Hobgoblin Associated Reconnaissance Korps—was that the Southern troops were just half a day away. Catharine had arrived with Brom and her army the preceding evening, and the beggars had been resting a full day already. They were, in fact, so primed and ready that Tuan was having a little trouble holding them in check; they were all for marching south and attacking the noblemen on the run.

''Still,'' said Rod, tugging at his lip, ''I don't see why we should wait for morning to do the fighting. We could ambush them tonight, when they're drawing up their troops.''

''Attack at night!'' Tuan gasped, horrified.

Rod shrugged. ''Sure, why not? They'll be tired from a day's march, and won't know where we are. We'd stand a much better chance of winning.''

''Aye, and you would stand a better chance of killing a man if you kicked at his head while he was down!''

Rod sighed and forebore saying that he had once

done exactly that, when the man was one of five excellently trained, seasoned killers who'd ambushed him. As a matter of fact, he'd fought dirtier than that with a lot less justification; but this didn't seem quite the time for telling it.

He did say, "I thought the point in fighting was to win."

"Aye," Tuan agreed, staring out into the fog toward the south end of the meadow, "but not by such foul means. Who would be loyal to a Queen who maintained her power thus?"

And that, Rod admitted, was the kernel of it. Prestige was everything on this world; and honor was the cornerstone of prestige.

"Well," he sighed, "you're the doctor."

Tuan frowned at him. "Doctor? I have no skill in healing."

"No, but you're an excellent practical psychologist. So I'll follow your lead when it comes to handling people."

Tuan smiled sadly, shaking his head. "Friend Rod, I have no skill at ruling."

Rod allowed himself a skeptical look. "Well, maybe not, but you're one hell of a leader."

"Ho!" a voice bellowed.

Rod turned and grinned at the huge shape that loomed in the fog. "Everyone happy over there?"

Big Tom shouldered his way out of the mist, grinning. "Most happy, master. They've ne'er in their lives drunk such wine, or so much of it."

"Hmmm." Rod tugged at his lip. "Better roll the wine away in a little while. We don't want them drunk so soon before battle."

But, "Nay," Tuan corrected, almost automatically, Rod noticed. "Let them drink their fill; 'twill put them abed sooner. Then rouse them early in the morning and give each a tankard or two—then they'll fight like the very demons.''

Well, Rod had to allow that was true. They weren't asking precision from the beggars, just wanted them to get out and beat up the enemy.

The night was pricked with the pinholes of watch-fires, softened by the lifting mist.

More dots of light sprang up to the south, where the noblemen and councillors were bringing up their army.

In the northern meadow, there was bawdy laughter and shouting, and the din of music, where the beggars were in the last stages of gleeful compliance with the order to get drunk as fast as possible.

On the hillside across the river there was a stern, disapproving silence, and the gentle glow of lamps within silken tents, where Catharine and her army of regulars went sober to bed.

But in the largest tent, Catharine's, things were anything but quiet.

''Nay, nay, and again I say nay!'' she cried, angrily pacing the floor.

She swung about, clapping her hands sharply. ''I shall have no more of your arguments! Have done, have done; for I *will* ride tomorrow at the head of my armies! I shall brook no further objection!''

Rod and Brom exchanged glances.

Tuan's face was beet-red with anger, frustration, and worry.

''Begone,'' snapped Catharine, and turned her back.

Reluctantly, the three men bowed, and filed out of the tent.

''What she will, she will,'' Brom growled. ''We three must guard her, then, and leave the plan of the battle to Sir Maris.''

''That's one sure road to defeat,'' Rod growled.

"His way of running a battle is as outdated as the phalanx."

Brom sighed and rubbed his eyes. "But as I have said, I will die by her. Yet mayhap we shall live, for I have a slight plan."

He stumped away into the darkness before they could question him, from which Rod inferred that his "plan" was limited to buoying up Rod's and Tuan's spirits by insinuating that there was yet hope.

"We shall die in her defense," Tuan whispered, drawn and pale. "Yet when we are gone, she will die too, and for that I am loath." He spread his hands helplessly. "But what can I do?"

"Well . . ." Rod pursed his lips, and looked back over his shoulder at the lighted tent. "I know one way to make sure she won't ride tomorrow. . . ."

"Tell it, then!" Tuan's face lit with frantic eagerness.

"Make sure she won't be able to sit down in the morning."

Tuan stared. A slow flush crept into his face, then drained away, leaving him pale and trembling. "What . . . dost . . . thou mean?" His voice was choked and threatening. He lifted a clenched, trembling fist.

Rod looked at him, frowned. "Why, spank her. Smack her so hard she'll have to stand till next Sunday. How else would you do it?"

Tuan's fist slowly dropped; the color came back to his face in a blush. "Oh," he said, and turned away. "I' truth," he said. " 'twould be well done."

"It's that, or let her die."

Tuan nodded, life coming back to him. He turned to the Queen's tent, paused a minute, then squared his shoulders. "That shall I do, then. Pardon me, friend

Gallowglass, for my anger; for a moment I had thought you meant . . . something else.''

He took a deep breath and stepped off briskly toward the tent.

He paused at the entrance, nodded at the guards, squared his shoulders again, and marched in.

Rod smiled, amused. "And I thought I had a dirty mind!''

He chuckled, shaking his head, and turned toward the witches' campfires, reflecting that Tuan's years in the House of Clovis had taught him a lot about life.

Gwendylon materialized out of the darkness (literally). She smiled shyly. "What amuses my lord?''

Rod grinned, caught her by the waist, and swung her up for a kiss, a warm kiss, and lasting.

"My lord!'' she said, blushing prettily, patting her hair back into place.

The night breeze wafted a sudden slapping sound to them, accompanied by squeals and cries.

The guards at the tent jerked bolt upright, then swung toward the tent. One put up a hand to swing aside the cloth of the doorway; but the second caught the hand and cried, "Does your Majesty require aid?''

"Stay out!'' squealed an agonized voice. "On pain of your life, do not enter!''

The sentries exchanged puzzled looks, then shrugged and turned back to their posts, albeit with some nervous looks over their shoulders.

The squeals became muffled, then turned into sobs. The slapping sounds ceased.

Then all was still.

Rod looked down at Gwen. "What are you grinning about?''

She looked up at him out of the corner of her eyes. "I

ha' told you, my lord, that I can hear all thoughts but yours.''

''Oh?''

''Aye. And there are most goodly thoughts in that tent at this moment.''

The lights in the tent went out.

Gwendylon giggled and turned away. ''Come, my lord. 'Twould be most improper to listen further. Come. Thou must be early abed this night.''

''Waken, Rod Gallowglass!''

Something jarred his shoulder.

Rod growled and levered his eyes open. ''What the hell do you think . . .''

He stopped as he saw the look on Brom's face.

''Aye,'' Brom growled. ''Now robe thyself and come with me.''

''I don't sleep naked on battle nights,'' Rod growled, and rose very carefully, so as not to disturb Gwendylon.

His face softened for a moment as he looked down at her. He touched his lips to her cheek. She stirred, murmured in her sleep, and smiled.

Then he rose, his face hardening.

Brom was already striding away through the chill predawn mist, beckoning curtly.

''All right, what's happened?'' Rod growled as he caught up with Brom.

''Nay, be still!'' Brom snapped, and was silent till they had climbed the hillside far above the tents.

Then he swung on Rod and snapped, ''Now tell me! Dost thou love her?''

Rod's face emptied.

Then he said, softly, ''You woke me just to ask that?''

"It is of some importance to me," Brom snapped. "Dost thou love her!"

Rod folded his arms, leaning back on one hip. "Just what the hell business is it of yours? What right have you to know my soul?"

Brom looked away, his face working; and when he spoke, the words seemed almost dragged out of him.

"She is my daughter, Rod Gallowglass."

He glanced up at Rod's stunned face, and a sardonic gleam came into his eye. "Aye. Thou scarce can credit it, canst thou?"

He turned away, looking out over the valley. His voice softened with memory and musing.

"She was naught but a servant-wench in the King's halls, Rod Gallowglass—yet I loved her. She was small, scarce half the height of another woman, yet still a head taller than I. And mortal, much too mortal.

"And she was beautiful, ah, so beautiful! And, strange though it may seem, highly desired by the men of the court. And yet"—Brom's voice took on a tone of wonder and awe—"yet she loved me. She alone, of all women living, elf or mortal, saw me not as dwarf, elf or Prince—but only as a man.

"And desired me . . .

"And loved me . . ."

He broke off, shaking his head in wonder.

He sighed. "I loved her, Rod Gallowglass, I loved her only, and begat a child within her."

His face darkened. He locked his hands behind his back and scowled at the ground. "When she proved by child, and her time grew apace, and she would soon be so swollen that all would know, and would shame her with cruel jests, though we were wed, I sent her away to the wild wood, to my people. And there, midwived by elves and leprechauns, she birthed a beautiful, laughing, part-elven child.''

His eyes misted over. He lifted his head, staring through Rod. ''She died. When her daughter was aged of two years, she died of a chill. And we buried her there, 'neath a tree in the forest. And yearly I come there . . .''

His eyes focused on Rod again. ''But I had, still, the child.''

He turned away, restless. ''Yet what should I do? Raise her near me, and have her know her father for a gnarled thing, and the butt of bad jests? Raise her to shame of me?

''She was raised in the woods, therefore, knowing her mother's grave and the elves, but never her father.''

Rod started to protest, but Brom waved him silent. ''Be still! 'Twas better so!''

He turned slowly, murder in his eyes. ''As 'tis still. And if ever she learns of it from thee, Rod Gallowglass, I'll hale out thy tongue by its roots, and lop off thy ears.''

Stone-faced, Rod studied him, and found nothing to say.

''And therefore, now tell me!'' Brom slammed his fists against his hips and lifted his chin. ''For know this: half-mortal am I, and may therefore be slain; and it may be that this day I shall die.''

His voice lowered. ''So tell me, tell a poor, anxious father, an thou wilt: dost thou love my child?''

''Yes,'' Rod said, low. Then, ''So it was no accident that I met her on my ride south?''

Brom smiled, sourly. ''Nay, of course not. Couldst thou ever have thought that it was?''

The east was reddening, embarrassed with dawn,

and the mist lifting as Rod rode into the beggars' camp to waken them.

But Tuan was there before him, going from pallet to pallet, shaking the beggars awake. A soldier was with him, placing a mug of hot mulled wine by each pallet.

Tuan looked up, saw Rod, and came up to him with arms outstretched and a grin a yard wide.

He clapped Rod on the shoulder, gripped his hand in a crushing shake. There was a deep, almost intoxicated quiet content in his eyes.

"My thanks, friend Rod," he said simply. "Dost thou wish my life? Thou mayst have it! Such is the debt that I owe."

Rod smiled slyly. "So you made double sure, did you? Well, all the better."

Tuan seemed to have things well in hand in the beggars' camp, so Rod turned Fess's steps toward the witches' lines.

All was in good order there; the baskets with ropes and harnesses stood ready; and the morning brew was passing from hand to hand. It was a potent beverage, something like concentrated tea with a touch of brandy, and served much the same purpose: a stimulant, to bring the witch powers to their peak.

Elves were underfoot everywhere about the camp, distributing good luck tokens and preventive-magic charms to all who would take them. Witches or no witches, the little folk argued, it never hurt to be sure. The charms could do no harm, and they might . . .

There was nothing for Rod to do there, either, so he rode in search of Gwendylon.

He found her seated in the midst of a knot of witches, old ones, as Gramarye witches went; they must have been into their twenties.

Gwendylon seemed to be explaining something to

them with great earnestness, marking diagrams in the dust with a pointed stick. They were hanging on her words as though every syllable might mean life or death.

It didn't look like a good time to interrupt.

Rod turned and rode through a maze of scurrying forms, cooking smells, clamor of voices and discordant bugle calls, out past the pickets into Breden Plain.

The first rays of sunlight slanted through the meadow now, burning away the last tatters of mist. The long grass was moist and chill with the dew, the sky clear and blue.

And the glitter of spear-points flashed from the south verge of the field. Sun gleamed off burnished armor. The wind blew him the metallic din, the horse-cries, and the mutter of a war-camp awaking. The councillors, too, were awake early.

Hooves approaching; Rod turned to see a page pelting across the meadows toward him.

"How now, my lad?" Rod called, grinning and waving for appearances.

"Thou must come to the Queen, Master Gallowglass," the page gasped, out of breath, as he clutched at Rod's stirrup. "My Lord O'Berin and the Lords Loguire are there already before you. 'Tis a council of war!"

The council of war was quickly over, no more than a summary of existent plans, and a brief prayer, plus the news that Catharine wouldn't ride after all. Rod had noticed that Catharine had stood through the meeting.

Then they were up and away, each to his station: Sir Maris to the center, old Duke Loguire to the right flank, and Rod to the left flank. Brom would stay high on the hillside with Catharine and Gwendylon, to direct the whole battle, an innovation Rod had recommended, and which Brom had accepted without reservation: the little man was a mighty fighter, but his legs weren't long enough to hold his seat in a joust.

Tom, offered the option of fighting with the beggars or staying by Rod, had chosen the latter option, probably because he wanted to be in the thick of the battle.

Tuan, of course, would stay with his beggars.

As Tuan swung into the saddle, Catharine stopped him with a hand on his knee. Rod saw her tie a veil of silk about Tuan's upper arm.

Then her hands lifted to him, pleading. Tuan caught them and pressed them to his mouth, bowed to kiss her lips, then wheeled his horse away, rode perhaps ten yards forward, then wheeled again.

They stood frozen a moment, the young Queen and the white knight. Then Tuan reared his horse, pivoted, and galloped after his ragtag-and-patchwork troops.

Rod smiled covertly.

"The time to feel smug is not yet, Rod," Fess reminded him.

Rod made a face. "Who do you think you are, Pinocchio's Cricket?"

He turned back for one last look at Gwendylon, standing near the Queen's tent; then he rode for the left flank.

He was the only horseman who rode without armor.

It was full, 14th Century plate armor, on both sides of the field; but the Southern armor was massed together in a solid, glaring wall, while Catharine's knights were spaced out, twenty yards apart, over the length of the enemy line.

Yes, there are a few holes, Rod thought. And the single line of foot soldiers behind the Queen's knights didn't compare too favorably with the packed masses that backed the rebel lords. No, it was not a sight to inspire confidence.

But the beggars weren't in sight. Nor, for that matter, were the witches. Or the elves.

The rebels were in for some very unpleasant surprises.

At the southern end of the field, a bugle called.

The rebel knights couched their lances.

The Queen's knights followed suit.

There was a long, straining, pause; then the horses plunged forward.

Horses' hooves muttered and rose to the roar of an avalanche as the two metal lines fell toward each other.

And as they fell, the North's line drew it upon itself till the knights rode shoulder to shoulder in the center.

A cheer went up from the rebel line as they saw easy victory coming; it would be easy for the rebel flanks to sweep around the Northern line and trap the Queen's forces.

The Queen's knights met the center of the rebel line with a grinding crash. Knights were unhorsed and blood spurted, but the center of the line held.

And with a victorious roar the rebels swung about to outflank the North. . . .

The yell broke into wild screams as the ground fell away beneath their mounts.

Knights and horses floundered in a six-foot trench.

The elves had done a good night's work.

The footmen came running up to their masters' rescue; but now the beggars broke howling from the trees at the sides of the field, with knife and sword and bludgeon, and fell on the footmen with extreme good will.

Still, they were vastly outnumbered.

But now the aerial arm got into the action. Teams of four levitating, fuzz-cheeked warlocks supported a swinging basket beneath them; and in each basket was a telekinetic witch. The warlocks fired arrows into the scrimmage at random, their hands freed by the leather harness at their waists; and pebbles flew out of the baskets, guided by the witches, to strike with more than enough impact to stun. Arrows speared up at them out of the Southern ranks; but the witches deflected them, and sometimes even managed to turn them back on their owners.

The simple, orderly battle deteriorated into hand-to-hand chaos.

But the Southern knights were still overly busy. The Code dictated that only a knight could fight another knight—a foot soldier could be killed just for trying it, and Heaven help him if he tried and won!

So Catharine's knights worked their way outward from the center along the rebel lines a large percentage of them dying on the way. But the percentage of rebels was greater, for Catharine, like her father before her, had seen fit to give her knights a little extra in the way of training.

Toby, the young warlock, suddenly appeared in the air just above Rod. "Master Gallowglass! The Duke Loguire is sorely pressed; you must come to him!"

He disappeared as abruptly as he had come. It might not have been the greatest form of military communication, but it was better than the rebels had.

Rod dispatched his current preoccupation with a parry and a thrust between breastplate and helmet and backed Fess out of the melee.

He ran around the lines to the other end of the line, where a spindly, armored-clad form with a glowing sword had just finished cutting its way through the troops to Loguire. One of the councillors was trying to save the day by eliminating the leadership. The sword had a strange, radiant quality. Rod didn't know what it was, but it was something mighty potent disguised as a sword.

Rod sailed into the ruckus, bulldozing his way through grappling pairs of beggars and soldiers, slipping in blood and loose heads.

Loguire saw the blow coming and threw up his shield to ward it off. The councillor's sword sheared through it silently, but missed Loguire. The old Duke yelled in pain as the heat was conducted through shield and armor to his skin and momentarily dropped his guard.

The councillor swung the sword up for the final blow.

Fess slammed full tilt into the councillor's horse. The animal went down and the councillor went flying with a scream of terror, sword flinging wide from his grasp.

Soldiers scurried back to be clear when the magic sword fell.

Rod, without the slightest tremor of conscience, wheeled about and trampled the councillor under Fess's iron hooves. The man gave a bubbling scream, choked off; and the scream rang on in Rod's mind.

Now his conscience began to clamor; but he locked it away till the battle was done.

He whirled about toward the sword, hearing the soldiers gasp "Witchcraft!"

"No, just magic," Rod shouted as he swung down, caught the sword, and remounted. "That's not so strange, is it?"

He threw the sword to Loguire hilt-first; the old nobleman caught it and saluted him, and Rod broke out of the lines again.

The battle clamored about him, steel on steel and bone and gristle, no quarter asked. The locked armies lay in the middle of the field like some great, pulsing, obscene amoeba.

Overhead the esper-witches turned and wheeled home, no longer able to tell friend from foe.

Rod charged back and forth through the battle-lines—Fess plowing his way easily through mere mortal flesh—guarding the three generals and as many knights as he could, directing the clearing of the wounded when he could, adding the weight of his arm to break deadlocks.

The beggars seemed to have the soldiers hopelessly outclassed; this was their kind of fighting. Many of them were killed, but seldom without having first accounted for six or more of the enemy, with wooden staves, rusty swords, keen knives, and total disrespect for age and/or rank.

Rod thought of Karl Marx and winced.

Big Tom had long since gotten lost in the battle. Rod hoped he was all right.

Then at the back of the rebel line, Big Tom rose up roaring "To me! To me!"

A thousand beggars rallied to him and began to chop their way through the Southern ranks.

The idea spread; beggar groups sprang up all along the line, and began to press the amoeba of war in on itself.

Big Tom was hewing his way through to a very definite goal.

Rod frowned and stood up in his stirrups, trying to plot Big Tom's course.

There, in the center of the battle, twenty frantic scarecrows labored furiously to construct some sort of machine: a spidery tripod topped by a wasp-waisted contraption with alien curves. It was the councillors, with their last hope.

Rod rapped with his heels, and Fess leaped—but the robot had responded a touch slow. With a sense of dread, Rod realized that the strain of battle was beginning to tell on Fess.

The horse bounded over the heads of the army and

plowed through to the force of councillors, just as Tom broke through from the other side, with only a fraction of his beggar troops.

A long, lurking moment of silence filled the little circle as the councillors saw their executioners.

Then the councillors howled, drawing back into a tight circle about the machine, the ferocity of despair in their eyes, their glowing swords leaping out.

Tom's boys circled out around the councillors and closed in.

The councillors' swords were deadly; but they had to hit to be effective, and the beggars were good at hitting and getting clear.

A lot of beggars dropped, cut in half; but a lot more lived. They outnumbered the councillors four to one. They whittled away at the ranks.

The councillors screamed, chopping, and died.

In the center of the circle, Rod could make out one lonely figure still working frantically at the machine—Durer.

Then, suddenly, there were only five councillors left.

Durer spun away from the machine with a shriek of despair and lugged something out of his wallet-pouch.

A laser-pistol.

Rod dropped down to Fess's far side, the bulk of the horse between him and the councillors, knowing that only a head shot could hurt the robot, and snapped open a hidden panel in his horse's side. In it was his last-ditch defense: the latest-issue DDT laser pistol.

He fumbled the weapon out, hearing the screams of the beggars as their legs were sheared off at the knee, and shot around under Fess's neck.

His shot creased Durer's leg. The scarecrow-man clasped his knee and fell, howling.

Tom bellowed.

The beggars stepped in. Oaken staves whirled, knocking the remaining councillors off their feet.

The staves rose high, poised a moment, and fell with a sickening, moist crunch.

Big Tom bellowed victorious laughter and scooped up a fallen councillor's sword.

Durer rolled back up to one knee and fired.

The red pencil of light caught Tom in the shoulder. He roared, spinning, and fell.

Half-crawling, half-leaping, Durer went for him, struggling to get a clear shot.

Rod snapped a shot at him, and missed.

Durer howled and dove behind a fallen body.

Rod slammed his heels into Fess. "Quick! Before he can recover to shoot!"

The horse leaped; the laser beam caught it in the belly—a hollow steel belly, no harm.

But the robot's legs stiffened, its head lolled forward, even while it was in the air.

Rod sprang free as Fess landed, crumpled, rolled.

Rod rolled too, came up to see Durer, risen to one knee, level the pistol at him.

Tom's huge body smashed into him.

Durer caromed away, pistol flying wide from his hand.

The same had happened to Rod's. He cast about him, frantically searching.

Tom rolled, came to his feet, lurched after Durer, catching up a fallen councillor's sword . . . and tripped over a body.

Quick as an eel, Durer was up, catching Tom's fallen sword, chopping down . . .

Rod dove.

His shoulder caught Durer in the belly, whipped the little man around; the sword landed harmlessly in the earth.

Durer leaned on the sword, kept his feet, and swung the sword up, turning to Rod.

Rod rolled to his knees, saw the sword coming. . . .

Tom bellowed, slammed into Rod, striking him out of the sword's path.

The glowing sword fell, shearing off Tom's shoulder and a third of his rib cage.

Rod screamed as he rolled to his feet and swung around. His arm locked around Durer's throat, his knee came up into the small of the back. Something snapped.

Durer screamed and went limp, screaming still, the sword falling from his fingers.

Rod threw him down.

Still screaming, the scarecrow groped for the sword.

Rod dropped to his knee and chopped down.

The callused edge of his hand smashed larynx and vertebrae.

Durer gurgled, convulsed, and lay still.

Rod stood, gasping, and turned, to see Tom's shoulder pumping blood in great gouts, the big man's face contorted in a silent grimace.

Rod was down again, groping frantically in the welter of blood and spare bodies.

He came up with the laser pistol and swung back to Tom.

The remaining beggars lurched forward, too slow; before they could reach him, Rod pulled the trigger and, holding it down, sliced off another half-inch along Tom's wound. Tom screamed.

Then they were on Rod, mauling and clubbing.

"Nay!" Tom rasped, a sickening parody of his former bellow. "Fools, let him be! Do y' not see! He stopped the blood!"

He sank back as the grasping hands hesitated, then loosened. Rod limped back to him, bruised on face and body, rubbing the worst of them—his scarcely-healed shoulder.

He sank to one knee by the gasping hilk of a man, face still wrenched with pain. The stink of cauterized flesh filled his head.

Tom forced his eyes open a fraction and tried to grin. " 'Twas . . . well meant . . . master. Two minutes ago, it . . . might ha' saved me.''

Rod jerked off his cloak, balled it up, thrust it under Tom's head. "Lie back and rest,'' he growled through a tight throat. "You're a healthy hunk, you'll make it. You haven't lost all that much blood.''

"Nay,'' Tom panted, "too much . . . lost. And the . . . body's shock . . .''

His face twisted with a spasm of pain. Rod turned away to Fess, slapped the reset switch and fumbled in one of the horse's hidden pockets for an ampul.

He limped back to Tom, slapped the ampul against the burned flesh.

Tom relaxed with a huge sigh as the anesthetic took hold. "My thanks, master,'' he murmured weakly. "That hast given me, at least, painless death.''

"Don't talk that way.'' Rod's face was frozen. "There's many a roll in the hay for you yet.''

"Nay, master.'' Tom shook his head, closing his eyes. "My time is nigh.''

"You're not going to die. You'll leave me in your debt if you do. I won't have it.''

"A pox on what thou wilt or wilt not!'' Tom spat, with a touch of life again. "I am not thine to command or deny now, lordling. He who now hath me in thrall is far more puissant than thou, and will one day command thee also.''

He sagged back on the pillow, heaving gasps of air.

Rod knelt silent by his side.

Tom's remaining hand groped over his belly to catch Rod's forearm. "Aye, thou'rt now in my debt, though 'twas not of my choice."

"Not your choice?" Rod scowled. "What are you talking about? You saved my life!"

"Aye, and thereby lost my own. But I would never ha' done so with a clear head."

"Clear head?"

"Aye. In battle, one sees and one does, whatever comes first to mind. 'Twas thee, or living my life longer to serve the House of Clovis; and in the heat of the battle I chose thee, in my folly!"

He was silent a moment, breathing hoarsely; then his hands tightened again. "Yet while I die, thou wilt live in my debt! And what thou canst not pay to me, thou must pay to my people."

Rod tried to draw his hand back. "No!"

"Aye!" Tom's eyes flew wide, glaring, angry. " 'Tis the payment I demand! Thy life for mine, thy life spent here on Gramarye, to work for the good of my people!"

"I'm not my own master . . ."

"Nay, thou art." Tom sank back, weary. "Thou art, and if thou knowest it not, thou'rt true fool."

"The price is too high, Tom. My death in battle, yes, gladly. But living here, all my days, I cannot. I too serve a dream. . . ."

" 'Twas my choice, also," Tom sighed, "the dream or the man. Nay, then, choose what thou wilt."

"I'm under a geas . . ."

"Then my geas also is on thee, freeing thee from the other. Thou must serve me and mine now . . ."

The dying face darkened. "I had thought I knew what was best for them . . . but now, as all darkens about me . . ."

He heaved up suddenly, body wracked with a spasm,

coughing blood. Rod threw his arms about the big man,
holding him up.

The spasm passed. Tom clutched weakly at Rod's
arm, gasping. "Nay, then . . . thy mind is . . .
clearer . . . thou must decide . . ."

"Be still," Rod pleaded, trying to lower him again.
"Don't waste what little life is left—"

"Nay!" Tom clutched at him. "Let me speak! Espers . . . Tribunal . . . they'll make it . . . work
. . . We . . . fight them . . . here . . . in the . . ."

"Be still," Rod pleaded. "Save your breath, I know
what you're saying."

Tom craned his neck to look up at him. "You . . .?"

Rod nodded. "Yes. You told me the last little bit I
needed, just now. Now lie down."

Tom sagged in his arms. Rod lowered him gently,
letting his head rest in the blood-soaked cape.

Tom lay panting. "Tell me . . . I must know . . . if
you know . . ."

"Yes, I know," Rod murmured. "The DDT will
win out. You can only fight it back here. And you fight
each other as well."

"Aye." Tom nodded, a barely perceptible movement. "Thou . . . must decide . . . now . . . and
. . . master . . ."

He mumbled, too soft to hear, and labored for
another breath, eyes opening, anxious.

Rod bent forward, putting his ear to Tom's
lips.

"Don't die for . . . a dream . . ."

Rod frowned. "I don't understand."

He waited, then said, "What do you mean, Tom?"

There was no answer.

Rod straightened slowly, looking down at the vacant
eyes, the loose mouth.

He touched the base of the throat, the jugular.

He let his fingertips rest there long minutes, then slowly reached up to close the man's eyes.

He stood, slowly, and turned away, his eyes not seeing.

Then, slowly, his eyes focused. He looked around at the staring, pathetic beggars, their eyes fixed on the huge body.

A slight, slender shape stepped hesitantly into the ring. "M-master Gallowglass?"

Rod turned, saw, and stepped forward as the beggars began to move in, to kneel by Tom's body.

Rod moved away from them, head hanging heavily.

He raised his eyes. "What is it, Toby?"

"Milord . . ." Toby's face was strangely tragic in its confusion as he looked at the group of beggars, disturbed without knowing why. "Mlord, they . . . They cry for quarter, milord. Shall we give it them?"

"Quarter? Oh, yes. They want to surrender." Rod nodded, closing his eyes.

He turned and looked at the group of beggars. "Oh, I don't know. What does Brom say?

"My lord O'Berin says, aye, grant it them, but the Queen says nay. The Lords Loguire are with Brom."

"And still the Queen says nay." Rod nodded, bitterness tightening his mouth. "And they want me to break the deadlock, is that it?"

"Aye, milord."

The circle of beggars parted a little. Rod saw Tom's waxen, still face.

He turned back to Toby. "Hell, yes. Give 'em quarter."

The sun had sunk behind the hills, leaving the sky a pale rose, darkening to the east.

The twelve Great Lords stood, bound in chains, before Catharine.

Near her sat Loguire and Tuan, Brom and Sir Maris.

Rod stood a little distance away, leaning back against Fess, arms folded, chin sunk on his breast.

The old Duke Loguire's head was also bowed, deep misery in his eyes, for his son Anselm stood a pace in advance of the rest of the lords, directly before the Queen.

Catharine held her head high, eyes shining with triumph and pride, face flushed with the joy of her power.

Rod looked at her and felt a twist of disgust in his belly; her arrogance had returned with her victory.

At a sign from Brom O'Berin, two heralds blew a flourish. The trumpets whirled away from their lips, and a third herald stepped forward, loosening a scroll.

"Be it known to all by these presents, that on this day the miscreant vassal, Anselm, son of Loguire, did rise in most vicious rebellion against Catharine, Queen of Gramarye, and is threfore liable to the judgment of the Crown, even unto death, for the crime of high treason!"

He rolled the scroll and slapped it to his side. "Who speaks in defense of Anselm, chief of the rebels?"

There was a silence.

Then old Loguire rose.

He bowed gravely to Catharine. She returned his courtesy with a glare, astonished and angry.

"Naught can be said in defense of a rebel," Loguire rumbled. "Yet for a man who, in the haste of hot blood, rises to avenge what he may consider to be insults to his father and house, much may be said; for, though his actions were rash and, aye, even treacherous, still he was moved by honor, and filial piety. Moreover, having seen the outcome of rash action, and being under the tutelage of his duke and his father, might well again realize his true loyalties and duties to his sovereign."

Catharine smiled; her voice was syrup and honey. "You would then, milord, have me enlarge this man, upon whose head must be laid the deaths of some several thousand, once again to your protection and discipline; to you who have, as this day has proved, failed once already in these duties?"

Loguire winced.

"Nay, good milord!" she snapped, face paling, lips drawing thin. "Thou hast fostered rebels against me before, and now seek to do it again!"

Loguire's face hardened.

Tuan half-bolted from his chair, flushed with anger.

She turned to him with a haughty, imperious look. "Has milord of the beggars aught to say?"

Tuan fought for calm, grinding his teeth. He straightened and bowed gravely. "My Queen, father and son have this day battled valiantly for you. Will you not, therefore, grant us the life of our son and our brother?"

Catharine's face paled further, eyes narrowing.

"I thank my father and brother," said Anselm, in a clear, level voice.

"Be still!" Catharine fairly shrieked, turning on him. "Treacherous, villainous, thrice-hated dog!"

Rage came into the Loguires' eyes; still they held themselves silent.

Catharine sat back in her chair, gasping, clasping the arms tight, that her hands might not tremble. "Thou wilt speak when I ask thee, traitor," she snapped. "Till then, hold thy peace!"

"I will not hold my peace! Thou canst not hurt me more; I will have my say! Thou, vile Queen, hast determined I shall die, and nothing will sway thee! Why, then, slay me!" he shouted. "The penalty for treason is death! I had known as much before I rebelled; slay me and be done with it!"

Catharine sat back, relaxing a trifle. "He is sentenced by his own mouth," she said. "It is the law of the land that a rebel shall die."

"The law of the land is the Queen," rumbled Brom. "If she says a traitor shall live he shall live."

She spun to him, staring in horror. "Wilt thou, too, betray me? Will not one of my generals stand beside me this day?"

"Oh, be done with it!" Rod stormed, looming up over the throne. "No, not one of your generals will support you now, and it seems to me that might give you some slight hint you're in the wrong. But oh, no, not the Queen! Why hold a trial? You've already decided he'll die!" He turned away and spat. "Come on, get this farce of a trial over with," he growled.

"Thou too?" she gasped. "Wilt thou also defend a traitor, one who hath caused death to three thousand . . ."

"*You* have caused the death of three thousand," Rod bellowed. "A noble man of low birth lies dead in that field, his right side torn away, the birds pecking at him, and why? To defend a willful child who sits on a throne, not worth the life of a beggar! A child who is so poor a queen she gave birth to rebellion!"

Catharine cowered back in her throne, trembling. "Be still!" she gasped. "Was it I who rebelled?"

"Who was it gave the nobles cause to rebel by too-hasty reforms and too-lofty manner? Cause, Catharine, cause! There is no rebellion without it; and who but the Queen has given it?"

"Be still, oh be still!" The back of her hand to her mouth, as though she would scream. "You may not speak so to a Queen.!"

Rod looked down at the cowering Queen. His face twisted with disgust.

He turned away. "Ah, I'm sick to the belly! Let them

live; there has been too much death this day already. Let them live. They'll be loyal, without their councillors to needle them. Let them live, let them all live. They're schooled now, even if you're not."

"This cannot be true!" Catharine gasped.

"It is not!" Tuan stepped forward, his hand going to his sword. "The Queen gave cause, aye, but she did not make the rebellion."

Catharine's eyes leaped up to him with a look of radiant gratitude.

"Speak truth," Tuan went on, "and you may chastise her. But when you charge her with that which she hath not done"—he shook his head slowly—"I cannot let you speak."

Rod ached to spit in his face.

Instead, he turned again to Catharine, who sat straight again, regaining her haughty look.

"Do not forget," he said, "that a queen who cannot control her own whims is a weak queen."

She paled again, and "Walk wary!" Tuan snapped.

Rage surged up in Rod, higher and higher as he stood rigid against it, till it broke some bond within him and drained away, leaving an icy calm and a great clearity, a clarity in which he saw what he must do and why . . . and what the consequences to himself must needs be.

Catharine was almost smiling now, smug and haughty again, seeing Rod hesitate at Tuan's threat.

"Has more to say, sirrah?" she demanded, lifting her chin.

"Yes," Rod said between his teeth. "What kind of queen is it who betrays her own people?"

His hand whipped out and slapped her.

She screamed, falling back in the chair, and Tuan was on him, fist swinging square into Rod's face.

Rod ducked under the blow and grappled Tuan to him, shouting "Fess!"

Tuan's fists slammed into his belly, trip-hammer blows; but Rod held on, seeing the other generals rushing up.

But Fess got there first.

Rod tried to forget what a nice, clean young kid Tuan was and drove his knee into Tuan's groin.

He let go and leaped to the saddle as Tuan fell, doubled with pain, rattling in his throat.

Fess spun and leaped over the heads of the approaching Guardsmen.

He landed and stretched into a gallop. Rod heard Catharine screaming Tuan's name and grinned savagely.

Then his grin stretched into a silent scream as pain exploded in his wounded shoulder.

Turning, he saw the nock of a crossbow bolt sticking out of his shoulder.

And, beyond the bouncing shoulder, in the midst of the circle of Guardsmen around the throne, Catharine bending over Tuan, who knelt, still curled around his pain, with a Guardsman's crossbow dropping from his hand.

They came back to a hill overlooking the field as dusk gathered, having run a long circle through wood and field and waded a mile of stream to hide their trail.

Rod slumped out of the saddle as Fess came to the edge of a grove. He limped to a large tree and sat, leaning back against the trunk, hidden from eyes in the field below by the gathering gloom.

He looked down over the glowing fires on the field, listening to the faint sounds of the victory merry-making.

He sighed and turned to the problem at hand, or more accurately, at shoulder. He opened his doublet and probed the shoulder gently, wincing with the pain that he felt even through the anesthetic he'd applied on the run.

The barbed bolt-head seemed buried just in front of collarbone and joint; by some miracle, it had missed both bone and artery.

There was a faint puff of air, like a miniature shockwave, and he looked up to see Gwendylon bending toward him, tears welling from her eyes. "My lord, my lord! Art badly hurt?"

Rod smiled and reached up to pull her head down to his. He held her against him for a good, long time.

"Nay, then," she said, blushing as she drew away, "I warrant thou'rt not so sorely wounded as I had feared."

"Ah, lass, lass!" Rod leaned back, cradling her in his arm. "I was lonely, on that ride."

"I'd ha' come to you sooner, lord," she said apologetically, "but I must needs wait till you'd come to rest.

"Now to that shoulder." She took on a brisk, almost businesslike air. " 'Twill hurt some, my lord."

Rod ground his teeth as she stripped the blood-soaked tunic off his shoulder. "Bandages in the saddlebag," he gritted as she finished.

She turned to Fess, brought out the small metal box, frowned. "What is this red cross here, my lord?"

"Just a symbol," Rod wheezed. "Means it's a, uh, healing kit."

She knelt by his side again, very still.

Rod frowned, wondering what she was doing.

Then pain lanced him again, and he felt the bolt-head receding, withdrawing slowly along the channel it had cut on its way in, and, seemingly, all of its own accord.

Through a pain-blurred haze, a random thought burrowed: these witches were the answer to the surgeon's prayer.

The bolt-head eased itself past his skin, then suddenly whirled spinning through the air to smash itself against a stone.

"Thus," she hissed, "may I serve all who would harm thee, my lord."

Rod shivered as he realized the extent of the power he'd been dallying with.

She reached for the bandages.

"No, no!" Rod touched her arm with his good hand. "The powder in the silver envelope first. It'll stop the bleeding."

"I would rather use compress of herbs," she said dubiously. "But as thou wilt have it, my lord."

Rod shuddered as the sulfa bit into him.

Then the pain numbed, and she was winding the bandage.

"It seems you're always bandaging that shoulder," Rod muttered.

"Aye, my lord. I would that thou wert more chary of it."

Someone coughed, somewhat delicately, nearby.

Rod looked up and saw a squat silhouette lurking in the shadows.

Rod's mouth tightened. "Well, if it isn't the Atrophied Ajax himself!"

Gwendylon laid a reproving finger gently on his lips.

Rod gave a short nod, irritated at himself; the fingers lifted away.

He beckoned with his good arm. "Well, come on and join the party, Brom. But be careful; the fruits of victory are sour tonight."

Brom came forward, hands locked behind him, head bowed, and sat on a nearby root.

Rod frowned. There was something sheepish, almost furtive, in the dwarf's manner. "What's eating you?" he growled.

Brom sighed and rested his hands on his knees. "Thou hast caused me much heartache this day, Rod Gallowglass."

Rod smiled, one-sided. "Sounds more like a bellyache. I take it you weren't too pleased at the way things went?"

"Oh, nay, I was most enormously pleased! And yet"—Brom rested his chin on his clenched hands, looking sheepish again—"I confess that at first I was somewhat wroth with thee."

"You don't say!"

"Aye; but that was before I realized your plan."

"Oh?" Rod raised one eyebrow. "But you did figure out what I was up to?"

"Nay. I grow old, Rod Gallowglass . . ."

Rod snorted.

"My thanks." Brom inclined his head. "But 'tis truth; I grow old, and must needs be shown."

"And what were you shown?"

"Oh, 'twas a most touching scene!" Brom smiled with a touch of sarcasm. "At first Catharine could but cry, 'My love, thou'rt hurt!' and call for doctors and herbs, till Tuan managed to rise, saying his hurt was but slight; and then she fell to weeping on his shoulder, the while crying him her lord and protector and the guard of her honor, and would not be comforted till he'd swore he would wed her!" Brom's smile softened, "Aye, 'twas most tender to look upon."

Rod nodded wearily, closing his eyes. "When's the wedding?"

"As soon as they shall be thrice called in a church. Catharine would have had it right then, but Tuan cried no, that she was Queen and the flower of womanhood, and must be wed as befitted her estate.''

"A promising beginning.''

"Oh, 'twas more promising still! For Tuan then turned to the twelve lords and, quoth he, 'And how shall we deal with these?' And Catharine cried, 'Oh, as thou wilt, my lord, as thou wilt! But be done with them right quickly, and come away!' ''

"Very auspicious," Rod agreed. "What did he do with them?''

"Struck off their chains, and bade them once more take up the care of their demesnes. But he required of them each a hostage, of twelve years old or less, of their blood and body and legitimate household, to dwell in the Queen's castle.''

Rod frowned, nodded. "Should work. He gets a deterrent, and a chance to raise a new generation very loyal to the throne.''

He leaned back against the rough bark, feeling totally drained. "Glad it worked.''

"Aye.'' Brom's eyes glowed "This land shall stand ever in thy debt, Rod Gallowglass. Thou hast saved us our Crown, and banished the ghost of a long and full bloody civil war; and, moreover, thou has given us a King.''

"And a Public Enemy No. 1,'' Rod said bitterly.

A shadow darkened Brom's face.

Rod lifted an eye to him. "You must admit that I'm slightly *persona non grata*.''

"Aye,'' Brom growled, "yet ever wilt thou find sanctuary in the land of the elves.''

Rod smiled weakly. "Thanks, Brom.''

"Yet tell me!'' Brom hunched forward, frowning. "How is it thou hast come? When all looked bleak in our land, and hope had been exiled, then did you come, falling from the skies like an answer to prayer—you, who had no stake in our countryside, no manor to defend. Our cares were not yours, yet you made them so.''

He thrust his head forward, eyes burning. ''Why hast thou saved us?''

Rod's smile soured. ''For the Dream.''

Brom frowned. ''How . . . ?''

Rod looked up at the stars. He hesitated a moment, then said, ''Fess, record this.''

He turned to Brom, then to Gwendylon, lifting his good arm to point to the sky.

''Look up there. See those stars? Each one has worlds circling about it, worlds like this one, where lovers meet and men feud, and kings topple.

''But most of them are united under one rule, one government—the Decentralized Democratic Tribunal. And the voice that commands is that of the people themselves.''

''Nay!'' Brom boomed. ''How can that be?''

''Because each man's voice can be heard, his opinions adding weight to those of his fellows. That's the key, communications. You can't have that kind of government here because your communications are lousy, which is strange, because you've got the potential for the best system, if you'd just use it.''

He folded his arms and leaned back. ''But they've got bad trouble up there. They're growing, you see. Every day, at least one new world joins the Tribunal. At that rate, they'll have reached the limit of their communications. After that, they'll start running downhill to dictatorship.''

''But how is this thy concern?'' Brom growled.

''I work for them. I'm the salesman. I'm the boy who goes ou and gets new planets ready for membership

. . . if they want it, which they always do, *once they're ready!''*

"And what is this readiness?" Brom smiled, fighting for tolerance.

"Communications, as I told you, but even more than that, learning. Education.''

He sighed. ''The education, we've got licked. Took a long while, but it's licked. Communications, though, that's another matter.

'' 'Cause there's one other ingredient to freedom: a frontier. It prevents a stratified society—never mind what that is, my Lord O'Berin, King of the Elves—and a stratified society is another road to totalitarianism.

"So the Tribunal's got to keep growing. But if it grows much more, slowing communications will be its death. And I, very personally, don't want that. Because the Dream has a name, you see—Freedom. That's my Dream. And that's why Gramarye means so much to me.''

Brom scowled. ''I do not comprehend.''

Rod turned to him, smiling. ''The witches. Their power to hear thoughts. That's the communications system we need.''

He watched understanding, and a certain dread, dawn in Brom's face, then turned away.

''We need them,'' he said, ''we need lots of them. Up till now, their numbers have been growing slowly. But, under Catharine's protection, they'll grow faster; and from their winning in today's battle, they'll begin to be respected, and before too long, every parent will be hoping for a witch to be born in the family. Then their numbers will soar.''

Brom scowled. ''But how is it this world alone, of all the ones you speak of, hath witches?''

''Because the men who brought life to the land, your

ancestors, who dropped from the skies, selected only those persons who had at least a trace of witch-power in them, to come here. They didn't know they had it, it was too little, and hidden too deeply, to be seen; but as the generations rolled and they married one another again and again, that little bit grew and grew, until at last a witch was born."

"And when was that?" Brom smiled tolerantly.

"When the elves appeared. Also the banshees, werewolves, and other supernatural fauna. Because there's a strange substance on this planet, called witch-moss, that shapes itself to the forms a witch thinks of. If the witch thinks of an elf, the moss turns into an elf."

Brom paled. "Dost thou say . . ."

"Don't feel bad about it, Brom," Rod said quickly. "All men were once just pulsing blobs floating in the sea; it's just that in your remote ancestor's case, the process was speeded up a trifle, through the witches. And it was your first ancestor, not you; my guess is that the critter formed out of the moss is such a perfect copy, it can breed true—and even cross-breed with mortal men."

He leaned back and sighed. "Be proud, Brom. You and your people are the only ones who can claim to be real native citizens."

Brom was silent a long moment; then he growled, "Aye, then, this is our land. And what wouldst thou do with it, warlock from the skies?"

"Do?" Rod cocked an eye. "Only what you yourself are trying to do, Brom, through the reforms you've suggested to Catharine. Equality before the law, isn't that your aim?"

"It is, aye."

"Well, it's mine, too. And my job is to show you the least bloody road to it, which job I have just finished."

He scowled, suddenly brooding.

Brom studied him. Gwendylon touched his head, stroking the hair, worried.

Rod looked up at her and tried to smile.

He turned to Brom. "That's why I fought for Catharine, you see: because she protects the witches, and because she's a reformer; and so is Tuan, thank Heaven.

"And that's why the councillors and the Mocker fought against her."

Brom scowled. "I am old, Rod Gallowglass. Show me."

Rod looked up at the stars again. "Someday the Tribunal will govern all the stars you can see, and a lot more that you can't. And almost all the people who live on those worlds will be witches, because they'll have the blood of Gramarye flowing in their veins.

"How's that for a laurel wreath, Brom? 'Father to a Galaxy . . .'

"But some people won't be witches. And because they're not, they'll hate the witches, and their government, more violently than you can imagine. That kind is called a fanatic.

"And they'll go for any system of government, any, as long as it isn't democracy. And they'll fight democracy with every breath in their bodies."

"If it is to be as you say," growled Brom, "these men will lose; for how could they fight so many worlds?"

"They can't," Rod answered, "unless they kill it before it's born."

"But how shall they do that? For to kill the witch in the womb, they must come to the womb, here to Gramarye, and try to . . . why . . . to slay . . ."

Brom stared, horrified.

"Catharine," Rod finished for him, nodding sourly.

"Right, Brom. The councillors and the leader cadre of the House of Clovis are somebody's great-great-fifty-times-great-grandchildren."

"But how could that be?" Brom gasped. "What man can visit his ancestors?"

"They can. They've got a thing called a time machine. There's one of them hidden somewhere in the House of Clovis, and another in the haunted tunnels of the Castle Loguire.

"So guard those four men in your dungeon very carefully, Brom. They might have a few surprises in store."

"Be assured that I will!"

"And the councillors are all dead." Rod leaned back, eyes closing. "Which nicely wraps up the report. Send it home, Fess. Oh, and corroborative material: a description of the time machine, and descriptions of the witches' main tricks—you know, telekinesis, levitation, telepor—"

"I do know, Rod," the robot's voice reminded him.

"Umph. Some self-effacing retainer *you* are. Well, send it home."

The warp transmitter deep within Fess's basketball brain spat a two-second squeal at the stars.

All was silent a moment; then Gwendylon said, hesitantly, "My lord?"

Rod lifted an eyelid and smiled. "You shouldn't call me that. But I like it."

She smiled, shyly. "My lord, you ha' finished your work here . . . ."

Rod's face darkened.

He turned away, glowering down at the earth.

"Where will you go now, Rod Warlock?" Brom murmured.

"Oh, cut it out!" Rod snapped.

He turned away again, sullen. "I'm not a warlock,"

he growled. "I'm an agent from a very advanced technology, and as such have a bag of tricks like you wouldn't believe, but they're all cold iron and its breed. I haven't a witch trick to my name, and I certainly don't have the tiniest shred of witch power."

He lifted his eyes to the stars again. "I'm not a warlock, not the slightest bit, not so much as the meanest of your peasants. I don't belong here."

He felt a tearing in him as he said it.

"I chose this life," Rod growled. "I take orders, yes, but I do it voluntarily."

"A point," Brom admitted, "but a weak one. By choice or not by choice, thou'rt still enslaved."

"Yes," Rod admitted. "But some must give up their freedom, so that their children may have it."

But it didn't even sound convincing to him.

Brom gusted a sigh and slapped his thighs, standing. He gazed at Rod, his eyes weary and old.

"If thou must go, thou must go; a geas is a thing no man can deny. Go on to the stars, Rod Gallowglass, but be mindful: if ever thou seekest a haven, 'tis here."

He turned and strode away, down the hillside.

Gwendylon sat quietly beside him, clasping his hand.

"Tell me," she said after a little while, "is it only one dream that takes you away from me?"

"Yes. Oh, yes." Rod's hand tightened on hers. "You sort of blotted out any other dreams."

She turned, smiling tremulously, tears glittering on her lashes. "Then may not I accompany you to the stars, good my lord?"

Rod clamped down on her hand, throat tightening. "I wish that you could; but you'd wither and die there, like an uprooted flower. You belong here, where they need you. I belong there. It's as simple as that."

"No." She shook her head sadly. "You go not for belonging, but for a geas. But, good my lord"—she turned, tears flowing now—"is not my geas as strong as your dream?"

"Look," he said tightly, "try to understand. A man has to have a dream. That's the difference between animals and man, a dream. And a man who's lost his dream is something less than a man, and worthy of no woman. How could I dare claim you if I wasn't a man?

"A man has to prove his worth to himself, before he can claim a woman, and the dream is the proof. As long as he's working for it, he's got a right to her, because he's worth something. I could stay here and be very, very happy with you. But in my depths I'd know I didn't deserve you. Because I'd be a drone, a male with no purpose. How could I father children if I knew their mother was more valuable to the world than I am?"

"Then it wouldst be thou who wouldst wither and die?" she murmured.

Rod nodded.

"But the geas, my lord, if not mine alone, is not Big Tom's geas added to it, and the old Duke Loguire's enough to balance the geas of the stars?"

Rod sat rigid.

"They bade you watch over their people," she murmured. "And what would become of them, lord, if these fiends from tomorrow come again? As surely they will, if they hate as deep as thou say."

Rod nodded, very slowly.

"And what of the Dream then, my lord?" she murmured.

Rod sat rock-still for a moment.

"Fess," he said quietly.

"Yes, Rod?"

"Fess, send them my resignation."

"Your *what?*"

"My resignation!" Rod snapped. "And hurry it up!"

"But Rod, your duty . . . the honor of your house . . ."

"Oh, stuff it! The councillors might be back, Fess, even if we smash the time machines. They did it once, they can do it again. Send it!"

Fess obediently beeped at the stars.

Then, slowly, Rod's head lolled forward.

"My lord?" Gwendylon gasped.

Rod raised a hand weakly. "I'm all right. I've done the right thing, and the one that'll make me happiest. For the first time in my life, I'm working on my own.

"And that's it. I've cut myself off. They're not backing me anymore—the house, the clan, Big Brother watching over me . . ."

"Thou hast a house here, lord," she murmured.

"I know, I know. And in a little while this'll pass, and I'll be happier than I ever have been. But now . . ."

He looked up at her, smiled weakly. "I'll be all right."

"Rod," Fess murmured.

He lifted his head. "Yes, Fess?"

"They have replied, Rod."

Rod tensed. "Read it."

"*Report accepted. Request send coordinates for veryifying expedition.*"

Rod nodded, mouth twisting back with bitterness. "Send 'em. Go on."

"*Request you reconsider resignation. Accept permanent assignment planet Gramarye guard against further infiltration-subversion.*"

Rod straightened, staring. "What?"

"They would like to make your chosen position official, Rod," the robot replied.

"What is it, my lord?"

"They want me to stay on," Rod answered mechanically.

He turned to her, life replacing the stunned look. "They want me to stay on!"

"Stay on where, my lord?" she asked, catching the first traces of his enthusiasm.

"Stay on here!" he bellowed, jumping to his feet and flinging his arm wide to include the whole planet. "Here on Gramarye! As an agent! Gwen, I'm free! And I'm home!"

He dropped to his knees, spinning to face her, hands biting into her shoulders.

"I love you!" he bellowed. "Marry me!"

"At once and forever, my lord!" she cried, clasping his face in her hands, and the tears poured.

He grabbed for her, but she held him off with a palm over his lips. "Nay, my lord. Only a warlock may kiss a witch."

"All right, I'm a warlock, I'm a warlock! Just kiss me, will you?"

She did.

He locked his hands in the small of her back, grinning.

"Hey," he said, "is it true, what they say about farm girls?"

"Aye, my lord." She lowered her eyes and began unbuttoning his doublet. "You'll never be rid of me now."

A BRIDE FOR ANNA'S PAPA

Also by Isabel R. Marvin

Bridge to Freedom
Josefina and the Hanging Tree
The Mystery of Green Fire
Saving Joe Louis
Shipwrecked on Padre Island

A Bride for Anna's Papa

Isabel R. Marvin

Illustrations by Kay Sather

MILKWEED
EDITIONS

First Published 1994 by Milkweed Editions
Printed in the United States of America
Cover design by Christian Fünfhausen
Cover photographs courtesy of the Minnesota Historical Society
Interior design by Don Leeper
Interior illustrations by Kay Sather
The text of this book is set in Minion.
04 05 06 07 08   5 4 3 2 1

Milkweed Editions, a nonprofit publisher, gratefully acknowledges support from Emilie and Henry Buchwald; Bush Foundation; Cargill Value Investment; Timothy and Tara Clark Family Charitable Fund; DeL Corazón Family Fund; Dougherty Family Foundation; Ecolab Foundation; Joe B. Foster Family Foundation; General Mills Foundation; Jerome Foundation; Kathleen Jones; Constance B. Kunin; D. K. Light; Chris and Ann Malecek; McKnight Foundation; a grant from the Minnesota State Arts Board, through an appropriation by the Minnesota State Legislature, a grant from the National Endowment for the Arts, and private funders; Sheila C. Morgan; Laura Jane Musser Fund; an award from the National Endowment for the Arts, which believes that a great nation deserves great art; Navarre Corporation; Kate and Stuart Nielsen; Outagamie Charitable Foundation; Qwest Foundation; Debbie Reynolds; St. Paul Companies, Inc., Foundation; Ellen and Sheldon Sturgis; Surdna Foundation; Target, Marshall Field's, and Mervyn's with support from the Target Foundation; Gertrude Sexton Thompson Charitable Trust (George R.A. Johnson, Trustee); James R. Thorpe Foundation; Toro Foundation; Weyerhaeuser Family Foundation; and Xcel Energy Foundation.

Library of Congress Cataloging-in-Publication Data

Marvin, Isabel R.
    A bride for Anna's Papa / Isabel R. Marvin.
      p. cm.
    Summary: In 1907, thirteen-year-old Anna tries to find a bride for her father who works in the iron mines of northern Minnesota.
    ISBN 1-57131-650-7
    [1. Finnish Americans—Fiction.   2. Minnesota—Fiction.]
    I. Title
PZ7.M36815Br 1994
[Fic]—dc20

                                                                    93-41175
                                                                         CIP

This book is printed on acid-free paper.

*Dedicated to the people of Chisholm
and the iron range, where we
spent many happy years.*

A BRIDE FOR ANNA'S PAPA

ONE

~

EARLY FRIDAY AFTERNOON, the most dreaded sound on the Mesabi Iron Range destroyed the peace of a warm July day—the whistle that announced mine accidents. The shrill warning pierced the air, stabbing its listeners' ears. Then a distant church bell began to toll, repeating the tragedy for those farther from Chisholm's Monroe-Tener mine.

Anna punched down the bread she was making. It wouldn't hurt to let it rise again, and she had to find out what had happened. It couldn't be Papa! He was a blacksmith now and didn't have to work underground anymore. But if he had gone down in the mine to deliver tools—.

Without removing her apron or looking in the mirror to see if her braids were neat, she paused only to shut the front door. Her little brother Matti was playing with friends, but he would hear the whistle and know there had been an accident. Mrs. Sevnick, the next-door neighbor who had been so helpful when their mother died, ran out of her house at the same time. Her baby, Mary, began crying as Mrs. Sevnick and Anna joined the housewives and children rushing toward the mine. Some carried babies; all ran with fear in their hearts that the mine had taken their husband, father, son, or brother.

Accidents happened often in the underground mines. Anna's papa, Toivo Kallio, had told her many times that the engineers and owners did not take enough precautions to keep the men safe.

"It would cost money," he said, "and there are always new workers to take the place of those who are crippled or killed."

Anna ran toward the mine with her neighbors until a group of workers stopped the frightened families. The men were covered with red ore dust, but she knew one man well—Pat Casey.

"Wait here," Mr. Casey told Anna, one big hand on her shoulder. "You'll only get in their way."

"Where—?" Mrs. Sevnick gasped. "Who?"

With a warning glance at Anna, Mr. Casey turned away. Did his expression mean it would be bad news for Mrs. Sevnick? Or was it aimed at her? Anna touched the woman's shoulder and indicated she would hold the baby. When she gathered little Mary into her arms, the mother did not seem to notice. Anna realized Mrs. Sevnick was bracing herself for bad news, even as Anna's own mama had countless times.

"Blasting is the most dangerous part of the workers' job," Papa had explained once. "The miners do their own blasting, and dynamite is tricky. Then, of course, the mine owners never use enough timbers to shore up the walls underground. If there's a collapse, men are buried or badly injured. Sometimes when they dump ore, it goes the wrong way—to a side they don't expect. If that's where the worker's standing—you can imagine what happens."

Anna shuddered. The baby must have felt the uneasiness and panic of the crowd of women, for she began crying. She was soaking wet besides, Anna realized bleakly. She walked and bounced Mary to keep her quiet.

Someone had driven a large wagon up to the underground shaft to wait for the injured. Within the next few minutes, the pulley began operating, and the cage in the center of the shaft rose into view. Women pushed closer to see who was on the stretcher, but until the bearers walked out of the elevator, no one was sure. Then there was a general muttering as the women, joined now by several miners from the elevator, parted to allow the stretcher and its carriers through to the wagon.

Breathless with anxiety, Anna moved closer to see who was lying so still. Then Mrs. Sevnick cried out in horror. As she screamed, the knot of wives around her closed in and one woman held her tightly.

"Shhh. Shhh. It's Danny, but he's alive!" the friend soothed.

"His leg! Oh, my God, what happened?" Mrs. Sevnick tried to escape her friends and run to the wagon. Before a blanket was laid over the figure on the stretcher, Anna could see that blood covered the man's right side. Mary began to cry again as if she, too, sensed what had happened. Anna jiggled the baby gently to calm her.

"They'll take him to the hospital in Hibbing," Mrs. Casey said. "I'll hitch up the buggy and drive you over." She put her arm around Mrs. Sevnick to urge her toward home.

The elevator came to the surface again and delivered several workers. Almost as if in answer to Anna's prayer, her papa came over the hill from his blacksmith shop.

Anna felt weak with relief. After her papa talked to the

men closest to the shaft, he stood for a moment searching the crowd. Then he walked toward her. She handed Mary to a helpful neighbor who hurried off after Mrs. Sevnick.

"What happened, Papa?"

"Timbers caved in. Caught his right leg. He'll probably lose it. He was lucky, though. They're bringing out two bodies now—Albert Maki and Charlie Lubica."

Anna gasped. Two men dead! She knew the Makis and the Lubicas. How could their families bear such news?

She hugged her father, grateful to feel his arms around her.

"Can you come home now, Papa?"

He shook his head. "Some of the men are having a meeting. I'll be home later."

Anna trudged home and opened the front door with a grateful sigh. If you have only one parent, she thought, you're always scared you'll lose him.

She looked around the familiar living room, as neat and clean as her mother had always kept it. The beloved Finnish rocker sat in the corner, the only piece of furniture Anna's parents had been able to bring with them from the old country. By now, they had added a few other pieces, a little table and an old chair Papa had mended. The ladder to the loft where she and her brother slept extended up the side wall. The kitchen opened off the living room, and she suddenly noticed that the cover over the dough in the familiar yellow bowl had puffed far above the rim.

The bread. She better get the bread in to bake. She just had time to flatten the dough, form it into loaves, and place it into Mama's battered pans when the door burst open and nine-year-old Matti ran in, caught his sister around the waist, and shoved his blond head into her apron front. Anna held him tightly for a few minutes.

"It's not Papa," she said softly.

Matti pulled away from her, rubbing his blue eyes with grubby hands.

"There'll be warm bread in a while," she said. "Then you can take a loaf to Sevnicks and see if there's anything they need. I'll go over later."

Matti gave his hands a quick wash and wiped most of the dirt on a towel. Tears dried on his small face as he drank a glass of milk. Then he grimaced.

"Daisy's been in the ragweed," he said. "This tastes funny."

"Then you can take her to graze tomorrow," Anna said. "And be careful where it is." He nodded. "Tomorrow's Saturday, and you have to help with the washing before you do anything. Kindling, too," she added. "You need to pick up sticks in the woods again."

Several hours later, Papa's familiar footsteps sounded on the wooden porch. She ran to open the door and watched her papa take off his boots and place them side by side on the front stoop. Next door, people were going in and out of Sevnicks' house, taking care of the children or bringing food, she supposed. Since the location houses were only four feet apart, you always knew when the neighbors were coming or going. The land that the location houses were built on was so rich with iron ore that the mining companies used as little as possible for homes.

Papa carried in his lunch pail and thumped it down on the table. Then he washed his face and hands in the basin with fresh water Matti had carried in from the pump.

"You're tired," Anna said and pulled out the chair in front of the place laid for him on the plain wooden table. He answered her with a grunt. She hurried to dish up his fish and potato stew. Today she had put in rutabagas and carrots, which he loved.

"There," she said. "Eat your *mojakka* while it's hot. Matti's already asleep." She knew her father liked to see both his children at supper, but when she noticed Matti's eyelids drooping, she had ordered him to bed.

She filled her papa's bowl again and cut some sour-rye bread for him. There was no butter; she would have to churn tomorrow. Then she sat down at the table with him. Her mama always had, and Anna sensed how lonely he was.

"Papa, don't you think I could go to school this year when it starts in September? I can get up early and do the cleaning and cook breakfast. I can wash on Saturdays—and bake bread, too." She hated to mention their loss, but she knew it was her strongest argument: "Mama wanted me to graduate from high school," she reminded him. "It meant a lot to her."

"You're lucky to get through the sixth grade," he said. "I didn't get that far. Your mama never had time for anything but housework and caring for us. And if you'll remember, you tried to go back last fall, and you couldn't do the work and go to school."

He looked at her set face. "I'm sorry! I wish I could think of something—or someone—to help us keep going, but I can't."

Her frustration grew. He knew how important education was! Hadn't he and Mama always told her the only way to succeed in their new country was to get an education? So why wasn't he more concerned about the months she had already stayed home? If he wouldn't help her get back into school, who would? If only Mama hadn't come down with diphtheria last summer, she thought bitterly, our lives would be so different.

He finished the bowl of *mojakka* and dark bread, then shook his head to the offer of more.

Anna picked up his dishes and clattered them into the tin dishpan before washing them. She didn't think he even noticed she was angry. He sighed.

"What's wrong?" she asked.

"The men are talking strike," he said slowly.

"Strike! Now I'll never be able to go to school! Oh, Papa, what will happen to us?"

"I've been lucky to keep working," he told Anna. "Since the dock strike in Duluth, no one's been able to ship ore. Today Oliver Mining discharged two hundred union men at the Mountain Iron Mine. We have to stand together in Chisholm for our group, which is mostly Finns, you know."

"But what will happen to us?" she asked again.

"The mine boss told us today that if we go out, we'll be blacklisted and never work in an iron mine again."

Anna was horrified. "Do you believe him?"

"Yes, I have a friend who angered the bosses several years ago. He gets hired on at one mine, works for two weeks, gets laid off for no reason, goes to another mine. He'll never have a permanent job again."

Anna gave the table one last wipe. "What are you going to do?"

"Some of the men plan to buy a little farm, but we have no money for that. Anyway, farming here on the Mesabi is almost impossible. The ground is too rocky."

"And the growing season is so short," she added.

"Like Finland," he said, "but you wouldn't remember that. You were only three when we came to Minnesota."

That was true. She didn't remember.

Papa got up from the table. "We're meeting at Dickie's Bar after work tomorrow to decide about the strike." He held out his arms for a hug. "Good night, Anna. I'll come home before I go to the saloon."

"Good night, Papa." She kissed his rough, whiskered cheek. After he had gone into the downstairs bedroom, Anna banked the kitchen fire with ashes and, putting her cloth shoes next to the wall, climbed the loft ladder to the narrow bed next to her brother's. She avoided the third rung of the ladder. It tended to twist underfoot and throw the climber back to the floor. She reminded herself to ask Papa to fix it. He never went to the loft so he probably did not know about it.

Although she was tired, she couldn't go to sleep right away. What would become of them if Papa went out on strike? Their house belonged to the mining company. Everybody who lived in the location, or "*lukeesi*" as the Finns called it, was in the same situation. The families owned only a few pieces of furniture and the clothes on their backs. Where would they go?

She wondered what the Sevnicks would do now. Mr. Sevnick would never work again as a miner. The Oliver owners might give the family a few hundred dollars—a grand sum—but that wouldn't last long. Papa had told her that Mr. Sevnick's brother farmed in Alango, about twenty miles from Chisholm. She said a silent prayer for the family.

She yawned. The Kallios' relatives all lived in Finland. At thirteen, she was too young to go to work, and anyway, she had too much to do at home. Papa simply could not afford to go out on strike.

No matter what, strike or not, she was going to figure out a way to go to school! But she knew her wish was a desperate one.

TWO

~

ANNA AWAKENED EARLY the next morning. She pulled her everyday dress of nutmeg brown homespun over her head although it was quite short and a little too tight. Her papa had suggested she take her mama's clothes and sew them to fit.

"If you can't fix them yourself, Anna," he had said, "ask Mrs. Sevnick. Lempi used to say she was the best seamstress in Chisholm."

When Papa told her that, she had gone into her parents' bedroom and opened the top drawer of the one good family dresser. The lovely scent of potpourri packed in with Mama's clothes—rose petals, dried lavender, and lemon verbena—brought back all the pain of her loss. She pulled out her favorite dress, a blue long-sleeved, high-necked dress that her mother had worn to church or square dances or meetings at the temperance hall. If anyone was going to touch her mama's dresses, Anna wanted it to be herself. It was too soon, though, after Mama's death. Tears had burst from Anna's eyes, and she wiped them with the hem of the precious blue cloth. Someday. Someday.

Anna went down the loft ladder, slipped her shoes on, and tiptoed out the door to the outhouse. It was so cool—

even for late July—that she wished she had taken her shawl. The place had begun to smell. She would bring some ashes from the stove and throw them into the hole as Mama had always done.

While she was outside, she took a look at her garden. Tomatoes were coming along. Soon string beans would be ready to can. Maybe Matti would weed today.

Next to the outhouse was their sauna with an adjoining barn for Daisy, their cow, and a dozen chickens. Beyond the small buildings, the blue of spruce trees stood out against the green of tall pines. Here and there a stately white birch tree made a long exclamation point in the woods. Pink hollyhocks bloomed against the log walls.

Mama had been proud of the sauna Papa had built. "A good Finn like you, Toivo," she used to tease, "can never get clean except in a steam bath. Sometimes I think you were born in one!"

A mournful moo sounded from the barn.

"I'll be back in an hour to milk you, Daisy," Anna called. A small toad hopped across the path worn around the house, and she almost stepped on it.

Anna paused at the pump in front. After she worked the handle rapidly to prime it, she held the bucket under the stream of water. She took the pail into the house, set it by the kitchen stove, and returned to the porch to collect kindling and short pieces of wood. Soon she had the smoldering fire in the cast-iron kitchen stove popping and blazing with renewed vigor. Anna began making the oatmeal.

"Good morning," Papa said as he emerged from behind the curtain hanging in his bedroom doorway. "Is it a nice day?"

"Cool," she said, "but clear. No rain today."

As soon as the oatmeal bubbled in the pan, Anna set it to the side and made Papa's lunch. Then she called, "Matti, time to get up! Breakfast's ready."

The slender boy descended the ladder, rubbing the sleep

from his eyes with one fist. He hopped down to avoid the third rung and gave his family a brilliant smile before running outside to the outhouse.

"The golden boy with the diamond eyes," Mama had always called him. Anna looked more like Papa with her dark blond hair and dark blue eyes—so dark that sometimes they appeared black, especially when she was upset, or so Mama had told her once. Both she and Matti had small noses and full lips. Although Papa wasn't tall, he was quite muscular; they thought their papa was the handsomest man in Chisholm.

Papa finished his breakfast quickly. "After this last accident," he warned grimly, "they'll vote strike. And if the owners close the bars like they threatened, we'll have to meet at the Finn Temperance Hall today. They don't want a bunch of drunk miners making decisions."

Anna and Matti exchanged a significant glance. Both remembered a few times when Papa had had too much to drink—but it hadn't happened since Mama died, thank heavens. That would really be something to worry about!

Papa reached for the coffeepot. "They've never had a miners' strike on the iron range. All we want is a minimum wage and an eight-hour day." He added bitterly, "And we want to be on contract and paid by the day, not for the amount of iron ore we dig out. Is that so much to ask?"

"No, Papa. Are all the Chisholm mines striking?"

"Just the Oliver Iron Mining Company—but they have mines all across the iron range, not just in Chisholm." He ground his teeth. "The workers are sick of having to pay bribes to the foreman to get a safe assignment!"

Anna kissed her papa good-bye and then stood on the small front porch wondering what to do. This strike was the last straw. She missed the variety of school life. Her life was so dull. No games outside at recess, no friends to talk and laugh with, no wonderful books to feed her dreams.

She could imagine it: I'll live here, taking care of Papa and Matti. Then Matti will be old enough to work in the mines—just what Mama didn't want for him—and I'll do this forever or marry some miner and keep his house! Either way, I have no chance for a different life.

After breakfast, Anna wadded old papers for the circle of rocks in back of the house and laid small sticks of wood on top. When she had the fire going, she put a grate across the rocks and set the copper boiler on it.

She went to the front door and called in to Matti. "I need you to haul water for the boiler and the tub." He ran quickly out to help her. "Try not to get completely soaked," his sister scolded. She suspected he liked that job because he could play in the water.

When the water was hot enough, she shaved what was left of her mother's homemade soap into the boiler and began washing the clothes. She would have to figure out how to make soap. She rinsed the clothes in a big tub of cold water set on a stump and wished again for an attached hand wringer. The day was bright and sunny, and a breeze began gently drying the clothes she had hung on the line.

As she stood there with her hands in the cold rinse water, a gray squirrel holding an acorn in his tiny paws scolded her loudly from beneath a pine tree.

"Don't forget where you bury it, silly," she warned him and laughed when he stopped chattering to listen.

By noon the clothes were dry, and she gathered them into a large basket and carried them inside. She pushed her face into the clean laundry; clothes dried outside smelled so nice.

As she folded towels and sheets, she thought about how much easier it was to wash in July than in winter. Then she had to hang everything outside to freeze first so water wouldn't drip in the house all day. Papa hated wet clothes slapping him in the face. She tried to take them down before he came home. In the winter, her hands were always chapped and red—like Mama's had been. She hadn't realized how hard Mama had worked.

After everything was put away, Anna remembered to shovel a few ashes into a can so that she could throw them down the privy hole. She churned as well, so now they had fresh butter. Then she took some butter over to Sevnicks. She had to force herself to walk up to knock on the door but she was glad when she had done it. She knew it was what her mama would have done.

Papa was late coming home from work and looked so stern that Anna was afraid to ask what had been decided. He always became very quiet when he was upset or angry, and then the children were careful not to cross him. They must be striking, she decided, and her heart sank.

THREE

~

ANNA DECIDED TO wait to ask about the strike until after the family took their Saturday sauna. That always put Papa in a good mood. Maybe she had misread his expression. Perhaps things weren't so bad after all.

Anna and Matti enjoyed their weekly sauna, but Papa loved it. First he built a fire in the stone fireplace of the steam bath. As soon as the fire burned low and the rocks were hot, the family took clean underwear to the small front room to put on after the sauna. They took off their clothes and placed them in a pile for the wash.

"Cedar boughs, Matti," Papa said. "Did you remember them?"

Matti grinned and handed them proudly to Papa. He had fanned three small cedar branches and tied them together at one end. They took turns striking each other with the switch as preparation for the bath. It brought the blood to the surface and started the perspiration flowing. Then they went into the steam room.

"Let me throw the water on the rocks," Matti asked eagerly.

Papa handed him the tin cup, and Matti prolonged his

task by throwing a little at a time. The water hissed loudly when it hit the hot rocks. Soon heat filled the room as all three sat on the bottom bench of the row along the wall.

The hotter it got and the more steam rose, the better Papa liked it. He moved quickly to the top shelf where it was hottest. Matti nudged Anna.

"Look how red Papa's face is!" The children grinned at each other.

Anna was beginning to enjoy the relaxing bath when she noticed the door was ajar a tiny crack.

In disgust, she poked Matti. "See, you left that open. The steam will all go out."

"You were the last one in," he retorted. Before anyone could get up to push the door shut, it opened a little wider. Then a small animal poked its face into the warm moist air.

"Hold still!" Papa commanded in a harsh whisper. "It's a skunk. Don't either of you move!"

While Anna and Matti sat perfectly still in horror, the young skunk ambled into the room. Now that the door was open a little more, Anna could see the two white stripes down the animal's back. She caught her breath.

If it sprayed in here, they would never get the odor out! They watched, transfixed, as the skunk explored the perimeters of the room, waddling slowly around the crack where the walls met the floor, sniffing and occasionally scrabbling at some unseen delicacy. It carried its tail low, and their eyes were riveted on it. When the skunk found itself close to the fire, it turned and went all the way back around the room. It seemed to take an eternity. Just as Anna thought she would have to scratch or sneeze, the skunk found the open door and wandered out.

Papa let out his breath in a prolonged sigh. Then he crept

to the door, looked through it, and went into the front room. Anna heard the outer door close; then he came back into the steam room and shut that one, too.

"Anna!" Papa said in a reproving tone.

"I'm sorry, Papa. I'll make sure no one leaves them open again!"

Then they all had to laugh and describe the ordeal over and over to each other.

When Anna, Matti, and Papa had had enough of the hot steam, they went outside and dipped cold water over themselves from the rain barrel standing at the sauna door. In winter, many Finns simply went outside and rolled in the snow. Anna remembered doing that when she was quite young. Now that she was thirteen, she preferred pouring the water over herself for a more dignified and gradual cooldown.

Relaxed and clean, the family had dinner and then sat around the kitchen table while Papa tried to teach Matti to play Smear, one of the miners' favorite card games. Anna had played cards with her parents often, but Matti had been too young to learn. Papa seemed to be in a good mood; she better talk about the strike now.

When the last card had been played, Anna dared to ask, "What did the union decide?"

"We set July 20, day after tomorrow, as the strike date, and until this is over, I can't work for Oliver Mining."

She caught her breath. "Do you have to strike?"

"The Finns are running it, and I wouldn't dare go back to my job. Some of us are going over to Buhl to try to get work at the lumber camp. We can go most of the way by train."

"Where will *we* stay, Papa?" Matti asked.

"Here, I hope." Papa looked at them for a moment, then said hesitantly, "I have to work somewhere. None of the striking workers will get credit at the Chisholm stores while we're out. Up to now, the storekeepers have been good about letting us charge. They know we settle up on payday."

"Then how will we pay for food?" Matti's blue eyes grew enormous.

"We'll be all right," Anna said. "It's summertime, and we have a garden. You can start to worry if the strike goes into the winter—"

And, she thought, you can worry if we run out of basic

supplies like flour and salt pork. This fall would be the hardest one yet if the strike went on. No school for sure, she thought in despair.

"Papa," Matti began with a puzzled look, "when people strike, what do they do?"

"We've been talking about this for a couple of days. Where were you?" Anna snapped.

Papa explained, "All we've done so far is march from one mine to another to persuade men to obey the strike—which really means we refuse to work until they give us more money, a shorter work day, and better working conditions."

"Oh," Matti said in relief. "I thought it meant hitting somebody."

"Like I'm going to strike you if you don't get yourself to bed?" Papa teased.

Matti laughed and kissed his father, then climbed the loft ladder.

After he left, Papa confessed his biggest worry. "I'm afraid the Oliver will put us out of our house if I go to work at the lumber camp. The location houses belong to them, you know."

Anna asked quietly, "What would we do?"

"I have no idea. I'm hoping they'll be so busy trying to run the mine without union workers that they won't notice. If I don't work," he reminded her, "we won't have any money!"

After she went to bed, Anna tried to imagine where they would go if they lost the house, but she could think of no place.

Within a week, Papa found a job at the lumber camp in Buhl.

"They need another blacksmith," he said before he left for his first day's work. "The horses have to be shod—the ones that take the heavy logs to the railroad—and harnesses have to be kept in good repair. That and the sharpening of tools."

"You were lucky, Papa," Anna said.

"Yes. I was glad to get on as a blacksmith's helper, though I know it's temporary."

They were all relieved he was working, but Papa would be coming home only on the weekends, which troubled him.

"Are you and Matti going to be all right without me?" he asked anxiously.

"Yes," Anna said firmly. "But are you going to be safe? I heard two loggers were killed last week."

He hugged her as she stood like a statue. "Try not to worry. Nothing will happen to me—nothing. The only miserable part is we have to live in tents, and we can't be with our families. They feed us, though."

Anna accepted what her father told her, but she felt as if they were constantly on the edge of hearing bad news. Violence seemed to hover in the air. If she and Matti were left alone, without a place to live . . .

Late one Saturday night in August when Papa was home, a thunderous knocking on the front door awakened Anna. She sat up in amazement and waited for him to go to the door. When the knocking continued and someone began shouting, she crept down the loft ladder.

"Who is it?" Matti whispered from his bed, white-faced.

"I don't know. Stay there," she whispered back.

She lit a lamp and went to open the door as Papa came from his bedroom, buttoning his trousers. Together they approached the unlocked door, but it burst open before they could answer it.

Three men advanced into the room, hands at their waists hovering near the pistols thrust into their belts.

Anna gasped. "Papa?"

He stepped forward. "You're frightening my daughter," he said quietly. "What do you want here?"

"Are you Teofilo Petriella?" the tallest man demanded.

"You mean the union organizer?"

"You know very well who we mean. Is he here?" The men separated and began searching the house, roughly overturning the kitchen chairs and yanking the family's coats off the hooks to toss them on the floor. One fat man looked at the loft ladder, then back at the man in charge.

Papa spoke quietly but menacingly. "I'm Toivo Kallio, and only my son is up there. Don't bother him. Do you have a warrant to search my house?"

"Don't need one," the tall man said. "Oliver Mining sent us." He motioned the third man to go outside, obviously to look in the sauna and barn shelter for the person they were after. "You better come with us and tell us where we can find Petriella."

Anna spoke up. "No one but our family is here. My father works in Buhl at the lumber camp." Then she wondered if she should have told them that. Now they might lose their house.

The tall man appeared surprised. "Is that true?"

"Yes, it is," Papa said. "Please leave my home."

Matti's frightened face appeared at the top of the loft ladder. The fat man climbed the first two rungs and then stepped onto the faulty rung, which turned just enough to send him sprawling. He groaned loudly while from above Matti exchanged a delighted glance with his sister.

The climber got up with clenched fists and turned to his companions. "Let me—" he said and nodded toward Papa. Matti's smiling face disappeared from the top of the ladder as he pulled back.

Anna panicked. There must be something she could do to keep them from taking Papa and perhaps beating him up. She inched her way to the front door.

"Here! Where do you think you're going?" the tall man snarled at her.

She could hardly speak. Fear had made her breathless. "To the privy. I have to go."

"Hurry up, then." The man almost pushed her out the door, but as she feared, he followed her.

Outside Anna stood for an instant, wondering what to do. Mr. Casey! Get Mr. Casey. He was probably the biggest miner in the location. But first she had to get out of the yard. She ran toward the back of their house where the privy stood. At the door she glanced back quickly to see if he was still watching her. It was so dark she could hardly see him. She opened the door and left it open, hoping he would think she had gone in. Then she sped around the other side of the house and straight ahead through the next row of houses. In a few seconds, she was on the Caseys' front stoop. Her heart pounded. No footsteps followed her, though, so she assumed the man was waiting for her to return from the privy.

Everyone was asleep. No light leaked from any of the houses in the location. She pounded on the door until she heard Mrs. Casey call, "Just a minute." Then the door opened, and Mr. Casey stood in the doorway rubbing sleep from his eyes, red hair on end.

"It's Papa!" Anna gasped. "Three Oliver men came for him. They think he's a union organizer."

Mr. Casey reached for his boots by the door. "Shawn," he called, "we're needed. Get your pants and boots on and bring our hunting rifles."

As soon as they were ready, Anna hurried back through the narrow walkway with the two big Irishmen behind her. At the door, Mr. Casey gently pushed her aside and cautiously opened the door. The tall man was tying Papa's hands behind him as the other two looked on. The man who had been watching Anna must have given up and gone inside.

Mr. Casey leveled the rifle almost casually at the three men. His oldest son Shawn entered and stood with his back to the wall, also holding his rifle ready.

"Untie him," Mr. Casey said in an even tone, "and get out of this house." The men looked up in surprise, but none of them pulled a gun. "Now!" Mr. Casey said angrily.

The leader said quickly, "We must have the wrong information. Let's go."

At the door, the man looked back at Papa with a warning. "If we find out you're Petriella or he was here—" he paused with a threatening scowl.

"You won't do anything," Mr. Casey said. "Out!"

Papa put his arm around Anna, who had run to his side. "We know nothing about Petriella."

When they had gone, Papa and the two Caseys held a low-voiced discussion on the porch. Then Papa came back in and bolted the door.

"We shouldn't forget to lock up tightly, Anna. We're

used to trusting our neighbors, but the strike is getting ugly now." He looked up at Matti. "Get back in bed, son. They came to the wrong house."

He sat down at the table with a cup of coffee, always available on the stove. "Anna, why did that man fall off the loft ladder?"

She giggled. "We've been meaning to have you fix the third rung. It's loose. I'm glad we didn't tell you before!"

She sat down at the table. "Why would they come here in the middle of the night?"

Wearily he answered her. "Ours is probably not the only house they searched. I heard they were trying to stop the strike by putting the leaders in jail, and this Petriella is an Italian organizer. He's from New Jersey, but he's living in Hibbing during the strike. I've heard him speak at our temperance hall, but I have no idea where he is right now— probably seven miles away in Hibbing!"

"Was it dangerous for me to tell them you were working in Buhl? Will they put us out of our house?"

"I don't know," he said slowly. "I wondered, too, but perhaps they're strangers who may not understand the Oliver's housing arrangement. Of course, if they wanted to find out I was working somewhere else, it would be easy. We'll hope they have too much to do to worry about us and our house."

Anna blew her breath in a long sigh. "I'm sorry," she said. "I shouldn't have added to your problems. How's the strike going?"

"Not very well," he said. "Strike breakers from Europe are arriving—Serbians and lots of Montenegrins; also, a few Italians and Greeks have started to work at the Monroe. The miners call strike breakers 'scabs.' "

Anna asked, "How do all those men talk to each other? They speak different languages."

He smiled. "We call it 'mine talk.' It's a kind of pidgin English—a few words in their own language, a few terms in English. On the iron range, almost everyone speaks a different language."

"Yes," she said thoughtfully, "all these languages seem natural to me. But I wonder what it was like before the iron mines started up."

"You must know about that from school," Papa told her. "Before iron was discovered, the French-Canadians were here trading furs. You would have heard French spoken if you had lived here then."

"And way back, of course, the Indians. It must have been beautiful then," Anna said wistfully, "without all this machinery and piles of dirt."

"Yes. Your mother and I often talked of how it must have been when the Indians, the Dakota or Sioux, could live off the land, fishing, hunting, and trapping. Then came the Chippewa Indians—or they're sometimes called the Ojibwa. There are lots of names for them."

"Matti and I used to think you and Mama were like the Chippewa when you went bow hunting in the fall for deer." Anna smiled at him.

Papa heaved a sigh. "We felt that way, too. What a shame to spoil such a beautiful land with all this digging. But people have to make a living, and so do I." He hesitated, then said, "If the longshoremen's strike in Duluth gets settled with the railroad, we're done for. We'll all have to move."

"Why?"

"Longshoremen load the ore from railroad ore cars into boats so it can be shipped," he said patiently. "We'll have to

34

give up if the scabs are able to ship ore. We either go back to work or move from here."

"Then everybody will go back to work."

Papa sighed heavily. "If—if—they let us go back. That's the question."

Anna thought bleakly, And I didn't know things could get any worse!

FOUR

~

THE FAMILY WAITED anxiously to see if Papa would get his old job back. Anna stood under the calendar on the kitchen wall, tracing the days of the past month with her finger. The Lake Superior dock strike was over, shipping had returned to normal, and the Oliver mines had reopened—using the strike breakers.

When Papa's friends asked for their jobs, most of them were turned away. They were also told they would never work for Oliver Iron Mining again. She hoped that because Papa was a skilled blacksmith, he would be luckier when he went to see about his old job.

She wondered again and again as she made soap—thanks to Mrs. Casey's instructions—baked bread, washed clothes, milked Daisy, and gathered eggs how she would ever find time to go to school when September came. Cooking, cleaning, and carrying water were unending tasks. Even making the sour-rye bread took a day and a half.

Late one Saturday afternoon in August, Anna met Papa at the door. "Have you heard anything about your mine job?" she asked eagerly.

"No," he barked. "I'm going—going to Dickie's. I won't be back for supper."

36

"Oh, Papa, don't—" She wondered how far she could go in asking her father not to drink. She remembered that Mama had sometimes argued with him about drinking. But she was only thirteen. What could she say?

"Don't go," she coaxed. "Let's have a sauna. You'll feel better after that. I thought you said the bars were closed."

He only shook his head and left without a word. When he returned late that night, the children heard his stumbling feet cross the room downstairs to the bedroom. The next morning was Sunday, fortunately. After looking down at her unshaven father sprawled across his bed still in yesterday's clothes, Anna didn't think she could have awakened him to go to work if it had been Monday morning.

"I wish they had left the bars closed," she whispered to her brother.

"I've got an idea," Matti said. "I heard something I've been wanting to tell you."

"Shhh. Let's go out back. He might hear us."

"Good idea," Matti agreed.

Anna perched on the stump in the backyard, and Matti sat on the ground.

"Over at the temperance hall," he began eagerly, "the bachelors in Chisholm are signing up to send for brides from Finland." His blue eyes sparkled. "Let's send for one for Papa!"

"You're crazy!"

"No, I'm not," Matti insisted. "He misses Mama, and he's worried about his job. He's afraid we might not be able to live here if he can't get back on at the Monroe. That's why he got drunk."

"I suppose. But how do we get him signed up?"

"That's the problem," Matti said slowly. "I don't think he

would sign up himself. We'll have to do it for him."

"We can't do that!" Anna was amazed that Matti would even consider signing Papa's name to anything. Then she thought about the condition he was in at this very moment. And maybe he would do it again and again and be like—well, she could think of several fathers in the location that she didn't want him to be like. She squared her shoulders.

"All right. What do we do to get him one of those brides?"

Matti said, "I don't know exactly, but Mike Ojala told me it was going to happen tomorrow evening at the hall."

"Mike's got a Pa and a Ma. What does he care?"

"Richard! His big brother." Matti's blue eyes blazed. "Richard says, 'Ain't no good-looking women around here. Might as well send for some.'"

"If any women are that desperate," Anna scoffed, "they won't be good-looking."

Matti shrugged. "Maybe the women over there *are* desperate. How do we know? Maybe Finland has too many women."

They thought about it for a few minutes. Then Anna slapped her knee. "Let's do it! Let's go down to the hall tomorrow night and put Papa's name down for a bride!"

Matti got up and began dancing around the stump. "I hoped you'd say that. Soon we'll have somebody to clean and cook and haul water and—"

"You rotten little boy! You aren't thinking of Papa. You're trying to get out of work!"

"And you want to go to school and leave at least some of the work for someone else," he reminded her.

She did. She wanted more than Mama had ever had, which had been a husband and children and the need to spend every waking moment taking care of them. There must be other things that could fill a woman's life. Reluctantly she agreed. Tomorrow, then. They would send for a bride for Papa!

A tremendous crowd of men packed the temperance hall, laughing and joking. When Anna saw Mr. Casey there, she realized that some were married men who had come simply to watch the single men sign up. Trying to be inconspicuous, the two Kallio children stood at the end of the line. Anna was a little uncomfortable and noticed a few stares, but no one said anything to them. After they had waited for about thirty minutes, Matti stuck his head out of the line and reported that there was a list on the desk in front.

"All the bachelors are signing up," he said. He looked at Anna with a strange expression.

"What? What's the matter?"

"They're giving money to the man behind the desk," he said. "I wonder what it's for."

Anna guessed. "To pay for the women's passage here on a ship," she said sadly. "I knew it couldn't be this easy!"

"How much money do we have?" Matti asked.

"None. There's nothing we can do with your fine idea. Come on home. We're wasting our time here."

"Wait a minute," Matti said. He stuck his head out again for a few minutes and watched the hopeful signers. "I know. We'll wait till Big Willie's woman gets here and take her!"

"Big Willie thinks he's going to get a wife!" Anna was amazed. "He must weigh over three hundred pounds!"

She leaned out to study Big Willie. His bald head was huge and his neck almost nonexistent. She wondered if he could even turn his head without also moving his body. Rolls of flesh hung over his belt, which was set so low that she wondered how his pants stayed up at all. His arms were enormous, his fingers like fat sausages. "What woman would look at him?"

Matti squinted his eyes for a moment. "None of them, but when his bride gets here, she won't have any place to go. You know she won't want to marry Willie, and she might not have the money to go back to Finland. We'll grab her, and she can move in with us!"

The two children left the line and went outside to walk home in the summer darkness. "Not too bad an idea," Anna mused. "She'll take one look at Big Willie and wish she was back home. Papa can pay Willie back for her ticket later."

"She'll like Papa," Matti said. "He's about the best Finn here in Chisholm!"

Anna said nothing more. They would have to wait and hope.

FIVE

~

WHEN SCHOOL STARTED in September, they learned that the brides were not due until late November. Anna almost cried when Matti left for school without her. She felt hopeless. She was busy every hour of every day, it seemed. Perhaps if she were a more experienced housekeeper—or if Matti were a girl and older. She couldn't fault Papa for not helping. He was working long hours and his job wasn't even in Chisholm. When he had time off on the weekends, she could see he was exhausted.

She and Matti had many plans for Papa's new wife.

"Maybe she can sew," Matti said one day as he contemplated his ragged pants.

"If you didn't fall down on your knees so much," Anna scolded, "no one would need to patch your pants every week."

"I do not," he said automatically.

She gave him a stern look. "Hand them here," she sighed. "I'll do the best I can." As she stitched on a patch, she said, "I bet she'll know all about canning. I'm never sure if the food is going to keep. And she'll know about gardening and baking."

"Maybe she'll play games with us and read us stories," Matti added.

"And make butter and soap—" Anna added to the list.

"I forgot to tell you. In two weeks there's gonna be a box social at school," Matti informed her as he stood waiting for his pants, "just before Halloween. It's to raise money for our Christmas at school."

"So?"

"So, you have to be thinking of some dish to take. Everybody that doesn't take a decorated basket to auction off has to take a dish to pass. What can you make?"

Anna thought for a moment. "How about deviled eggs?"

"I like them." He accepted his pants from her and began putting one leg into them. "We can look over the unmarried women there," he suggested, "in case Big Willie's bride decides she wants to stay with him."

"That's a good idea. I'd better find a dress to wear."

Papa wanted to know what the box social was for and when it was.

"Two weeks from Saturday. To raise money for a Christmas party for the students. There's a program and everything." Anna turned anxiously to him. "We're going, aren't we?"

Papa groaned. "I suppose so."

Both children noticed that their father was becoming quieter and quieter when he was at home, a sure sign he was upset. They began tiptoeing around him until he roared at them.

"What are you doing? You act like you're afraid of me. When did I ever beat either of you?"

42

"Sorry, Papa," Anna hastened to say. "We thought perhaps you wanted us to be quiet."

"I will tell you if that's the case," he snapped.

Anna and Matti exchanged glances, then went outside. "Come with me to graze Daisy," she suggested. "Then we can plan."

It was Saturday, a beautiful Indian summer day, a week before the box social. Anna led Daisy out of the shed next to the sauna, and the three walked toward the pasture beside the Chisholm lake. Anna draped the rope over a tree branch without tying it.

"She won't go anywhere," Anna said. "She's a nice cow."

"What if we have to eat her some day?" Matti asked with a devilish grin.

"Stop it," she said. "Now, we have to make plans. How many unmarried women do you think will be at the box social?"

"Let's see." Matti began counting on his fingers. "There's the widow Maki." They looked at each other simultaneously and spoke in unison, "No."

"Too old," Anna said. "Who else?"

"There's Mr. Seppala's oldest daughter. I don't know her name," Matti put up another finger.

"Too young. She can't be more than four years older than I am."

Matti's face brightened. "There's the teacher! The new one!"

Anna looked scornful. "That Cousin Jack? He'd hate her. You know how the miners and their families feel about all those Cousin Jacks from Cornwall!"

His face fell. "Oh, I forgot. She's from England all right.

Everybody says they get all the best jobs 'cause they can talk English so good. He wouldn't take a second look at her. Too thin, anyway, and real tall." Then he added after a careful glance at his sister, "Mean, too."

She was immediately suspicious. "Why? What have you been doing at school to make the teacher mean to you?"

"Nothing," he insisted. "Anyway," he added, "if she's teaching school, how's she going to take care of us?"

Anna grew impatient. "They'd soon have their own baby and she'd have to stay home."

Their own baby. She was sorry she'd ever thought of that. Anyway, Papa wouldn't like the teacher. Maybe she was already married.

The two sat on a fallen log. The ground was too cold for sitting after a hard freeze, and they'd already had two so far this month. Finally Matti had an inspiration.

"How about the widow Marinelli? She's the right age."

"Italian." Anna shook her head. "He needs a Finn or at least a Swede-Finn. Besides—" but she couldn't think of any other problem with the lady he had suggested. According to rumor, the widow was a fine housekeeper, and Anna thought she was nice looking.

"Well, if she's there Saturday night," Anna said slowly, "we'll have a chance to see her. Then if we like her, we'll somehow get her over to talk to Papa."

"Then what?" Matti wanted to know.

"Then . . . then," Anna didn't have an answer to that. "Let nature take its course." She had heard someone say that once, and it seemed to fit the situation.

Matti looked puzzled, but just then, Daisy wandered over to the lake for a drink.

"I'll get her," he said. He jumped up and ran to lead the cow back.

On Thursday, after Anna had taken the dark Finnish bread out of the oven, she began to worry about what she would wear to the box social. Finally in desperation, she went into her parents' dresser again, and although she wasn't ready to do anything to the beautiful blue dress, she found the white one she remembered had been tight on her mother. She pulled out the dress, carefully folded everything else up again, and closed the drawer.

She held it up in front of herself and tried to see how she looked in the small mirror nailed to the wall. Even by jumping up and down, she couldn't see all of herself. She took off her brown everyday dress and slipped on the white one. It felt delicate and floaty, like a party dress. If she turned up the hem about two inches, the sleeves about an inch, and took in the waist a bit, it would fit her!

She carried the dress into the big room and sat down with her mama's sewing basket. It was hard not to be sad when she looked at the buttons she remembered, the scraps of lace from a dress that had been her mother's and all the needles neatly stuck through a bit of red flannel. If only—but there was no use thinking that.

She considered taking out the hem and putting it up properly but, on second thought, decided a temporary folding would be best.

"I'll grow some more," she said to the dress. "Then it will be easy to let down the hem."

Saturday was going to be an important night for their family. It might change their whole lives!

SIX

~

THE EVENING OF the box social, Anna was nervous. She didn't want to answer the questions she was sure to get about why she wasn't in school, and, more important, she and Matti had to choose someone as a second possibility in case the bride from Finland didn't work out. They were determined to find someone for Papa to marry. And soon. She wanted so much to be in school with her friends. She and her mother had talked about Anna's graduating and going on to become a nurse or a teacher.

"Get up on this stool," Papa instructed Matti on Saturday evening. "You need a haircut before we go."

Matti, who hated having his hair cut, complained, "You cut it before school started! You don't have to do it again so soon."

"It's been almost two months," Papa said sternly. "Up on the stool now."

"We *both* want to go to the social, don't we, Matti?" Anna reminded her brother.

Matti hopped up on the stool, grimacing. Anna went into Papa's bedroom to dress for the box social, but she could hear the barber and his customer's loud argument.

"Stop wiggling! I'll cut your ear, and it won't be my fault!"

"I'm not wiggling. That's enough for now. I don't need any more cut."

"Hold still. I'll be the one to say what's enough."

"This is as still as I can sit!"

When she had put on her mother's white dress, she came out to show them, twirling around as she did. She hadn't been sure how to take it in at the waist, so she had pulled the dress in with a red sash.

"See how pretty it turned out?"

Papa, sweeping hair into a dustpan, paused and smiled admiringly. "Nice. You look very nice in Mama's dress." Then he ducked his head, but not before they had seen the tears in his eyes.

"See," Anna whispered to Matti as they left the house behind their father. "Remember our job: to find somebody for Papa." Her brother nodded.

When they arrived at the schoolhouse, many buggies and wagons were already outside. A box social was an exciting event in the location, and everyone would be there, even those who had no children in school. It was their way of supporting the school and having a good time besides.

Music greeted them as they walked in. On a raised platform, two people performed. Old Mr. Kangas was playing the concertina, as he always did for functions like this, and someone Anna didn't recognize was accompanying him on the piano.

"Who's that?" she whispered to her brother.

He made a terrible face. "My teacher—Mrs. Williams. I told you, too thin and tall."

Anna looked the teacher over. Dark brown hair braided

around her head, upright posture, long, slim fingers on the piano keys. Anna wished she could play the piano, too. No, not too tall, and not all that thin. She looked old enough to be married already, though.

"Is she married?"

"Who'd have her?" Matti said scornfully.

"Well, do you know if she is?"

"She might be," he said vaguely. Then, before he ran over to his friends in the corner, he told his sister, "She always says 'Missus' Williams when she gives her name, but she lives in one room at Hintsalas' place, so we figure she doesn't have a husband now."

Anna sighed. Obviously Matti wasn't going to be much help. She put her deviled eggs with the other dishes on the table. About twenty decorated baskets sat close to the end of the table by the platform. Soon Mr. Kangas would begin auctioning them.

Papa and Anna found seats at the table with the Suhonens, old friends of the Kallios. Then she looked around for unmarried prospects. Soon she pulled Papa's sleeve. He bent down to hear her whisper.

"Papa, isn't that Makis' oldest daughter—over there in the corner? She's been away at nursing school. Must be home for the weekend."

He looked where she indicated. "I guess," he said, shrugging.

"I think her name's Siiri. She's pretty, isn't she?"

He glanced toward the short, vivacious woman. "I suppose so."

"You're as bad as Matti," Anna muttered. Her father looked puzzled but then became caught up in conversation with his friend Mr. Suhonen.

"You bet," he answered Mr. Suhonen's invitation. "We'll go deer hunting as soon as we have an inch of snow on the ground."

Anna looked around the room for the widow Marinelli. She located her, finally, and began admiring the widow's fine clothes and posture. Then she realized that standing self-consciously next to Mrs. Marinelli was the storekeeper, Mr. Potash, recently widowed himself. Mentally Anna eliminated that possibility. Matti must be right. The men here had to send away for their brides unless they had brought them along to the iron range.

The musical program of polkas and schottisches came to an end, and Mr. Kangas picked up the first basket, a pink-ribboned one.

"What am I bid?" he called. "Who'll start me with twenty cents?"

Although bidders weren't supposed to know whose basket they were bidding on, everyone present knew the pink ribbons signaled plump Esther Ikola's property. They also knew the basket held the best fried chicken anywhere around, and the bidding became lively.

"Bid on that, Papa," Matti advised. "I love fried chicken." His father grinned but did not respond to Matti's request.

The bidding for the baskets went quickly, and soon Mr. Kangas was down to the last two: one, decorated in black and orange, symbolizing the near arrival of Halloween; the other, an old shoe box tied with a long shoestring.

"Papa! Bid on that pretty one," Matti suggested. "I know whose the other one is, and you don't want it." His father looked at him and frowned. "It's my teacher's," the boy explained. "I saw her put it on the table. She's mean. She makes me stay in if I don't know my spelling. And she won't let us talk at all. I don't like her."

Anna glared at him. "Since when have you had trouble with spelling? Just you bring that list home to me. I guarantee you'll be able to spell every word!"

The orange and black basket went to Andy Bonacci, a young miner. He smiled widely at the teacher, obviously thinking it was hers. She returned the smile, but devilishly, Anna thought. As Matti had said, she was tall, but she wasn't bad looking. Maybe she really was unmarried—or widowed.

The shoe box was last, and although both children rolled their eyes, Papa was the successful bidder. When the men went to pay for the baskets they had won, everyone laughed when Andy's colorful basket turned out to belong to old Mrs. Kangas, wife of the concertina player. With a resigned but friendly grin, Andy sat down with Mrs. Kangas to eat.

Papa picked up the shoe box and looked around for its owner, but no one came forward. Anna and Matti helped themselves from the dishes displayed on the long table, and finally the family found places at a corner table and sat down to eat. Anna looked with curiosity toward the teacher. She was willing to bet that she had prepared the box. Why wasn't she owning up to it?

Papa untied the shoestring wrapped twice around the old box and tied in a knot. A heavenly aroma floated up. Matti sighed happily.

"I get my fried chicken after all." Then he paled as his teacher sat down with them. She smiled at the family.

"I'm sorry to be late. Several parents wanted to talk to me. I'm Mae Williams," she introduced herself, "Matti's teacher." She smiled at Matti, who scowled darkly at his plate. She turned to Anna with a surprised look in her large brown eyes.

"I haven't seen you in school," she said. "Are you Matti's sister?"

"Yes," Anna said. "I—uh, I haven't been able to come to school this year."

"Our mother died," Matti said belligerently. He glanced at his teacher's left hand where Anna had already noticed a wide gold band. "Where's your husband?"

Gently the teacher said, "I lost him two years ago. But I am interested in your attending school, Anna. Perhaps we can work something out."

Anna was uncomfortable under the teacher's scrutiny. Papa seemed to sense her problem.

"This looks wonderful," he said cheerfully. "Does everyone have a plate?"

The fried chicken was delicious, but Anna escaped as soon as she had eaten. Something about seeing her father sitting side by side with Matti's teacher bothered her. There seemed to be a tension between them. They must just naturally dislike each other, Anna decided. Sometimes that happens between people. Also, Papa had begun questioning Mrs. Williams about his son's activities in school and his recent inability to spell, or to be quiet, according to her. Only Anna and Matti knew this was a sure sign their father was upset. A stranger would have thought him perfectly calm.

They're not getting along, Anna thought as she sought out her former school friends. We'll have to wait for the brides and hope we find someone.

SEVEN

◞

O N FRIDAY, THE week after the box social, Matti
didn't come home for supper. Anna wondered
where he could be. He had checked in with her at
the usual time after school, so the teacher wasn't keeping
him late. He must be playing somewhere and had forgotten
the time. Papa had talked to both children rather sternly
after their mother died, telling them they must know where
the other was at all times.

"We have to take care of each other. No running off without thinking, Matti," he warned.

Anna thought Matti had been pretty good about that.
Now she paced the kitchen wondering where he could have
gone. The stew was on the stove keeping warm. For the
moment she had no other duties except to wait for Matti
and for Papa to arrive from Buhl. New carrots, onions, potatoes, and some squirrel meat simmered in the pot. It had
been a struggle for the two of them to clean the squirrel
Matti had killed, but at least they hadn't had to buy the
meat.

Gradually darkness stole in around the house, until Anna
realized that her brother was not only late, he was missing.
She chewed her thumbnail wondering what to do.

She made up her mind. She'd go to all her brother's friends' houses to ask if they knew where he might be. She moved the stew to the back of the range and propped a note up on the kitchen table for Papa to find when he came home from Buhl:

Papa
I'm looking for Matti. He isn't home yet.
Anna

Then she went to knock on the doors of houses where Matti played regularly.

"No, haven't seen him today," Mrs. Pouchak said. "John, have you seen Matti Kallio this afternoon?" A distant "No" came from the back of the house. "Sorry."

Mrs. Aho invited Anna in. "Jimmy isn't home yet, either. Where could they have gone?" She added, "His father's going to blister him when he gets here. If Matti is with him, I'll send him straight home."

Anna thanked her and ran through the location to the Suhonens with an anxious heart.

"No, and Arthur isn't here," Mr. Suhonen said angrily. "I wish I knew where that varmint was! We better look for them. Is your father back yet?"

"I don't know," Anna said weakly. "I'll go home and see. I'll send him over if he's there."

Papa had arrived and was eating a bowl of stew when she returned from her frustrating search. She had been to see ten families, and no one knew anything about Jimmy, Matti, or Arthur Suhonen. She explained what she had learned to her father, who looked like a thunder cloud by the time she was through.

"You stay here and wait for him," he ordered, getting up

to go to Suhonens. "I knew something would happen if I left you two here alone. Even with the neighbors watching, it isn't right."

Her eyes filled with tears. "I know I'm the one who's responsible," she said and gulped. "We've been fine until now."

Her father patted her shoulder. "I'm not blaming you, Anna. I'll go over to Suhonens to see what I can find out."

Anna couldn't eat. She paced and paced, then picked up some mending to keep her hands busy. By the time Papa came back, she had darned five socks.

She knew the moment her father came in that something dreadful had happened.

"Papa—?" she said quickly. "Tell me."

He sagged into a chair. "One of the Popovich boys saw them playing around the Shennago mine."

She was alarmed. "And?"

"There's an underground shaft that they could have gotten into without going down in the cage. We think they went into one of the drifts."

Anna knew about drifts, the tunnels that went off in various directions horizontally. Some of those drifts had old timbers that could come down on those boys! And the boys could be anywhere inside a tunnel.

"If they go too far in and run out of air—oh, Anna!" He buried his face in his hands. "I promised Lempi I'd take care of you children!"

"Don't, Papa! Everybody will look for them. Don't blame yourself!" She put her arms around him, trying to comfort him in spite of her own growing fear.

"But think what it must be like for those three down there in the dark. They'll be scared to death! It's as black—as black as death in those underground mines if you don't have candles," her father told her. "If the back should fall on them—" He groaned.

Anna patted his shoulder. "Maybe they have some candles." But she was thinking about how dangerous the back was, there at the top of the stopes—those rooms where miners worked when they were digging. The back was like a ceiling made of iron ore. Sometimes after blasting, not all of the ore comes down right away. It could fall on them!

Papa grabbed his coat and unhooked a kerosene lantern from beside the door. He stuffed several candles into his pockets.

"But it's still daylight," Anna said.

"It's never daylight in an underground mine," he said, and every word hurt her heart. In the early years of his work, this was the job he and his friends had done every day, and it was unbelievably hard and dangerous.

"Suhonen is coming for me in his wagon," he added. "Six of us are going over to the mine to search. Give me a blanket, will you?"

She looked at him, puzzled.

"Hurry, Anna. It's always around fifty degrees underground, and those boys may have been down there several hours already. And it's wet, too."

She caught her breath in anxiety but without comment found him a blanket and a warm coat for Matti.

"When men are working underground," he explained, "air is pumped in and water out. Even so, we used to get pretty wet. We always had to change our clothes in the drying room before we came home. Those boys could get pneumonia or worse."

"The sun was shining and it wasn't freezing today," she

said, trying not to cry, "so he didn't wear his heavy coat when he went out to play." She looked up pleadingly, "Papa, can't I come, too?"

"No, honey. You wait here in case we're wrong, and he comes home from somewhere else." But they both thought they knew where Matti was.

At first Anna paced and wrung her hands. It was no use going to bed; she would never be able to sleep. Then she decided to find something to do so that time might pass more quickly. She went into Papa's bedroom to look through Mama's clothes again. This time she resolutely pulled out the blue dress she loved, but when the odor of potpourri floated into the air, she began crying.

"Mama, I feel so alone. How can I do all this without you?" She held the dress to her face trying to get some comfort from it. Finally she dried her tears and examined it.

She tried it on and then pinned the hem, sleeves, and waist. She firmly turned up the sleeves and hem and sewed them. She had trouble with the waist and decided to leave it until someone could help her. Then she hung the dress up in Papa's closet so the wrinkles would begin to come out.

An unfriendly darkness seemed to press around the house. Where was Matti, and would they find him before it was too late?

EIGHT

~

*I*T WAS THE LONGEST night Anna had ever spent. If only they had taken her along! In her anxiety, she cleaned corners she had never before noticed needed attention. She even got the hammer and pounded the outside bars of the ladder together so the third rung would not turn. Still no one came to the door to bring her news. Finally she went in and curled up on Papa's bed, hoping she would soon hear him come in the door with Matti.

Several times she got up and opened the front door. The November air was frosty, the night silent. From far off, an owl hooted in the darkness. She closed the door again but did not lock it. If they came, she did not want to delay their entrance.

Anna thought about Matti. He was bright, kind, and a joy to her and her father. The few little problems he had—with spelling, for example—were not serious. He couldn't be gone now; he couldn't! His life had only begun. Maybe he had told her where he was going, and she hadn't been listening. No. She would have remembered that. In fact, if he had told her they were going down in the mine, of course she would have said no!

Maybe he hadn't gone into the mine. They might be

looking in the wrong place. Longyear Lake hadn't frozen over yet. Could they have . . . no. He and his friends wouldn't have gone into the lake when the water was this cold. What if this had happened during the week while Papa was in Buhl? How would she have felt then? And what would she have done?

She wore herself out imagining Matti's condition. Before she knew it, she fell into a sleep full of terrible dreams. She was lost in a mine, running down tunnels, looking for a way out. It was dark and cold. She woke up suddenly.

Was that someone outside? She listened carefully for a few seconds. Definitely several men were talking quietly in the street outside the house. She got up, smoothed her rumpled brown dress, and opened the door to see who it was.

Papa came in cradling Matti in his arms. He turned back to call softly, "Thanks, Suhonen, I will see you tomorrow." Then he carried his precious burden across the kitchen and into his bedroom.

Anna followed him quickly, turned down the bed she had been lying on, and said, "Put him here." She watched Papa roll Matti cautiously into the covers, pulling off the extra blanket he had been wrapped in. Then they looked down at the boy.

He was white, paler than Anna had ever seen him. A large blue bruise marred his high forehead, and he was dirty—filthy.

"Can I sponge him clean with warm water, Papa?" she asked, wanting to do something, anything for her little brother.

Papa shook his head. "He needs sleep now, and warmth." He nodded toward the range. "Put plenty of wood in the stove. He's been shivering all the way home." Indeed, Matti shook as Anna watched. "We'll need to put dry clothes on him."

"Is he all right?" she asked anxiously.

Papa nodded. "We think so. His friend Arthur has a broken ankle, but they're in good condition for the ordeal they've had." After he changed Matti into flannel pajamas, he nodded toward the kitchen, and they went out to sit at the table. Anna poured a cup of coffee for him, which he accepted gratefully.

"It was so cold down there for little boys," he murmured. "And their candles had all gone out. They were really frightened!" He looked at Anna's anxious face. "No use scolding him. He's learned a lesson. None of those boys will ever try that again."

She sat down with him. "I'm so glad—I mean, it's wonderful—he's all right," she said. "All I could think of is—. For anything to happen to him—" She began to sob in relief.

Papa patted her shoulder. "I know. We're lucky he came through it without any real damage." He looked at the clock and sighed. "In an hour I have to leave for Buhl."

"But today's Saturday!"

"Overtime," he said, "and if I hadn't promised to go back, I wouldn't. I'll leave right after work and be home tonight as early as I can."

"If you're going to work, I'll make your breakfast." She nodded toward the bedroom. "What about him?"

Papa shook his head. "Sleep and warmth are the best medicine for him. He may not feel very well when he wakes up."

Anna ran out to the chickens in their shed with Daisy and returned with two eggs. Then she fried potatoes. Papa ate and dressed for work.

60

When she kissed him good-bye, he whispered, "Your mama would have been proud of us, I think, for the way we took care of Matti. Don't blame yourself." Then he squeezed her extra tight before he left.

After she washed the dishes, she went in to check on her brother and listen to his breathing for a few minutes.

She looked down at Matti and wondered if he really was all right. There was a hoarse sound to his breathing that she didn't like. When he had been much younger, Matti used to get croup every time the weather turned cold or rainy. He hadn't had croup for two years, but he sounded very much as if he had it now. She wondered what she should do. Hesitantly, she went back into the kitchen. How had Mama treated croup?

She thought about putting a pan filled with water on the stove, but it would take too long to boil. She searched the shelf above the stove for some idea of what to use. To the far left, a small alcohol lamp sat. That's what her mother had done! She lit it and finally found the croup kettle on a bottom shelf in the kitchen. She filled the kettle with water and carried both into Matti's room, then lit the lamp. The kettle began sending out steam as she watched. She went back to the kitchen medicine shelf.

Her hand hovered above each bottle of patent medicine. What had Mama put into the water when Matti got sick? Her hand paused over the bottle of camphor oil. She picked it up and sniffed.

Awful! It had the same awful odor she remembered. She took it into the bedroom to put a little into the croup kettle, but she was standing too close to the mixture. She inhaled a large whiff of camphor and gagged. It was horrible, but that was what Mama had used. She would never forget that smell.

61

It had penetrated everything in the house, but the camphor oil had kept his throat and chest clear.

If it helps him, she thought, we can stand it! She looked at him once more and then climbed to the loft to try to sleep for a little while. By the time the light woke her up, the sun was high in the sky, and Matti was coughing and crying.

Anna went down to Papa's room and leaned over Matti to listen to his chest. Every noisy breath was an effort. She kept the water boiling; she didn't know what else to do. She carried a pan of warm water into the bedroom and tried to sponge off his filthy face and hands. He thrashed around so much as he tried to catch his breath that she finally had to stop washing him. Matti woke up as she knelt by the bed, and he looked around the room in amazement.

Hoarsely he whispered, "I'm home! Did I just have a bad dream, Anna?"

"No, Matti, you really were down in a mine. Papa and some of his friends went in for you. Could you eat something?"

"I need to go to the privy." He started to get up, then fell back.

Anna reached under the bed and pulled out the chamber pot. "Use this. I don't think you should go out in the cold again. You have the croup."

She helped him get up, then left the room. "I'll make you some hot milk with bread in it, the way Mama used to when we were sick. Do you think you can come into the kitchen to eat it?"

He nodded weakly. Then he whispered hoarsely, "I'm sorry, Anna. We didn't think when we went into the mine. We dared each other to go." He shuddered. "It was awful.

You don't need to worry about me ever doing that again."
He began coughing.

"Stay quiet," she advised. "When you talk, you start to cough. After you eat something, I'll read you a story."

When he had eaten and returned to bed, she sat by his side reading aloud for awhile from a book of Greek myths, his favorite. He fell asleep, and she tiptoed out to take care of Daisy and the kitchen chores. Sleep's the best thing for him now, she told herself, but she was relieved when Papa came home right after dark.

Papa came through the door, shutting it against the cold wind. "There's snow in the air," he said. "How's Matti?" He hurried to the bedroom before she could answer.

Matti was awake and each breath was audible. They stood by the bed and listened to the rasping noise of his breathing. Papa sniffed the air a few times.

"What is that awful smell?" he asked.

"Camphor oil," Anna told him.

She showed him the pan on the alcohol burner. "Mama used to do that when Matti had the croup. I thought it would help."

"Steam," Papa said thoughtfully. "If steam will loosen up his chest, why don't we take him into the sauna?"

Anna stared at her father. "That's a wonderful idea! But I don't think he should cool off suddenly. He should be kept warm, don't you think?"

"You're right. I'll go fire up the sauna. You keep this wood stove going pretty hot, and I'll take him out wrapped in a blanket. Back the same way. We won't let him get a whiff of cold air." He looked anxiously at Anna. "Do you think we're doing the right thing?"

She shrugged helplessly. "Mama always said croup should be caught right away or it might turn into pneumonia. I think it's a good idea." As Papa turned to go out to the sauna she said, "We can get him clean in there at least. I don't know when he's been any dirtier!"

Papa smiled. "You sound just like your mother." Then he hurried outside. Anna stoked the kitchen range, refilled her pan of water, and got a blanket to roll Matti in for the trip to the sauna and back. She also set out warm socks and long underwear to dress him in afterwards.

Within an hour, Papa had the sauna ready. He explained to Matti what they were going to do and rolled him into the blanket.

"Put your face under there, too," Papa warned. "We don't want you to breathe in any cold air." Obediently Matti snuggled under the blanket, and Papa carried him out, followed by Anna with clean clothes for all three of them and a pail of warm water.

Papa placed Matti on the bottom bench and helped him take off his clothes. As soon as they were ready, Anna threw a cup of water on the heated rocks. When Matti didn't scold her for taking his job, she knew he was really sick. She handed him a rag and put the pail next to him so that he could wash himself. After a few halfhearted swipes with the rag, Matti lay down on the shelf, so Papa finished the job.

"Should I put some of that medicine on the rocks?" Anna wondered aloud.

Papa wrinkled up his nose. "I doubt if we would ever get that horrible odor out of here," he said. "It would be almost as bad as the skunk spray would have been. I honestly believe the hot air is the best thing for him—with or without the medicine." He smiled at Anna. "Your mama always thought if anything tasted or smelled bad, it was good for you."

After about an hour, Papa looked at Anna in satisfaction. "Sounds better," he whispered, "doesn't he?"

She listened for a few minutes to the boy's peaceful breathing. Matti was half asleep again.

"I think so," she said slowly. "Let me dress and make sure the house is really warm before you bring him in. I'll be back in a few minutes."

She cooled herself off with a few dippers full of water, dressed, and went into the house to put more wood in the range. Then she returned to the sauna and nodded to Papa.

He had himself and Matti dressed by then, so he wrapped the boy up completely and hurried into the house. He laid Matti on the downstairs bed, then unwrapped him.

"He isn't so feverish," Papa said, "and he isn't coughing. I'll keep him here in my bed tonight so that I can watch him. Give him something more to eat if he wants it, and we'll let him rest now."

Matti shook his head to the offer of more food, and his eyes closed as they watched. They tiptoed out.

Anna prepared a supper of sausage and potatoes for Papa and herself. After she cleaned up the kitchen again, she said good night to Papa and went up the loft ladder.

By this time, she was so tired that she couldn't even stay awake to worry. Only time would tell if Matti was going to be really sick or not.

NINE

~

B Y SUNDAY MORNING, Matti was much improved, but Papa and Anna knew croup was still potentially dangerous. Several Chisholm children had died from croup. Papa didn't think the boy should go to school the next day, but now that Matti had permission to stay home, he wanted to go.

"Anna will walk over to the school and talk to the teacher," Papa promised him. "She'll bring back any lessons you should do. We want to be sure you're all right before you go back."

"How did you bruise your forehead?" Anna asked. "Do you remember?"

"Sure. We each had a candle at first; then only Jimmy's was left. We were walking along a tunnel, and all of a sudden, we fell over a bunch of rocks."

"Iron ore," Papa said grimly. "Fallen from the stope."

"Ore," Matti agreed. "Jimmy's candle went flying, and we were in the dark." He looked at Anna and explained, "It's not like nighttime dark. It's black! I fell on my head. Arthur hurt his ankle, and Jimmy just started crying 'cause he's scared of the dark." Matti looked at his father. "I think he wet his pants," he said.

"I wouldn't doubt it." Papa exchanged an amused glance with Anna. "So then what did you do?"

"We found each other again and decided to hold hands until somebody found us."

"That was smart," Anna said. "And do you know what else would be smart?"

"Yes," Matti said and sighed. "Never to do that again. Is Arthur all right?"

His father promised to go over to find out during the day. Later, when they had eaten and Papa left for Suhonens', Anna reminded Matti that they had to go to the temperance hall at the end of the week.

"The brides are coming," she said, "Remember?"

"Oh, yes." Matti sat up. "I'll be fine."

Anna nodded, but in her heart she wondered if she really wanted Papa to find a new wife. Seeing him sitting by Mrs. Williams at the box social had made her realize that she was of two minds about finding someone for Papa. He needs a wife, she thought, but do we really want a stranger here? But she did, definitely, want to finish school. She sighed. She didn't know what she wanted.

The next day, after she gave Matti his breakfast and warned him about what he shouldn't touch while she was gone, she put on her coat and walked over to the Monroe Location School. Their house was about as far from there as one could get in the location, but it was a nice day for a walk.

Anna arrived at recess while the teacher was outside with the children. She stood hesitantly on the edge of the playground, feeling quite left out. Never before had she not been a part of this world. School had been a big part of her life, she realized.

All of the leaves had fallen from the maples edging the

yard, and the tamaracks had lost their needles. Birches had long ago dropped their yellow leaves and stood skeletonlike against the November sky, spidery black limbs tracing strange patterns against the blue.

Her best friend, Elinor Petaja, called to her and beckoned. Elinor and her younger sister Marta had been dependable friends, but Anna merely waved and shook her head, then continued toward the front steps. She knew she mustn't be away from Matti too long.

She moved up the steps to the door to wait there. Mrs. Williams hurried up behind her.

"Welcome! How is your brother? We all heard about his adventure."

"Thank you. He is fine," Anna said, "but he needs his lessons at home for a few days. Papa doesn't think he should go out in the cold air for a while. He's had the croup."

The teacher took her inside. "This is a good time to talk. I have a few minutes to gather up everything he needs. I've been keeping his lessons on my desk. I thought you might come." She picked up a packet on her desk.

Organized, Anna recognized. This teacher knows where everything is and has it at hand.

"Jimmy came back today," Mrs. Williams said, "but Arthur's ankle is broken, they say."

She sat down beside Anna and showed her what Matti should accomplish for the week. When she finished, she handed the papers and a book to Anna and looked at her thoughtfully.

"And what about you?" she asked. "I'd like to see you try to come back to school. Don't you think you could work it out—even if only for a few days a week?"

Anna picked up the homework. "I don't know," she said

slowly. "I want to, but I don't have much free time. Maybe when Matti is well and back here, Papa and I can talk about my coming back."

"Good!" Mrs. Williams smiled at her. "I'd be glad to come over and add my voice to yours. Let me know if it's needed."

Anna glanced around the large room before leaving. Neat and clean, it smelled as usual of chalk dust and lunches sitting near the potbellied stove. Just as she remembered it. For a moment, she thought she would cry. She turned at the door and called, "Thank you, Mrs. Williams. Matti should be back by the end of the week."

She scuffed through the dry leaves and watched them scurry across the school yard over the hard ground. The wind was picking up, and it did smell like snow, just as Papa had said. Now he and Mr. Suhonen will go deer hunting and we'll have venison to smoke and to eat, she thought. But a deep feeling of sadness threatened to overwhelm her.

Why couldn't everything have gone on the way it was? Mama was so sweet and kind to us. Why did she have to die and leave us? I should be in school, not trying to decide what to cook for supper or if I've milked the cow and all the rest.

For the first time, she realized that she resented having to grow up so fast. It isn't fair, she thought. Then she felt disloyal to her mother's memory. I'm sorry, Mama, she thought, but I'm only thirteen.

Why, why—? But there weren't any answers to questions like that.

For the rest of the week after the underground expedition, Matti stayed home out of the cold. When Anna lifted the front window curtain to look outside on Friday morning, she called excitedly to her brother.

"Snow! Matti, look at the beautiful snow!"

They stood together at the window, gazing at the sparkling layer of silvery white covering the frozen earth. It transformed everything. Anna caught her breath. She always forgot how beautiful winter was here. Papa said northern Minnesota was like Finland, but Anna couldn't remember Finland.

She looked up into the trees. The weather had to be perfect, she thought, to produce this wonderful scene. A narrow rim of white edged the top of each black tree limb and the side of each trunk. She wished she could paint such a picture.

"Papa can go deer hunting now," Matti said. "Then we'll have venison to eat!"

"Yes, and he can give the storekeeper part of it so we can get credit again," his practical sister said. She dropped the curtain.

"After we eat breakfast," Matti asked eagerly, "can I get dressed and go outside to play in the snow?"

"It'll still be there tomorrow," she said. "Papa will be home tonight, and you can ask him then."

"You're not my mother!" he growled, but she ignored him.

Papa came home fairly early and laid his paycheck on the table. "This is the last one," he said.

Anna looked at him in horror. "Oh, Papa!"

"Their blacksmith doesn't need me any more," he said. "We knew this work wouldn't last. I'm hoping I can get back at the Monroe by early spring. Anyway, it's time to go deer hunting!"

Matti jumped up and down. "I knew you'd say that. Can I go this year?"

Papa shook his head. "Maybe next year. You'll be ten and you'll be stronger than you are right now. I want you to be careful for a while."

Matti scowled, but Anna thought he should have expected this answer. She turned to look at the calendar, tapped the November page, and shot her brother a conspiratorial glance. He looked puzzled for a moment. She pointed at the date, and he smiled at her.

"Papa," she said as she began putting supper on the table, "would you like to go to the temperance hall tomorrow night?"

"Is that the night the Finnish brides arrive?" he asked.

"You knew!" Matti said in astonishment.

Papa laughed. "The whole community knows they're coming! Sure, let's go over to the hall and watch the fun."

Matti and Anna looked at each other with expectation. Tomorrow was the night that could change their lives forever.

TEN

~

THAT SATURDAY NIGHT was Matti's first step into the world outside his house since going into the mine. His father hadn't thought playing in the snow during the day was a good idea. Bundled up warmly, the three Kallios walked to the hall after supper to be greeted by many neighbors and friends. Anna was glad to see that Matti tolerated the women's hugging without objecting. Usually he showed his dislike of that kind of emotion, but Matti seemed to know that the miners and their families had been genuinely worried about him and the other boys. The hall was crowded with excited people.

How do these men who sent for brides endure the suspense? Anna wondered. She peered around people to get a glimpse of the other end of the hall where several men handled the ledger that listed the incoming women and their intendeds. She looked all around but saw no strangers. Then an outside door opened, and a man ushered a number of women into an adjoining room. The curious audience craned their necks to see through the doorway of the room. The man then signaled to the person sitting at the desk.

"The train," Papa said. "The train bringing the brides must have just arrived."

Anna could hardly breathe she was so excited. Their

whole lives could change! She looked at Matti. He was nervous, too. Did they really want Papa to get married again? And to a stranger? It might be someone they didn't like. Or who wouldn't speak English. They would probably have to teach her English.

"Anna—?" Matti began.

"Shhhh. They're calling the men's names," she said.

One by one each man who had paid a bride's passage from Finland walked up to meet his wife-to-be. A group wedding would be held here on Sunday, a speaker announced. The ladies would stay at the O'Neil Hotel in Chisholm tonight. Anna knew what would happen next. After the ceremony, the miners would visit their newly married friends' homes and make as much noise as possible outside each house. To *shivaree* the newlyweds, they would pound on tin pans and other noisy objects.

Matti poked her when Richard Ojala's name was announced. The young miner walked gravely to the desk as a young woman emerged from the back room. Friends and relatives of the Ojalas applauded as the two young people blushed and tried not to look each other over too obviously.

"He was lucky," Matti whispered. "Big Willie's next."

"William Lampala," the speaker intoned, and the bathed, dressed-in-his-best Big Willie plodded toward the desk as the crowd of miners and their families went wild. Applause started almost as soon as he began walking, each large foot tromping solidly on the wooden floor of the hall.

From the back room, a woman of the same gigantic proportions came toward him. She had a sweet, smiling face and dimples, and she was dressed in lavender. The two met in front as Willie called out something in Finnish to her. The crowd roared in approval as she answered.

"What did they say, Papa?" Matti asked breathlessly. Neither he nor his sister spoke the language, and they could understand only a little of what they heard. Mama had thought learning English more important than trying to maintain their Finnish language and customs.

Papa was laughing hard—along with most of the crowd. "Willie said, 'You're just as beautiful as your picture,' and she answered, 'So are you'!"

Anna and Matti exchanged a disappointed but accepting glance. If ever the Lord had matched a man and a woman, it was these two. In fact, the entire crowd must have agreed because there was vigorous applause when Willie and his lady sat down. Anna noticed they were already holding hands.

"Well," she said to Matti, "that idea didn't work."

"What idea?" her father asked.

"Nothing, Papa. You wouldn't be interested. If you help *shivaree* anybody, you should go to Big Willie's house."

Papa looked puzzled. "Sure, if I go."

Now what? Anna wondered. She would never get back to school full-time, but maybe she could set up a few lessons during the week, she decided. That at least she could do.

On Monday morning, after Anna got Matti off to school and the bread set to rise, she combed her long blond hair and rebraided it. The homespun dress would have to do; aside from her mother's white dress that she had worn to the box social, she had very little that was suitable for anything but housework. She put on a warm jacket and scarf and walked over to the school. She tried to time her visit again for recess, but when she got there, no one was outside.

Slowly she made her way up the steps. She listened at the door for a few minutes, then slipped inside. Elinor noticed her and waved. A few of the older girls also turned to smile at her, turning back again as Mrs. Williams tapped her desk with a ruler. The teacher nodded toward a chair next to the wall, so Anna sat down to wait. Although she was self-conscious, she soon found herself engrossed in the geography lesson. She had been missing lessons so much!

"While we're talking about Finland, class, did you girls know that women got the vote there last year—1906?"

Anna and her friend Elinor Petaja exchanged delighted smiles. There was a general murmuring of approval from the students.

"Finland is the second country to allow women to vote," Mrs. Williams added.

"What was the first?" an excited Michael Casey asked, without bothering to raise his hand.

"Michael!" his teacher warned.

"I'm sorry," he said, "but was it Ireland? I bet it was!"

The class laughed. Mrs. Williams smiled, too. "No, it was New Zealand." He was clearly disappointed. Then she continued the lesson.

Within half an hour, each student had something to work on, and the teacher made her way toward Anna.

"You came!" Mrs. Williams whispered. "I'm so glad. Wait about twenty minutes, and they'll all go out for recess. I can take a little time, and we'll talk about your courses. You are going to try to attend school, aren't you?"

Anna nodded. When the students went outside, she watched them longingly. Then she went up to sit beside Mrs. Williams' desk to look through the seventh grade books.

After questioning Anna closely about what she had done in school and what she liked and did not like, Mrs. Williams set several books aside.

Without looking at Anna, the teacher asked, "How is your father?"

Anna could tell she was asking only to be polite. It had been obvious to her and Matti that the two adults had been somewhat stiff in their conversation. They had hardly looked at each other.

"He's well, but his job in the lumber camp has finished."

The teacher dropped the subject. "Now," she said, "since you think you can come for only part of three days, I think we should concentrate on arithmetic, geography, and history. I'll give you plenty of books to take home to read for

English. Your records indicate you have been a superior student in English."

Anna ducked her head and smiled shyly.

"You love to read, don't you?"

Anna nodded. "I'm all right in spelling, too, but I'd like my brother's lists so I can help him. Should I write something about each book as I read it?"

"Yes! That's a good idea," Mrs. Williams agreed. "What days are best for you?"

"I'll have to come about ten on Tuesdays, Thursdays, and sometimes Friday mornings. I'm sorry it can't be more."

"I suspect you're a very good student, Anna," Mrs. Williams said. "We'll see how this goes. Can you stay for a little while today?"

Anna nodded. She could hear the shouts from the school yard.

"Why don't you go play with your friends for a few minutes," Mrs. Williams suggested. "It must be a long time since you've done that."

As Anna went down the steps to join her friends, she thought the teacher must have read her mind. Being with her friends was definitely something she had missed. Elinor and Marta waved and called to her. As she ran over to them, she thought, this will work. It has to!

She was determined to graduate from high school. As for Papa, maybe it would be better if he didn't get married again. She could take care of the house and the family and still go to school. She could do it.

ELEVEN

~

THE WEEKS UNTIL Christmas vacation were happy ones for Anna, now that she was back in school, even for a few days a week, working hard to pass the seventh grade.

Papa and many of his friends were laid off until March.

"It's normal," he reminded his children. "If you'll remember, we didn't work last winter for three months. When the lakes freeze over, ore boats can't operate."

"But will you be able to work for Oliver Mining?" Matti asked with big eyes.

"That's what they promised me," he said. "Most of the scab workers who were taken on can't do skilled jobs—like blacksmithing, for instance. They need me. At least while I was working in Buhl," he muttered, "I was able to miss one part of my old job at the mine. It was time to bring the Monroe mules up and shoe them. I always hated that."

"Why, Papa?" asked Matti.

"You know," he explained, "the mules that pull the loaded ore cars underground. They stay down there at least six months in the dark. Somehow when they come up to be shod, they sense they have to go back down."

Anna wrinkled her brow. "The dark—?" she said slowly.

"They go blind," Papa said shortly. "Great care has to be taken so they don't lose their sight. Before they come up, gunny sacks have to be tied around their heads and eyes and a layer taken off every few days so that their sight will gradually come back. Sometimes that isn't done."

The children were horrified. "No wonder they don't want to go back down," Matti said.

"Yes," Papa agreed. "They kick and scream when it's time to return."

Anna shuddered. Even animals didn't like working underground.

Now that the snow had arrived to make tracking easier, Mr. Suhonen and Papa spent several weeks deer hunting. Finally they were successful and shared the big buck that Papa shot. They dressed it and took part of the meat to the store to exchange for credit for both families. Mr. Suhonen had not worked at all during the strike, so his family was especially happy to have the venison.

Papa looked so sad the night after taking the venison to the store that Anna brought him a second cup of coffee and sat down with him, even though it was after her bedtime.

"Aren't you glad, Papa, about the deer?"

Papa nodded but looked even more glum.

"What's wrong?" she asked.

For a moment he didn't answer her. Then he said, "I was thinking of the year before your mother died—do you remember when Lempi and I used to get up early and bow hunt?"

Anna smiled. "Yes. We always thought it was unusual that both our parents went deer hunting."

"It was. That was one of the things I loved about your

mother. We did everything together." There was a faraway look in his eyes as he began to tell her about his last deer hunt with Mama.

"Each fall we took a different trail, but we usually came back with enough venison to last all winter. We didn't always get our deer the first day, but we were patient hunters. One morning we left the house with our bows and arrows and a slip I had made to carry the deer home on."

Anna had seen the slip, which was like a large flat sled, stored in the barn.

He continued, "We went north of Chisholm to investigate the hunting there. For three miles we pushed through the woods as silently as possible. It was a place we had talked about hunting but never had."

"Where were Matti and I?"

"Still in bed. Your mama always left milk and warm rolls for you when we went hunting. Your school lunch pails were on the table. She knew you would go to school as usual, and we always told you where we'd be."

"Tell me what happened that day."

"We stepped out of the forest into a clearing. Ahead of us lay a small lake surrounded by white pine, spruce, and birch trees on three sides, a lake we didn't even know existed. We were excited—it was our own private place! As we stood quietly, a six-point buck and a doe came out of the trees on our left.

"No more than sixty feet away, I decided. I nocked a broadhead arrow to my bow. I told myself to wait for a broadside shot. I don't think the deer were even aware of us. The buck lowered his head to drink from the lake. Then he watched over the doe as she drank.

"I looked at Lempi, but she shook her head. I couldn't

figure out why she didn't want me to shoot. We stayed there without moving until the deer disappeared back into the woods."

Tears glittered in Papa's eyes. "We sat on a fallen tree. I was surprised she hadn't wanted me to take the buck. I asked, 'Why—?'

"Lempi looked around. 'Toivo, this place belongs to the animals. We'll get our deer,' she said. 'Don't worry. But not here.'

"We sat for an hour, watching raccoons dip food into the deep pool. Then a fox drank from the lake. It was a place untouched by humans. Then it got late, and we had to get back. We promised each other we'd come again next season. We got a deer within the week, but in another woods, far from our secret lake.

"When bow hunting season came the next fall, Lempi was gone." He sat quietly without speaking. Anna patted his hand resting on the table.

Anna hugged her father. "That's one of your special memories of Mama. Don't be sad. We have our deer now, just when we really need him." She saved her tears until she went to bed. Papa was so sad that she didn't want him to see her cry. She missed Mama so much!

The next day they smoked part of the meat, hung some out to freeze, and Anna began learning to cook venison. She worried about Christmas, though, and saw no solution to one problem. She and Matti had no way to get a present for their father. Matti's thoughts were fixed on whether or not Papa had a gift for him. Anna kept teasing him about the Joulu pukki, an old Finnish custom.

The pukki was a straw goat who was supposed to watch children and, if they were good, bring them presents at

Christmas. If they had been naughty, the pukki would bring a rutabaga, a vegetable much like a turnip and one that Matti hated. Traditionally, it should have been on the mantel in a Finnish home, but because the Kallios had no fireplace, their pukki sat on a small table in the corner of the downstairs room.

"A rutabaga for sure," Anna said to Matti the day before Christmas, "maybe a whole bag of them!"

Her brother looked up at her. "I don't think one bad thing deserves a rutabaga. I've been good since—well, since the mine."

"Oh, but the pukki has a long memory," she said with a smile. Then when she saw he was close to tears, she relented. "Maybe he's forgotten the mine," she said.

"I hope so." He stepped back from the small Christmas

tree Papa had set in the corner. "Are there enough strings of cranberries on it?"

"They look just right," his sister assured him. "And your paper chains from school are fine. But we don't have any present for Papa except those cards we made at school." She pointed to them, already hanging on the tree.

Matti looked sad. "I know. I've thought and thought, but we don't have any money at all. Do you think he has something for us?"

She shook her head. "Probably not. It's been a hard year for everyone."

"I wish Mama were here," Matti muttered. "She would have knitted something, at least."

"I do, too. But it's no use even talking about it." She began tidying up the room after their afternoon of decorating. "I have to get the venison roast ready, and you can help peel the potatoes." She hoped Papa had something for Matti. She had invented a game for her brother, but she wasn't sure he would like it.

Mrs. Williams had found a square board for the game, and using crayons, Anna had colored squares all around the edge of the board. Then she had taken two pretty rocks from her rock collection to use as tokens for the players.

"You need to make up some rules," Mrs. Williams had suggested, "and perhaps include dice to roll for each turn." When Anna had not been able to find dice, the teacher had produced a pair. Now the game was wrapped and ready. "Matti likes to win occasionally," the teacher had reminded her with a smile, "so the rules had better be written, or he'll argue." Mrs. Williams knew Matti pretty well, Anna thought.

At supper that day, Matti told his father again about the skating party on Longyear Lake.

"I know," Papa said, eating his supper.

"But we don't have any skates," Matti said gloomily.

"I know," Papa said again.

"It doesn't matter, Papa," Anna said hastily. "We don't mind not going."

"I know."

Anna exchanged a puzzled look with Matti. Didn't their father care at all that it was the party of the year?

On Christmas morning, Papa lighted the few candles that had been tied to the branches of the tree. Then they ate breakfast in the glow of the tiny flames.

"It's beautiful," Anna said.

"We are together," Papa said, smiling at them both.

After the dishes were cleared from the table, washed, and left to drain, Anna put the venison roast and potatoes into the oven and gave Matti his new game. He was delighted.

"Can we play after dinner?" he asked, his blue eyes sparkling. "Like we did a couple of years ago when Mama—" he stopped. "I'm sorry," he said.

Papa walked silently out the door.

"See, you said the wrong thing," Anna scolded. "You reminded him of Mama. You shouldn't have done that!"

"I'm sorry. I wasn't thinking."

Their father came back in with two bulky packages.

"What? What?" Matti breathed, grabbing the one Papa gave him.

"Papa? What have you done?" Anna asked.

Papa sat down and smiled as they ripped off the brown paper.

"Skates! Skates!" Matti yelled exultantly. "How did you buy these?"

"Yes, Papa, how?" Anna slipped her shoes into the skates.

A perfect fit—as were Matti's.

"I didn't buy them," Papa said, very pleased with himself. "I made them after work at the camp in Buhl. Have you forgotten I'm a blacksmith!"

The children laid their wonderful skates on the floor and rushed to hug him.

"We can go to the skating party!" Matti shouted. "We can go!"

Anna asked her father. "Do you have skates, too?"

"Yes." Papa looked happier than the children had seen him in a long time. "I'm a good skater. Your mother and I used to skate often in Finland. I should have made skates for you long ago."

Anna picked up her skates. "We better not put them on in the house," she told her brother. Then she hesitated. "Papa, we don't have a gift for you. We didn't have any money." Both children looked miserable.

"You don't have anything for me?" Papa said in astonishment. "Look at that beautiful tree! Didn't you two decorate it?"

"Yes," Matti said, "but—"

"And dinner. Didn't the two of you prepare it?"

"Yes," Anna said, "but—"

"You both study hard and take care of the house and me. Isn't that a gift?" Papa asked.

Once again they hugged him, and Anna went out to the privy so that neither of them would see her cry. She had worried about Christmas, but it was going to be fine.

TWELVE

~

THE PROMISED SKATING party took place on the day after Christmas. The Suhonens came in their bobsled to take the Kallios to Longyear Lake. It was not far, and Papa protested that they could walk, but Mr. Suhonen said, "We need some firewood for the party, too. That's really why I came by. Have any to spare?"

Papa went back for several huge armfuls of sticks and a few logs. When everyone had climbed in, Matti said, "We could sure use a horse and wagon."

Papa smiled and exchanged an amused glance with his friend Mr. Suhonen. Anna had a pretty good idea that her father had already decided to get a wagon. There were so many times when one had been needed.

"The horse could go in the barn with Daisy and the chickens," she said.

"You want a horse, too!" Papa said and laughed. "We'll see."

When they arrived at the lake, the fathers of some of the students had been busy shoveling and then sweeping the snow off a section of the lake to make a large round skating rink. Papa and Mr. Suhonen got busy building a huge bonfire at its edge. Many families arrived, and the fire builders

had more help than they wanted as small children tossed in sticks and debris. Papa snatched up one tiny child who staggered too near the flames. He carried him to his father who accepted him with a grin. The fire was not only to keep the spectators warm, but to roast food the skaters had brought. For that, the fire had to burn down to coals.

As soon as the ice was as smooth as the men could get it, the children who were old enough put on their skates and took to the rink. Papa spent some time teaching both his children, and soon they were skating on their own, if a bit shakily.

"I wouldn't play any crack-the-whip or snake if I were you," he advised, grinning.

"Noooo," Anna called as she wobbled away from him. Because she was falling about every hundred feet or so, this was good advice. But as she slid down and struggled up, she kept a fascinated eye on her teacher, Mrs. Williams.

Dressed in a long red skirt and black jacket, the teacher glided around the circle, encouraging her students. It was clear to Anna that Mrs. Williams had been on skates many times.

Whoops!

"Slow and easy," the teacher said, gliding over to help Anna up. "I'll hold on to you for a few steps."

"Where did you learn to skate?" Anna panted.

"Michigan." Mrs. Williams held Anna's arm and skated slowly with her. "My father was a copper miner there—my husband, too. Are you steady now?"

"Yes. You can let go." Slowly, cautiously, Anna fought to keep her feet moving. Soon she was falling less often and beginning to enjoy the skating. My ankles will be sore tomorrow, she thought.

She and the Petaja sisters joined hands and skated together around the outskirts of the cleared circle. They avoided the far section of their rink where many of the older boys laughed and shouted as they played crack-the-whip in the crisp air.

The day was perfect: sunny, cold, with blue skies overhead. The men had the fire under control by now and began to come onto the rink themselves. Out of the corner of her eye, Anna watched her father glide onto the ice, then execute several perfect figure eights. But when she turned around to see him better, down she went.

As she picked herself up, her admiring eyes again sought him, but he was no longer alone. Skating with him, matching him stroke for stroke, was a skater in a bright red skirt who was almost as tall as he was. Anna stood for a few moments at the edge of the lake to watch. Many others watched also because the two skaters were well matched. Each took turns skating backwards, then shifted again to cross arms and glide together.

That's interesting, Anna thought, for two people who behave as if they didn't like each other! The next time she looked, Mrs. Williams was skating with someone else. When she located her father, he was kneeling by a small crying child, refastening the little boy's skates. It was only a temporary joining—Papa and the teacher. For some reason that she could not understand, she was very relieved to notice that it did not happen again.

Later, when a few of the party-goers began placing small pieces of venison or potato on sticks to roast in the fire, she made a point of asking him about Mama.

"Did you and Mama skate together?" she wondered, hoping her words carried to the teacher, who stood nearby assisting one of her younger students pierce a morsel of meat with a sharpened stick.

"In Finland, yes, but we never seemed to have time after we came here. We loved to skate!" He smiled at her. "I'm glad your teacher planned this outing. We should do more of this. I should have made skates for you long ago."

The sky began to darken quite early that afternoon, and icy particles flew through the air to sting the faces of the skaters. Parents gathered up their children to make their way home before the snow began falling in earnest. Since the bonfire was far from any buildings, the men decided to leave it burning.

Anna looked back through the swirling snow, which was beginning to batter them, and tried to remember the sight of the fire's rosy glow against the darkened sky. It had been a wonderful party. Why did she feel so uncomfortable about it?

A blizzard howled around the house all night Sunday, and the next morning Papa had to shovel a path to the outhouse and the barn. The wood piled on the front stoop was somewhat protected by the roof, but the wind had blown the outermost logs full of snow. He had to bring several armfuls of wood inside and stack them against the wall to be sure they would have dry wood during the storm.

By Monday afternoon more than three feet of snow had fallen and the temperature had dropped well below zero. Unable to go outside, Matti and Anna decided to play the new game.

"What do the white squares mean?" Matti asked.

"Almost all the colors mean problems: if you land on

white, it means there's a blizzard and you lose two turns."

"Two turns!"

"Yes. You can't go anywhere for two days after it snows a lot, right?" she questioned.

"That's true. The blue squares?"

"That's night. You have to wait out one turn."

"The yellow?"

"Sunshine. You get another turn because it's a nice day."

"How about red? I know. That's a happy time, like a birthday or something, and you get two turns."

"You've got it. Now let's play."

Papa had an errand in Chisholm that he said would take him all afternoon. When he returned several hours later, he proudly drove a brown horse and a bobsled to the front door.

"Papa, Papa! Are they ours?" Matti shouted.

Papa couldn't stop smiling. "Yes, and the horse is named 'King.' One of the men I work with traded the outfit to me for blacksmithing work I've been doing for him. We've got wheels as well as these runners." He got down from the wagon and patted the horse. "Isn't he nice?"

The children stroked the old horse tenderly. "He's wonderful," Matti said. "And now Daisy will have some company."

"We can plow a bigger garden," Anna said. "If," she added, "we can borrow a plow."

"Suhonens'," Matti said cheerfully.

Papa led the horse around to the tiny barn and unhitched him. Anna and the delighted Matti followed him in.

"Daisy doesn't mind," Matti observed as the cow moved over to make room for King. "What are we going to feed him?" he asked anxiously.

"We'll buy more hay," Papa said.

"We can haul supplies so much easier," Anna said happily. "Just think how many times we've had to ask Suhonens for help!"

"Suhonen is a good friend," Papa said. "Now we can give him and his family a ride sometimes!"

By the following Sunday, the weather had settled down to bitter cold, and the snow had stopped.

Monday morning, Anna fixed her brother's lunch pail before breakfast and then hauled him out of bed. He came down to breakfast grouchy.

"I don't think I should go to school today. It's too cold, and I might get croup again."

She addressed him with her hands on her hips. "That won't work. You're well!"

He ate his hot cereal, saying not quite under his breath, "I'll get sick again. You'll be sorry."

"It didn't take you long to get spoiled," Anna teased. Sleigh bells jingled outside. She ran to the window to lift the curtain.

"Get into your coat and mittens. Papa has the bobsled hitched up, and he's taking you and some of your friends to school. You don't have to walk. Today you're lucky!"

Eagerly he obeyed and ran out to the sled.

Anna felt left out not to be going along. She tried to shake off the feeling and began working furiously so that she could go to school as usual on Tuesday. As she fed the animals, she made a mental note to tell her father that the cow needed to be freshened. Until Daisy was bred and had a new calf, she wouldn't have much milk. When Anna walked back to the house, she noticed that the sky had darkened. Soon the wind began to beat at their walls.

When Papa came back he said, "I don't like the looks of this storm. If the snow lets up, I may go back and bring the students home. The school's close enough to their homes so they could walk, but not if there's a blizzard. It didn't look this bad earlier."

All morning the wind howled and blew snow against the windows. Anna couldn't see anything but white when she looked outside. She gave her father his meal while he tried to decide whether or not to go back for the children. Then at noon, a glint of light caught her eyes.

"Look outside! The sun is shining, and the snow has stopped. Can you believe how suddenly the weather changed?"

Papa went out to check on the condition of the sky, but he was frowning when he came in.

"The sky looks good right now, but these storms usually come from the northeast," he said, "and it's dark in that direction. I think we'll get more snow." He stood looking out the window. "I wonder if the teacher will send them home while it's nice enough to walk. She might think it's stopped storming for the day. She doesn't know much about iron range blizzards because this is her first year here."

"Are you worried, Papa?" Anna asked.

"A little," he admitted.

Matti did not come home early. The weather gradually worsened outside until Anna and Papa looked solemnly at each other and began worrying aloud. The teacher must have decided not to send the children home.

"They'll be warm," Anna assured Papa. The school had a huge wood pile that the parents kept up.

When Papa came back in after getting an armload of wood in the early afternoon, the wind tore the door from his hand and slammed it back against the inside wall. Together they shut and locked it.

"Phew!" he whistled. "I wonder how long this will keep up."

All afternoon, was the answer. The wind screamed and pounded against their house. When she stood very quietly, Anna could hear the walls creaking in the cold. The large trees around back made snapping noises constantly. She shuddered. Anyone out in that storm would freeze to death. Around four o'clock, Papa decided he should take the bobsled and help get the children home.

"Any distance is too far in this blizzard—especially for the younger children," he said. "I'm going over to see what Suhonen thinks."

"Then I'm coming with you," she said, and nothing he could say would convince her to stay at home and wait.

At Suhonens', they were welcomed heartily. Mrs. Suhonen insisted on giving them coffee and bread.

"The children are all right," the adults comforted each other. "They're warm and safe. The teacher was right to keep them at school when it got so bad out. There was only a short time, when the sun was out, when it was safe for any of them to walk home."

Then Anna voiced what had been at the back of their minds all afternoon.

"What if the teacher didn't keep them? What then?"

THIRTEEN

~

T HE GROWNUPS LOOKED at each other uncertainly. Mrs. Suhonen started to cry.

"That's all I've been able to think about," she wailed. Her husband put his arm around her shoulders.

"Mrs. Williams has plenty of common sense, Dorothy," he reminded his wife. "She wouldn't have let those children walk out in this weather, and you know it!"

"I know," she sobbed, "but all five of our children are in that schoolhouse. I can't help worrying."

"Me, too," Papa agreed and turned to Mr. Suhonen. "Let's try to get to the school. It doesn't seem so bad right now. What do you think?"

"Yes," Mrs. Suhonen said eagerly. "You might get stuck there tonight, but I'll know the children are safe if you two are there." She hurried around the kitchen, gathering up food as she went. "Take this kettle of homemade stew—and here's a haunch of smoked venison and some bread."

"No, that's too much fussing," her husband announced. "We'll take the students home a few at a time! That's all."

"Stick your head out the door, Stephen. It's the middle of the afternoon and already starting to get dark. Pretty soon those children will be hungry. They can have sandwiches and stew, at least. And here's some coffee for the adults in case you can't get back tonight."

"I guess we're going," Mr. Suhonen said with a shrug. He grimaced at his friend. "Dorothy thinks eating makes everything better. I'll get ready."

"She may be right, you know. Take some lanterns," Papa advised. "Anna, you stay here."

"I'm coming with you," she said firmly. "I'm just as anxious as you are."

"But—"

She insisted, however, and as soon as the food and a pot of coffee were packed, they carried everything out to Papa's bobsled.

"If you need to eat supper there, you can heat the coffee and soup on the school stove," Mrs. Suhonen called as they went out.

Every few minutes, the wind let up and allowed them to see where they were. If it hadn't been for those few glimpses of the landscape, they would have been lost immediately. The snow seemed to get deeper as they drove the bobsled toward the school. Soon the horse was up to his knees in the drifts.

"We're off the road," Steve shouted, "and I don't know where it is."

On they went, bending their heads against the snow being driven into their faces. Ice gathered on the scarves across their mouths. Periodically, Anna worked her arms and legs so they wouldn't freeze.

She shouldn't have come, she admitted to herself. She had known that from the beginning, but Matti and Papa were all she had. The sky was slowly darkening, a sure indication that more snow was coming. What would happen if they became completely lost? Freeze to death, that's what.

96

Better not think about it. Think instead of how warm the schoolhouse would be and how happy the students when they got there. Think about that—and pray.

They slogged on in the storm. The horse traveled slowly; the drifts were deep. Anna felt numb, partly from the cold, but also from her growing fear that they might have made a terrible mistake coming out in this blizzard. She had trusted her father's decision to try to get to the school. If he hadn't thought they could make it, would he have tried?

King finally stopped, and Papa got down to coax him on. He walked beside the horse for a few moments, and suddenly the wind let up again and all three of them saw a light ahead. Twilight had come early with the storm. Papa patted the tired horse and got back into the bobsled.

"Lantern in the window," he shouted against the wind and snow. "I think it's the schoolhouse!"

King must have sensed deliverance, because he lowered his head and moved a little faster. All three passengers watched the light until they were sure they were approaching the school. At the front steps, King stopped as if to say, "I'm through."

Mr. Suhonen and Papa jumped out and helped Anna down. Carrying the basket of food and the coffee pot, they struggled up the icy steps. The door was locked—probably to hold it shut—and they had to pound on it. Two surprised students opened it.

"It's the Kallios and Mr. Suhonen!" a little girl called to the teacher.

"Pa! It's Pa," came from several voices.

At the far end of the schoolroom, a boy stood beside Mrs. Williams, who was sitting at her desk. She smiled at the welcome visitors.

97

"Come in!" she said, rising. Mrs. Williams smiled over Anna's head at her unexpected guests. Anna looked up to see her father smiling back.

"Look who's here," she said, but the students were already cheering loudly. "Someone to help you get home." A few of the students groaned. It must have been an unusual school day, Anna thought, if they wanted to stay.

Mr. Suhonen took one long look at his friend and smiled. "I'll put King around back in the woodshed out of the wind."

Papa nodded without looking at Mr. Suhonen, and he and Anna walked up the center of the schoolroom to where the teacher stood. He set the basket on the table and looked around for a place to put the coffeepot. Anna gave him a disgusted look and took it from him. Couldn't he see the stove? Because he continued to stand by Mrs. Williams without speaking, Anna also carried over the big pot of stew.

The students gathered around Anna, everyone talking at once about the storm and the games and the songs they had been singing.

"I wasn't scared a bit," Arthur Suhonen bragged.

"Oh, not much!" his friend Jimmy Aho teased.

"Was not!"

"Were, too!"

"Mrs. Williams let us play games," Matti told Anna, "but only after three o'clock. I guess she has to be strict when it's schooltime." For a few seconds, Matti watched the two adults smiling at each other, then he went over to stand by his teacher. Anna followed him curiously.

"If the snow lets up, we'll make several trips," Papa said, speaking to Mrs. Williams. "We'll make sure the children get home safely. But if the storm keeps blowing, we'll stay here and keep your fire going and help feed everyone. I suppose you know there are community cups and plates stored in the cloakroom."

"Yes, thank you," Mrs. Williams said softly. "I should have sent the students home at noon when the storm lightened up, I guess."

"Not all of them would have made it before the blizzard hit again," Papa insisted.

"I'm so glad you came. We've been needing someone with a bobsled for times like this during the winter," Mrs. Williams said. "Maybe the school board will pay you a little something to help us out occasionally."

"Hay for the horse?" Papa suggested with a grin.

When neither adult looked at him, Matti finally pulled on Mrs. Williams' sleeve. She looked down at him. "Yes, Matti?"

"Can you sew?" he asked.

She laughed and, once again turning her head to face Papa's eyes, answered, "Yes, and I can teach Anna to make her own dresses if she would like to learn."

Papa leaned forward, smiling at Mrs. Williams. He wouldn't! Anna thought in horror. Not here—in front of all these kids! As she watched, he moved back.

Matti was watching Anna wide-eyed. He looked as uncomfortable as she felt. The decision was out of their hands now, unless they could change Papa's mind. She wondered why they had ever embarked on such a mission as finding a bride for Papa. Life was becoming complicated, and Anna, for one, was no longer looking forward to any changes.

FOURTEEN

~

WHILE THE BLIZZARD raged outside, Mrs.
Williams organized the students into teams to
serve supper and clean up afterwards. Both of
the men had decided the storm was too fierce for them to
take anyone home. The day had turned dark, and it was clear
they would not be able to find their way until morning light.
They were reasonably sure no one would try to come for the
children until tomorrow, but they wished for some way to
get word to the other parents. Chisholm had telephone service, but that service did not as yet extend to the Monroe
location.

The older girls and boys took out the dishes in the cup-
boards and set one long table as a buffet. Any students with
leftover sandwiches, fruit, or sweets donated them to the
table, and soon the stew Mrs. Suhonen had sent was hot. As
each student stepped up to the table with a small bowl, Mrs.
Williams filled it with the delicious-smelling stew. There was
water for the children to drink and coffee for the adults.
Soon everyone was eating and talking in a kind of holiday
atmosphere.

Anna thought bleakly that it was a good thing the students couldn't go home right this minute. They were so

excited to be eating and staying at school late that their mothers would never be able to calm them down. She didn't realize that she was glaring at her father and the teacher until her friend Elinor mentioned it.

"What did your papa do to get you so mad at him?" Elinor wanted to know.

"Nothing!" Anna snapped.

Elinor looked surprised but suggested that after supper they clean the blackboards and put up the next day's assignments. "The fourth and fifth graders have to wash the dishes," she said. "We already did our share."

After a few hours of games that became wilder and wilder, the two fathers strongly urged the children to get some sleep. The boys laid their outer clothes on the cloakroom floor and lay down on them. Some of the girls sat with their heads resting on their desks. Others placed their coats on the floor as makeshift beds. Anna could hear excited whispers for a while; then silence gradually stole over the schoolhouse.

From where she sat at a desk, resting her head on her left arm, she could watch her father and Mrs. Williams playing card games with Mr. Suhonen at the teacher's desk. The men kept the fire in the wood stove going, and although the wind dashed frozen snow against the windows from time to time, most of the children finally went to sleep. Anna's last conscious thought was of poor Daisy waiting in vain for more feed. Fortunately, she didn't need to be milked again until after her calf arrived next fall.

In the morning, the sun blazed down on the snowdrifts. The men shoveled the path again to the outhouse, where one end of a long rope that stretched from the schoolhouse was fastened to a nail on its door. During the night, any child who needed to go out had held the rope so that no one would wander off the path. An adult had accompanied the very young students.

"I'll alert a few of the other families," Papa told Mrs. Williams at the door as she made sure the children were bundled up warmly. "We'll soon have several bobsleds to help us take everyone home."

Anna tied a scarf around one small girl's mouth. She tried not to notice that Papa was gazing at the teacher again. The sight made her uncomfortable.

"I'll take you home after we've delivered the children," Papa promised Mrs. Williams. She smiled at him and nodded.

"Yes," she joked, "the captain should be last to leave the ship."

Along with the teacher, Anna and Matti were the last to be taken home. Papa left them outside their house with a request to shovel paths to the front door, barn, and outhouse. The shovel was frozen in place on the tiny front stoop, but Anna finally wrenched it free.

"Here," she told Matti. "I'll get the fire going and then go out to the barn. Shovel the barn path first, please, and I'll help you as soon as I take care of poor Daisy and the chickens. There's another shovel in the barn."

The work seemed to take hours, but soon the hollow scraping of shovels ceased, and the two of them went inside to thaw.

"Shake your outside clothes on the porch," she said crossly. "I don't want all that snow in the house."

Matti gave everything a quick flutter outside the front door. Then he looked at her belligerently.

"I don't see what you're so mad at," he said. "You wanted Papa to find a wife. Well, it looks to me like that's what has happened. She's not so bad," he said. "Yesterday we had fun. And she tells good stories, too."

Anna refused to answer him. She angrily tossed her braids and tried to think of what she should cook for supper.

"Until it happens," she finally reminded Matti, "I'm the one who has to do it all. Now go into the pantry and bring me a jar of tomatoes and one of string beans. Then you can go collect the eggs."

"You don't do it all!" he retorted and then skipped quickly out of her way.

In early afternoon, Anna heard her father come home. The sounds of King being unhitched from the sleigh and put into the barn with Daisy reached her ears clearly now in the crisp air. The sun shone brightly, and although it would never heat the frigid outdoors, the sun on the snow was pleasant to see. She finished her preparations for supper and laid her books on a corner of the kitchen table to study.

Papa stomped his boots free of snow and came in.

"Wet," he said. "My feet are half frozen." When she didn't look up or answer, he added, "There's school tomorrow. Suhonen and two of the other parents will go around with bobsleds to pick up the children. I'll take you and Matti and a couple of your friends. The school board agreed to give us hay for our horses if we drive the children to school until Easter or until we go back to work."

"Yes," Anna said stiffly. "Tomorrow is Tuesday, and that's one of my days at school. I'll be too busy to go on Wednesdays and even on Fridays from now on. I have the washing and bread-making, you know."

She could feel his gaze on her bent head, but she didn't look up. He reached for the coffee pot and poured himself a steaming cup, then he sat down beside her.

"You're too young to bury yourself in housework, Anna," he said cheerfully. "We'll have to see what we can do about that."

"I don't mind," she said in a cool, dismissive way. Then she picked up the book she planned to read and walked determinedly to the ladder.

"Call me if you need anything," she said in what she hoped was a dignified and adult manner. "I'll be reading upstairs until it's time for supper."

His swift glance showed his surprise at her retreat, but Anna pretended not to see it. She climbed the loft ladder quickly before the threatening tears could fall.

Everything was going to change now. Everything.

FIFTEEN

~

ANNA WAS AMAZED that Matti didn't notice Papa was constantly gone at night and absent on the weekends.

"You know where he goes!" she shouted at her brother one Friday night when Papa vanished immediately after supper.

"So?" Matti inquired, shrugging his shoulders.

"So he's with *Her*."

Matti shrugged again. "He likes her. And so do I."

Anna was enraged. "Well, I don't! We were doing fine before he got this wonderful idea."

"No, we weren't," Matti contradicted. "We wanted someone here to mend and cook and do those other things that needed doing and be with Papa and take care of us. I say she's all right."

Anna glared at him. "You wash the dishes tonight," she said angrily. "And don't get water on the floor!"

It was true. Papa was courting the teacher. He seemed happier, too, Anna had to admit, than he had been since Mama died. He went around humming to himself or whistling a tuneful melody. He also tried to help Anna more with the housework. If that involved carrying something heavy, like buckets of water, she let him help her. When he tried to set the table or sweep the floor, she discouraged him.

"You don't know how I like it done," she would say and motion him away from the task.

Papa gave her a keen look each time but remained cheerful. It was the cheerfulness that made Anna feel bad.

She wanted Papa to be happy; she truly did. But she wanted to be the one who made him happy. Mrs. Williams was a stranger. Perhaps if she refused to accept the teacher as his—friend—he would give her up. Somehow, though, she knew he wouldn't.

On Shrove Tuesday, their favorite Finnish festivity was to take place—Laskiainen Day—but because the children had school and the fathers had to work, the community had decided to celebrate it the following weekend.

On Saturday morning, all the Finnish families in the location were going to go sliding down a nearby hill, using large pieces of cardboard because toboggans or sleds were too expensive. Matti had been looking forward to this day all winter and was ready far too early.

"Wake up, Anna," he said eagerly. Anna opened her eyes to see Matti standing beside her bed fully dressed in his cap, coat, and mittens.

"What in the world?" She blinked at him and then sat up in amazement.

"Laskiainen Day," he explained patiently.

She threw her head back down on the pillow. "For heaven's sake! It's not time yet. Go take off your outside clothes. I'll make breakfast. Then Papa will take us over to Blueberry Hill."

"All right," Matti said, "and then this afternoon Papa's going to pick up Mrs. Williams and bring her too."

Hearing that made Anna truly cross. She jumped out of bed and smoothed the blankets rapidly. "Of course he will! We can't go anywhere without her!"

"I like her," he said.

"I know you do!" She stomped down the ladder to the kitchen.

It was a wonderful day, though, she had to admit. The sun turned the new snow into dazzling glitter. Since it was a special day, most of the adults who climbed the hill, dragging the large pieces of cardboard, lapsed into speaking Finnish. Their children climbed and slid and screamed all the way to the bottom. Fortunately, no one slid far enough to hit any of the large pine trees at the foot of the hill.

For the first few hours, Anna was happy and carefree; then her father arrived in the sleigh with Mrs. Williams. Some of the adults gave them a sidelong glance, but Anna believed everyone in the community knew that Toivo Kallio was courting the teacher. Certainly her classmates knew.

Anna watched the couple when she thought no one would notice. She loved her father and wouldn't want her neighbors to know how she felt about the—friendship—between him and Mrs. Williams.

Darkness put an end to the sliding all too soon, and the miners and their families climbed into the bobsleds, tucked the thick blankets all around them, and drove home.

For a long time, Anna had felt as if bad news was hanging in the air, or misfortune was about to strike. Finally, the day she had been dreading came. At the end of Lent just as spring began to make itself felt and Easter was about to arrive, Papa said that he had a special surprise for the family.

On Saturday afternoon, while they were waiting for the

sauna to heat up, he said in a determinedly cheerful tone, "Tomorrow I'm going to take you both to dinner at the O'Neil Hotel in Chisholm. How would you like that?"

"Dinner in the hotel?" Matti was thrilled. Never, never in his life had he eaten in a restaurant. "Papa, that's wonderful!" He began dancing around the kitchen.

"Stop it," Anna commanded crossly. "Just you and Matti and me?" she asked cautiously.

"Noooo," Papa said slowly. "I've, ah, invited your teacher to have dinner with us. Her only relatives live in Michigan, and she can't go home for Easter." He smiled at Anna and tried to pat her shoulder. "You won't have to do a thing but eat and enjoy it."

She shrugged her shoulder away and turned to put a dish in the cupboard. "Go ahead. I don't mind. I'd rather stay home. I have a lot of homework to do."

"Mrs. Williams didn't give anybody homework over Easter," Matti reminded her. "Don't be that way."

Papa looked so hurt and bewildered that Anna relented.

"All right," she said briefly. "I'll go." But I won't enjoy it, she promised herself silently.

She wore her mother's blue dress, and both Matti and her father told her how nice she looked. She didn't even answer them. Papa hitched King to the sleigh, and the family rode silently to the hotel on Lake Street, which ran straight through the center of Chisholm. Anna wondered if they would see the place where Mrs. Williams stayed. Surely Papa would pick her up before they got to the hotel. But he didn't. He hitched King to a post outside the hotel and ushered the children into the small lobby. Sitting on a couch was Mrs. Williams, dressed for the occasion in a green dress that Anna had not seen before.

108

Papa reached for Mrs. Williams' hand and drew her to his side. "I don't have to introduce you three. Mae sees more of you than I do," he said.

"Hello, Mrs. Williams," Matti said shyly and smiled.

"You look so nice," the teacher said. "And Anna does, too! Blue becomes you."

Anna ducked her head and mumbled something. She felt her face turning red. The waiter saved her by approaching to show them to their seats at a table covered with a red-and-white checkered cloth.

Ordering was not a problem, because the waiter immediately brought each of them a ham dinner, evidently the Easter special. Anna made brief answers to the teacher's questions but offered nothing on her own. After they had eaten their dessert of cherry pie and the dishes had been removed, Papa reached for Mrs. Williams' hand once again and held it on top of the table. Anna noticed that his own hand was shaking slightly.

"We have something to tell you," he began. Mrs. Williams smiled at him encouragingly.

"I know, I know," Matti interrupted. "You and Mrs. Williams are going to get married, aren't you?"

Papa smiled in relief. "Yes," he said.

Anna did not speak. Her worst fears were coming true. What could she say? That their engagement was bad news and she wished they would forget about it? She couldn't make her father unhappy. And Mrs. Williams would be very embarrassed. Matti was so excited that she really did not need to speak. He chattered on about the things they could do together. Finally he ran out of ideas, and everyone turned to Anna.

"I hope you'll both be very happy," she managed to say.

Her father picked up Anna's hand. "We're *all* getting married," he said, "not just Mae and me. We want you both to be pleased about it. You're very important to us."

Anna tried to smile. "We are pleased," she said politely, "but you'll have to give us time to get used to the idea."

Mrs. Williams nodded. "You'll have plenty of time," she said. "We'll wait until school's out in June. That will give me more time to make my dress and Toivo—" she blushed "—your father, I mean, will have time to make a piece of furniture, which he seems to think is necessary." She looked at Anna. "Would you do me the honor of standing up with me? I have no relatives here in Minnesota. We can decide on our dresses together. What do you think about that?"

For a minute Anna allowed herself to become excited. Part of a wedding! None of her friends had ever been a bridesmaid. Then she looked down so no one would see her excitement.

"That will be lovely," she said stiffly.

Papa sighed despairingly.

"What do you two think about going to the program at the temperance hall this afternoon?" Mrs. Williams suggested. "There's going to be a juggler and a team of dancers."

"Yes!" Matti said and leaped up. "Let's go now."

The two adults looked anxiously at Anna.

"Yes," she said quietly. "I would like that."

But she refused to let her enthusiasm show. It was their wedding, not hers, no matter what Papa said. And if the wedding wasn't until June, anything could happen. Maybe they would change their minds by then, she thought hopefully. She could not accept their decision as final. She would not.

SIXTEEN

~

MRS. WILLIAMS TOOK Anna on the train to Hibbing to shop for dress material for the wedding. Although Anna had ridden the train during her original trip to Minnesota, she had been too young to remember it. The passengers had to board the Duluth Missabe and Northern train in the Clark Location because there was no passenger service to Chisholm itself. This ride was only the beginning of the excitement.

In and out of the Hibbing stores they went, feeling materials, discussing colors and prices. In spite of Anna's practical side, which was a strong part of her character, she fell in love with a rose-colored material that seemed to float in the air. She held it in front of her eyes.

"You can even see through it!" she said in astonishment.

Mrs. Williams hesitated a moment. "Can you think of other places you could wear it?" she asked, feeling the delicate material between her thumb and forefinger.

"No," Anna said reluctantly, "and I need clothes so much that I should buy something I can wear all the time. Or, at least," she added hastily, "as a good dress."

"We'll work on some of your mother's clothes," Mrs. Williams offered, "if you want to adjust them for your own

111

use. We can even take them apart and lay out a different pattern on the material."

"You can do that?" Anna was impressed.

The teacher smiled. "I have," she said. She picked up a length of pale tan material and held it beside her face. "Now this shantung would make a nice tailored suit for me, a sensible addition to my wardrobe. But," she added with a shy laugh, "I could add one of those new lace jackets!"

Anna studied the material, noting Mrs. Williams' fine brown eyes and the dark braids wound around her head. She thought most people would call the teacher attractive.

"Oh, yes! That would be beautiful!" Anna agreed. "The lace would be perfect for a wedding, and then later without it you wouldn't always be so dressed up."

If I don't watch myself, I'll like her as much as Papa does. But what would be wrong with that? a small voice questioned. She quickly turned her thoughts again to the materials.

They purchased the tan shantung and a few yards of matching lace for Mrs. Williams' dress, then decided on pink for Anna—but not the sheer rose.

"I like this," Anna said, "and I'll be able to wear it often."

Mrs. Williams insisted on paying for everything, and they spent several hours looking at dresses and the high collars that were so popular. Anna became more excited as the day went on and especially when they ate lunch in the Hibbing hotel.

She tried to tell Mrs. Williams "Thank you" when they reached Clark location, where Papa was waiting for them with the wagon.

The teacher hugged her. "I loved being with you. It's always more fun to shop with a friend. We'll begin sewing

112

next weekend, if you like." She hesitated, then asked, "May I bring my sewing machine over to your house? I live in one room, and it's so small for such a large project."

"Of course!" Anna said, only later realizing that it would be the beginning of Mrs. Williams' moving in with them. But that was going to happen. There was nothing to stop the wedding now.

Preparations were under way for the big day, June 10. Anna and Mrs. Williams spent hours cutting, sewing, and fitting their dresses. Papa bought a navy blue sailor suit for Matti, who pretended not to like it. Anna, however, noticed that he couldn't contain his glee at having a new suit with pants that buckled at the knees.

Papa's preparations—besides having Anna press his only good suit—were to build a wardrobe for an unused corner of his bedroom. "Mae has a lot of clothes," he ventured with a smile.

"Should I take Mama's clothes out of your dresser and keep them upstairs until we can work on them?" Anna's lower lip quivered.

He looked at her pleadingly. "Would you do that?" he asked. "It would probably be a good idea. I know that it hurts you to look at them, but you're sensible to try to use them. She would want you to." Tears stood in his eyes.

Anna turned her head away so that he would not see her tears. It hurt so much to remember Mama. Would it ever get any better? And what would she call her new mother? She had been calling her "Mrs. Williams" at school, but things were changing. She wondered what name would be best.

One Sunday afternoon in May, because that was the only free time the two had to work together, she voiced the question. "What would you prefer us to call you?"

Mrs. Williams laid down the lace jacket that she was stitching and reached for the scissors to cut her thread.

"I've thought about that. 'Mrs. Williams' is all right until school is out. Then you can call me 'Mother' "—at Anna's expression she hastened to add—"or 'Mae' would be fine."

"What if I slip and call you 'Mae' in school next year?"

"Oh, that won't be a problem. The school board won't give me a contract once I get married."

Anna was horrified. "You have to give up teaching?"

114

Mrs. Williams shrugged. "The board will look for an unmarried teacher. If they can't find one right away, they'll let me teach until they do."

"But why?"

"Times are hard, Anna, as I'm sure you know. If the husband is working, more than likely no one will hire the wife."

Anna studied Mrs. Williams' face. "How do you feel about that? You love teaching, don't you?"

"Yes, I do. But as I see it, there's a good chance they won't be able to find a qualified unmarried applicant. If they do, there's nothing I can do about that. But you, Anna, you would make a fine teacher! Why don't you plan to take a course in high school when you're a senior and teach here yourself?"

Anna looked out the window and squinted her eyes. Yes, she could see herself as a teacher. That was a long way off, though. She would be in the eighth grade next year—unless she got skipped. Six weeks after Anna had begun going to school again, Mrs. Williams told her that she had finished all the seventh-grade curriculum, and since then Anna had worked very hard on eighth-grade material.

For the first time in Anna's life it occurred to her to wonder if her mother had ever wanted to be anything other than a wife and mother. Dimly she remembered that Papa had a collection of poems her mother had written when she was growing up in Finland. Had Mama had ambitions to write? And had she simply taken her role because she fell in love— or because that's what women always did? Anna decided that she would have to think about this question again. Suppose you had a dream of doing something else? Somehow she knew that her mother had died with unrealized dreams.

Mrs. Williams picked up the jacket again. "My job is here, taking care of my new family. Don't worry about me not teaching. We *could* use the money, of course," she said wistfully.

But Anna felt the injustice of it all. If a person was a good teacher, why should marriage prevent her from continuing? That rule was wrong, there was no question about it.

Will I have to choose between marriage and teaching someday? That choice isn't fair. She supposed Mrs. Williams had not said anything about the possibility of losing her job because she wasn't a complainer.

And I am, Anna thought guiltily. I certainly am.

SEVENTEEN

~

T HE DAY OF THE wedding finally arrived along with bright sunshine, a perfect June day. Papa and Mae had decided to hold the ceremony in the school so that all the students and their parents could attend. Mae's mother and father arrived on the train that morning from Michigan and would stay in their daughter's rented room at Hintsalas'. The entire family would gather at the O'Neil Hotel for a wedding supper, and the bride and groom would spend the night at the hotel. Then the couple were going to Duluth on the train for a two-day honeymoon.

Anna and Matti were excited, if somewhat apprehensive, to have grandparents visiting.

"We don't know our grandparents," Matti informed the elderly Mrs. Williams, who looked just like his teacher, only older. "They live in Finland. I was born here."

"Someday," she told him, "you and Anna will have to persuade your parents to bring you to Michigan. We would love to have you come."

"Yes, absolutely," echoed her husband, a tall, portly man. "We have no other grandchildren."

That was something Anna and Matti had worried about. What if they had to get along with cousins who were strangers? Matti was thrilled.

"When? Maybe we can come this summer. Can we, Papa?"

Papa laughed. All of them, except Mae, were gathered around the kitchen table where Anna had served breakfast before the wedding. "Don't get too eager, son. We'll see."

When everyone was dressed and ready to go, Anna felt a little like a bride herself. The soft pink dress had midlength sleeves with large ruffles falling over her elbows. The dress was not to the floor like the bride's but fell below her knees. She loved it! And everyone told her that her eyes looked especially blue when she wore it. She let her hair fall loose, unbraided, and felt very grown up tossing it behind her.

Papa was handsome in his good dark suit, but Matti looked like a stranger. His navy blue sailor suit was the height of fashion.

"I've never seen you look so grand," Anna told her brother. "Now, walk; don't run or you'll tear the knees out of those pants before anyone ever gets to see them." He glared at her, but she noticed he walked around a little more carefully after her warning.

Mae dressed at the Hintsalas' house and appeared at the school in her new glory, escorted by Mr. Suhonen, who was going to stand up for Papa and who had insisted that the groom not see his bride until the actual wedding.

The creamy lace jacket topped the bride's floor-length tailored suit of tan shantung. The suit itself had a high collar and full-length sleeves, tight at the wrists. Mae had added a wide lace hat trimmed in pink that was the same hue as Anna's dress, and she carried a single rose to match.

Anna smiled. "Beautiful! I didn't know you were going to wear a hat."

"Do you like it?" Mae turned around so that everyone

could get the full effect, then she took a deep breath as Mr. Kangas began playing "Here Comes the Bride" on his concertina. "Here we go, Toivo. Too late to back out now!"

Anna, who was first, processed slowly down between the rows of chairs, basking in her girlfriends' admiring smiles. At the raised platform, she paused and stepped slightly to the left. Mr. Suhonen and her father stood at the right. When Mae approached the makeshift altar, she handed Anna the rose.

After the brief ceremony, the students crowded around their teacher, each wanting her attention. Punch and cookies finally captured their interest, and within an hour, the musicians' lively playing invited everyone to dance. After dancing several times with her new husband, Mae sat down at the piano and played a few schottisches and polkas with Mr. Kangas.

Anna was looking forward to piano lessons. "I don't think it would be a problem if we stayed after school a few afternoons," Mae had told her. "Then I could get you started."

Mae's parents left on the train the next day, and Anna threw herself into cleaning house so that Mae would know she was a good housekeeper. Once, when the reality of the new life struck her, she sat down in her mother's small Finnish rocker to try to imagine what things would be like when the newlyweds returned.

Hardly aware of what she was doing, she stroked the wooden arm of the rocker. It was their first piece of furniture and had come on the ship with her parents. Her mother had insisted on bringing it, so Papa had taken it apart and packed it in a box. When they settled into the company house at the Monroe-Tener Location, one of his first jobs had been to glue the rocker together.

Anna looked down at the worn arms of the chair. She remembered Mama sitting here nursing or rocking Matti. Everything was different now. No use mourning, she thought, and she got up quickly and went to scour the stove. She would never give her new stepmother an opportunity to say the house was dirty when she moved in.

If Anna hadn't been so tired that night, she would no doubt have worried about how the jobs would be divided up between Mae and herself. When she awoke the next morning, the thought was on her mind. Would Mae order her around? She had every right to. Somehow Anna couldn't imagine that happening. But how would they handle the division of chores? No solution suggested itself to her.

Papa and Mae arrived at the depot on the third day after the wedding, met by Mr. Suhonen who drove them home. After the bustle of arrival, the family sat down to eat the supper Anna had prepared.

"You're really a fine cook," Mae said, complimenting her stepdaughter. "I'll clean up the kitchen. Afterwards we should sit down together and decide who does what around here."

So. It was going to be as simple as that, Anna thought, vastly relieved.

Sitting at the kitchen table later, Matti sulked to learn he had his usual jobs: taking care of the garbage, making his bed, drying dishes, shoveling snow in winter, weeding the garden, and helping cut wood for the kitchen stove.

"Add gathering the eggs to that," Anna said, and Matti groaned.

"It seems to me I shouldn't have to do anything," he said. "There's plenty of workers around here without me."

"Matti!" his father said. Those words and a stern look took care of future complaints—at least where adults could overhear.

Anna offered to get the evening meal during the week, because Mae usually stayed after school to prepare the next day's lessons. Then Mae said she would clean up the kitchen and fill the lunch pails during the week. They decided to clean house together, which Anna agreed would make it an easier job.

"And we'll all plant the garden," Mae concluded the discussion. "I have so much to learn about gardening, things the three of you already know."

These plans sounded as if they would work, Anna thought, and they would free her time considerably. What about taking saunas with the family, though? Both she and Matti had discussed this at length before the wedding. Saturday would inevitably arrive, they knew. Some part of the ritual would have to change or it would be the embarrassment of their lives!

Traditionally, Finnish families took saunas together without clothes, just as one would take any bath. What about this new person in their family? On Saturday afternoon, Matti helped his papa start the fire in the stove. Both he and Anna had agreed they would feel miserably uncomfortable being unclothed in Mae's presence or, worse still, seeing her unclothed. Soon they would be faced with the bare facts, as it were.

When the sauna rocks were hot, Papa cleared his throat.

"Matti, you and Anna go first. Then when the sauna's good and hot, Mae and I will take our turn." He turned to his new wife. "Have you ever taken a sauna, Mae?"

She blushed and laughed. "No, but you've told me enough to scare me to death."

He smiled at her. "I'll let you sit on the bottom step while I go to the top. You'll like it," he promised, "as soon as you get used to it."

The children could see that she was nervous about going into the steam bath. Cheerfully, both began to describe how red Papa's face got, how tough he had to be to sit on the top shelf, and about the skunk visitor.

When they were alone in the bath, Anna told her brother, "She was more afraid of the sauna than we were of going in with her!"

Matti laughed. "We got so caught up helping her that we forgot our own problems."

Anna leaned her elbows back on the bench above their seat and thought. That's the secret to getting along with her, I guess, to think more about her feelings than my own.

Anna was surprised at herself. I'm growing up, she decided in amazement. Six months ago, I wouldn't have cared what she felt.

When their father knocked on the door, they quickly cooled themselves down with dippers of cold water, dried off, dressed, and made way for Papa and Mae to take their first sauna together.

Everything, however, was not as easily solved as the sauna problem.

EIGHTEEN

~

PLANTING THE GARDEN, taking care of Daisy until she produced her calf in the fall, and doing the normal summer chores made June and July fly by. Anna noted that Matti had completely succumbed to his new stepmother's charms.

"It's time for my story, Mama," Matti reminded Mae each night shortly before his bedtime. Smiling, Mae would follow the now-ten-year-old boy up the loft ladder.

He's too old for that, Anna grumbled to herself silently, but she wanted everything to go smoothly, so she said nothing aloud. She wondered sometimes if Mae knew how she felt about the new marriage. I don't hate her, she thought, but I sometimes wish it hadn't ever happened. We were doing fine without her. Anna tried to forget how lonely she had been when she could not go to school every day and when she had had the pressure of being responsible for much of their family life.

She began to make it a point to keep her mama's memory alive by telling stories from the past. "Mama always used to take us berry-picking every summer. Then we would help her make jam."

And another time, when they discovered that although

Mae was a fine pianist she could not sing, Anna mentioned nearly every song Mama had ever sung to them. "Matti especially liked to hear Mama sing 'Daisy,' " she would say, "or 'Beautiful Dreamer.' " Papa, who didn't seem to realize that Anna was being deliberately cruel to his new wife, sang Finnish songs to the family.

"At least we didn't have to teach her English," Matti told Anna cheerfully as they led Daisy to graze.

"No," she said shortly, "she teaches *us* English!"

"What's wrong with that?" he demanded.

"You're too young to understand," she informed him loftily.

"You're jealous," he said. "I know that much."

"I am not!"

Matti looked at her and smiled in a way she truly hated, but he dropped the subject.

One pleasant August day about two weeks before school was to start, Mae stood in the pantry counting the jars of canned vegetables and preserves.

"Over one hundred!" she said. "I could never have done that by myself, Anna. Do you think we need more jam or jelly?"

Anna shrugged. Generally she tried not to venture an opinion. Finally she admitted, "Papa loves preserves."

"Then let's go pick some wild raspberries!" Mae began taking off her apron. "Soon I won't have time for any of this, so we'd better go now."

The school board had not been able to find a replacement for Mae, and although she would be working without a contract because of her marriage, she would still be the teacher for the Monroe School. She had qualified Anna as a ninth grader, so Anna would no longer be in the location school but at Central, the new school in Chisholm for high school students. Anna was pleased, because her friend Elinor Petaja would also be at Central. Elinor's sister Marta, a year younger, would remain at the Monroe.

"Would you like to pick berries with me?" Mae asked.

"I guess so."

Be careful, a small voice in her brain said, or you'll begin to enjoy all this.

"Matti?" Mae called out the back door where he was weeding in the garden. "We're going to look for raspberries. Want to go?"

"Of course," he said and instantly dropped the hoe he was holding and ran to the door.

"Go put that hoe away before someone steps on it and is hurt." Anna pointed sternly at the back door. Reluctantly he retraced his steps, then carried the hoe to the barn.

By the time they were ready, Papa had returned from town and decided to go along. They took the wagon and drove out toward Blueberry Hill where they had gone sledding on Laskiainen Day. Matti chattered without needing any answers, and Anna tried not to notice that Papa and Mae were holding hands. Mae finally signaled their stopping place and Papa tied King to a low tree branch.

"The bushes are across that path," Mae said and pointed. Her husband came around to her side of the wagon and lifted her down gently. Another hug, Anna thought. Don't they ever get tired of each other? She reached into the back and took out two pails, giving one to Matti.

"We're going across the road," Anna said. "Come on,

Matti. The berries are thick there." While Papa and Mae wandered off into the brush hand in hand, Anna dragged Matti in the opposite direction.

The sun was bright, cardinals and finches whistled and chittered from the pine trees, and bees buzzed around the raspberry bushes as the children picked the ripe berries. Soon the plunk, plunk of fruit into the buckets gave way to almost soundless deposits. Anna picked rapidly and tried to keep her skirt from the thorny branches. Suddenly Matti cried out.

"Ow! A bee stung me!"

She straightened and watched him rubbing his forearm. "We'll put baking soda on it when we get back." She bent to her task. About fifteen minutes later, she realized Matti was no longer picking berries. "Why—" she began, then she realized something was wrong. He lay on the grass, scuffing his feet together. She went over to him.

"What's wrong?"

His face was swollen, his fingers were like fat sausages, and he seemed to be trying to scratch his feet.

"A bee bit me, and I itch inside, Anna," he whimpered. "I feel strange."

She knelt beside him. "Where did the bee sting you?"

Feebly he indicated his right forearm. The swelling was much more pronounced around the bite area. She thought she should try to remove the stinger but could not see it.

"I'm going to get Papa," she told him and ran back to the road and through the brush to find their parents.

"Papa!" she called several times, but fear made her so breathless that she realized her voice wasn't very loud. She broke through some tall brush into a small meadow. Papa lay with his head in his wife's lap. Mae leaned down to kiss him just as Anna appeared.

She was disgusted. What good are parents if they aren't there when you need them!

"Papa! Matti's been stung by a bee, and he's all swollen. He's just lying on the ground."

Mae and Papa jumped to their feet and ran toward Anna.

"That happened once when he was almost three," Papa panted as they ran behind Anna across the road. "He was very sick."

When they reached him, Mae gasped. In the short while it had taken Anna to go after them, his face and hands had become even more swollen and blotchy. He was having difficulty breathing, too.

"The doctor!" Mae commanded. "Carry him to the wagon, and let's take him to town right away."

Papa picked up the half-conscious boy, and the family ran to the wagon. Anna untied King, and Papa urged the old horse back onto the road toward Chisholm. They were several miles from town, and no doubt the same thought was on all their minds: Would they be in time to save Matti?

It seemed an eternity before the wagon pulled up to Doctor Schmidt's office. Quickly Papa carried the boy inside.

"Wait here," he told Mae and Anna.

They clutched each other's hands for a long twenty minutes. Then Papa came out, pale and clearly upset.

"The doctor gave him something called 'epinephrine,'" he explained. "I think he's going to be all right. Doctor Schmidt said he's never seen such a severe reaction to a bee sting."

"Thank heaven we brought him right in," Mae said. She put her arms around Anna who was crying openly now. She turned to her husband. "Matti will recover, won't he, Toivo?"

Papa hugged them both. "Yes, but the doctor will keep him here for a few hours to watch him. He says we can see him now."

They went into the small office, then into a back room that held one narrow bed. Matti lay quietly, his face bloated almost beyond recognition. His swollen hands lay on his chest. When they leaned over him, he opened his eyes and tried to speak.

"Shhhh," Mae said. "Don't try to talk, honey. We'll stay right here until we can take you home. You certainly frightened us!"

Matti tried to smile. Mae put her arm around Anna and said softly, "Your sister did exactly the right thing—coming for us. You're going to be fine, but picking berries is not a good idea if bee stings make you this sick. From now on, we'll do the picking."

Anna thought that again they had come close to losing Matti! Yet the picture that stayed in her mind was of Papa's head in Mae's lap.

NINETEEN

~

F OR WEEKS BEFORE school started in the fall of 1908, brush and trees burned northwest of Chisholm. Matti had been out on the west side visiting a friend and was worried.

"What if houses start to burn?" he asked his father anxiously.

"Don't worry, son. If there were any real danger, they would tell us. Every year a few fields get burned off; you know that," Papa soothed him. "And our house is way over on the east side of Longyear Lake."

Anna was excited about going to Central School. It's so big, she exulted. Fourteen teachers and over five hundred students! She had never gone to a school any bigger than the one in the Monroe Location. She walked over to her new school with Matti before it opened on August 31. The school was far from home, but she supposed there would be some kind of transportation in severe winter weather.

"See," she said, "someday you'll go to high school here. It's huge and way up on a hill. This is the nicest building in Chisholm."

Matti was still thinking about the possibility of fire.

"Anna, where would people go if there was a big fire in Chisholm?"

"Oh, you silly!" She turned to look back at the school as they walked away. "I suppose a lot of people could get in there. It's probably as safe as anywhere. Stop worrying."

Around noon on Saturday, Matti was not the only one who noticed the fires burning to the north and west of Chisholm. The rumor was that firefighters from the town of Hibbing, west of them, were out fighting them. By four o'clock, a neighbor told Mae and Anna that the fire was in the Pillsbury Location, to the southwest, and might burn that community out.

"People are standing on the sidewalks looking toward the northwest and talking about what might happen," the neighbor said. "I don't think the fires will get as far as the city limits of Chisholm, though."

"Good!" Mae said in relief; then she and Anna looked at each other and frowned. "Your father's still at the mine," Mae said slowly, "but where's Matti?"

Anna's lips felt stiff. "He's visiting a friend on the other side of the lake," she said. When Mae looked concerned, Anna hastened to say, "He asked for permission. You weren't here, but I thought it was all right to let him go."

"I'm sure it was, then," Mae told her. "But I hope he comes home soon."

One of the neighbors next door to the Kallios came racing down from a small hill where he had been looking toward the fire site. "Huge clouds of smoke over the west side of town!" he gasped. "I heard the fire alarm calling out the volunteers. We're going to the lake." Then he ran inside to get his wife and baby daughter.

131

"We'll wait a little while to see if Matti and Toivo come home," Mae said. "Then maybe we should go to the lake, too."

They waited in vain. At about five-thirty, they went out to the garden. Anna wet her finger and held it up.

"Wind's changed," she said breathlessly. "Everyone thought the fire would pass north of town. I wonder—"

"Anna, I have a bad feeling about this," Mae said. "Do you think we should go to the lake now? But what if they come back and we're not here?"

Anna smelled smoke, and she doubted if any place near Chisholm would be safe. She thought hard.

"Matti asked me the other day where to go in case of fire, and I said I thought Central School would be safe. It's on a hill," she reminded Mae, "and it's a new building. Let's go there. We'll leave a note in case one of them comes back, and I'll harness King."

She hurried to the barn and put the bridle and harness on the horse with trembling hands. After she cinched the belly band, she backed him into the shafts, then put them into place on the harness. It's a good thing I've helped Papa do this before, she thought.

"Get in," she said to Mae, but after her stepmother had climbed into the wagon, Anna held her hands to her mouth.

"Daisy!" she gasped. "We can't lose her now! She's almost ready to have her calf."

"Leave her," Mae urged. "The fire is in the west. Maybe it won't come this far."

But Anna ran back into the barn, led the cow out, and tied her to the back of the wagon. Leading Daisy might slow them down, but it was necessary, she decided. She was fourteen now and felt she could make that decision.

Smoke billowed over the horizon as they went to the road across Longyear Lake. People came from everywhere to go down the same road. Some were carrying precious belongings they wanted to save. They passed a woman running with a bird cage in her hand.

"Poor thing," Mae murmured, "the door is open and her cage is empty!"

"Should we tell her?"

Mae shook her head.

As they neared Chisholm, it was clear that many of the fleeing families were heading toward the Great Northern depot. No passenger trains ran from there normally, but surely with this emergency, they would be able to get out of the path of the fire some way, even if it was in a boxcar.

At the lake, many frightened escapees had run their buggies into the water in the hope that they would be safe there. One woman counted and recounted a huge stack of bills as she sat on her buggy seat at the edge of the lake.

"She runs a boarding house," Anna told Mae. "Everybody that lives there must have given her their money to keep safe!" Then she pointed up ahead. Telephone poles were bursting into flames, and as they watched in awe, fire engulfed several stores. Glass windows blew out and crashed to the ground.

"The wind's carrying burning debris and when it lands, something else catches on fire," Mae shouted above the noise.

Anna wondered if the school had been a good choice. Then some of the people fleeing ahead of them turned left after they crossed the lake, and she realized that they, too, were going to Central. Through the falling debris and black smoke she urged the nervous horse toward the school. When they were within a short distance, she stopped to unharness King and untie Daisy.

"What are you doing?" Mae cried.

Once he stood free, Anna slapped the horse's rump, and he immediately began running toward the lake. She urged Daisy in the same direction although the cow went more slowly.

"They'll be safer in the water," she said. "Come on. Let's get to the school."

She helped Mae down from the wagon seat. Her stepmother was white with fear and worry.

So far the school had been untouched, Anna observed as she and Mae climbed the steps. Inside, people were being sent to various rooms. When there were no more seats in one room, one of the teachers, whom Anna recognized from her first week in the school, sent people into the next. Evidently many others had decided that Central was a fairly safe building.

After she and Mae were placed in a room, Anna took charge. "I'm going to look for Matti and Papa. Please stay here."

Mae urged. "You go ahead. I'll be all right."

When Anna tried to leave the room, a teacher ordered her back inside.

"But I have to look for my family," she cried. "Please, let me look!"

"We can't have people milling around in the building any more than they already are," the woman said. "Now, please, don't give us a problem."

Anna went back to sit by Mae, although now she had to sit on the floor because the seats were filled.

"We're going to be fine," Anna said. "As soon as no one's watching, I'll sneak out to look for Papa and Matti."

The noise and the smoke never stopped. Newcomers streaming down the hall reported the fire's progress to the listeners.

"Great Northern sent fifteen cars to take people to Hibbing," one man yelled. "Maybe there'll be another train!"

"Chisholm's about gone," a woman told a friend. "It's burning to the ground. Our house isn't there any more. What will we do?" She burst into loud sobs.

"They tried to fight it, but they ran out of water," one said. "I bet the pumping station burned. Thank God we live on the east side. Maybe the lake will protect us."

East side, Anna thought. That's us! Maybe the Monroe Location won't burn.

Just then, a man who worked with Anna's papa walked by the doorway and spotted Anna in the classroom. "Your father is down the other hall," he called out to her. "Everybody from our shift came over here," and he pointed.

"Thank you!" Anna breathed fervently. "Is my little brother Matti with him?" But the swiftly moving stream of people had carried the man away.

Mae caught Anna's hand with both of hers. "We have to look for them," she said. "Won't they let us out of here?"

Anna shook her head but waited quietly for her chance to slip out. Soon she stood up, squeezed Mae's shoulder, and whispered, "Stay here." Then in the confusion, she eased past the woman at the door.

She found it impossible to hurry. Too many people pushed against her. It took many minutes to find the room her papa's friend had indicated. Inside, leaning against the wall, Papa and Matti stood with smoke-blackened faces and clothes.

"Anna!" Papa said and hugged her until she squealed. "Where's Mae?"

Matti's tearstained face brightened when he saw her. "Is Mama with you?"

"Yes!" Anna exhaled in relief. "I'll take you both to her, but it won't be easy getting through the crowd."

When the three had pushed their way back to the room where Mae waited, once again the teacher stopped them.

"You can't go in there," she said. "The room is full."

"Our mother's in there," Anna said fiercely, "and we're going in!"

In they went, and Mae jumped up when she saw them. Papa reached for her, and somehow the little family wrapped themselves in each other's arms.

"God answered my prayers," Mae sobbed.

"And mine," Papa said fervently. "We're all safe!"

Anna leaned her head against Papa's arm. She would always mourn her mother, but Mae was now an important part of their family, someone she had come to accept and even to love. Their house might not be standing after this fire, but they were together, a family. For an instant the beloved rocking chair flashed across her mind. There'll be other chairs, Anna thought. As long as we have each other, we'll be all right.

AFTERWORD

~

W HEN MY HUSBAND DAVE, an elementary school principal, our little girl, and I moved to Chisholm in 1949, the iron mines operated at full capacity and schools were crowded. The town had been rebuilt of fireproof materials wherever possible after the 1908 fire and had everything any town should have: a library, good schools, many churches, banks, and thriving businesses.

We found Chisholm, and in fact the entire Range, unique. Never before had we lived where there were so many different nationalities, quite a few of whom preferred to speak their own language. Since most of the parents had needed to go to work as youngsters, they insisted their children should have a better education, so school was important to them.

After sixteen years and two more children, we moved away. Fortunes were changing on the Range: taconite was just beginning to be mined, schools were closing, and my husband felt that we should leave before he too was out of a job. All of us hated to go.

When I returned to research this book, I talked to many former mine workers and engineers. I visited Iron World and at the Iron Range Research Center listened to tapes made by mining retirees. I descended into the Soudan Underground Mine on the Vermillion Range, half a mile down in three minutes, an experience that gave me the deepest respect and empathy for the lives of underground miners and their families. I decided that my book should be about a Finnish family, since Finns were present in large numbers and I have always been intrigued by Finnish customs and heritage.

My imaginary Anna and her family became quite real to me, and I knew that her education would be important to her and to her parents. Although Anna had to deal with the difficulties and challenges of a very different time, I believe her courage, ingenuity, and love of family are as welcome today as they would have been in a small northern mining town at the beginning of this century.

—Isabel Marvin

ISABEL R. MARVIN (1924–2000) earned her BA and teaching credentials from the University of Minnesota at Duluth and for twenty-two years taught English, journalism, and Spanish to high school and middle school children in Farmington and Chisholm, Minnesota. Isabel began her writing career at age fifty-seven and published her first short story two years later. Over the course of fifteen years she published numerous short stories and articles and ten novels, and in 1994 she won the Milkweed Prize for Children's Literature for *A Bride for Anna's Papa*. In 1995 she was nominated for a Minnesota Book Award.

**IF YOU ENJOYED THIS BOOK, YOU'LL ALSO WANT TO
READ THESE OTHER MILKWEED NOVELS.**

To order books or for more information,
contact Milkweed at (800) 520-6455 or
visit our Web site (www.milkweed.org).

THE $66 SUMMER
John Armistead

MILKWEED PRIZE FOR CHILDREN'S LITERATURE • NEW
YORK PUBLIC LIBRARY BEST BOOKS OF THE YEAR: "BOOKS
FOR THE TEEN AGE"

A story of interracial friendships in the seg-
regation-era South.

THE RETURN OF GABRIEL
John Armistead

A story of Freedom Summer.

THE OCEAN WITHIN
V. M. Caldwell

MILKWEED PRIZE FOR CHILDREN'S LITERATURE

Focuses on an older child adopted into a large,
extended family.

TIDES
V. M. Caldwell

The sequel to *The Ocean Within,* this story
deals with the troubles of older siblings.

ALLIGATOR CROSSING
Marjory Stoneman Douglas

Features the wildlife of the Everglades just before it was declared a national park.

PERFECT
Natasha Friend

MILKWEED PRIZE FOR CHILDREN'S LITERATURE

A thirteen-year-old girl struggles with bulimia after her father dies.

PARENTS WANTED
George Harrar

MILKWEED PRIZE FOR CHILDREN'S LITERATURE

Focuses on the adoption of a boy with ADD.

THE TROUBLE WITH JEREMY CHANCE
George Harrar

BANK STREET COLLEGE BEST CHILDREN'S BOOKS OF THE YEAR

Father-son conflict during the final days of World War I.

NO PLACE
Kay Haugaard

Based on a true story of Latino youth who create an inner-city park.

THE MONKEY THIEF
Aileen Kilgore Henderson

NEW YORK PUBLIC LIBRARY BEST BOOKS OF THE YEAR: "BOOKS FOR THE TEEN AGE"

A twelve-year-old boy is sent to live with his uncle in a Costa Rican rain forest.

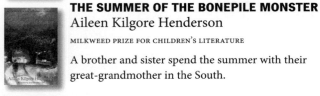

HARD TIMES FOR JAKE SMITH
Aileen Kilgore Henderson

A girl searches for her family in the Depression-era South.

THE SUMMER OF THE BONEPILE MONSTER
Aileen Kilgore Henderson

MILKWEED PRIZE FOR CHILDREN'S LITERATURE

A brother and sister spend the summer with their great-grandmother in the South.

TREASURE OF PANTHER PEAK
Aileen Kilgore Henderson

NEW YORK PUBLIC LIBRARY BEST BOOKS OF THE YEAR: "BOOKS FOR THE TEEN AGE"

A twelve-year-old girl adjusts to her new life in Big Bend National Park.

I AM LAVINA CUMMING
Susan Lowell

MOUNTAINS & PLAINS BOOKSELLERS ASSOCIATION AWARD

This lively story culminates with the 1906 San Francisco earthquake.

THE BOY WITH PAPER WINGS
Susan Lowell

A story about a feverish boy's imagined battles. Includes paper-folding instructions.

THE SECRET OF THE RUBY RING
Yvonne MacGrory

A blend of time travel and historical fiction set in 1885 Ireland.

EMMA AND THE RUBY RING
Yvonne MacGrory

A time-travel tale to nineteenth-century Ireland.

MINNIE
Annie M. G. Schmidt

A cat turns into a woman and helps a hapless newspaperman.

THE DOG WITH GOLDEN EYES
Frances Wilbur

MILKWEED PRIZE FOR CHILDREN'S LITERATURE

A young girl's dream of owning a dog comes true, but it may be more than she's bargained for.

BEHIND THE BEDROOM WALL
Laura E. Williams

MILKWEED PRIZE FOR CHILDREN'S LITERATURE • JANE ADDAMS PEACE AWARD HONOR BOOK

Tells a story of the Holocaust through the eyes of a young girl.

THE SPIDER'S WEB
Laura E. Williams

A young girl in a neo-Nazi group sets off a chain of events when she's befriended by an old German woman.

INTERIOR DESIGN BY DON LEEPER.

TYPESET IN MINION

BY STANTON PUBLICATION SERVICES.

PRINTED ON ACID-FREE 55# NATURAL PAPER

BY EDWARDS BROTHERS.